That night I dreamed that I was being married. I was standing at the altar at Eversleigh waiting for my bridegroom. He came out of the shadows and waves of emotion swept over me. I was in love . . . passionately in love.

He was beside me. I turned, but his face was in shadow. I cried out to him to come to me.

Then I awoke. . . .

Fawcett Crest Books
by Philippa Carr:

THE ADULTERESS

KNAVE OF HEARTS

LAMENT FOR A LOST LOVER

THE LION TRIUMPHANT

THE LOVE CHILD

SARABAND FOR TWO SISTERS

THE SONG OF THE SIREN

VOICES IN A HAUNTED ROOM

WILL YOU LOVE ME IN SEPTEMBER?

THE WITCH FROM THE SEA

THE RETURN OF THE GYPSY

Philippa Carr

FAWCETT CREST • NEW YORK

A Fawcett Crest Book
Published by Ballantine Books
Copyright © 1985 by Philippa Carr

Library of Congress Catalog Card Number: 84-24768

ISBN 0-449-20897-4

This edition published by arrangement with G. P. Putnam's Sons

Manufactured in the United States of America

First Ballantine Books Edition: August 1986

Contents

Romany Jake   1

The Verdict   33

Tamarisk   78

The Blind Girl   127

Riot   168

The Debt   185

After Waterloo   221

Blackmail   263

Suicide or Murder?   303

The Understanding   340

Romany Jake

I believe that very few people who lived through that summer and early autumn of the year 1805 will ever forget it. Throughout the entire country was a feeling of dread of what might be our fate, which was only surpassed by a determination to prevent it. We were a nation preparing for invasion from the most formidable foe any country had ever had to face since the days of Attila the Hun. The Corsican adventurer, Napoleon Bonaparte, had shown the world that he was determined on conquest, and, having subdued the greater part of Europe, was now turning his attention to our island.

His name was on everybody's lips; any little rumour about him was magnified and passed around; he was generally known as Boney, for nothing is such an antidote to fear as contempt—even if it is assumed—and he was slightingly referred to as The Little Corporal; but the most ominous warning a mother could give to a naughty child was: "If you are not good, Boney will get you"—as though Boney was the devil himself. Boney was the bogey-man and there could have been few in England at that time who did not contemplate his coming to our land with considerable apprehension.

Bands were formed all over the country; weapons were collected and hidden. We looked at the sea which lapped our shores, and whether it was calm and blue, or lashing our beaches in a grey fury, we thanked God for it. It was our great ally because it separated us from that mass of land over which the Emperor Napoleon's battalions had ranged and where, it seemed, none could deter him.

Enemies became allies in the only cause that mattered. We were all one great family, determined to maintain our independence. We were no little European state to be lightly overrun. Until now we had ruled the seas—and we were going to carry on doing so. We were—we hoped—impregnable in our little island, and thus we were going to remain.

There was talk of little else in our household, and we would sit over meals listening to my father discussing the state of affairs. My father was very much the head of our household. He was the patriarch, the master of us all, one felt. There were only two in the family who knew how to soften him; my mother was one; I was the other.

He was quite old at that time—sixty in fact—for my mother was his second wife, and although they had been in love with each other in their youth, there had been a previous marriage for both of them. My mother already had a grown-up son and daughter by her first marriage—and I was the result of that long delayed union.

This made complicated relationships in our family. For instance, my constant companion, Amaryllis, who had been brought up in the nursery with me, and who was only a month younger than I, was in fact my niece; her mother, Claudine, being my mother's daughter by her first marriage.

I always felt this gave me a certain superiority over Amaryllis—one month's superiority plus the fact that I was her aunt.

I used to call her Niece sometimes until Miss Rennie, our governess, told me not to be ridiculous.

"But it is a fact," I would insist.

"There is no need to stress it," retorted Miss Rennie. "You are both little girls, and there is scarcely any difference in your ages at all."

I was not such a pleasant little girl as Amaryllis was. She was fair, with a face rather like the angels of the coloured pictures in our Bible. I sometimes expected to see a halo spring up about her curly head. She was pretty in a fragile way, with blue eyes and long fair lashes, a little heart-shaped face, and hair that curled about her head—hyacinthine locks, someone once called them and the description fitted.

2

She was very kind and loved animals; her mother, my half sister, Claudine, doted on her, and so did David, her father, who was my father's son. The relationship seemed more and more complicated whichever way one looked at it. But we were a very close family and few in it were closer than Amaryllis and myself.

We were in the schoolroom together; we had our ponies on the same day; we learned to ride under the tuition of the same riding master; we shared a governess; we were as sisters. But although we were related and scarcely ever out of each other's presence, we were not in the least alike in looks and temperament.

I was very dark—with almost black hair and dark brown eyes, heavy dark brows and lashes. In our family there were very dark-haired and very fair-haired women. The picture gallery bore witness to this. Some of the dark-haired ones had blue eyes, which was a very attractive combination. My ancestress Carlotta and my mother were two of these. They were the dramatic ones, the ones who struck out from conventions when they wanted to. I was one of that kind. Then there were the gentle ones with their pleasant *good* faces. They were quite a contrast to the dark side of the family.

Amaryllis and I seemed to fit quite neatly into these categories. We were surrounded by love. Amaryllis was the sort of daughter most parents would have chosen had they been given a choice; but I believe my father and mother preferred me as I was. They knew that I might be a little rebellious, that I might act in an unpredictable manner. My mother might have been like that once. As for my father, he had always been bold and determined to get his own way, so he would want a daughter who was a little like himself.

That Amaryllis and I were the best of friends was largely due to her unselfish and forbearing nature. When I seized the more exciting toy or demanded more than my fair share of the rocking horse, she had merely stood aside. It was not that she had no spirit. I was sure that, in a good cause, she would have had a good deal. Perhaps she was wise and from an early age saw the futility of screaming for something which was after all not worth the effort; perhaps she was far sighted enough to realize that after I had taken the prize from her, it had already lost its value because she did not want it as desperately as I had done.

Well, whatever it was, Amaryllis was Amaryllis and I was

Jessica, and the two of us were as different as two children brought up together and sharing a nursery and schoolroom could be.

I suppose my parents were not conventional, Dickon, my father, in particular. He made the rules his way and in our household they were law.

When we were eight years old he decreed that we were too old to eat in the nursery with Miss Rennie and we joined our parents at table.

"I like to see the family assembled," said my father.

Our parents encouraged us to talk and listened to our opinions. I was a great talker, egged on by my father who would sit back watching me with his mouth moving almost involuntarily as though he were trying to stop himself laughing. He would argue with me, trying to trip me up, and I always plunged in, stating my views without considering whether they were his or not, for I knew that the more I disagreed with him the more he liked it.

My mother would sit enraptured, her eyes on us both.

And it was the same with Amaryllis; her parents were as proud of her as mine were of me. I could imagine them in their bedrooms alone at night and I could hear my father's comment: "Amaryllis hasn't our Jessica's spirit. I'm glad we have a girl like that." And in that other bedroom: "What a difference in the two of them! I'm glad Amaryllis is not so forward. Jessica can be almost insolent at times."

But most important to me, we both had love, the most important thing a child can have.

It was alarming to think that an alien force might intrude on our cosy way of life. My parents were aware of the threat and so, as I have said, was the whole of England. Patriotism flourished. It is only when people are afraid of losing something that they realize how precious it is.

That was what was happening to us in those memorable days of that year.

There is something very comforting about a big manor house which has been the home of a family for generations. Eversleigh was such a house. It overawed me to think that the house had been here long before any one of us was born and it would be there long after we had all gone.

It was also comforting to have the whole family there—my parents and Amaryllis's. David's twin brother Jonathan had died a long time before, and his wife Millicent had gone to live with her parents some miles away taking her son Jonathan with her. They should really have stayed at Eversleigh for Jonathan was the heir. I was next in succession and after me Amaryllis. I was a little resentful that Jonathan should come before me just because he was a boy. I was older than he was, and I never forgot to remind Amaryllis that she was a month younger than I. However, Millicent wanted to go to her old home, but although she lived at Pettigrew Hall with her parents she was often at Eversleigh.

I loved the place, especially the antiquity of it, and I often thought of the members of my family who had lived here. I had read so much about them, and I felt I knew some of them personally—generations and generations of them—right back to the days of the great Elizabeth when it was built—the E-shaped building dated it without doubt. I loved the old hall with the two wings on either side. Dear Eversleigh!

I found the neighbourhood of immense interest. For one thing the sea was not very far away. I loved to gallop along by the frilly waves and feel the salt sea breeze in my face. "Race you!" I would shout to Amaryllis. I always wanted to race and it was of the utmost importance to me that I win. Amaryllis would come riding along, a pace behind me, smiling happily, not caring in the least who won. Winning was not important, she would say. It was the ride that mattered. Wise Amaryllis!

There were two houses close to ours and I found their inhabitants quite intriguing.

At Enderby was Aunt Sophie, a very sad and tragic figure; she had been badly burned during a fireworks display in Paris at the time of the marriage of Marie Antoinette to the Dauphin who soon afterwards became the ill-fated Louis XVI.

Aunt Sophie was a recluse, living there with her faithful friend and companion-servant Jeanne Fougère. I was not encouraged to visit her often; though she had a certain fondness for Amaryllis. It was an uncanny house. Terrible things had happened there. It was haunted, said the servants; and I could well believe it. Even my half sister, Claudine, looked strange when we called on Aunt Sophie; and I noticed she looked about her almost as though she was seeing something which was not there.

Aunt Sophie had had a very tragic life. She had not only been terribly scarred but had lost her lover and she never forgot it. She liked to mourn over the past and I had a notion that if things were going well she was not so pleased as she was when they were going badly. All the talk of possible invasion seemed to take years off her life. She herself had come out of revolutionary France with her jewels sewn into her clothes—a story I loved to hear in detail. We did not speak of it often because of Aunt Sophie, and Jonathan my father's son, who had shared in that adventure, was dead, so he could not tell of it.

Enderby, house of shadows, shut in by tall trees and thick bushes, uncanny, redolent of the past, was a house of mystery and tragedy which must stay so because that was the way Aunt Sophie wanted it.

I should have liked to prowl about that house all alone, for I always enjoyed frightening myself. I felt there was evil in that house. Amaryllis did not feel it. I suppose when one is good—fundamentally good—one does not sense these things as quickly as someone who is more inclined to sin.

But I felt there was something there. Often I would look quickly over my shoulder, expecting to see a sinister figure hastily disappearing. I loved to linger in the minstrels' gallery for that was said to be especially haunted.

I liked to make Amaryllis call me up from the kitchen when I was in one of the bedrooms for there was a speaking tube connecting the two rooms. Claudine heard us once and asked us not to do it. Amaryllis immediately desisted but I wanted to do it more than ever. It had a fascination for me and when I was younger I used to ask one of the servants to talk to me through the tube.

The other house that interested me was Grasslands—and again it was not the house which fascinated me so much as the people who lived in it. Grasslands was an ordinary small manor house—pleasant without being impressive. There was nothing special about the house itself to arouse my interest. Its inmates were quite another matter.

Old Mrs. Trent, for instance. I was sure she was a witch. She rarely emerged from the house, and it was said she had become a little strange since the suicide of her elder grand-daughter. It was a tragic story and she had never got over it. She lived in Grasslands with another granddaughter—Dorothy Mather, whom we all knew as Dolly.

Dolly was a strange creature. One met her riding about the countryside; sometimes she would return our greeting; at

6

others pass us by as though she did not see us. She ought to have been attractive; she had a neat figure and pretty, fair hair, but she had a facial disfigurement. One eyelid was drawn down at one side and her face seemed slightly paralysed in a way that gave her a somewhat sinister appearance.

I told Amaryllis that she gave me the shivers and even when she smiled, which was not often, that malformation gave her a mocking look.

Claudine was always trying to be kind to her and telling us we must be the same. "Poor Dolly," she used to say, "life has been cruel to her."

Amaryllis would always stop and talk to her and oddly enough Dolly seemed to be a little fascinated by her. She looked at Amaryllis as if she knew something about her which she could tell if she wanted to.

So we lived in our little community which was now threatened by the possibility of invaders who would disrupt our pleasant existence.

It was a lovely September day. There was just a little chill in the air, which was full of the scents of autumn. Amaryllis and I had ridden away from Eversleigh in the company of Miss Rennie, and had come as far as the woods. It was lovely riding under the trees on a carpet of golden and russet leaves. I liked the scrumbling noise the horses' hooves made as they walked through them.

Miss Rennie was a little breathless. As we had approached the woods I had pressed my horse into a gallop, which always alarmed Miss Rennie. She was not so sure of herself on a horse as she was at the schoolroom desk and was greatly relieved on those days when one of the grooms took over the duty of escorting us.

I was thoughtless in those days and I liked to tease her. It made up for the withering contempt she sometimes had for my scholastic achievements. It was like turning the tables and I am afraid I often set my horse galloping ahead of her, for I knew she had great difficulty in keeping up.

"Race you!" I had cried to Amaryllis; and we were off. Thus we reached the woods a little before Miss Rennie, which was why we came face to face with the gypsy.

"Don't you think we should wait for Miss Rennie?" cried Amaryllis.

"She'll catch up," I replied.

"I think we should wait for her."

"You wait then."

"No. We should keep together."

I laughed and pushed on. And there he was, sitting under a tree. He was very colourful and yet somehow blended in with the landscape. He wore an orange-coloured shirt, open at the neck. I caught a glimpse of a gold chain and there were gold rings in his ears. His breeches were light brown; he had dark hair which curled about his head and brown sparkling eyes. I noticed the flash of very white teeth in a sunburned skin. He began to strum on a guitar when he saw us.

I pulled up my horse and stared at him.

"Good afternoon, my lady," he said in a musical voice.

"Good afternoon," I replied.

Amaryllis was now beside me.

He rose and bowed. "What a pleasure to meet not only one beautiful lady—but two."

"Who are you?" I asked.

"A gypsy. A wanderer on the face of the earth."

"Where have you wandered from?"

"From all over the country."

"Are you encamped here?"

He waved his hands.

I said: "These are my father's woods."

"I am sure the father of such a charming young lady would not grudge the poor gypsies a spot on which to rest their caravans."

"Miss Jessica! Miss Amaryllis!" It was Miss Rennie. She was close by.

"We're here, Miss Rennie," called Amaryllis.

The gypsy looked on with some amusement as Miss Rennie came into sight.

"Oh there you are! How many times have I told you not to go on ahead of me? It is most unseemly." She stopped short. She had seen the man and was horrified. She took her duties very seriously and the thought of her charges coming into contact with strangers—and a man at that—momentarily stunned her.

"What . . . what are you doing?" she stammered.

"Nothing," I replied. "We have just got here and have met . . ."

He bowed to Miss Rennie. "Jake Cadorson, at your service, Madam."

"What?" cried Miss Rennie shrilly.

"I am Cornish, Madam," he went on, smiling as though he found the situation very amusing, "and Cador in the Cornish language means Warrior. So Cador son . . . the son of a warrior. For convenience my gypsy friends call me Romany Jake."

"Very interesting, I am sure," said Miss Rennie, recovering her composure. "Now we must get back or we shall be late for tea."

He bowed again and resuming his seat under the tree he began to strum on the guitar; as we turned away he started to sing. I could not resist looking back. He saw me and putting his fingers to his lips blew me a kiss. I felt extraordinarily excited. I rode on in a sort of daze. I could hear his strong and rather pleasant voice as we went on to the edge of the wood.

"I must insist that you stay with me when we are riding," Miss Rennie was saying. "That was an unfortunate encounter. Gypsies in the woods! I don't know what Mr. Frenshaw will have to say about that."

"They always have permission to rest there as long as they are careful about fire—and there is not much danger of that after all the rain we have had," I said.

"I shall report what we have seen to Mr. Frenshaw," continued Miss Rennie. "And I must ask you, Jessica, to be more obedient to my wishes. I do not wish to have to tell your parents that you are disobedient. I am sure that would grieve them."

I thought of my father's receiving the news and I could picture that look on his face when he was trying not to smile. His daughter was very much what he must have been at her age, and parents like their children to resemble them even in their less admirable qualities; so I did not think he would be greatly grieved.

As for myself, I could not stop thinking of the man under the tree. Romany Jake! A gypsy . . . and yet he did not seem quite like other gypsies I had seen. He was like one of the gentlemen who were friends of my parents . . . only dressed up as a gypsy. He had fascinated me. He was very bold. What would Miss Rennie say if she knew he had thrown me a kiss when I had looked back? I toyed with the idea of telling her, but desisted. Perhaps that would be something which would be unwise to come to my parents' ears.

True to her word she told either my father or my mother and the subject was raised at dinner that night.

"So we have gypsies in the woods," said my father.

"They always come south towards winter," commented David.

My father turned to me. "So you saw them today."

"Only one. He said he was Romany Jake."

"So you spoke to him."

"Well, just for a few minutes. He had an orange-coloured shirt and a guitar. There were rings in his ears and a chain about his neck."

"He sounds like a regular gypsy," said David.

"I think you should avoid the woods when the gypsies are there," said Claudine, looking rather fearfully at Amaryllis.

"But the woods are so lovely now," I cried. "I love scrumpling through the leaves."

"Nevertheless . . ." said Claudine, and my mother nodded in agreement.

"I wish they wouldn't come here," she said.

"They can make a bit of a mess of the land," added my father. "But they've always been allowed to bring their caravans into the clearings. As long as they don't make a nuisance of themselves they can stay. I expect they'll be round to the kitchens with their baskets and oddments to sell—and telling the maids' fortunes."

"Mrs. Grant will deal with all that," said my mother.

Mrs. Grant was our very efficient housekeeper who ruled the nether regions as despotically as Pluto ever did his. I had rarely seen so much dignity contained in such a small body—for she was under five feet and rotund with it—and the very crackle of her bombazine jet-decorated gown, heralding her approach, was enough to set a servant shivering and wondering what misdemeanour could be laid at his or her door.

So the gypsies could be left safely to Mrs. Grant.

During the days that followed I learned a little more about the gypsies. The best way to get news of such matters was through the servants and I had developed a very special relationship with them. I saw to it that there was always a welcome for Miss Jessica in the kitchens. I chatted to them, made a point of knowing what was happening to them and of encouraging their confidence. I was enormously interested in their lives; and while Amaryllis was studying the exploits of the Roman generals and the Wars of the Roses, I would be seated at the kitchen table hearing what was happening when Maisie Dean's husband came home suddenly and caught her with her lover, or who might be the father of Jane Abbey's child. I knew that Polly Crypton, who lived on the edge of the woods in a cottage surrounded by her own special herb garden, could cure other things besides earache, toothache and indigestion; she could get rid of warts, give the odd love potion; and if a girl was in a particular sort of trouble she could do something about that too. There was much mysterious talk about this activity, and when they found themselves discussing it in my presence there would be nods in my direction, followed by an infuriating silence. Still, at least I was aware of the powers of Polly Crypton, and this I told myself was Life, and as necessary to the education as a knowledge of past battles. Moreover, I could always copy Amaryllis' notes. She was very good about such matters.

So it was not difficult to learn something about Romany Jake.

He was, according to Mabel, the parlourmaid, "a one," and I knew enough of the vernacular to understand that that meant a person of outstanding fascination.

"There he was, sitting on the steps of the caravan playing that guitar. His voice . . . It's a dream . . . and the way the music comes in . . . Real lovely. Romany Jake they call him. He's from foreign parts."

"Cornwall," I said. "That's not exactly foreign."

"It's miles away. He's been up in the North and come right down through the country . . . all in that caravan . . . with the others."

"He must know the country very well."

"I reckon he's been wandering all his life. One of them came round this morning, telling fortunes, she was."

The other servants started to giggle.

"Did she tell your fortune?" I asked.

"Oh yes . . . Even Mrs. Grant had hers done—and gave her a tankard of cider and a piece of meat pie."

"Was it an interesting fortune?"

"Course, Miss Jessica. You ought to have yours done. I reckon they'd tell *you* something."

The servants exchanged glances. "Miss Jessica is a regular one," said Mabel.

I felt warm and happy to be awarded the highest accolade which could be bestowed.

"Now, Miss Amaryllis . . . she's a little darling . . . so pretty and gentle like."

I was not in the least jealous. I would much rather be "a one" than pretty and gentle.

The servants left me with no doubt in my mind that there was something special about Romany Jake. I could tell it by the manner in which they spoke of him and giggled when his name was mentioned. Although they were fairly frank with me, there were times when they remembered my youth, and although that did not prevent their talking, it curbed their spontaneity and they spoke in innuendoes which I sometimes found difficulty in deciphering.

But I learned that the coming of Romany Jake was one of the most exciting things which had happened for a long time. He must have driven from their minds the thoughts of invasion for he was now the main topic of conversation in the servants' hall.

He was no ordinary gypsy. He was a Cornishman—half Spaniard, they reckoned, and I remembered that at the time of the defeat of the Spanish armada many of the Spanish galleons had been wrecked along the coast and Spanish sailors found their way ashore. So there was a sprinkling of Spanish blood in many a Cornish man or woman. It was evident in those dark eyes and curling hair and their passionate natures—all of which attributes were possessed, so I was told, by Romany Jake.

"Romany Jake!" said Mabel. "What a name to go to bed with!"

"I always think of him just as Jake," said young Bessie, the tweeny. "I don't think he's a real gypsy. He's come to it because he likes the wandering life."

"He looks like a gypsy," I said.

"Now what would you know about that, Miss Jessica?"

"As much as you do, I suppose," I retorted.

They've made quite a little home for themselves in that clearing. They're shoeing their horses, setting up their baskets and doing a bit of tinkering. You can't say they're lazy, and Romany Jake, he plays to them and sings to them . . . and they all join in the singing. It's like a play to see them."

"At least," I said, "he has stopped you all talking about the invasion."

"I reckon Romany Jake would be a match for Boney himself," said Mabel.

And they all laughed and were very merry. That was what the coming of Romany Jake had done for them.

I saw him once when I was alone. I had been down to the cottages to take a posset to Mrs. Green, wife of one of the stablemen who was suffering from a chill, and on my way back there he was. He had no right to be on our land, of course, and he was carrying something in his coat pocket. I believed he had been poaching.

His eyes sparkled as he looked at me and I was aware of an acute pleasure because I fancied he was admiring me and as I was growing older I was becoming rather susceptible to admiration and experienced a kindly feeling towards those who expressed it. But it seemed particularly pleasant coming from him.

So I had no desire to run away from him, nor to reprove him for poaching on our land.

"Good day to you, little lady," he said.

"Good day," I replied. "I know who you are. You're Romany Jake. I met you in the woods the other day, I believe."

"I am certain of it, for having once made your acquaintance that would be something I should never forget. But that such a great lady as yourself should remember me . . . that is as gratifying as it is remarkable."

"You don't speak like a gypsy," I said.

"I trust you will not hold that against me."

"Why should I?"

"Because you might think that every man should keep his place . . . a gentleman a gentleman . . . a gypsy a gypsy."

I fancied he was laughing at me so I smiled.

"I know you live in your caravan in the woods," I said. "Are you staying long?"

"The joy of the wandering life is that you go where you will when the spirit moves you. It is a great life lived under the sun, the moon and the stars."

He had a musical voice not in the least like any gypsy I had ever heard. There was laughter in it and it made me want to laugh too.

"You're quite poetic," I said.

"The life makes one love nature. It makes one conscious of the blessings of nature—of the life on the open road."

"What about winter?"

"Ah, there you have spoken. The north wind will blow and we shall have snow and what will the gypsy do then, poor man. I'll tell you. He might find some warm and cosy house and a warm and cosy lady who will open her doors to him and shelter him there until the cold is past and the spring comes."

"Then he wouldn't be a wandering gypsy, would he?"

"What does that matter as long as he is happy and those about him are happy. Life is meant to be enjoyed. You agree with me? Yes, I know you do. You will enjoy life, I see it in your eyes."

"Do you see the future?"

"They say, do they not, that gypsies have the powers?"

"Tell me what you see for me."

"All that you want it to be. That's your future."

"That sounds very good to me."

"You'll make it good."

"Have you made yours good?"

"To be sure I have."

"You seem to be rather poor."

"No man is poor when he has the good earth to live on, and the sun to warm his days and the moon to light his nights."

"You have a great respect for the heavens," I said.

"Well, from thence comes the source of life. I'll tell you something if you will swear never to mention it to a soul."

"Yes, yes," I said eagerly. "I promise."

"I took to you the moment I saw you. I said to myself: She'll be a fiery beauty, that one. I'd like to steal her away and take her off with me."

I burst out laughing. Of course I should have scowled at him and ridden off immediately; but I did not. I just wanted to stay where I was and indulge in this conversation which was fascinating to me.

"What! You think I would leave home and become a gypsy."

"*I* did," he said. "It's a good life . . . for a while."

I shivered. "What about the north winds blowing and the snow coming?"

"You'd have me to keep you warm at nights."

"Should you be talking to me like this?"

"I am sure some would say I shouldn't but between ourselves it depends on whether you want to hear it."

"I don't think I should stay here."

"Oh, but is it not the things which we are supposed not to do which we enjoy doing? I'll swear you have often done that which you should not have done . . . and loved the doing of it."

Someone was coming. I looked at the bulge in his pocket. He was about to disappear when Amaryllis came into view.

"This is my lucky day," he said. "Once more two beautiful ladies."

"Why, it's Romany Jake," said Amaryllis.

"You are the second lady to do me the honour of remembering my name . . . and all in an hour."

Amaryllis looked at me and said: "We ought to go in."

"I was just going," I replied.

"Good day, Mr.—" began Amaryllis.

"Cadorson," he said. "Jake Cadorson."

"Well, good day, Mr. Cadorson," I said.

Amaryllis pulled at my arm and I turned away with her. I was aware of his watching eyes as we went towards the house.

"What was he doing there?" asked Amaryllis.

"I don't know."

"Did you see what he had in his pocket?"

"There was certainly something there."

"A hare or a pheasant, I think," said Amaryllis. "He must have been poaching. Do you think we ought to tell your father or mine?"

"No," I said firmly. "They have to eat. Do you want them to starve?"

"No, but they should not poach. It's stealing in a way."

"Don't tell, Amaryllis. My father would be angry and turn them away. They must be very poor."

Amaryllis nodded. It was always easy to arouse her compassion.

The next time I saw him was in the kitchen at Grasslands.

Claudine took a special interest in Mrs. Trent and was always sending something over to her. I had heard Claudine say that Mrs. Trent had never been the same since the death of her granddaughter Evie. She just seemed to lose her grip on life. Amaryllis never liked going there very much which I thought odd for she was always eager to share our comforts with the people of the estate. They liked to see her, too. She had the face of a ministering angel, and was also patient listening to accounts of their ailments. She had more aptitude than I for that sort of thing. "You're the ideal sister of mercy," I told her. And so she was . . . except at Grasslands.

I asked her why she did not like going there and she said that Dolly had an odd way of looking at her.

"She makes me shiver sometimes," she said. "I'll look up and her eyes will be on me—at least the one that is wide open. And I always wonder what that other eye can see. It is almost as though it sees what other people can't."

"I always thought you were so reasonable and logical," I said. "I don't expect you to have flights of fancy."

"That's how I feel . . . just uncomfortable. So will you go and take them whatever my mother wants to send to them?"

Although I was not the perfect visitor of the sick, I did like going to Grasslands—just as I did to Enderby. It was not that I wanted to spend a good deal of time with Mrs. Trent and Dolly or Aunt Sophie; but the uncanny atmosphere which prevailed in both houses intrigued me.

"We are lucky to have two such houses in the neighbourhood," I said to Amaryllis.

"It is not the houses," she replied. "It's the people in them. I wouldn't mind Grasslands at all without Dolly."

I thought a good deal about what she had said and I wondered why Dolly was so interested in Amaryllis, because most people simply thought Amaryllis sweet and angelic, and paid more attention to me. Dolly did, however, have a certain interest in me. Once she said: "You were ever such a lovely baby."

"Do you remember me then?" I asked.

She nodded. "You were so pretty . . . and could you scream! If you couldn't have what you wanted . . . You should have heard."

"I probably did hear myself."

"And when you smiled . . . oh you were lovely then."

But even so her real interest was in Amaryllis.

So it was that I took the sloe gin to Mrs. Trent.

I looked in at the front door and there was no one there so I went round to the back. I could hear voices. The door was open so I went in.

In the Grasslands kitchen, seated at the table, his legs stretched out before him, sipping from a tankard, his guitar on the table before him, was Romany Jake.

Dolly was sitting at the table some little distance from him.

He rose when he saw me and said: "Well, if it isn't the lady from the big house."

Dolly said: "Oh Jessica, it's you then."

She needed no answer to the obvious so I put my basket on the table and said: "Young Mrs. Frenshaw thought your grandmother might like to try her sloe gin."

"She'll appreciate that," replied Dolly. "Would you like a little wine?"

"No thank you."

Romany Jake surveyed me with his laughing eyes. "Too proud to sit down with a gypsy?"

"I never thought . . ." I began; but he had turned to Dolly.

"Perhaps you should be taking your guest into the parlour which is more suited to her."

I said firmly: "I *will* take a little wine, Dolly . . . here "

"You are as gracious as you are beautiful," he said. "Grace and beauty. What a joy to find the two together!"

"Jake brought in a basket I ordered," said Dolly, explaining his presence.

"And how is your grandmother today?" I asked, as she poured out a little wine which she handed to me.

"She is brighter, thank you. I'll tell her you called. She'll like the sloe gin."

Romany Jake, who had kept his eyes on me, then raised his glass. "A long and happy life to you, Miss Jessica," he said.

"Thank you." I lifted mine. "And to you."

"Jake was telling my fortune," said Dolly.

"I hope it was a good one."

"I have told Miss Dolly what I tell all . . . and there is no great skill in it. What comes to you is largely of your own making. The good life is there . . . if you have the wit to take it."

"It is a comfortable way of looking at life if you believe it," I said.

"And wouldn't you believe it, my lady Jessica?"

"I suppose you are right in a way, but so many things happen in life that one has no control over. Acts of God they call them."

Dolly said: "Earthquakes, floods, death . . ."

"I wasn't only thinking of them," I said.

"She is wise, our lady Jessica."

"Jake told me I had a good life ahead of me . . . if I took the right road to it," said Dolly.

"That applies to us all," I retorted.

"Ah," said Romany Jake, "but we don't all have the opportunity to take the golden road."

"If it is golden why should we turn away from it?"

"Because it is not always seen for what it is at the start. You have to have the wisdom to see it and the courage to take it."

"Shall I?" asked Dolly.

"It is for you to decide, Miss Dolly."

He held out his goblet and she went to him to refill it.

There seemed to me then a sense of unreality in that kitchen. I wondered what my family would say if they could see me sitting at a table drinking wine with Dolly and Romany Jake. He seemed to guess what I was thinking and to be amused by it.

He said: "Look at me now. Romany Jake, sitting at this table drinking wine with two ladies. Now if I were a man who turned away from his opportunities, I'd have touched my forelock and declared myself to be unworthy of the honour."

"I have a feeling that in your heart you think yourself worthy to sit down with the highest in the land," I said.

"And what would a lady like you know of a poor gypsy's heart?"

"I think Mr. Cadorson, that I know a little about you."

"Well, it is clever you are and I've never doubted that. You'll have a great life because you're bold and you are going to take what you want with both hands. It will be a lucky man who shares that life with you."

He looked at me very steadily when he said that. I felt myself flushing.

"And what of me?" asked Dolly.

"You are more timid than my lady Jessica. She has a fine opinion of herself, this one. She's precious . . . and she knows it. And she will make sure others don't forget it either."

"You are still talking about *her*," interrupted Dolly somewhat peevishly. "Why are you so interested in her?"

"I am interested in the whole world—you, gentle Miss Dolly, and the not so gentle lady Jessica . . ."

With that he set down his goblet and picked up the guitar. He strummed a few bars and began to sing a song about beautiful ladies. We sat there in silence watching and listening.

Then he started to sing about a high-born lady who was discontented with her life until she met a gypsy in the woods. Then she left the luxury of her home and all that went with it to live a life of freedom under the moon and the stars and the sun . . . among the trees of the forest.

His tenor voice vibrated with emotion; and all the time he was singing his eyes were on me and I was sure he was singing for me rather than for Dolly.

I clapped my hands when he had finished but Dolly was silent.

I said: "I daresay she didn't find it so very wonderful. It is all very well to change a soft feather bed for the earth . . . but the earth can be very hard and uncomfortable with creeping crawling things in the summer and frost in winter. It is just a pleasant song."

"Oh, but my lady Jessica, there are great comforts in a gypsy's life which I haven't sung about."

"Well, I think she would soon have been regretting it."

"Not she. She learned more about love and life with her gypsy than she ever would with her high and mighty lord."

"Perhaps high and mighty lords would think differently."

"What an argumentative lady you are and how hard to convince. There is only one way of getting you to agree."

"And what is that?"

He looked at me very boldly and I knew what he was going to say before he said it. He leaned closer to me and said quietly: "To show you."

"Have some more wine," said Dolly, still peevish.

She filled his goblet; he sipped it thoughtfully, looking at me with that amused smile; then he picked up his guitar and his deep rich voice echoed round the Grasslands kitchen. Some of the servants came down and stood at the door listening.

When I saw them I remembered it was time I went home.

I stood up hastily and said I must go. "I only came to bring the sloe gin."

He rose and bowed, giving me that disturbing enigmatical smile. I hurried out and as I walked away I heard the sound of the guitar.

I felt very exhilarated by the encounter.

When I arose that October morning there was no indication that this was going to be an important day not only for my family but for everyone in England. But with one glorious stroke our fears disappeared when the news of the victory at Trafalgar Bay was brought to us.

Even my father was deeply moved. We were assembled at the table and the talk was all about what this would mean to us and our country. Lord Nelson had beaten the French at Trafalgar Bay. He had so crippled their fleet that there could no longer be a question of invasion. He had shown the world that Napoleon was not invincible.

The saddest news was that, in giving England freedom from fear, our great admiral had lost his own life. Therefore our rejoicing was tempered with sorrow.

But even that could not stem the jubilation. We had checked Napoleon. We alone, in threatened Europe, had shown the bombastic Emperor that we were the unconquerable.

My father was eloquent. "Never, never in all its history has our country lain at the foot of a conqueror."

David mentioned the Norman Conquest and was immediately rounded on by my father. "We English are the Normans. The Vikings . . . for mark you they were not French . . ." I smiled at him. My father had an unreasoning hatred of the French because my mother had married a Frenchman before she married him. I could well imagine him in a winged helmet, sailing to these shores in a long ship. He guessed my thoughts and grinned at me. "No," he went on. "Not French. The Normans were Vikings who had been given Normandy by the King of the Franks to stop them invading the rest of France. The Vikings along with the Angles and the Jutes mingled their blood with the Saxons and created the Anglo Saxon race . . . *us,* my son. And we have never allowed a conqueror to set foot on this soil . . . and by God's grace never shall. Napoleon! Napoleon would never have been allowed to come here. But this matter of Trafalgar Bay has saved us a lot of trouble."

Then we drank to the great hero, Lord Nelson, and to our

own Jonathan who had died for his country. Claudine was overcome by emotion and I saw the glitter of tears in her eyes.

"There will be bonfires all over the country tonight," said my mother.

"We must see them," I cried.

"Well," went on my mother, "I suppose we could all go out. They won't light them until after dark."

"I want to go out and see them, don't you, Amaryllis?" I cried.

"Oh yes," she answered.

Our parents exchanged glances and my father said: "We'll take the carriage. It will be near the coast . . . right on the cliffs, so that any watchers from the other side of the water may be able to see them. Bonfires all along the coast telling the plaguey French what we think of their Napoleon. David, you can drive us. We'll all go."

The elders looked relieved. I followed their thoughts. There would be revelry round the bonfires tonight and they did not want their daughters to be out of sight.

At dusk we set out. The excitement was intense. People were making their way to that spot on the cliff top where the bonfire was to be lighted. Already there was a crowd assembled there. Driftwood and rubbish of all sorts had been piled up, and on the top of the heap was an effigy of Napoleon.

The crowd made way for our carriage.

"Down with the Boney Party!" shouted someone.

There were cheers for our carriage. My father waved his hand and called a greeting to some of them. Nothing could please him more than this display of feeling against the French.

Our carriage pulled up some yards from the bonfire.

People were looking anxiously at the sky. It must not rain. It occurred to me that people who had such a short time before been worried because they feared an invasion, now seemed equally so about the weather.

We were lucky. The rain held off. The great moment had come.

Several men approached carrying flaming torches. They circled the heap and with a shout threw their torches into the mass of accumulated rubbish and paraffin-soaked wood. There was a burst of flame. The bonfire was alight.

The air was filled with shrieks of delight; people joined hands and danced round the bonfire. Fascinated, I watched. They looked different in the firelight. One hardly recognized the sober people one had known. They were servants, most of them. I saw the little tweeny, wide-eyed and wondering. Her hand was seized by one of the stable boys and she was whirled off into the dance.

"They are going to get wilder as the night progresses," said David.

"Yes," replied my mother, "there will be some merry-making tonight."

"I trust the aftereffects will not be more than some of them have bargained for," added my father.

"Crowds scare me a little," said my mother.

My father looked at her tenderly. "This is rejoicing, Lottie," he murmured gently.

"I know. But crowds . . . mobs . . ."

"Would you like to go?" he asked.

She looked at me and Amaryllis. "No," she replied. "Let's wait awhile."

I felt a great desire to mingle with the crowds, to dance round the bonfire. Two of the men had brought fiddles with them and they were playing songs we all knew—*The Vicar of Bray* and *Barbara Allen* and the one which set them all shouting with fervour as we all joined in:

> When Britain first, at Heaven's command
> Arose from out the azure main,
> This was the charter of the land,
> And the guardian angels sang the strain:
> "Rule Brittania, rule the waves
> Britons never will be slaves."

The words rang out into the night air; below the waves washed against the white cliffs.

"Never, never, never," chanted the crowd, "Will be slaves."

All the pent-up emotions of the last months were let loose as the fear of the havoc an invading army could wreak evaporated from their minds. Not that any of them would admit that they thought it could really happen, but the relief was intense, and I could hear it in those words. "Never . . . never, never . . ." they went on singing.

22

The music changed. Now the fiddlers were playing a merry tune:

Come, lasses and lads, get leave of your dads
And away to the maypole hie . . .

It was not Maytime but the tune would do for a dance and the lasses and lads had joined hands and were dancing round the bonfire as though it were a maypole.

I saw some of the gypsies mingling with the crowd and yes! there he was. He was hand in hand with a sloe-eyed gypsy girl. Creole earrings flapped in her ears; she wore a red skirt and had wild dark hair.

He danced gracefully, leaping round the bonfire. He came close to our carriage and saw me. For a few seconds his eyes met mine. He released the hand of the girl with whom he was dancing and she went leaping on without him. He stood there just looking; and although he did not beckon I knew that he was telling me how much he wanted me to be down there dancing with him. His gaze implied that our acquaintance was a secret . . . a delightful secret—something daring and forbidden.

My father said: "The gypsies are here."

"Well, I suppose there is no reason why they shouldn't be," replied my mother.

"They seem to be enjoying the occasion," added David.

I was amazed to see Dolly in the crowd. I would not have expected her to venture out on such a night, and certainly not to come to the bonfire. She was standing on the edge of the crowd, looking frail and pretty because her deformity was not discernible. She looked like a young girl though she must be past her mid twenties.

I whispered to Amaryllis: "Look, there's Dolly."

And at that moment Romany Jake was beside her. He seized her hand and, drawing her along with him, began to dance.

"Dolly . . . dancing," said Amaryllis. "How very strange."

I followed them with my eyes for as long as I could. Once or twice as they came round the bonfire they were quite close to the carriage. Dolly looked ecstatic. He glanced my way. There was something I did not understand in his expression but I knew he was telling me how much he wanted me to be dancing with him round the bonfire.

I waited for them to come round again, but they did not. I continued to look for them but I did not see them again.

"This will go on through the night," my mother said.

"Yes." My father yawned. "David, take us home now. I think we have had enough. This sort of thing becomes monotonous."

"It is a good thing that they all realize what dangers we have come through," commented David. "There can't be a man or woman in England tonight who is not proud to be English."

"For tonight, yes," said my mother. "Tomorrow may be another matter."

"Lottie, my dear," said my father, "you have become a cynic."

"Crowds make me feel so," she replied.

"Come along, David," commanded my father, and David turned the horses.

So we rode the short distance back to the house through the lanes which were illuminated by the light from the bonfire. We could see other bonfires spread along the coast like jewels in a necklace.

"A night to remember," said David.

What I would remember most was the sight of Romany Jake standing there almost willing me to leave the carriage and go to him; and then hand in hand with Dolly he had disappeared.

A few days later there was trouble.

One of the gamekeepers came to see my father. He had caught two gypsies stealing pheasants in the wood. There was a definite boundary between those woods in which the gypsies were allowed to camp and those in which the pheasants were kept. There were notices in every conceivable spot warning that those who trespassed in the private woods would be prosecuted.

These two men had been seen by the gamekeeper with pheasants in their hands. He had given chase and although he had failed to catch them he had traced them back to the gypsy encampment.

As a result my father rode out there and warned the gypsies that if any more attempts were made to encroach on the land which was forbidden to them and if those stealing his pheasants were caught, they would be handed over to the law and suffer the consequences; and the gypsies would be moved on and never allowed to camp on his ground again.

He talked of them over dinner that evening.

"They are a proud race," he said. "It's a pity they don't settle down and stop wandering over the face of the earth."

"I think they like the life under the sun, moon and stars," I said.

"Poetic, but uncomfortable," said Claudine.

"I suppose," added David, who always brought a philosophical turn to the conversation, "that if they did not prefer it they would not continue with it."

"They're lazy," declared Dickon.

"I am not sure," contradicted my mother. "They have been doing it for generations. It's a way of life."

"Begging . . . scrounging . . . making use of other people's property!"

"I believe," I put in, "that they have an idea that everything on earth is for the use of everybody in it."

"A misguided philosophy," said my father, "and only adhered to by those who want what others have got. Once they have it, they would endeavour to keep it to themselves with more vigour than any. That is nature and no philosophy on earth is going to change it. As for the gypsies, if they are caught in any more mischief, they'll be out. They're an insolent lot. There was one fellow . . . He was very different from the rest. He was sitting on the steps of one of the caravans playing a guitar of all things. I thought he might have got up and done a bit of work."

"That would be Romany Jake," I said.

"Who?" cried my father.

"He's one of them. I've seen him about. In the kitchen they talk about him a great deal."

"Colourful character," said my father. "He was a sort of spokesman for them. He's certainly not at a loss for words."

"I saw him at the bonfire," I added. "He was dancing."

"He'd be good at that, I daresay. It would only be work he was shy of. I shall be glad when they've moved on. Thieves, vagabonds, most of them."

Then he started to talk about what might happen on the Continent. Napoleon would be anxious for success in Europe.

He had to restore the people's faith in the invincible Emperor whose fleet had been crippled beyond redemption at Trafalgar.

It was a week or so after the bonfire. We were all at dinner when one of the servants came rushing in crying that the woods were on fire.

We left the table and as we came out into the open air we were aware of the smoke and the acrid smell of burning. My father soon had the servants rushing out with water. I went to the stables and mounting my horse galloped in the direction of the fire. I knew that it was in those woods where the gypsies had their encampment.

A scene of wild disorder met my eyes. The grass was on fire and the flames were running across it towards the trees, licking at their barks while I watched in horror.

My father was in the midst of the mêlée shouting orders; cottagers who lived nearby were running out with buckets of water.

"We have to stop it reaching the thicket," cried my father.

"Thank God there's hardly any wind," said David.

I could see how the difficulty of getting water to the scene made us helpless. This went on for some time and the fire fighting method was most inadequate. I was sure that part of the woods could only be saved by a miracle.

And it came. The rain began to fall, a slight drizzle at first which soon changed to a downpour.

There was a shout of relief from everybody. We stood, faces uplifted, letting the precious rain fall on us.

"The woods are saved," said my father. "No thanks to those plaguey gypsies."

He noticed me and cried: "What are you doing here?"

"I had to come, of course," I replied.

He did not answer. He was watching the flames being beaten out. Then he shouted to the gypsies: "You'll be off my land tomorrow."

He turned and started to ride away. I followed with David.

My father was up early next morning, and so was I. He was preparing to go out and I said to him: "What are you going to do about the gypsies?"

"Send them packing."

"What? Now?"

"I'm riding out in a few minutes."

"Are you going to blame them all because one or two were careless?"

He turned to me, his eyes narrowed. "What do you know about it? These people nearly burned down my woods. If it hadn't rained how much timber do you think I would have lost? I won't have them burning down my trees, stealing my pheasants. Thieves and vagabonds, the lot of them."

"The woods weren't burnt down. And I don't suppose you'll miss a pheasant or two."

"What does all this mean? Why are you making excuses for a band of gypsies?"

"Well, they have to stay somewhere. If people won't let them camp, where can they go?"

"Anywhere, but on my land."

With that he strode out. I went to my room and hastily put on my riding habit. I ran down to the stables. There, they told me that my father had left a few minutes before.

I hurried out and caught up with him before he had reached the woods. He heard my approach and looking round pulled up sharply and stared at me in astonishment.

"What do you want?"

"You are going to see the gypsies," I said. "I am coming with you."

"You!"

"Yes," I said. "I'm coming."

"You'll turn right around and ride straight home."

"I don't want you to go alone."

I saw the familiar twitch of his lips. At least he was amused.

"What do you think they are going to do to me? Truss me up like a pheasant and eat me for supper?"

"I think they might be dangerous."

"All the more reason why you should not be there. Go back at once."

I shook my head.

"So you would disobey me, would you?"

"I am coming with you. I am afraid for you to go alone."

"Do you know," he said, "you get more like your mother every day. Plaguey daughters! I don't know why I put up with you."

"I'm coming," I said.

He was laughing inwardly, well pleased. He turned his horse and started to trot towards the woods. I fell in beside him. It was far from his mind that there would be any trouble or he would then have insisted that I go back. He must have been dealing with gypsies all his life and I doubt he had ever known rebellion, either from them or anyone else with whom he came into contact.

We came to the gypsies' encampment. There were four caravans there—brown and red—together with a van which was laden with baskets, clothes pegs and plaited rush mats. A fire was burning and over it sat a woman stirring something in a pot which smelt like a stew. Several horses were tethered in the bracken and four or five men were seated near the fire watching us.

It was clear that no preparations for departure had been made.

I felt a shiver of apprehension as I glanced at my father. The blood had rushed into his face. He was going to be very angry and show these people who was the master here.

He said in a voice of thunder: "I ordered you off my land. Why are you still here?"

The group near the fire did not move and the woman went on stirring. They just behaved as though my father was not there. This was the quickest way to anger him. He urged his horse forward towards the group of men. I followed.

"Get up, you louts!" he shouted. "Stand up when I speak to you. This is my land. I'll not have you despoiling it . . . stealing my birds. Take your horses and your caravans and go. Go, I say. You were here with my permission. That permission is now withdrawn."

One of the men got slowly to his feet and sauntered towards us. There was insolence in his very movements. Colour burned under his brown skin and his eyes were fierce. I saw that his hand rested on a knife in his belt.

"We do no harm here," he said. "We go when we are ready."

"No harm!" cried my father. "You call setting fire to my woods no harm! No harm . . . stealing my pheasants. You will go when I say and that is . . . this minute."

The man shook his head slowly. He stood there threateningly but my father was not to be threatened.

My throat was dry. I tried to whisper that we must go at once. The gypsies in this mood were dangerous; they were a wild people and we were unarmed. It was folly to stay here. They were so many and we were but two.

"Father . . ." I whispered.

He made a gesture with his hand. "Leave me," he said. "Get away . . . at once."

"I will not go without you," I answered fiercely.

Another of the men stood up and started to come towards us. Others followed. Four . . . five . . . six, I counted. They came very slowly. It was as though time had slowed down and they were taking a long time to reach us.

"Do you hear me," cried my father. "Start packing . . . *now*."

"The land belongs to the people," said the man with the knife. "We've got a right."

"Much right as you have," shouted one of the others.

"Fools! Knaves! I'll have the law on you. I'm going straight now to see about it."

He had my horse by the bridle and was about to turn it when a stone hit my saddle. I caught my breath. It was too late for retreat now. I was aware of them closing in around us, and for the first time in my life I saw fear in my father's face. It was for me, of course. He was terrified that he would not be able to protect me.

Then suddenly there was a shout from one of the caravans. We all looked towards it. Romany Jake was standing on the steps—colourful in his orange-coloured shirt and the gold glittering in his ears.

"What's to do?" he shouted.

Then he took in the scene—my father with me beside him, the angry gypsies surrounding us.

"His lordship wants to drive us off the land, Jake," said one of the men.

"Drive us off? When we're going in good time?"

He sauntered towards the crowd and came close to us. Even in such a moment his eyes held mine, slightly mocking, full of hidden meaning. "Good sir," he said, in loud ringing tones, "I and my friends will not harm your land. Last night there was an accident. It was not our intention to cause damage."

"But you did," said my father. "And you'll get out . . . now."

"In good time we will pass on."

"Not in your good time but mine. And that is now! This day, and, by God, if you continue to defy me I'll have the law on you. It's time some action was taken. I'll get you shipped to Botany Bay, the whole lot of you. Perhaps you'll be prevailed upon to do a bit of honest work out there."

The man with the knife stepped nearer. I saw it flash in his hand as he lifted his arm. At that moment someone threw another stone.

"My God . . . Jessica . . ." murmured my father. I think he would have killed the man who threw the stone if he could have caught him. I felt numb with fear. I had always thought of him as invincible. He had always been a power in our household; he had lived a life of adventure; he had faced the French mob in the Terror and brought my mother out from under their noses; but here he was, unarmed, completely outnumbered . . . and vulnerable . . . because he was afraid . . . afraid for me as he could never be for himself.

They were cunning, these gypsies. I think some of them sensed the weakness in him.

One of them came close to me and laid a hand on my thigh.

My father made an attempt to seize him but then Romany Jake spoke.

He said in loud tones which rang with authority: "Stop that. Leave the girl alone."

The man who had touched me fell back.

There was silence, tense and ominous.

"Fools," said Romany Jake. "Do you want to get the law on us?"

I was aware of the effect he had on the gypsies. The knife had been ready and was for my father. The man stood still with it in his hand.

"Get back," said Romany Jake.

The man with the knife seemed to be some sort of leader. He said: "It's time to show them, Jake."

"Not now . . . not before the girl. Put that knife away, Jasper.

The man looked at the knife and hesitated. It was a battle of wills, and I sensed that a great deal hung on this moment. Those watching people were ready to follow either man.

Jasper wanted revenge, wanted to wreak his anger against those who owned land and whose permission had to be granted before the gypsies could rest their caravans. What Romany Jake felt on that subject I was not sure. He had spoken as though it were solely on my account that they were to hold off. What would have happened to my father if he had come alone?

My father remained calm. He said: "You seem a reasonable man. Be off my land by nightfall."

Romany Jake nodded. Then he said quietly: "Go. Go now."

"Come, Jessica," said my father.

We turned our horses and walked them slowly away from the gypsy encampment.

When we had left the woods my father pulled up and turned to me. I saw that the rich colour which had suffused his cheeks while he was talking to the gypsies had receded and he was pale. There were beads of sweat on his forehead.

"That was a near thing," he said.

"I was terrified."

"And had every reason to be. And another time when I tell you to do something, I expect obedience."

"What do you think would have happened if I hadn't been there?"

"Ha! You may well ask. I would have given my full attention to those rogues."

"Romany Jake saved us. You have to admit that."

"He's a rogue, like all of them. If they are not off by dawn tomorrow, there'll be trouble for them."

"That man with the knife . . ."

"Ready to use it, too."

"And, Father, you had nothing."

"I wish I had brought a gun with me."

"I'm glad you didn't. You had me instead, I was better than a gun."

He laughed at me. I believed he was very touched because I had insisted on going with him.

"There's no doubt whose daughter you are," he said. "Jessica, forget I said this, but I'm proud of you."

"I'm so glad I insisted on coming with you."

"You think it would be the end of me if you hadn't, don't you? You're kidding yourself. I've been in tighter spots.

What beats me is that such a thing could happen on my land in broad daylight. Another thing . . . not a word of this to your mother.''

I nodded.

And as we rode home each of us was too emotionally stirred for words.

The next morning the gypsies left and there was lamentation in the kitchen because of the departure of Romany Jake.

The Verdict

Life seemed quite dull after the gypsies had gone. We were all dismayed to hear of Napoleon's great victory at Austerlitz that December. It seemed that he was not beaten yet. Trafalgar had merely robbed him of sea power and he was anxious to show that his armies were supreme.

However, we settled into the usual routine: lessons, rides, walks, visiting the sick of the neighbourhood with comforts. It was only with the preparations for Christmas that life became eventful again. Bringing in the log, hunting for mistletoe, cutting the holly, and all the baking that went on in the kitchens; selecting the gifts we were giving and speculating on what would be given to us: the usual happenings of the Christmas season.

Christmas came and went and it was January, three months after the gypsies had vacated our woods. I had not forgotten Romany Jake; I believed I never should. He had made a marked impression on me. I found myself thinking of him at odd moments. I was sure he had been attracted by me in a special sort of way; and there was no doubt that he had had an effect on me. He made me feel that I was no longer a child; and that there were many things I could learn and which he would teach me. I felt frustrated because he had gone before I could understand the meaning of this attraction between us.

The winds were blowing in from the north bringing snow with them. We had fires all over the house. I loved fires in the bedrooms; it was pleasant to lie in bed and watch the flames in the grate—blue flames which were due to the salty wood which was brought up from the beach after storms. It was great fun going down to collect it and to burn the pieces we had personally found; I always said that the pictures in the blue flames were more beautiful than any others.

Outside the wind buffeted the house; and there we were warm and cosy with our fires round which we sat roasting chestnuts and telling uncanny stories—the same which we told every year.

It was the middle of January, during an icy spell, when Dolly Mather came over to Eversleigh in a state of panic. She asked for young Mrs. Frenshaw. She seemed to have a special feeling for Claudine. I happened to come in just as Claudine was coming down to the hall, so I heard what was wrong.

"It's my grandmother . . . Oh, Mrs. Frenshaw, she's gone."

"Gone!" For the moment I thought she was dead for people say "gone" because they fight shy of saying the word "dead" and try to make the act of dying less tragic by calling it something else.

Dolly went on: "She's gone. I went to her room and she's not there. She's just gone . . ."

"Gone!" echoed Claudine. "How can she be? She found it hard to get about. Where could she have gone on a day like this? Tell me exactly . . ."

"I think she must have gone last night."

"Oh no . . . Dolly, are you sure?"

"I've searched the house. She's nowhere to be found."

"It's impossible. I'd better come over."

"I'll come too," I said.

Claudine went up to her room to get her coat and snow boots. Dolly looked at me, staring in that disconcerting way she had.

"I don't know where she can have gone," she said.

"She can't be far off. She was almost bedridden."

Claudine came down and we walked over to Grasslands. There were only two servants there; the man who managed the small estate lived in a cottage half a mile away and his wife also helped in the house.

Dolly took us up to Mrs. Trent's bedroom.

"The bed has not been slept in," I said.

"No. She couldn't have gone to bed last night."

"She must be in the house somewhere."

Dolly shook her head. "She's not. We've looked everywhere."

Claudine went to the cupboard and opened the door. "Has she taken a coat?" she asked.

Dolly nodded. Yes, she had taken a coat.

"Then she must have gone out."

"On a night like last?" asked Dolly. "She would have caught her death."

"We've got to find her," said Claudine. "She must have had some sort of breakdown. But where could she have gone?"

Dolly shook her head.

"I'll go back to Eversleigh," said Claudine. "We'll send some men out to look for her. It's going to snow later on. Where on earth can she be? Don't worry, Dolly. We'll find her. You stay here. Get a fire going in her bedroom. She may need to be warmed up when she gets back."

"But where is she?" cried Dolly.

"That's what we have to find out. Come along, Jessica."

As we trudged back to Eversleigh, Claudine said: "What a strange thing . . . That old woman. She had difficulty in walking up and down the stairs. I can't think what this means. Oh dear, I do hope she is all right. I can't think what will become of Dolly if anything happened to Mrs. Trent."

"It's Dolly who really cared for Mrs. Trent."

"But Dolly . . . all alone in the world."

"She can't be far away," I said.

"No. They'll soon find her. But if she has been out all night . . . in this weather . . ."

"She must have sheltered somewhere."

As soon as we returned to Eversleigh and told them what had happened search parties were organized. As predicted it started to snow and the strong winds were making almost a blizzard. The search went on all through the morning, and it was not until late afternoon when Mrs. Trent was found, not by one of the searchers, but by Polly Crypton. Polly had been out—bad as the weather was—to take a potion to old Mrs. Grimes, in one of the cottages, who suffered terribly from rheumatism and had run out of her medicine. Coming back Polly had stumbled over something close to her garden gate.

To her horror she had discovered that it was a woman, and looking closer had recognized Mrs. Trent.

It was clear to Polly that she had been dead some time. She hurried to give the alarm, and at last Mrs. Trent was brought back to Grasslands.

Several of us were there—my mother, Claudine, David, Amaryllis and myself. The doctor had come. He said that the effort of walking so far would have put a great strain on her impaired health; it was his opinion that exhaustion had been the main cause of her death; and even if that had not been the case she would have frozen to death.

"Whatever possessed her to go out in such weather?" cried Claudine.

"She must have been temporarily out of her mind," said my mother.

"It is Dolly who worries me," went on Claudine. "We shall have to take special care of her."

Poor Dolly! She was like one in a dream. She spent a great deal of time at Enderby where she was warmly welcomed by Aunt Sophie—herself the victim of misfortune, she was always ready to show sympathy to those whom life had treated ill.

The day of the funeral came. Claudine arranged it all. Dolly had listlessly stood aside and accepted help. We all attended the church and followed the coffin to the grave. Poor Dolly, chief mourner, she looked so frail and white; and at times of emotion that deformity in her face seemed more prominent. Even Aunt Sophie attended in deep black with a black chiffon hood hiding half of her face; she looked very strange standing there at the grave like some big black bird, a prophet of doom. But Dolly kept close to her and clearly drew more comfort from her than from Claudine who was doing so much to help.

Claudine had insisted that the funeral party come back to Eversleigh, so there they all were, talking about Mrs. Trent and how well she had cared for her granddaughter, and how well she had managed Grasslands, not an easy job for a woman even though she had a good manager. We remembered all the pleasant things about Mrs. Trent as people always do at funerals. I had heard people say—when she was living—that she was an old witch and that if she had been different, her granddaughter Evie would never have committed suicide when she found herself pregnant, and that poor

Dolly had a "life of it" looking after her. But she was dead and death wipes away a person's faults and gives virtue in their place.

But Mrs. Trent's virtues were discussed with not so much fervour as was the reason for her sudden departure from the comforts of Grasslands to go out into the bitterly cold winter's night.

Claudine said that Dolly must stay at Eversleigh for a few days, but Aunt Sophie insisted that she go to Enderby; and it was clear that this was Dolly's preference. So Dolly stayed with Aunt Sophie for a week after the funeral and then she returned to Grasslands. Claudine said that we must all keep an eye on her and do what we could to help her over this terrible tragedy.

One day when Claudine returned home from visiting Aunt Sophie, she looked very grave and I saw from her expression that something had happened. She went straight to my mother and they were closeted together for a long time.

"Something is going on," I said to Amaryllis and she agreed with me.

"I'm going to find out," I added. "It's something about Aunt Sophie because it is since your mother came back from there that it started."

I made a few tentative enquiries in the kitchens but I could glean nothing there so I decided to ask my mother.

I had always been treated in a rather special way by my mother. It may have been that she was older than most mothers are when their children are born, and she did tend to treat me more as an adult than Claudine and David did Amaryllis. It may have been that I was more anxious to be regarded so than Amaryllis. "Pushing," as some of the servants called it.

So when I found my mother in one of what I called her dreamy moods, I asked her outright if there was something going on, some secret adult matter which was considered to be not for the ears of the young.

She looked at me and smiled. "So you have noticed," she said. "My goodness, Jessica, you are like a detective. You notice everything."

"This is rather obvious. Claudine went to Aunt Sophie and came back, well . . . secretive . . . anxious and *strange*."

"Yes, there is something, but it is not Aunt Sophie. You will have to know in due course, so why not now?"

"Yes, you might as well tell me," I agreed eagerly.

"It's Dolly. She is going to have a baby."

"But she is not married!"

"People occasionally have babies when they are not married."

"You mean . . ."

"That is what is troubling us. Dolly herself is happy enough, almost ecstatic. That's a help in a way but it is more unfortunate. Your Aunt Sophie will help all she can. We shall all have to be gentle with Dolly. She has had a very hard life. She adored her sister who drowned herself because of her own pregnancy. So now you see why we are worried about Dolly."

"You don't think Dolly will kill herself?"

"On the contrary. She seems delighted at the prospect."

" 'My soul doth magnify the Lord' . . . and all that," I quoted irreverently.

My mother looked at me intently. "Perhaps I shouldn't be telling you all this. Sometimes, Jessica, I forget how young you are."

"I'm quite knowledgeable. One learns about these things. I knew about Jane Abbey's baby before she had it."

"Your father thinks you are wise beyond your years."

"Does he?"

"But most parents think there is something special about their offspring."

"But my father is not like most parents. He would only think it if it were so."

She laughed and ruffled my hair. "Don't say too much about Dolly, will you? Not just yet. Of course it will come out and there'll be a lot of gossip. But don't set it going."

"Of course not. I'll only tell Amaryllis; and she never talks about anything if you tell her not to."

I went away and thought a good deal about Dolly. Oddly enough I was to talk to her soon after my conversation with my mother.

I went over one day to see Aunt Sophie. Jeanne told me she was sleeping so I went into the garden to wait for a while and whom should I see there but Dolly.

She looked different. There was no thickening of her figure yet but there was a certain transformation in her face. The drawn-down eye was less noticeable. There was a little colour in her cheeks and the visible eye shone with a certain delight and, yes . . . defiance.

She was more talkative than I had ever known her.

I did not, of course, refer to the subject. It was she who brought it up.

"I suppose you know about me?"

I admitted I did.

"I'm glad," she said. She gave me that odd look. "In a way you're to blame."

"I? What have I done?"

"When you were a little baby I kidnapped you. Did you know that?"

"Yes," I said.

"I thought you were the other one. I was going to kill her."

"Kill Amaryllis! Whatever for?"

"Because she was alive . . . and oh . . . it's an old story. But my sister had lost her lover and she killed herself. It was all mixed up with them at Eversleigh. It was their fault that it had happened. She was going away with her lover and I was going with her to look after the little baby."

"You mean . . . you wanted revenge through Amaryllis?"

"Something like that."

"But Amaryllis . . . she is the most inoffensive person I ever knew. She would never do anyone any harm."

"It was because she was a baby and I'd lost Evie's. But I took you instead . . . the wrong baby, you see. I had you up in my room hidden away. I was afraid you were going to cry. You were the most lovely baby I had ever seen. I used to try to make myself believe you were Evie's baby. You used to smile at me when I spoke to you. I just loved you when you were a baby. That was when above everything I wanted a baby of my own. It was you who started it. And now I'm going to have one."

"You seem very happy about it."

"I always wanted a little baby . . . ever since I took you. I thought I'd look after Evie's. I don't care what people say. It will be worth it to have a little baby. You'd like to know about it, wouldn't you?"

I did not speak for a moment. I looked into her face and I thought of her dancing round the bonfire on Trafalgar night.

"And . . . the baby's father?" I said weakly.

She smiled, reminiscently, I thought.

I said: "Was it . . . Romany Jake?"

She did not deny it. "He used to sing those songs for me. No one ever cared about me before. He said life was meant for enjoying. There should be laughter and pleasure. 'Live for today,' he said, 'and let tomorrow take care of itself.' The gypsies lived a life of freedom. It was what they cared about more than anything. And so . . . I was happy . . . for the first time in my life, really. And now . . . there is going to be a little baby . . . mine and Jake's."

I felt deflated; betrayed. I could see him so clearly standing there in the light of the bonfire. I had felt he was calling to me . . . to *me* . . . not to Dolly. He had wanted me to be down there dancing with him and I had wanted to be there. Only now did I realize how much.

"Dolly," I said, "did he ask you to go off with the gypsies . . . with him . . . ?"

She shook her head.

"It was such a night . . . It was the people dancing and singing . . . and everything somehow not quite real. I've never known anyone like him."

"You will love the baby, Dolly."

Her smile was ecstatic. "More than anything on earth I wanted a little baby . . . a little baby of my own," she repeated.

I thought what a strange girl she was! She had changed, grown up suddenly. Though she was adult in years, there had always been a childishness about her, perhaps because she was so vulnerable. I was angry suddenly with Romany Jake. He had taken advantage of her innocence. He had called to me with his eyes, with his presence . . . but I was too young . . . I was guarded by my family and so he had turned to Dolly. It was wrong; it was wicked . . . but it had given Dolly what she wanted more than anything on earth.

She said: "I have nightmares about Granny. You know how you feel when it's your fault . . . in a way. I could say I killed her."

"You!"

"I didn't know where she had gone . . . not then. But now I know and I know why. There was a terrible scene that night before she died. I've got to tell someone so I'll tell you because it was partly your fault for being the baby you were . . . and it was your family who made Evie do what she did. But for the Frenshaws at Eversleigh, Evie's lover would never have been found out and he would have gone to France with Evie and me and she would have had the dear little baby . . . so it was the Frenshaws' fault in a way."

"Tell me what happened that night when your grandmother went out in the cold."

"She thought there was something wrong with me and she questioned me. When I said I was going to have a baby she nearly went mad with rage. She kept saying, 'The two of you. It's happened to the two of you. What's wrong with you . . .' That seemed to upset her so much that it took her right back to the time when Evie had died. She always thought afterwards that if she had been different Evie would have come to her with her trouble and something could have been sorted out. She blamed herself and that was why she was so ill. She kept shouting, 'Who was it?' and when I told her she cried out, 'The gypsy! God help us, I can't bear this. You . . . and the gypsy . . .' I told her that he was a wonderful man and that there was no one I'd rather have for the father of my child, and the more I talked the more mad she became. She kept saying she had failed with us. She had planned for us; she had wanted so much for us . . . and I was going the same way as Evie. She kept on and on about Evie. I thought she really had gone mad. I didn't know she had left the house. She told me to leave her alone and I did. 'Go away,' she said. 'I've got something to do. Go away and leave me in peace to do it.' She was so upset I went out and left her and in the morning she had gone. I know now where she had gone. She was making her way to Polly Crypton. Polly knows what to do to get rid of babies. She had done it before for girls in trouble. That was where my grandmother was going on that night. She was going to Polly Crypton to get her to do something to destroy my child."

"Oh, Dolly, what a terrible story! Poor Mrs. Trent, she cared so much for you."

"It was the wrong sort of caring . . . with Evie and with me. Evie was afraid to tell her. I shall never forget the day she learned that her lover was dead and we shouldn't be going away with him after all. She kept saying, 'What shall I do?' I said we'd tell Granny and we'd stand together and we'd manage somehow. But, you see, she could not bring herself to tell Granny. She chose to drown in the river instead. Granny blamed herself for that, and when she knew that I was going to have a child it brought it all back to her. She was going to stand by me. That was why she went to Polly Crypton's on that night.''

''I'm so sorry, Dolly. You know we'll do everything . . . everything we possibly can.''

''Yes. Madame Sophie wants to help me. So do the two Mrs. Frenshaws. I'll be all right.''

Jeanne was calling that Aunt Sophie was ready to see me. I touched Dolly's hand gently and as I ran into the house I was still seeing Romany Jake standing there in the light of the bonfire and wondering what would have happened . . . if I had danced with him as Dolly had done.

By the time spring came, people ceased to talk much about Dolly and her coming child. No one seemed to think very harshly of her. I suppose it is only when people envy others that they revel in their misfortunes. Nobody ever envied Dolly. ''Poor Dolly,'' they all said, even the most humble of them. So if she had had her hour of abandoned passion and this was the result—about which she was delighted—who was to grudge her that?

She spent a great deal of time at Enderby. Aunt Sophie was quite excited at the prospect of the coming child. Jeanne Fougère made all sorts of nourishing dishes, and Dolly seemed to like to be cossetted. Aunt Sophie said that when the time came she must go to Enderby. The midwife should be there and Jeanne would look after her. My mother commented that she had rarely seen Sophie so happy.

Soon it was summer. The war with France dragged on. One grew used to it and a little bored by it. It seemed there was always war with France and always would be.

It was the end of June. Dolly's baby was expected in July. Aunt Sophie insisted that Dolly leave Grasslands and take up her residence at Enderby and Dolly seemed happy to do so. She was completely absorbed in the coming baby and it was wonderful to see her so contented. For as long as I could remember she had been mourning her sister Evie and had been very much her grandmother's prisoner. Now she was free and that which she wanted more than anything—a child of her own—was about to come to her.

''It's a strange state of affairs,'' said my mother. ''That poor girl with her illegitimate child . . . the child of a wandering gypsy . . . and there she is for the first time in her life really happy.''

"Yes," added Claudine, "even in the days when Evie was alive, she was overshadowed by her. Now she is a person in her own right . . . about to be a mother, no less."

"I do hope all goes well for her," said my mother fervently.

Jeanne had taken one of the cradles from the Eversleigh nursery and had made flounces of oyster-coloured silk for it. It was a glorious affair by the time Jeanne had finished with it. There was a room at Enderby called "the nursery"; and Aunt Sophie talked of little else but the baby. Jeanne was making baby clothes—very beautiful ones at that—and Aunt Sophie embroidered them.

It certainly was an extraordinary state of affairs, as my mother said.

The few servants who had been at Grasslands resided chiefly at Enderby now, going to Grasslands only a few times a week to be sure the place was kept in order.

When I walked past it I thought it had a dead look. It would soon have the reputation Enderby used to have. David had said that a house acquired a ghostly reputation because the shrubs were allowed to enshroud it, giving it a dark and sinister appearance. It was not the houses themselves which were haunted; it was the reputation they were given, and people usually saw to it that those reputations were enhanced. Things happened in supposedly haunted houses because people imagined they would.

With July the weather came in hot and sultry. Late one afternoon I had been over to Aunt Sophie with a special cake our cook had made and to enquire after Dolly's health. When I came out of the house I noticed the heavy clouds overhead.

One of the servants called to me: "You'd best wait awhile, Miss Jessica. It's going to pelt down in a moment or two. There's thunder in the air, too."

"I'll be at Eversleigh before it starts," I replied.

And I set out.

There was a stillness in the air. I found it rather exciting. The calm before the storm! Not a breath of wind to stir the leaves of the trees . . . just that silence, rather eerie . . . ominous in fact. It was the kind of silence in which one could expect anything to happen.

I walked on quickly. I was near Grasslands. I glanced at the house . . . empty now. I stood for a few seconds looking up at the windows. Some houses seem to have a life of their own. Enderby certainly had. And now . . . Grasslands.

Eversleigh? Well, there were always so many people at Eversleigh. Enderby had had an evil reputation before Aunt Sophie had gone there, and a woman whose face was half hidden from sight because of a dire accident could hardly be expected to disperse that. Grasslands? Well, people had said that old Mrs. Trent was a witch; and her granddaughter had committed suicide and now the other was going to have an illegitimate child. It was stories like that which made houses seem strange . . . influencing the lives of the people who lived in them.

There was a faint rumbling in the distance and forked lightning shot across the sky. Several large drops of rain fell on my upturned face. The black clouds overhead were about to burst.

I was flimsily clad. I ought to take shelter. The rain would pelt down but it would very likely soon be over. I looked about me. "Never shelter under trees in a thunderstorm," my mother had often warned me.

I turned in at the gate. I could find adequate shelter under the porch at Grasslands.

I started to run towards the house; the rain was coming down in earnest now. I looked up. Then I stopped short for there at one of the upper windows, I saw . . . or thought I saw . . . a face.

Who could be there? Dolly was at Enderby, so were all the servants. There were only three of them and I had seen them all that afternoon.

A dark face . . . I could not see clearly. It had moved swiftly away as I looked up. Was it a trick of the unusual light? A fancy? But I was sure I saw the curtains move.

I reached the porch and stood there. I was quite wet already. Who could be in the house? I wondered.

One of the servants? But I had seen them all at Enderby just before I left. I pulled on the somewhat rusty chain and the bell rang. I could hear it echoing through the house.

"Is anyone at home?" I called through the keyhole.

There was no answer—only a loud clap of thunder.

I rapped on the door. Nothing happened. It was a heavy oak door and I leaned against it, feeling that something very strange was happening. I am not particularly scared by thunderstorms, especially when other people are there, but to see that lightning streaking across the sky and to wait for the violent claps of thunder which followed and to watch the rain violently hitting the ground when behind me was a house which should have been empty . . . well, I did feel a strange sort of fear which made my skin creep.

I stood for a while watching the storm as it grew wilder. My impulse was to run, for suddenly I knew that there was someone on the other side of the door.

"Who is there?" I called.

There was no answer. Did I hear heavy breathing? How could I? The storm was too noisy, the door too thick.

What was it I was aware of? A presence?

I would brave the storm. They would scold me. Miss Rennie would say, How foolish to run through it. You should have stayed at Enderby till at least the worst was over . . .

I shivered. My thin damp dress was clinging to me, but I was not really cold. It was just the thought that there was someone in that house who was aware of me . . . and that it was very lonely here.

I turned to the door and put my hands against it. To my amazement it opened.

How could that be? It had been shut. I had leaned against it. I had rapped on it and now . . . it was open.

I stepped into the hall.

It was dark because of the weather. I looked up at the vaulted ceiling which was rather like ours at Eversleigh but smaller.

"Is anyone there?" I called.

There was no answer and I had the feeling that I was being watched.

I advanced cautiously, crossing the hall to the staircase. I heard a movement and hastily turned round. There was no one in the hall. The door swung shut with a bang. I ran over to it. Someone was in the house and I had to get out quickly. I had to run home as fast as I could, never mind the storm.

A figure appeared at the top of the stairs. I stared.

"Are you alone?" said a voice.

"It's . . . it's . . . ." I stammered.

"That is right," he said. "You remember me."

"Romany Jake," I murmured.

"And the lady Jessica."

"What are you doing here?"

I'll tell you. But first are you alone . . . Is anyone with you? Anyone coming after you?"

I shook my head. I was no longer afraid. Waves of relief

were sweeping over me. I could not feel afraid of Romany Jake—only a tremendous excitement.

He came down the stairs stealthily.

"It was you who were behind the door. You were at the window . . . You opened the door so that I would come in. What are you doing here?"

"Hiding."

"Hiding? From whom are you hiding?"

"The law."

"What have you done?"

"Killed a man."

I stared at him in horror.

"You will understand when I tell you. You will not betray me, I know."

"Why did you come here?"

"I thought Dolly would help me. There was no one in the house so I got in through an open window on the first floor. I was hiding until she came."

"She is staying at Enderby."

"Where are the servants?"

They are there, too. They only come now and then to see that the place is all right."

"What does it mean?"

"Aunt Sophie is looking after her until the baby comes."

"The baby?"

"Your baby," I said, watching him closely.

He stared at me incredulously. "What do you mean?" he asked.

"Dolly is going to have your baby. She wants it very much and so do Aunt Sophie and Jeanne, and my mother says it is not such a bad thing."

He was silent, running his fingers through his thick dark hair. Then he murmured: "Dolly!"

I said: "You say you have killed someone."

"I want you to understand. But first . . . Dolly? Is she all right?"

"She is with my Aunt Sophie."

"And she told you that?"

"That it was your baby, yes."

"Oh . . . my God," he said quietly. "What a mess."

"She wants it. She's happy about it. She'll be all right. They'll look after her and the baby, and my mother says she has never been so happy in her life. Tell me what you have done.''

A loud clap of thunder seemed to shake the house.

''No one will come here in this storm,'' he said. ''Sit down here and let us talk.''

I sat beside him on the stairs.

''You must decide whether you will go straight back to your father and tell him I am hiding here . . . or whether you will say nothing and help me.''

''I want to hear all about it. I don't think I would tell my father. I think I should want to help you.''

He laughed suddenly and he was like the merry man I had known before he went away. I was happy to sit close to him.

He said: ''First Dolly. It happened you know, suddenly . . . These things sometimes do. You won't understand.''

''I think I do.''

He took my chin in his hands and looked into my face. ''I believe you are very wise,'' he said. ''From the moment we met I wished you were a little older . . . not much . . . just a little.''

''Why?''

''Then I could have talked to you . . . You would have understood.''

''I can understand now.''

He smiled and kissed me lightly on the cheek. ''I must tell you what happened. We were encamped in a forest near Nottingham. The local squire had a nephew staying with him. I killed the nephew.''

''Why?''

''Because I caught him assaulting one of the gypsy girls. He would have raped her. He thought the gypsy girls were fair game. Leah is fourteen. I know her father. He adores his daughter. He is a good man. You may be surprised but morals are very strict among the gypsies. Leah is a beautiful girl. The squire's nephew had marked her out no doubt and he just lay in wait to catch her alone. What he did not know was that I was not far off. I heard Leah scream. I hurried to her. He had torn her blouse off her shoulders and had flung her to the ground. I just went for him. I caught him and we rolled over and over on the grass. I was mad with rage against him and all of those people who call themselves nobility and think that gives them a right to take any girl they fancy providing she is not one of their own class. When I had finished with him nothing could have saved him. I took Leah back to the camp. Her father wanted us to move on and we all saw that that was the best thing possible. But we were too late. The law caught up with us. I was arrested on a charge of murder.''

"But it was not an ordinary murder. You did it to save Leah. They would have to take that into consideration."

"Do you think they would? The squire is a man of great influence in the neighbourhood. It was his nephew who was killed."

"But it is against the law to commit rape."

"Does that apply to squires and gypsy girls?"

"To all, surely," I said. "The real criminal is that squire's nephew."

"Do you think you could get a court to believe that?"

"There will be Leah to give evidence."

"That would carry no weight. No. I could see it was the hangman's noose for me." He touched his neck wryly as though he could feel the rope about it. "I have a strong desire to go on living."

"What happened?"

"Before they took me away, Penfold, Leah's father, swore the gypsies would never allow me to be hanged. They knew where I was in jail and they had a horse waiting nearby in case I could make my escape. They were aware that if I came up for trial it would be over for me. My chance came . . . a drunken guard, a little bribery . . . and I was out and there was the horse waiting for me . . . and I was away. I want to get out of the country. I'll never be safe here. I was making my way to the coast. I came this way because I thought Dolly would help me. But I found the house empty . . ."

I was silent, then I said: "You will be safe here for tonight. Tomorrow the servants will come. How will you get out of England? There is a boat in the old boathouse. I've seen it fairly recently, but you would never get across the Channel in it, and how could you go to France?"

"I would attempt it."

"The French will be watching the coasts. You know we are at war with them."

"I'd have to take the risk."

"If you could get to Belgium . . . but that is a longer crossing."

"First it would be for me to get the boat."

"The boat is there. You'd have to row yourself . . ."

"The case is desperate. I'll try anything rather than fall into the hands of those who will condemn me before the trial starts." He took my hands and looked steadily at me. "You will not betray me, little Jessica?"

"I never would," I cried with fervour. "I'd always help you."

He kissed me tenderly.

"You are a wonderful girl," he said. "I never knew a girl like you before."

He had a certain effect on me. I forgot Dolly and how he had seduced her. I forgot that he had killed a man. Soldiers killed in battles. The enemy, they called them, although they had no personal quarrel. This man had killed another who would have harmed a young girl. He was protecting the innocent against the wicked. He had been right to use whatever methods were necessary to save the girl. I was on his side. I had a feeling that no matter what he had done I should have been.

"You should be out of this house before the morning," I said.

He nodded. "After dark, I shall go down to the shore and find that boathouse. Perhaps I could take the boat along the coast and find a ship going somewhere . . ."

"You should go round to Ramsgate or Harwich. There you might get to Holland. Do you have any money?"

"Penfold brought me money with the horse."

"It would have been better if you had made for the east coast."

"I could not choose my way. I was being hunted."

"If you went abroad, it would mean you would never come back."

"These things are forgotten with the years. Tell me, when will the baby come?"

"Very soon now."

"And Dolly, how is she?"

"Very happy. She wants the baby desperately. I think if you came back, she would be perfectly happy."

"What a neat little ending that would be to a midnight frolic round a bonfire."

"Is that what it was to you?"

He was silent. Then he said: "Please don't think too badly of me. You were there, weren't you. Do you remember?"

"Yes, I do remember."

"Sitting in the carriage with your parents. I went on thinking of you . . ."

Neither of us spoke for some time. I was thinking of him in a cart, being taken to some place, and the crowd looking on while they strung him up by his neck. I had never witnessed a public hanging, but one of the servants had. She had come from London and seen it at Tyburn. She had given a graphic description.

That must not be the fate of Romany Jake.

I turned to him impulsively. "You must get away from here as soon as it is dark. I'll bring you some food. Go to the east coast . . ."

"There is food here in the pantries. I was sure Dolly would not grudge me that. Where is the old lady? Has she gone with Dolly?"

"She died. She was horrified because Dolly was going to have a baby. She went out into the snow and was out all night. It killed her."

He put his hand to his head. "So that is something else I have to answer for."

"We all have to answer for all sorts of things."

"How wise you are and how lucky I am to have your friendship. It is an unusual story. The lady of the manor befriending a poor gypsy who is running from the law."

"There have been stranger stories. There is that one you sing about the lady who left home to join the gypsies."

"You have not gone so far as that!"

The hall was suddenly illuminated by lightning which was immediately followed by a clap of thunder.

"I thought that one was for us," he said.

"As soon as the storm is over I must go back. They'll be wondering where I am."

"They wouldn't expect you to be walking through the storm."

"No."

"So we are safe for a little while."

"Tell me about the gypsies," I said. "It seems such a strange life for a man like you."

"I'll tell you a secret. I'm not a gypsy, born and bred. I joined them two years ago because I wanted a life on the open road. I had never liked the restricted life. I wanted my freedom. I could have had an easy life . . . slept in my goose-feather bed . . . sat down at table and feasted like a lord. This is the story over again. This is not the lady who left her home to follow the gypsies; but the man who left the family home to join them.''

"Why did you do that?''

"I quarrelled with my brother. He is fifteen years older than I. As our parents were dead he was in a sense my guardian—and I was a rebel. I ran away from school; I consorted with the menials on the estate. I made their grievances my concern; and after a serious family quarrel I realized that I did not want to go on doing things just because that was the way they had been done for hundreds of years. I wanted to be free . . . my own man. I did not want to obey a lot of social laws which seemed absurd to me, so I joined the gypsies. They have accepted me and some of the best friends I ever had are among them. I cut myself off completely from the old life. There were no regrets I believe on either side. My brother was relieved to be rid of one who brought nothing but trouble. It was just that I cannot endure being shut in whether it be by iron bars or conventions.''

"I understand.''

"Well, now this could be the ignoble end of a useless life.''

"Don't say that,'' I cried. "In any case it wasn't useless for Leah. You saved her, remember. And this is not going to be the end. You can get out of the country. Get to Harwich. I am sure you will be able to get across to Holland. You have the horse.''

"I took the liberty of putting him in the stables. I fed and watered him there. He is resting . . . ready for the long ride to Heaven knows where.''

"You must get to Harwich. Take the byways. They would not think of looking for you along the east coast. You'd have a good chance there.''

"I'll leave when it is dark. Can I trust you to tell no one I am here?''

"Of course.''

"I hope to lie in hiding for a while until the hue and cry has died down.''

"Leave tonight,'' I said; and I added: "I shall be thinking of you.''

"That gives me comfort, a determination to succeed, and when you are older I shall have so much to tell you.''

"Tell me now. I hate waiting."

"I hate waiting too . . . but this will have to wait."

We sat in silence for a while. Then I noticed that there had been no thunder for some little time and that the heavy rain had ceased.

"I must go," I said reluctantly. "They mustn't know that I have been here. Goodbye. Good luck. You are safe here for the rest of the day."

"I will be watchful . . . and leave as soon as darkness falls. Thank you, my dear little girl. I shall think of you constantly . . . my beautiful young benefactress."

He took my face in his hands and tenderly kissed my forehead. I felt very emotional. I wanted to do so much for him; but there was nothing I could do but remain silent.

I went across the hall. I stood at the door for a moment looking back, smiling at him.

I felt frightened suddenly, wondering if that was the last I should see of Romany Jake.

When I arrived home there was great consternation. Where had I been? My mother had sent the carriage over to Enderby to bring me back.

"Dear Mother," I said, "I am not made of sugar."

"And then we learned that you had already left."

"I sheltered."

She felt the sleeve of my gown. It's damp," she announced. "Get it off at once. Where is Miss Rennie? Oh, Miss Rennie, see that Jessica puts her feet in a hot mustard bath at once."

"Certainly Mrs. Frenshaw."

I protested. "Really, this is absurd. I'm just a little wet." And I was thinking, They sent the carriage over. Suppose someone had seen me go into Grasslands? Suppose they had come and found him?

I felt sick at the thought.

I must protect him.

I sat in my dry gown holding it above my knees while my feet were immersed in the hot mustard bath. Miss Rennie filled it again with hot water, when she thought it was getting a little cold.

"You should have stayed at Enderby. You could have come home in the carriage."

"Such a fuss . . ."

How was he faring? Nobody else would call at the house this day and by nightfall he would be off.

I could not get out of my mind the horrible thought of his hanging by a rope. It must never be.

My mother came into the bedroom to see if her instructions were being carried out. She herself dried my feet, and while she was doing so there was the sound of voices below. She looked out of the window.

'It's a stranger,'' she said. ''Oh, there's your father. They're talking earnestly together. I daresay this will mean a guest for dinner. I'll go down and see. Now put on your stockings quickly. You'll be heated from the mustard. You don't want to catch cold.''

''Really, Mother,'' I protested. ''All this because of a little rain.''

''I don't want you in bed with a cold. I have enough to do without that.''

In a way it was pleasant to be looked after and made to feel precious.

Then my thoughts were back with Romany Jake.

I went downstairs to see who had arrived. The whole family were gathered there with my father and mother. Claudine, David and Amaryllis. They were talking excitedly.

My father said: ''This is my daughter Jessica. Jessica, this is Mr. Frederick Forby.''

Mr. Forby bowed and my father went on: ''Do you remember the gypsy they called Romany Jake?''

I felt dizzy. I hoped I did not show how shaken I was.

''Mr. Forby is looking for him. We have to be on the watch.''

''Romany Jake?'' I repeated.

''I thought he might come this way,'' said Mr. Forby to my father. ''We're going to all the old haunts and I believe they were here last year.''

''Yes,'' said my mother. ''It was October. I remember they were at the Trafalgar bonfire.''

''October,'' repeated Mr. Forby. ''And not since?''

''Oh no, not since,'' said my mother. ''We should have been aware of them if they had been here.''

''They set my woods on fire,'' put in my father. ''I turned them off the land after that.''

''They say he is wanted for murder,'' said David.

''That's so,'' said Mr. Forby.

"He's a real villain then."

"These gypsies have to be watched, sir. It's usually petty crimes. Murder! Well, I have to say that's rare enough. But we're determined to get him."

"Who was the victim?" asked Claudine.

"He was the nephew of the local squire. They were encamped near Nottingham."

"Oh dear, that's bad," said my mother. "I thought perhaps it might have been a quarrel in the camp."

"Oh no, the gypsy attacked the young man and killed him."

"I hope they catch him," said my mother.

I heard myself say in a rather high-pitched voice: "Why did he kill this man . . . the nephew of the squire?"

"Some quarrel over a girl. They're a hot-blooded lot, these gypsies."

I had to control myself. I wanted to shout: A quarrel over a girl! The squire's nephew tried to rape her. Romany Jake was quite right to do what he did. Any man of chivalry would have done the same.

I must be careful. I must not betray the fact that I had seen him. I should somehow have to warn him that this man Forby was in the neighbourhood. I must be wary. He never should have come here.

They were talking about him. "A colourful sort of fellow as I remember," said my father.

"I gather he is not a real gypsy."

"What's he doing living with them then?"

"It's all rather odd. In fact he's an odd fellow. We've been making enquiries. It seems he comes from quite a good family . . . somewhere in Cornwall. He's known as an eccentric."

"Who goes round committing murders," said my mother.

"We don't know of any others," I said. "And it wasn't murder. It was this girl . . ."

"Murder is murder, my dear young lady," said Mr. Forby. "It is my job to see that the guilty are brought to justice."

"But you said it was a quarrel over a girl. Perhaps . . ."

My father was looking at me with raised eyebrows and Mr. Forby went on: "We expect a bit of trouble with the gypsies. He seems to be a sort of leader in spite of not being one of them. Cornish name of Jake Cadorson. Romany Jake is just a nickname."

"I remember the fellow," said my father. "I quite liked his manner. He was reasonable enough when I went to order them off my land."

"Hot-blooded," said Mr. Forby.

"Where are they searching for him?" I asked.

"All along the coasts. I've got my men out. We're determined to get him. He'll try to leave the country. I think he'll make for the east coast. Harwich most likely. But for the war I'd have expected it to be the south coast. But he couldn't very well get to France at a time like this. No, I reckon he'll make for Harwich."

I felt myself tremble. I thought: He will go straight into the trap.

I had to see him.

"I'm going to all the houses round here," went on Mr. Forby. "I'm warning them to keep a look out. If anyone should see this man we want to know right away."

I made an excuse to get away. I went to my room, got into my riding habit and slipped out of the house. I saddled my horse and rode out.

The trees were still dripping with moisture and the ground was damp after the storm. The bushes looked as though they had had a battering. Why does one notice these things when one's thoughts are deeply involved elsewhere?

I reached Grasslands. It was very silent. I dismounted and tied my horse to the mounting block. I went to the door and rang the bell. I called through the keyhole: "It's all right. It's Jessica . . ."

I heard his footsteps. The door was opened and he stood there.

Just at that moment there was a shout. My father and Mr. Forby were galloping towards the house.

"No, no!" I cried.

Romany Jake looked at me and the pain in his eyes hurt me more deeply than I had ever been hurt before.

They had leaped from their horses. Mr. Forby produced a gun.

"It's all up," he shouted.

I felt as if I were going to faint. My father put his arm round me. "It's all right," he said. "I'm here."

Two men appeared as if from nowhere. I had never seen them before but I knew that they were Mr. Forby's assistants.

I could not bear to see what was happening.

My father said: "I'll take my daughter home."

I turned to Romany Jake. I could not speak. I shook my head. I could scarcely see him. My eyes were full of tears . . . tears of horror, remorse, frustration . . . and deep sorrow. I wanted above all things to talk to him, to explain. I could not bear him to think that I had betrayed him.

Quietly I rode back with my father.

We went to the stables and my father lifted me out of the saddle. He held me against him. He was not naturally demonstrative. The grooms took our horses and we went into the house.

My father said: "I think you had better tell me, don't you? What is your part in all this?"

I said: "We've got to save him."

I wanted to talk to him. All my life he had been the most powerful being in the world. We all knew of how he had brought my mother out of France: he had always behaved as though he were a superior human being with such conviction that we had believed him to be.

Now I thought: He can save Romany Jake. He was my hope. I had to let Romany Jake know that I had not betrayed him. What had he thought when he opened the door and saw me and the men behind me? What could he have thought but one thing? That I had betrayed him.

"Come into my study," said my father. "You can tell me all about it."

When we were there he shut the door and said: "Well?"

"It was not murder," I told him. "It was not what you think. The squire's nephew was going to rape the gypsy girl. Jake found them. There was a fight and the nephew was killed during it."

"Who told you this?"

"He did."

"You mean . . . the gypsy?"

"He's not a real gypsy. He joined them because he wanted to be free."

"You seem to know a lot about him."

"Why were you there . . . behind me?"

"I was riding with Forby. We went out together and saw you turn in at Grasslands. I said, 'That's my daughter,' and we rode after you."

"Why did you do that . . . oh why?"

"My dear girl, we were going to ask at Grasslands if anyone had seen the gypsy."

"But no one was there. Dolly and the servants were at Enderby."

"I thought some of the servants might have been there. They knew him . . . from when he was here before."

I buried my face in my hands. I felt so wretched.

"Come on," he said. "Explain."

"I went to Grasslands to shelter from the storm. I was going to stand under the porch till it was over. He was there. I thought I saw someone at the window and he saw me. He trusted me . . ."

"You mean you spoke to him?"

"Yes. I went into Grasslands and he told me what had happened . . . how he had killed that man. He said there would be no mercy for him. He, the gypsy, had killed the squire's nephew. I wanted to warn him that that man was in the neighbourhood and had his men all along the coasts. He was going to Harwich after dark. He would have walked right into the trap. And that is just what he did, and he will think that I . . ."

"You must not upset yourself. You did not mean to betray him."

"But I did."

"No, no. It just happened."

"What will they do to him?"

"They'll take him to Nottingham to face trial."

"And they'll find him guilty."

"He has killed a man. He does not deny it."

"But it was not murder."

"It is the usual term for describing such an action."

"But you don't see? There was this girl . . . What will they do to him?"

"Hang him, I expect."

"They must not."

"My dear Jessica, this man is nothing to do with you. A wandering gypsy. Colourful, I admit. Handsome . . . not without charm. This time next year you'll be wondering who he was."

"I shall never forget that he will believe I betrayed him. He trusted me."

"You foolish girl. You did no such thing. You just went there to warn him and we happened to be behind you."

"But he will think . . ."

"Very soon he will be past thinking."

"Oh, don't talk like that, Father. I want you to save him."

"I? What power should I have to save him?"

"When I was little I used to think you could do anything you wanted to. I thought you could make it rain if you decided to. I thought you could do just anything."

"My dear innocent child, you know differently now."

"I know you can't interfere with the elements, but I know there is very little else you cannot do if you really want to."

"I'm a lucky man to have a daughter who thinks so highly of me. She is very wise and almost correct. But at least you know I can't interfere with the weather. Nor can I with the law."

"I don't agree."

"Oh?"

"Laws are man-made."

"So it is only the gods I can't defy. You think I can cope with everything else?"

"Father, wonderful, dear, *clever* Father, you can do something."

"Dearest daughter, no blandishments you can offer me would enable me to save a man who is a self-confessed murderer."

"The circumstances make it no real murder. He had to save that girl. He is chivalrous. Do you remember when we faced the gypsies . . . you and I together and he was afraid of my getting hurt. I may have saved your life then."

"You think the gypsies would have murdered me if you hadn't been there to save me?"

"It could have happened."

He was silent for a while.

"There are means of influencing a court," I said.

"Bribery? Corruption? These things exist. Are you suggesting that I, a law-abiding Englishman, should commit such crimes?"

"You could do something to save him. If the judge knows that he killed this man defending a girl from rape . . . doesn't that count?"

"H'm," he said. "A gypsy . . . the nephew of a squire . . ."

"That's just it," I cried indignantly. "Suppose a nephew of a squire had killed a gypsy who was trying to rape his wife . . ."

"Ah, there you have a point."

"If this man hangs I shall never be happy again."

"You talk wildly. You're only a child, though I must say you make me forget it at times. How old are you. Eleven?"

"Nearly twelve."

"Heaven preserve us. What will you be at eighteen?"

"Please, Father . . ."

"Jessica, my dear?"

"Will you do something for me . . . the best thing in the world you could possibly do. Will you help me save this man?"

"There is little I can do."

"There is something then?"

"We could find the girl. Perhaps bring her forward."

"Yes, yes," I said eagerly.

"I'll go to Nottingham."

I threw my arms round his neck. "I knew you could do it."

"I don't know what I can do. I am just being bullied into taking actions which I feel cannot be fruitful—and all because of my overbearing daughter."

"So you are going to Nottingham. Father, I am coming with you."

"No."

"Oh yes, please . . . please. I want to be there. Don't you see, I must be there. He must know that I did not betray him. If he thought that, I could never be happy again . . . not in the whole of my life. So . . . I am coming with you to Nottingham."

He held me away from him and looked into my face. I saw that sudden twitch of the jaw.

"I used to think," he said, "that I was master in my own household. That's changed since I was misguided enough to beget a daughter."

I flung my arms round him and hugged him.

He just held me tightly to him. It was a great comfort to be loved so much.

The next day we set out for Nottingham. My father had told my mother everything and she wanted to accompany us. When I told her in detail what had happened she was almost as eager as I was to save Romany Jake.

We went by carriage and the journey took several days. It

would be about a week before the trial took place, my father reckoned, and we needed a little time to think out a plan of action.

It was dusk and we must have been about seven or eight miles from Nottingham and were gambolling along at a fair pace when our coachman pulled up sharply.

"What is it?" called my father.

"Well, sir, there's someone on the road. Looks in distress."

"Pull up," ordered my father.

My mother laid a hand on my father's arm.

"It's all right," he said, taking a gun from its place under his seat.

"Much better to drive on," said my mother.

"It might be someone in real distress."

"It also might be a trick. You never know with these gentlemen of the road."

I looked out and saw a man limping towards the carriage.

"I'm in trouble," he said. "Robbed of my purse and my horse . . ."

My father got out of the carriage and studied the man. "Get in," he said.

My mother and I sat closer together to make room.

When the man was seated, my father said, "Whip up the horses," and we were off.

The man was very well dressed, breathless and bewildered, and it was impossible then to suspect him of a trick. He was genuinely overwrought, and for some time found it hard to speak.

"I was riding along," he said at length, "when a fellow stepped out and asked me the way to Nottingham. I told him and as I was talking three of them came out of the bushes and surrounded me. They had guns and commanded me to dismount and to hand over my purse. I had no alternative. I gave them what they asked. They took my horse and left me. Thank you for stopping. I am most grateful. I tried to stop one other carriage but it drove straight on."

"Suspecting mischief," said my father. "These robbers are getting a pest. 'Tis my opinion that we law-abiding citizens don't get enough protection."

The man nodded agreement.

"Well, sir, where do you want to be taken?"

"My home is just outside Nottingham. If you could drop

me in the town where I am well known, I can find someone to take me home, I should be greatly obliged."

"We'll take you to your home," said my father. "Is it far?"

"About a mile outside the town."

"It will be simple to take you there. Just direct us, will you?"

"You are very good. My family and I will never forget your kindness."

"It is only what travellers owe to each other. There ought to be more supervision on the roads."

Our companion was beginning to recover. He told us his name was Joseph Barrington and he had a business in the town of Nottingham. "Lace," he said. "As you know, Nottingham is one of the headquarters for lace-making in the country."

"And your home is outside the town?"

"Yes. One would not want to live too near the factory. We are within easy reach and it is pleasant to be in the country. May I ask what part of the world you come from?"

"We come from Kent."

"Oh, some way south. Have you been to Nottingham before?"

"No. I have business there and my wife and daughter are accompanying me."

"That is a very pleasant arrangement. Could you ask your driver to turn off here. Straight ahead is the direct road into Nottingham. This road leads to my home."

In due course he pointed to a house. It was large, imposing and built on a slight incline for commanding views of the countryside.

We turned in at the drive. Now we could see the house clearly. It must have been built about a hundred years ago and was characteristic of that time with its long windows—short on the ground floor, very tall on the first floor, slightly shorter on the next and completely square on the top. Looking at the door with its spider-web fanlight I thought it had an air of dignity which our Tudor residence lacked. The aspect was of simple good taste and elegance.

The door opened and a woman came out. She stared in astonishment as Mr. Barrington alighted.

"Joseph! What is it? Where have you been? We've been so worried. You should have been home hours ago."

"My dear, my dear, let me explain. I have been robbed on the road . . . my horse and purse taken. Let me introduce these kind people who have rescued me and brought me home."

My father had stepped out of the carriage and my mother and I followed.

The woman was middle-aged and rather plump and at any other time would have been called comfortable-looking. Now she was anxious and bewildered.

"Oh, Joseph . . . are you hurt? These kind people . . . They must come in . . ."

A man came out of the house. He was tall and I guessed in his mid-twenties.

"What on earth . . . ?" he began.

"Oh, Edward, your father—he's been robbed on the road. These kind people . . ."

Edward took charge of the situation.

"Are you hurt, Father?"

"No . . . no. They only wanted poor old Honeypot and my purse. But there I was with nothing . . . nothing . . . and a good seven miles from home."

The young man turned to us. "We are deeply grateful for the help you gave my father."

"They must come in," said Mrs. Barrington. "What are we thinking of? We are just about to serve dinner . . ."

My father said: "We have to get to Nottingham. I have urgent business there."

"But we have to thank you," said Mrs. Barrington. "What would have happened to my husband if he had been left there . . . unable to get home."

"No one would stop . . . except these kind people," added Mr. Barrington.

"They were all scared to," replied my father. "They know something of these knavish tricks people get up to nowadays."

"You stopped," said Mrs. Barrington. "Otherwise my husband would have had to walk home. That would have been too much for him in his state of health. I don't know how to thank you."

"You must come in and have a meal with us," said Edward with the air of a man who is used to giving orders.

"We have to book rooms at an inn," explained my father.

"Then you must come tomorrow night."

My mother said we should be delighted.

"Very well, tomorrow. The name of the house is Lime Grove. Anyone will direct you here. Everyone in Nottingham will know the Barringtons.

We said goodbye and as we drove away my mother said: "I'm glad we stopped and brought him home."

"I have an idea," my father reminded her, "that you tried to persuade me not to."

"Well, those highwaymen can do such dreadful things."

"I was terrified when you stepped into the road," I added.

He gave me that look which I knew so well—slightly sardonic with the twitching of the lips.

"Oh, I was not in the least alarmed because I knew my daughter was there to look after me."

"You are a rash man," I said. "But I am glad you were tonight."

"I look forward to dinner," added my mother. "The family seem very agreeable."

Then we were on the road to Nottingham.

We found a good inn in the town and my father was treated with the utmost respect. He seemed to be known, which surprised me. I had always been aware that he had a secret life which was involved in matters besides banking and his various business interests in London as well as the management of the estate. The secret life had taken him to France in the past and involved him and his son Jonathan in numerous activities. Jonathan had died because of his involvement; and Dolly was somehow caught up in the intrigue through the French spy Alberic who had loved her sister Evie. None of us could be entirely unaffected by the smallest action of those around us.

But such activities clearly had their advantages which were now borne home to me. I believed my father was a man who was capable of taking actions which might be impossible for most men.

My spirits were rising. He would use his influence to free Romany Jake.

My mother whispered to me when we were alone in that room which was to be mine and which was next to my parents': "If anyone can save the gypsy, your father can."

"Do you think he will?" I asked.

"He knows your feelings. My dear child, he would do anything he possibly could for you."

That was a great comfort and I felt a good deal better than I had since that terrible moment when the door of Grasslands had opened and Romany Jake stood there while I realized that my father and the man Forby were behind me.

The very next morning my father was busy. He had discovered that the trial would not take place for a week.

"So we have some time at our disposal," he said with gratification.

He saw several people of influence and when we met over luncheon he told us that the victim was said to be a man of unsullied virtue by his friends.

"We have to prove him otherwise," he added.

"Would that save Romany Jake?" I asked.

"No. But it would be a step in the right direction. The girl will be represented as a person of low morals."

"How could they prove that?"

"Easily. They'll have friends to come forward and swear to it. I'll tell you what I plan to do. The gypsies are encamped outside the town. They are awaiting the trial. I'll see them tomorrow and I'll impress on them that if we can prove the girl to be a virgin, we may have a good case."

"Why not now?"

"My dear daughter, you are impatient. First I have to make inquiries. And have you forgotten that we have a dinner appointment for tonight?"

"Those nice Barringtons!" said my mother. "It will be interesting to get to know them."

"We are here to save Romany Jake," I reminded her.

"We'll do our best," said my father. "Now these Barringtons live in the neighbourhood. They are gentry . . . obviously. They might know the local squire and perhaps they were acquainted with his nephew. You have to tread cautiously in these matters. Leave no stone unturned. A little diversion this evening will do us no harm."

So that evening we drove out to the Barringtons', where we were most warmly welcome. Mr. and Mrs. Barrington with their son, Edward, were waiting at the door to greet us, and we were taken into an elegant drawing room on the first floor. Its long windows looked out over well-trimmed lawns and flowerbeds.

We were given wine and again effusively thanked by them all.

"We want you to meet the rest of the family," said Mrs. Barrington. "They are all anxious to express their thanks."

My father raised his hand. "We have had too many thanks already for what—on our part—was a very trivial service."

"We shall never forget it," said Mr. Barrington solemnly.

"Oh, here is my daughter Irene," said Mrs. Barrington. "Irene, come and meet the kind people who brought your father home yesterday."

Irene was a fresh-faced young woman of about twenty. She shook our hands warmly and said how grateful she was to us.

"And here is Clare. Clare, come and meet Mr. and Mrs. and Miss Frenshaw and join your thanks to ours. Miss Clare Carson is our ward and a remote relation. Clare has lived with us almost for the whole of her life."

"Since I was seven years old," said Clare. "Thank you for what you did."

"I think we might go in for dinner," said Mrs. Barrington.

The dining room was as elegant as the drawing room. It was rapidly growing dark and candles were lighted.

"This is a most unexpected pleasure," said my mother. "We did not expect to be invited out in Nottingham."

"How long do you stay?" asked Edward.

"For a week or so, I believe. We are a little undecided at the moment."

"It depends I suppose on how long your business lasts."

"That is so."

"Business is always uncertain," said Mrs. Barrington, "as we know to our cost, don't we, Edward?"

"That is very true," agreed Edward.

"You are involved in the making of lace," said my mother. "That must be quite fascinating."

"My family has been in the business for generations," explained Mr. Barrington. "Sons have followed sons through generations. Edward is taking over from me. Well, I would say he has taken over, wouldn't you, Edward? I have little say in matters now."

"My husband wants to get away from Nottingham," Mrs. Barrington told us. "He wants a place in the country somewhere, not so far away that he can't look in on the factory now and then. But his health has not been good. Affairs like that of last night are not good for him."

"They could happen anywhere," I said.

"But of course. He has not been very well lately . . ."

Mr. Barrington said: "I'm quite all right."

"No you are not. Bear me out, Edward. We've been discussing this. You come from Kent, I believe?"

"Oh yes," said my mother. "Eversleigh has been in our family for generations. It's Elizabethan . . . rather rambling . . . but we all love it. It's the family home. We're not far from the sea."

"It sounds ideal," said Mr. Barrington.

"Are there any pleasant houses for sale in your neighbourhood?" asked his wife.

"I don't know of any."

"Let us know if you do."

"I will," promised my mother.

"Kent would be rather a long way from Nottingham," said Clare.

She was pale, brown-haired with hazel eyes. I thought her rather insignificant.

"Indeed not," said Mrs. Barrington. "We should want to be a fair distance away otherwise Mr. Barrington would be running to the factory every day. It would be the only way of stopping him if there was a long journey to be made. In any case there are no houses for sale there. I think we shall look in Sussex or Surrey. I have a fancy for those areas."

"They are beautiful counties," said my father; and the conversation continued in this strain until Edward said: "The assizes are coming to Nottingham tomorrow. There is a trial coming up. A gypsy murdered a young man. Judge Merrivale will probably try the case."

"Merrivale," said my father. "I've heard of him. He's quite a humane fellow, I believe."

"He isn't one of our hanging judges."

I put in rather hotly: "It is wrong that there should be hanging judges. They should all be humane."

"So should we all," said Edward, "but, alas, we are not."

"But when it is a matter of a man's life . . ."

"My daughter is right," said my father. "There should be one standard for all. What chance do you think the gypsy has?"

"He hasn't a chance. He'll go to the gibbet. No doubt about that."

"That will be most unjust!" I cried.

My eyes were blazing and they were looking at me in some surprise.

"Perhaps I had better explain our business here," said my father. "I have come to do what I can for this gypsy. It appears that he killed a man who was attempting to rape one of the girls on the encampment. Unfortunately the man who was murdered was the nephew of Squire Hassett who is quite a power round here."

The Barringtons exchanged glances.

"He is not a very popular man," said Edward. "He drinks to excess, neglects his estate and leads rather a disreputable life."

"And what of the nephew who was killed?" asked my father.

"A chip off the old block."

"Dissolute . . . drinking . . . a frequenter of brothels?" went on my father.

"That would be an accurate description."

My father nodded. "You see, the gypsies encamped on my land. I met the fellow who is accused. He seemed a decent sort for a gypsy and his story is that this nephew was trying to rape the girl."

"It's very likely," put in Mr. Barrington.

"Oh! Could I get some information about him? Perhaps from people who have suffered at his hands?"

"I think that might be possible. There was one family up at Martin's Lane. They were very distressed about one of their girls."

"Wronged by this charming fellow, I suppose," said my father.

"No doubt of it. And there were others."

"Perhaps I could prevail on you to give me the names of these people."

"We shall be delighted to help."

I was getting excited. I believed that fate had led us to the Barringtons who were going to prove of inestimable value to us.

It was in a state of euphoria that we said goodnight to the Barringtons and rode back to the inn.

"What a charming family!" said my mother. "I wish they would find a house near us. I should like to see more of them. I thought Mr. and Mrs. Barrington so pleasant, Edward and Irene too. The girl Clare was so quiet. I would say Edward is a very forceful young man."

"He would have to be if he is running a factory," said my father.

"Clare was like a poor relation," I said.

"Poor relations can be a little tiresome because they find it hard to forget it," added my mother. "Everyone else is prepared to but they seem to get a certain satisfaction in remembering."

And so we reached the inn, talking of our pleasant evening. Mr. Barrington's ill fortune on the road had turned out to be very diverting for us.

The next day we all went to the gypsy encampment. I could smell the fires before we reached it, and a savoury smell came from a pot which one of the women was stirring. Other women sat about splitting withy sticks to make into clothes pegs. The caravans were drawn up on a patch of land and the horses tethered to the bushes.

"Is there a Penfold Smith there?" called my father.

A man came out of one of the caravans. He was middle-aged and swarthy; he walked towards us with the panther grace of the gypsy.

"I am Penfold Smith," he said.

"You know me," replied my father. "You camped on my land. I have heard that a friend of yours is in trouble and I have come to help."

"He was betrayed . . . near your land."

"No, no!" I cried. "He was not betrayed. I did not know . . ."

"My daughter wanted to help him. It was not her fault that she was followed. I am here to do what I can for this man. If you will help me we may get somewhere."

"What could we do . . . against the squire and his sort? He owns the land here. He's a powerful man and we are only gypsies."

"I have some evidence which may prove useful. I can prove that the victim was a man of disreputable character. It is your daughter, is it not, who was attacked by him?"

"It was."

"May I see her?"

Penfold Smith hesitated. "She has been very upset."

"She wants to save Romany Jake, doesn't she?"

"Yes, indeed, she does."

"Then she must help us."

"Wicked things are said against her."

"That is why we must do all we can to prove them false."

"Who would listen to her?"

"It is possible to make people listen to her."

"How?"

"May I see her?"

Penfold Smith hesitated a moment longer, then he called: "Leah. Come here, Leah."

She came out of the caravan. She was very beautiful—a young girl a year or so older than myself, very slim with black hair and dark eyes. I was not surprised that such a creature caught the fancy of the lecherous young man.

My father turned to my mother. "You speak to her. Tell her that we believe her. Tell her we want to do everything to help. Explain to her."

My mother knew what was expected of her. She laid a hand on the girl's shoulder. "Leah," she said, "believe me when I say we have come to help. We have already evidence of the nature of the man who would have attacked you."

She said gently: "Jake saved me. But for him . . ." She shivered.

"Yes," said my mother, "and now we must save Jake. We will do anything to save him. Will you?"

"Yes," she answered. "I will do anything."

"What we must do is prove that you are an innocent girl. Will you do that?"

"How? They won't believe me."

"There are tests. Not very pleasant but necessary. I mean . . . they would have to believe you if the evidence was there."

"Tests?" she asked.

"If the court is told that you are a virgin then all the stories which had been circulating about you would be proved false. We know that the man who died was a rake . . . a seducer, a rapist. If we could tell the court that you, on the other hand, are a virgin . . . Do you see?"

She nodded.

"Would you agree to this?" asked my father of Penfold Smith.

"Is it necessary?"

"I think it might be vital to our cause."

"I would do anything to save him," said Leah.

We went into the caravan and talked for a while. Leah told

us that she had been aware of Ralph Hassett before the attack. He had tried to talk to her and she had run away. Then he had waylaid her and the attempted assault had taken place.

"I think," said my father, "that we are getting somewhere."

Penfold Smith, who had at first been suspicious, now accepted the fact that we wanted to help. I think that was due to my mother.

We went back to the inn and we talked continuously about the possibility of saving Romany Jake.

Fortune seemed to go our way. A panel of respectable matrons agreed to make the examination and to our great joy declared Leah to be *virgo intacta*.

Edward Barrington came to the inn and told us that if he could be of any use he would be delighted. He knew that influential people in Nottingham would be eager to see justice done, and they would see that the evidence in Romany Jake's favour was brought forward and, what was more important, heard.

"All is going well," said my father.

I wished I could have seen Romany Jake. I wanted to assure him that it was through no fault of mine that he had been caught. I wanted him to know that I had come to Grasslands to warn him, and that I had no idea that I had been seen.

Then came the day of the trial.

My father attended. My mother and I stayed in the inn. My father was going to say a word in the accused's favour if possible. He was going to tell the court that he knew the gypsy because he had camped on his land and he was certain that he was not the young man to engage in a brawl without good reason for doing so.

He declared he would make them listen to what he had to say, and of course they could not fail to listen to my father. He was certain that when the evidence of Ralph Hassett's dissolute behaviour was brought to light and with it the proof of Leah's virginity, this could not be a hanging case.

My mother and I waited in the inn for my father's return. The tension was almost unbearable. If in spite of everything they condemned him to death . . . I could not bear to contemplate that.

We sat at the window of my parents' bedroom watching for his return.

Edward Barrington was with him. He had also been in court, and I warmed towards him for making our cause his.

As we saw them approaching I tried to judge from their expressions which way the verdict had gone, but I could not do so.

I sprang to the door. My mother was beside me. "Wait here," she said. "It won't be long now."

They came into the room. I stared at my father. He was looking solemn and did not speak for a few seconds. I feared the worst and I cried out: "What? What?"

"They've sentenced him."

"Oh no . . . no. It's unfair. It was my fault that he was caught."

My father took me by the shoulders. He said: "It could have been worse. A man was killed. That cannot be forgotten. He won't hang. We've stopped that. They've sentenced him to transportation . . . for seven years."

We were to leave Nottingham the following day. I felt deflated. I kept telling myself that at least they had not killed him. But to send him away for seven years . . . right to the other side of the world. Seven years . . . it was an eternity. I said to myself: I shall never see him again . . .

He had made a deep impression on me and I should never forget him.

The Barringtons persuaded us to dine with them on our last night. We did so—and the talk was all about the case.

"He was lucky," said Edward Barrington. "It's a fairly light sentence for killing a man."

"In such circumstances . . ." I began hotly.

"He did kill the man and it would be considered a light sentence. The girl made a good impression. She was so young and innocent . . . and quite beautiful."

"The fact that she was a virgin and we'd been smart enough to prove it knocked the wind out of their sails," said my father with a chuckle.

"The prosecution was out to prove that she was a loose woman. That was proved false and the evil reputation of Ralph Hassett could not be denied."

"Thanks for your help," said my father.

"You have been wonderful," added my mother.

"It is the least we could do," said Mrs. Barrington.

"Moreover," put in her husband, "it is good to see justice done."

"He'll be all right . . . that young man," said my father.

"He's one of the survivors. That I saw right from the beginning."

"But to leave one's country . . . to be banished . . ." I said. "When he should not have been banished at all, but applauded."

"The old squire was in a passion," said Mr. Barrington. "He wanted a hanging."

"Wicked old thing," said Mrs. Barrington.

"Well, I think they should set him free," I said.

"My dear girl, people cannot go about killing for whatever reason," said my father.

My mother smiled at me. "We saved him from the rope. Let us rejoice in that."

"Do you think he knew?" I asked.

"He saw me in court," explained my father. "He heard my testimony and he knew I was the one who had produced the evidence of the dead man's character and had proved the girl's innocence. And he would say, Why should he do that? He would know it is because I have a daughter who tells me what should and should not be done." He turned to the company. "She is a tyrant, this daughter of mine and she has made me her slave."

They were all gazing at us smiling, all except Clare Carson. In the turmoil of my thoughts there came the idea that she did not like me very much. I dismissed the thought at once. It was pointless and unimportant.

"They are a wild pair," said my mother, "my husband and my daughter. Jessica takes after her father and the odd thing is that I wouldn't change either of them even if I could."

"Remind me to remind you of that sometime," said my father.

"I think," put in Mrs. Barrington, "that we should drink to our meeting. It started in an unpleasant way and has turned out quite the reverse. I hope it will be the beginning of our friendship."

We all drank to that and I caught Edward Barrington's eyes on me. He was smiling very warmly and I felt rather pleased in spite of my sadness over Romany Jake, until I saw Clare Carson watching me.

I lifted my glass and drank.

The next day we left for home. We came out of the inn early in the morning. The Barringtons had requested that we call in to them on our way. There we were refreshed with wine and little cakes and it was agreed that we must visit each other at some time.

They all came out to wave us off and wish us a pleasant journey home.

My thoughts were melancholy. I had done everything I could to save him and at least he was not dead, but I wondered what it must be like to be banished to the other side of the world for seven years.

Ours had been a strange relationship and I knew that if I never saw him again he would live on in my thoughts.

He's a survivor, my father had said.

Those words brought me a certain comfort.

I went to Aunt Sophie's. One of us made a point of going every day. It was a different household since Dolly had gone there. Aunt Sophie was, as ever, at her best with misfortune, and Dolly had always been a special favourite of hers. Now that she was about to have a child and had no husband to help her through the ordeal, Aunt Sophie was in her element.

As I was given to pondering the strangeness of people's behaviour this gave me cause for consideration. One would have thought it was an unpleasant trait to thrive on the ill fortune of others and yet Aunt Sophie was assiduous in her care for those in trouble. Perhaps, I thought, nothing is wholly good, nothing wholly bad, but when we do good we get great satisfaction for ourselves, and the more benefits we bring to others, the greater our self gratification. It is vanity, self absorption in a way.

What a maze my thoughts led me into at times! If I went on in that strain it would be difficult to tell the difference between good and bad. Romany Jake had committed murder to save a girl from an injury which could have affected her whole life. Good and evil walked very closely together.

And now Dolly was hoping to have an illegitimate child. That was to be deplored. But on the other hand her rather sad life had taken on a new dimension and for the first time Dolly was happy.

I was very interested in this matter and discussed it with Amaryllis. She listened to me and told me I was making a complicated issue out of something which was very simple. Amaryllis only saw the good in people. It does make life simpler to be like that.

I wished I had not gone to Aunt Sophie's that day. I wished I had not had that talk with Dolly.

It had been decided that she should know nothing of Romany Jake's sentence. Everyone knew, of course, that he was the father of her child. It was hardly likely that his visits to Grasslands and their being together on Trafalgar night could have passed unnoticed. Romany Jake was a man to attract attention wherever he went, and the fact that he had selected Dolly for his attention would cause some surprise and would no doubt be discussed at length in the kitchens of Grasslands and Enderby as well as in all the cottages.

"To know would upset her," said my mother. "She will have to in time, of course, but let it be *after* the baby is born."

I went into the room which had been assigned to her. It was one of the bedrooms on the first floor—the one with the speaking tube which went down to the kitchen. Jeanne had said she should have that room so that if she needed help there was another way of letting people know. It was Aunt Sophie's room normally but she had given it up so that Dolly could have it. The midwife slept in the next room, but when the time grew nearer she was to have a bed in Dolly's room.

She was lying on the bed with the blue velvet curtains and I noticed as soon as I entered that she was not looking as serene as when I last saw her. Perhaps, I thought, she is growing alarmed now that the ordeal is coming nearer.

She said: "I'm glad you have come, Jessica."

"Everyone wants to know how you are. My mother is asking if you need another shawl."

"No thank you. Mademoiselle Sophie has already given me two." She went on: "I've been thinking a lot about . . . him, you know."

"Who?" I asked, knowing full well.

"The baby's father. I just have a feeling that something is wrong."

I was silent.

She said: "If the baby is a boy, he is to be called Jake after his father. If it's a girl she's to be Tamarisk. He talked about the tamarisk trees in Cornwall. He liked them very much. I've never seen one. The east wind is too strong here for them, he said. He liked the feathery clusters of pink and white flowers with their slender branches. He said they are

74

dainty . . . like young girls. So I shall call her Tamarisk. That should please him if he comes . . . when he comes . . .''

I remained silent but she gripped my hand. "I feel," she said, "that something is wrong."

"You mustn't," I replied. "You have to think of the baby."

"I know. But I can tell. I've always had something . . . I don't know what it is . . . but I know when something terrible is going to happen. I wonder if it is being not quite like other people . . . deformed in a way. Do you think if you are short of something Nature gives you something else . . . to make up?"

"Very likely."

"I've done some wicked things in my life."

"I expect all of us have."

"I've done especially wicked things . . . but all for love . . . in a way. I wish I hadn't. Taking you, for one thing, when you were a little baby. I know now what they must have gone through. I knew then, I suppose . . . but I wanted to hurt them."

"Don't think of that now. It doesn't seem to have done me much harm."

"I've done worse things . . . much worse. I wanted revenge. That's a bad thing."

"I suppose it is. People often say so."

"But I've always had a special feeling for you because of that time when I kept you in my room. I can see you as you were then. Those lovely big eyes and you just stared at me, you did . . . and then suddenly you'd break into a smile as though you thought there was something rather funny about me. I knew I couldn't hurt you then. Jessica, I want you to tell me about him."

"Tell you what?"

"There is a lot of whispering going on. I know something has happened. You went to Nottingham and it was something to do with him." She gripped my hand hard. "I sit here worrying. Tell me. I have to know. When I ask questions Jeanne pretends not to understand. She does that. She pretends her English isn't good enough. But she understands everything. And Mademoiselle Sophie, she won't tell me either. She keeps saying everything will be all right. I know something is very wrong and I believe it is about him."

I half rose and said: "I ought to be getting back."

She looked at me reproachfully.

"I thought you would have the courage to tell me. I lie here worrying. If anyone ought to know, I ought. They come south at the end of the summer. It will soon be summer. Something has happened to him, hasn't it? I hear the servants whispering. 'Don't let her know,' they say. 'Don't let her know till after the baby is born.' "

She was restless and there was a hot colour in her cheeks.

"You mustn't upset yourself," I began.

"I am upset and will be until I know. However bad it is, I've got to know. He killed a man and they caught him. He'll be tried. I know what that means. They think I don't hear their whisperings but I do."

I burst out: "He killed a man who was attempting to rape one of the gypsy girls."

She closed her eyes. "Oh then, it's true. They will hang him."

"No, no," I cried. I had to ease her mind. I was sure now that it was better that she should know than fear the worst. "He will be all right," I went on. "He will not hang. My father has saved him from that. Of course he could not get him freed entirely."

"Then he is in prison . . ."

"He has been sentenced to transportation."

She closed her eyes and lay back on her pillows. I was frightened. The colour had faded from her face. She was as white as the pillow on which she lay.

"It is only for seven years," I said.

She did not speak. I was afraid and called Jeanne.

That was the beginning. I was not sure whether the shock brought on the birth prematurely, but it was only two days later when Dolly's child was born.

I explained to my mother what I had done, and she assured me that there was nothing else I could have done in the circumstances. But I was sorry to have been the one to tell her.

The baby was a girl, healthy and strong. Not so, poor Dolly. The midwife said it was one of the most difficult deliveries she had ever undertaken. Aunt Sophie sent for the doctor. Dolly, he said, was not really suited to childbearing. In spite of the fact that she was in her mid-twenties, her body was rather immature.

She was very ill for a week—unconscious most of the time,

but there were occasions when she was able to hold the child in her arms.

At the end of the week she died and there was great sorrow at Enderby and indeed at Eversleigh.

Jeanne said: "She was so happy to have the child. I'd never seen her really happy before. And as soon as the child is born she leaves this world! Life can be cruel so often."

Claudine and my mother discussed at great length what should be done about the child.

"We will take her," said my mother. "The girls will love to have a baby in the nurseries. I shall like it, too. There is nothing like a baby in the house."

The child was to be called Tamarisk. I remembered Dolly had told me that she wished her to have that name. She must have told Aunt Sophie, too.

When my mother suggested that Tamarisk be brought to Eversleigh, Aunt Sophie was most indignant.

Indeed it should not be. *She* had decided to adopt Dolly's baby. She had always intended to look after her and Dolly. There was only Tamarisk now.

Jeanne took charge as usual and a beautiful nursery was prepared. Aunt Sophie was better than we had ever seen her before.

"It is a great interest for her," said my mother.

So Tamarisk lived at Enderby and flourished there.

Tamarisk

Now that Dolly was dead the question was what would happen to Grasslands. The baby Tamarisk was Dolly's natural heir and it was decided that as the house would not be needed because Tamarisk was to live at Enderby, it should either be let or put up for sale.

To let was not easy, and it seemed only reasonable that the house should be sold.

My mother said: "I wonder whether the Barringtons would be interested in it."

We all stared at her. We had forgotten that they had talked of looking for a house.

"It's just a possibility," went on my mother. "And think what pleasant neighbours they would be. Much nicer than having strangers here."

"There is no harm in letting them know about it," agreed my father.

Aunt Sophie was quite pleased when she heard we had a possible buyer in view but her interest now was centred on the baby and she gave little attention to anything else.

My mother invited the Barringtons for a visit, and she told them about the house. Both parents as well as Edward and Irene came; and of course Clare Carson was with them. They were enchanted with Grasslands and with the prospect of living close to us—all except Clare, who seemed somewhat guarded in her comments.

To our joy the Barringtons bought Grasslands and made it their main home. Clare came with them. Irene was shortly to be married to a Scot, so she would not be living in the house and Edward remained in Nottingham because of the business; but he often came down to stay with his family.

I thought a great deal about Romany Jake and often wondered how he was faring in the penal settlement.

My conscience was eased a little because we had saved his life but I would never be content unless I could talk to him and explain how it had all happened.

Life at Eversleigh passed pleasantly, unruffled by what was happening in the outside world.

It was April—one of my favourite times of the year because of the coming of spring.

We had lived fairly serenely since the death of Dolly Mather. We were no longer apprehensive about a possible invasion though Trafalgar had not put an end to Napoleon's ambitions. He had shrugged aside his failure at sea as he was making good his conquests on land and setting up his family to rule in the courts of Europe. Eager to found a dynasty of rulers, he had divorced his wife Josephine because she was barren and taken as his second wife Marie Louise of Austria in the hope of producing a son to carry on the line.

The wretched war dragged on. There were defeats and victories and one wondered whether it would ever end, though it did not affect us greatly except in increased taxation. The nation found a new hero in Arthur Wellesley who—after the victories of Oporto and Talavera about two years before—had been created Baron Douro and Viscount Wellington, and we were having spectacular successes on the Continent.

At home our poor old King was now blind and quite out of his mind; and in January of the previous year, the Regency Bill was passed, so that the Prince of Wales was now virtually the ruler.

One evening as we were sitting over dinner discussing topics of the day as we often did, my mother turned to a more frivolous topic: "It will soon be time for the birthday party and this year it will have to be a special one. Just think of it. The girls will be eighteen."

She looked at Amaryllis and me as though we had achieved something rather wonderful in reaching such an age.

"Eighteen!" said David. "Are they really? How time flies!"

"They are no longer little girls," said Claudine.

My father persisted: "Perceval's got a point. But now we are at war with America he's got to be cautious."

"Wars!" said my mother indignantly. "How stupid they all are! I don't even know what this one is about."

"It's all a disagreement about commerce," explained David.

My mother sighed. "You would have thought they had learned a lesson, when they quarrelled before about the colonies."

"History may repeat itself," said my father, "but it is certain that the lessons it teaches are hardly ever learned."

"One would have thought," said my mother, "that war with France would have been enough for those who are so enamoured of it."

"This war with France goes on and on," said Claudine.

"Perceval's a good man but I would say an uninspired one."

I said that it was strange that good people did not often make good leaders, and good leaders were often wicked in their private lives.

David, who loved this sort of discussion, instanced the two King Charleses. Charles the First such a good husband and father and about the worst King we had ever had, leading us to Civil War; whereas the second Charles's life had been one of moral scandal, and yet his rule had been really good for the country.

My mother interrupted with: "What colour would you like to wear for the party, Amaryllis?"

"I think perhaps blue."

"What about white, darling?" asked Claudine. "I can just see you in white. You will look like an angel."

"Jessica, are you going to have your favourite scarlet?" asked my mother. "Or is it going to be emerald green?"

"I'll have to think about it," I said.

"Such matters need weighty consideration," said my father, "while the country is plunged into war on two fronts."

"We should never do anything if we waited for those wretched wars to be over," commented my mother. "And the sooner they have finished one they start another. We'll go to London to choose the materials. I think we should give ourselves plenty of time. Where are we now . . . April . . .

Sometime in May. That will give us plenty of time to have the dresses made up. We'll fix a date. August would be best . . . somewhere midway between the two birthdays. That's fair enough.''

There had always been one party to celebrate the two birthdays as they came so close together—mine in August, Amaryllis' in September; and the parties were usually held at the end of August. Our mothers had started the practice when we were very young and had kept it up.

That was how we came to be in London in the May of that year 1812. There were my mother and myself as well as Amaryllis and Claudine; and as my father never liked my mother to go to London without him, he joined the party. So we all set out in the carriage and in due course arrived at the family house in Albemarle Street.

I had still retained that excitement which I felt when I came to London. The big city always seemed pulsating with life. Everyone appeared to be in a great hurry which always gave me a sense of urgency. I hoped we should visit the theatre while we were there.

The very first day my mother and I, with Claudine and Amaryllis, descended on the shops and after much debating a beautiful white silk was bought for Amaryllis' dress. It was more difficult to find the acceptable shade of red to enhance my darkness; but my mother said we should not be hurried.

My father always had business in London—rather mysterious business as well as his banking concerns, and one thing we had learned was not to ask questions. We did know that he worked less in the field than he had in the past and that his son Jonathan had lost his life because of his connections with this mysterious espionage. I knew that Claudine was delighted that David had no part in it. Amaryllis had told me so.

I often wondered whether Jonathan's son, also named Jonathan, who was at this time living with the Pettigrews, was also involved.

However, my father's interests did not absorb him so much that he could not pay a visit to the theatre and we had a glorious evening watching *A Tale of Mystery* which was not exactly new but was the first of the melodramas which had since become so popular. It had a wicked villain who the audience liked to pretend struck terror into them when he appeared; and although we laughed we could not help being caught up in the drama, particularly as it was accompanied by

81

the most expressive music which rose in volume for the villain and played sweetly for the unsullied heroine.

When the play was over we all returned home and sat up late drinking hot chocolate and discussing the improbabilities of the plot, laughing heartily at the actions of the villain and the gullibility of the heroine; and admitting that we had enjoyed every moment of it.

The next day was Sunday. We had attended church and afterwards walked in the Park; and my mother said that the following day we really must come to a decision about the material for my dress.

There were callers in the morning and an invitation to dine a few days later.

"And after that," my mother said, "we must think about getting home."

"It is a strange thing," I said, "that when we are at Eversleigh, a visit to London seems very desirable; and when we are here we think how nice it would be to get back."

"Perhaps anticipation is more satisfying than actuality," suggested Amaryllis.

"I think you may be right," I agreed.

"It reminds us that we should enjoy everything as it comes along."

"Amaryllis, if you are so wise at eighteen, you'll be a veritable sage by the time you are thirty."

The callers delayed our visit to the shops but my mother was determined that we should go, so about four o'clock we set out.

We examined bales of material—emerald greens and vivid scarlets, both of which my mother declared were my colours.

I had my mother's dark hair, but alas, not her vivid blue eyes. Mine were deep set, black lashed but of a deep brown; and I needed strong colours to set them off.

She was determined that I must look my best and she spent a long time selecting the right shade.

It was while we were in the shop, sitting at the counter, that a young man ran in. He was breathless and could scarcely stammer out the important news.

"The Prime Minister . . . has been shot. He's stone dead . . . there in the House of Commons."

As we came through the streets we realized that the news had spread. People stood about in little groups talking in shocked whispers. The Prime Minister assassinated! Surely not! This could not happen in England. That sort of thing was for foreigners. Spencer Perceval the Prime Minister had not been exactly one of the popular figures in politics. He was no Pitt or Fox. He had been rather insignificant but was no longer so.

My father was not at home when we arrived there. I guessed he would be occupied for a few days, perhaps delaying our return to Eversleigh.

There was a hush throughout the capital. News began to seep out. The murderer had been captured. It had been no difficult task to catch him for he had made no attempt to escape.

He was mad, it was said, a fanatic. Some avowed that it was merely fate that it happened to be the Prime Minister who was shot. It could have been any politician. The madman had a grudge against the government, not against any particular person. The Prime Minister had just happened to be in a certain spot at a certain time.

The trial took place immediately.

The murderer was John Bellingham, a Liverpool broker who had gone bankrupt, he declared, through government policies. He had recently visited Russia where he had been arrested on some trivial charge and when he had applied to the British Ambassador in St. Petersburg for help, it had been refused. Eventually he was freed and returning to England he had applied for redress for the wrongs he had suffered. When this was refused, he went crazy and vowed vengeance.

Now he was pleading insanity.

My father said that he would not get away with it. The whole country was shocked. We could not have our public figures shot at and be told that it was the work of a person of unsound mind. There had to be an example.

He was right. John Bellingham was sentenced to death and a week after the shooting he was hanged. We were in London on the day but we did not go into the streets.

My father's comment was: "The verdict was a wise one. Madman he may be, but we cannot have anyone with a grievance shooting our ministers and then being freed on a plea of insanity."

But the affair haunted me. The idea of that man's being so crazed with grief that he took a gun and shot a man dead depressed me. I could not shut out of my mind the image of his body dangling at the end of a rope. He had done the deed for revenge and two lives had been lost when there need not have been one.

My mother tried to disperse our gloomy mood by talking of other matters—chiefly the birthday celebrations. I responded but my thoughts could not be withdrawn from the tragedy of that poor madman and most of all I thought of the bereaved Perceval family who had lost a good husband and father. I heard there was a sorrowing wife, six sons and six daughters. He had been such a good man, people said; and even taking into account that aura of sanctity which invariably surrounds the dead, there appeared to be some truth in it.

To bear a grudge . . . a grudge which drives one to murder! I could not get that out of my mind.

Back in Eversleigh preparation began for the party. Eighteen was a coming of age. We were no longer children and I guessed our parents were hoping that suitable husbands would be found for us for that seemed to be the wish of all parents with nubile daughters.

The date was set for the end of August.

"The best time for a party," said Claudine, "for if the weather is good it can spill out into the garden."

We set about making out lists of guests.

"There is no need to send out invitations to the Barringtons," said my mother. "You two girls can go over and invite them personally."

A few days later Amaryllis and I set out together. On the way we passed the woods and I saw smoke rising from the trees.

"Look!" I said to Amaryllis.

"Gypsies, I suppose," she answered.

"It's a long time since we had them here. Not since . . ."

"That poor man . . ."

"Six years," I said.

My thoughts were back in that terrible moment when Romany Jake had come out of the house and been captured. It was a nightmare which had recurred in my mind in the past and even now came back to haunt me.

Amaryllis knew how I had felt and was very sympathetic; whenever the subject was mentioned she would remind me that I had saved his life.

I tried to believe I had; and indeed it seemed certain that if

I had not roused my father to take action, the death sentence would have been carried out.

Now the thought of the gypsies brought it back.

"Let's go and see," said Amaryllis, and she spurred on her horse.

I followed.

There in the clearing were the caravans. One of the women was lighting a fire and a few children were running about shouting to each other.

They were all silent when they saw us.

One of the men strolled over.

"Permission to stay is being asked," he said. "Now . . . this minute."

"You mean someone has gone to the house?"

The man nodded.

A girl emerged from a caravan and, looking curiously at us, strolled over. She was strikingly attractive with large luminous long-lashed dark eyes. Her hair hung in a thick plait tied at the end with red ribbon. I knew before she spoke who she was. She knew me too.

"Good day," she said. "Miss Frenshaw, is it not?"

I said: "You are Leah."

She smiled in affirmation.

"So you have come back."

"My father has gone to the house to ask permission for us to rest here."

"This is Miss Amaryllis Frenshaw," I said.

She bowed her head. Amaryllis gave her friendly smile. She had heard of Leah, of course, and knew what part she had played in Romany Jake's tragedy.

"Do you intend to stay long?" I asked.

She shook her head. "For a very short while. We are on our way to the West Country."

"Have you . . . heard anything of . . ."

She shook her head.

"It is so long ago."

"Six years," I said.

"In another year he will be free."

"Yes," I said. "Another year. I am sure my father will agree to your staying here."

"I think so," she said, and stood aside to let us pass.

We went on.

"What an extraordinarily beautiful girl," said Amaryllis.

"Yes. She looked sad, though. I suppose when something like that happens to you . . . when a man almost loses his life for defending you, it would make you feel strange . . . guilty in a way."

"It was not her fault. She should not feel guilty."

"No, but sometimes people feel guilty when things are not their fault. I mean . . . if they come about *because* of you."

"It may be so, but she certainly is lovely."

We had come to Grasslands. Mrs. Barrington had heard our approach and came out to greet us while one of the grooms took our horses.

"Edward is at home," she said. "He'll be so pleased you've called."

"Everyone will, I hope."

"I can assure you of that."

"Everyone is well?"

"In excellent form. We still miss Irene and wish we could be more together. She is pregnant again. Isn't that exciting? If only she were a little nearer!"

Edward had come out. "What a pleasure to see you," he said.

Edward had seemed to become much more mature since I had first seen him six years ago on that fateful trip to Nottingham. He was very sure of himself. His father said he was going to be one of the most influential businessmen in the country one day. "He has a flair for it," was his comment. "Much more than I ever had. Reminds me of my grandfather who founded the business."

I could well believe that. Edward constantly steered the conversation towards business; I imagined he found the trivialities of ordinary discourse a trifle boring.

I liked him though—mainly, I think, because whenever we met and Amaryllis was with me, although he was extremely polite to us both, he could not stop his eyes straying to me. That was pleasant. I think I was a trifle jealous of Amaryllis. She was so lovely and she had such a sweet nature; she was one of the good women of Eversleigh. I was of the other sort—not exactly bad, but rebellious, self-willed, selfish perhaps and decidedly vain. Yes . . . all those things and I really could not understand why so many young men—and older ones too—always showed more interest in me than in beautiful Amaryllis. It was extraordinary. Amaryllis would have made the perfect wife. She was domesticated, easygoing and extremely beautiful. I was none of these really. Yet it was to me they looked with a certain speculation which indicated they considered me desirable.

One of the servants once said: "You've got something, Miss Jessica. Miss Amaryllis is very pretty . . . beautiful as an angel . . . but you've got what they want. There's no putting a finger on it. It's just there. Miss Amaryllis is just too pretty, too much of the lady, too good, too nice. Men respect the likes of Miss Amaryllis but you're one of them they go after." The next remark was less flattering. "Men are such fools . . . never know what side their bread's buttered, they don't. Always go for them that's hardest to live with . . . and leave the good ones behind."

Amaryllis was undoubtedly one of the good ones.

"Come along in," said Mrs. Barrington. "Oh, there's Clare."

Clare Carson had come in. She smiled as though pleased to see us, but I always felt she was hiding her true feelings.

"You'll have to test the new elderberry," went on Mrs. Barrington. Ask them to bring it, Clare. Not a patch on young Mrs. Frenshaw's . . . but you might like to try it."

"We have come for a purpose, haven't we, Amaryllis?"

"We have," agreed Amaryllis. "It's to invite you to our birthday party."

"Oh, is it time then? How the days fly! It seems only yesterday when you had your seventeenth."

Mr. Barrington had come into the room and heard the last remark. "The older you get, the quicker time flies," he said. "Good morning to you, my dears."

"It will be in August, I suppose," said Clare.

"Yes," I replied. "Midway between the two birthdays. That's how it has always been."

"You can be sure we'll be there," said Mrs. Barrington. "The whole lot of us . . . except Irene. She would be if she could, but she's so far away . . . and there are the babies."

"I shall make sure I'm here for it," said Edward, smiling at me.

"A little relaxation will do you good," added his father.

"He wouldn't miss it for the world, I know," said his mother.

The servants brought the wine which Mrs. Barrington poured out. We sipped it and declared it exceptionally good.

Edward came over to me. "It's good to see you. You look blooming."

"With health and vigour," I said. "And you . . . you look a little preoccupied."

He drew his chair closer to mine. Amaryllis was in conversation with the others.

"A little trouble at the factory. It's the new machines. The work people don't like them."

"You'd think they would welcome them."

"They are afraid the machines will take over their jobs and there will be no work for them."

"And will they?"

He lifted his shoulders. "It may be so for a time. But if we don't have the machines we can't compete with the people who have and we should be out of business; so that would lose their jobs in any case."

"It must be worrying."

"We'll overcome it, but they are threatening. In some places they have actually broken up the machines."

"I did hear something about those people. Are they what they call Luddites?"

"Yes. It's a name given to them because some time ago there was a Ned Ludd. He was simple, quite mad. He lived in Leicestershire. One day, in the factory where he worked, someone teased him. He was frustrated being unable to find words to express his anger and he turned to the stocking machines and started breaking them up. He was just crazy. He felt there was something evil in machines and vented his wrath on them."

"But the present-day Luddites are not mad. They are just frightened men."

"You could say that they are short-sighted. They can't see that if we are to continue to be prosperous, we have to advance with the times, and if we don't there will be no work anyway."

Mrs. Barrington came over. "Is Edward boring you with talk about those people who are threatening to break the machines?"

Amaryllis wanted to know about them and it was explained.

"Poor men," she said. "It is so terrible to be afraid of poverty."

Edward said: "We have to move with the times."

"What will happen?" she asked.

"We shall have to wait and see. We must have the machines, that's certain. If the workmen become a menace we shall have to call in the troops or something like that."

Mrs. Barrington changed the subject. She was the sort of woman who hated the thought of trouble and seemed to believe that if one did not think of it, it ceased to exist. But I was rather disturbed thinking of the men who feared the machines would rob them of their livelihood.

"Clare said there were gypsies in the neighbourhood," Mrs. Barrington was saying.

"Yes. I saw them coming in this morning," said Clare. "The caravans were lumbering along the road."

"They plan to stay only a little while," added Amaryllis. "We saw them as we came along and spoke to one of them."

"It was Leah," I said. "Do you remember Leah?"

They were all puzzled for a moment.

"Six years ago," I reminded them. "When we all met. She must have been about fourteen then, I'd say. I recognized her at once. We were in Nottingham to do what we could for the gypsy. Leah was the girl in the case."

"I remember well," said Edward.

"They are asking my father's permission to camp in the woods."

"He'll give it," said Amaryllis, "with the usual injunctions about fire risks, of course."

The Barringtons did not seem to find the subject of the gypsies very interesting and Mrs. Barrington began to talk about the previous year's party at which rain had made use of the garden impossible.

At length we left.

As we came close to Enderby, I said: "Let's call in. There's time."

Amaryllis was agreeable.

As we approached the house we saw Tamarisk on her pony—a new acquisition for last Christmas. One of the grooms had her on a leading rein and she was trying to break away from him.

I could never see Tamarisk without thinking of Romany Jake. She was a very beautiful child, though not conventionally so. She had enormous expressive dark eyes with thick black hair and lashes. Her features were perfect. Her hair was straight and so thick that nothing could be done with it. Jeanne despaired of it. She would have liked soft curls. Jeanne herself cut it, as she said, in the only possible way. It was short with a fringe on the forehead, so that Tamarisk looked like a handsome boy. She was tall for her years—long limbed and graceful. She had a wild rebellious nature. My mother and Claudine said it was due to the fact that Aunt Sophie had spoiled her, for Aunt Sophie doted on her. My mother declared she had never known Sophie so contented with life. And it was all due to this naughty child.

She was bright and intelligent and had already taught herself to read, but there was nothing docile about Tamarisk. She would fly into rages if she was crossed. If anyone annoyed her she would fix those enormous eyes upon them and murmur in a deep voice: "You'll be sorry."

Jeanne both delighted in and despaired of her.

"I do not know what she will be like when she grows up," she said. "She is so rebellious now."

The governess said she was a handful though she had only been in the house a month. The previous one had stayed six weeks. Some of the servants blamed her parentage, saying: "She's the gypsy's child. What blood has she got in her veins? She could be a witch."

It was unfortunate that Tamarisk overheard these comments for instead of being disturbed by being thought of as a witch, she was delighted.

"I'm a witch," she was constantly reminding everyone. "Witches put spells on people."

She had revolutionized Enderby. It was no longer merely the home of a recluse and her maid. It was typical of Tamarisk that she should dominate the household.

"I don't want to be held," she was saying. "I want to ride properly."

I said: "Hello, Tamarisk."

The luminous dark eyes turned to us. "You have a proper horse," she said. "Why can't I?"

"You will when you are a little older," Amaryllis told her gently.

"I don't need to be older. I want it now."

"When you are seven perhaps."

"I want it now . . ."

"That is unfortunate," I said, feeling sorry for the poor groom.

Tamarisk glared at me.

"We are going to see Aunt Sophie," I continued. "Is she well?"

"I don't want a little horse like a baby. I don't want to be a child."

"Babies don't ride at all," pointed out Amaryllis.

"Some babies could. I could."

"Come on, Amaryllis," I said, turning away. "That child is getting impossible," I added.

"Poor little thing. It hasn't been easy for her."

"Not easy! With Aunt Sophie doting and Jeanne supplying all her needs!"

"Still . . ."

"You'd make excuses for the devil." I spurred on my horse and made for the stables.

Aunt Sophie was in her sitting room. In the old days before the coming of Tamarisk, she had scarcely stirred from her room. She looked almost normal or would have done but for the unusual hood she wore, which covered the scarred part of her face. This morning it was pale blue which matched her gown. Jeanne was with her.

"We have fixed the day for the party," I said, "and we've been over to Grasslands to issue the invitations."

We did not ask Aunt Sophie. We knew she would not want to be present, and if by some miracle she did decide to come, she would not need an invitation.

She asked after my mother and Claudine which was a formality really, because they had called on her only the previous day.

I said: "Edward Barrington is concerned about trouble in his factory. The people are threatening to break up the machines."

Jeanne flashed a warning look at me. We did not talk of such things in front of Aunt Sophie. It reminded her of what she had endured from the revolutionaries in her own country.

Amaryllis said quickly: "We saw Tamarisk on the way in."

It was a subject calculated to turn Aunt Sophie's thoughts away from all that was unpleasant.

"She sits a horse well," I said.

"Amazing child," murmured Aunt Sophie lovingly.

"Too fond of her own way," added Jeanne.

"She has spirit," insisted Aunt Sophie. "I'm glad of that. I shouldn't want her to be meek."

"She was complaining bitterly about being on a leading rein," I said.

"That one wants to run before she can walk," commented Jeanne.

91

"She is full of life," said Aunt Sophie.

We chatted a little about the weather and the party and after a while there was a commotion outside the door.

"I *will* go in. I want to see Amaryllis and Jessica. They are with Aunt Sophie. I will. I will. Let me go. I hate you. I'll put a spell on you. I'm a witch."

These words were followed by a crash on the door.

"Let her come in, Miss Allen," called Aunt Sophie. "It's quite all right."

The door burst open and Tamarisk stood there—beautiful in her riding habit, her eyes ablaze, her hair like an ebony cap on her perfectly shaped head.

"Hello, *mon petit chou*," said Aunt Sophie.

Tamarisk turned to us. "*Petit chou* means little cabbage, and in French that means darling and you are very precious. You thought I was going to be scolded, didn't you?"

"I thought nothing of the sort," I said.

"Yes, you did."

"How did you know what I thought?"

"I know because I'm a witch."

"Tamarisk," murmured Jeanne reprovingly, but Aunt Sophie was smiling, clearly applauding her darling's precocity.

"And what have you been doing?" she asked, giving her entire attention to Tamarisk.

"I've been riding. I can ride now. I won't have Jennings holding my horse. I want to ride on my own."

"When you're a big girl . . ."

"I want it now."

"Little one, it is only because we are afraid you will fall."

"I won't fall."

"No, *chou,* but you wouldn't want poor Aunt Sophie to sit here worrying that you might, would you?"

"I wouldn't mind," said Tamarisk frankly.

Aunt Sophie laughed. I looked at Jeanne who raised her shoulders.

Aunt Sophie seemed to have forgotten our presence, so I said we should be going and Jeanne escorted us to the door. Tamarisk was still telling Aunt Sophie how well she rode and that she wanted to ride by herself.

I said to Jeanne: "That child is becoming unmanageable."

"She is not becoming, she always was," commented Jeanne.

"Aunt Sophie spoils her."

"She loves her so. She has made all the difference to her."

"It is not good for the child."

"I daresay Aunt Sophie is very sorry for her," said Amaryllis. "Poor Tamarisk . . . it is awful not to have a father or a mother."

"No child could be better looked after," I reminded her.

"Yes . . . but to have no real father or mother . . . I understand how Aunt Sophie feels."

"It is good that we came here," mused Jeanne. "We had to leave our home . . . everything. But here there was first this house and that did a lot for her . . . and now the child. I think she will become better than I ever hoped . . . and it is due to the child."

"The child is storing up a lot of trouble for herself, and for Aunt Sophie, I should imagine," I said.

"Dear Jessica," put in Amaryllis, "you were a bit of a rebel yourself when you were young. I can remember you . . . lying on the floor and kicking out at everything because you couldn't have what you wanted. And look at you now!"

"So I have improved, have I?"

"A little."

"We do our best," said Jeanne, "Miss Allen and I. It is not easy. She *is* a difficult child. Sometimes I wish she were not so bright. She listens; she misses nothing. Miss Allen says she is quite clever. I wish she could be a little more serene."

"I'm afraid she won't be while Aunt Sophie spoils her."

We rode back to the house.

"Well, are the Barringtons coming?" asked my mother.

"The entire family . . . with the exception of Irene who could not possibly have accepted," I told her.

"I thought they would," she answered, smiling at me.

Riding near the woods I came face to face with Penfold Smith. I recognized him immediately as I had his daughter. I called: "Good day." He hesitated for a moment and then he swept off his hat and bowed.

"You're Miss Frenshaw," he said.

"Yes, that's right. We last met in Nottingham."

"Six years ago."

He looked older, I thought. There were streaks of white in the black hair, and his face was lined, more weather-beaten.

"We shall never forget what you did," he said.

"It was my father."

"Yes, but you, too. I think you moved him to do what he did."

"You know a great deal about us."

"Gypsies learn about life. It's wandering . . . seeing so many people."

"I should have thought you weren't long enough in any place to find out much about people. I saw your daughter a few days ago."

"Yes—a good girl."

"She has married, I suppose?"

He shook his head. "No, she has not married. She will take no man."

"She is very beautiful . . . strikingly so."

"I think so. I fear for her sometimes because she is so beautiful. But she knows how to take care of herself . . . now." His eyes glinted.

"You have never heard anything of . . . ?"

"You mean Jake?" He shook his head. "It would not be possible. He is well though."

"How do you know?"

"Leah knows. She has powers . . . the second sight. She knew that disaster was threatening us. Poor child, she did not know from what direction it was to come. She has grown in her powers. She was born with them. She is my seventh child. Her mother was a seventh child. In gypsy lore the seventh child of a seventh child is born with the power to see into the future."

"I thought a number of gypsies had that. Fortune telling is one of their gifts, I believe."

"Leah has special gifts. She has said she would like to look at your palm one day."

"She told you that?"

"Yes, after she had seen you. She said there were powerful forces round you."

I looked over my shoulder and he smiled.

"They are not for ordinary eyes to see. She said you interested her very much. The other young lady, too, but especially you."

"I am sure Amaryllis would love to have her fortune told. So should I. Tell her to come to the house tomorrow afternoon. If it is fine we will be in the garden. If the servants hear she is telling fortunes they would not give her a moment's peace."

"I will tell her."

"And you say she foretold . . . that terrible tragedy?"

"In a manner . . . yes. She knew that Jake was in danger, but she did not know that it would come through herself. Now she knows that Jake is well. He will come back, she says."

"She is waiting for him," I said. "Is that why she will not marry?"

"Perhaps. She keeps her secrets. But . . . she is waiting and she knows that one day he will come."

"I hope he understood that I had no part in betraying him."

"I am sure he understood. He knew that you were there, that you cared enough to try to save him. He knew what your father did and that he owed his life to that."

"But to be sent away . . . to that place . . . not knowing what would happen to him when he arrived . . ."

"Remember, he had been expecting the hangman's noose. Anything would seem good after that. Life is sweet and he had not lost his. He would always survive, and he will always be grateful."

"How cruel life was to him . . . just because he happened to be there . . ."

"He saved Leah. I think I should have been the one to kill that rogue if Jake hadn't."

"If he ever comes back he will find you," I said. "When he does will you please tell him that I had no hand whatsoever in his capture. I rode over to tell him that they were looking for him. My plan was to help him. I had no idea that they were there . . . right behind me."

"I'll tell him but he knows already."

"I think of it often and I hope and pray that life is not unbearable wherever he is."

"He will come through whatever happens to him."

"You are sure of that?"

"My daughter is and she is the one who sees beyond what ordinary people see."

"And you are all right in your camp?"

"Very comfortable, thank you. Your father has been good to us."

"He remembers too and wishes he could have done more at the trial."

"He has given us permission to stay for a few weeks, but we shall be moving on shortly."

"To the West Country, I believe. Your daughter told me. Will you remind her that we shall expect her tomorrow afternoon?"

I rode on.

When I told Amaryllis that Leah was coming over to read our palms, she was intrigued. Who does not like having one's fortune told? Even the men do, I think, though they would probably deny it.

However, there was no doubt of Amaryllis' interest.

The next day Jeanne came to the house with some embroidery she had done for my mother. To my surprise Tamarisk came with her. She wanted to see the puppies which had been born to one of the Labradors; and as Amaryllis and I were meeting Leah one of the maids was asked to take her to the kennels.

Amaryllis and I were in the garden when Leah arrived. She wore a red skirt with a simple white blouse; her hair was piled high to make a crown about her head and there were gold-coloured rings in her ears. About her waist was a thick leather belt. She looked quite regal. "The queen of the gypsies," I said to Amaryllis as we saw her approaching.

I said: "We are going to find a sheltered spot in the garden because if the servants discover that you are telling fortunes they won't give you any peace."

"I like only to tell when I have something to tell," she replied.

We walked across the grass to the summer house.

"Let's go in here," said Amaryllis.

"You may well have nothing to tell us," I said.

"I am sure there will be something."

"And for me?" asked Amaryllis.

"We shall see. There is serenity all about you. It is the best. It makes for happiness . . . but happiness often means that there is not much to tell."

We seated ourselves on the chairs in the summer house. There was a small white topped table there. As Leah sat down I noticed that her belt had a sheath attached to it. She was carrying a knife. I remembered what her father had said about her taking care to protect herself. The knife was such a startling contrast to her gentle demeanour. It was very understandable, I thought. If what had happened to her had happened to me, I should want to carry a knife in my belt.

First she turned to Amaryllis and took her palm. They made a charming picture—their heads close—one so fair, one so dark. Two of the most beautiful women I had ever seen—and so different. Amaryllis so open, so innocent in a way; Leah dark, brooding, her eyes full of secret knowledge—and wearing a belt with a knife in it!

"I see happiness," she said. "Yes, I felt it immediately. You walk through life calmly, as the young do. You are young in heart and that is a good thing to be. There are dangers all around you . . . below you . . . above you . . . but you walk straight through and you look neither up nor down, and because you see no evil, evil cannot harm you."

"It sounds a little dull," said Amaryllis. "I should like to know what all these dangers are."

Leah shook her head. "This is the best way. You are a lucky lady. That much I can tell you."

Amaryllis looked faintly disappointed but Leah could say no more.

Then she turned to me. I held out my palm and she took it.

"Oh yes . . ." She touched my hand lightly and looked up at me. Her dark eyes seemed to bore right through me and I felt my secret thoughts were revealed to her, my petty jealousies and vanities, my less than admirable nature.

She said: "You will be much sought after and there will be a choice to be made. So much will depend on that choice."

"Can't you see what I should do?"

She answered: "There is always free will. There are divided paths. It is for you to decide. If you take one you must beware."

"How shall I know which is the dangerous path?"

She paused and bit her lip. "You are strong in your will. Whatever happens to you will be your choice. You *can* come through. But you must be wary. All about you I see forces . . . forces of evil."

"What sort of evil?"

She shook her head. "I saw this . . . and I wanted to tell you. You must be careful. Do not act rashly. Be careful."

"How can I when I don't know of what to be careful?"

"Take care in all your actions. The time of choice will come, depend on that. You go one way and the evil will not be there. You take one path and then . . . it is there."

97

"What sort of evil? Death?"

She did not answer.

"So it is death," I insisted.

"It is not clear. Death could be there . . . Not yours. A death. That is all I can say."

"And you saw all this when you met me. You wanted to come and warn me."

"I did not know what I should find. I never know. But I had the strong feeling that I wanted to warn you."

She released my hand and looked at me helplessly; and at that moment the door of the summer house opened. I looked towards it in dismay. She had shaken me a little with her warning and I wanted to hear more.

It was Tamarisk who stood there. She was dressed in a red dress with a light navy blue cloak. The combination was beautiful. Jeanne made most of her clothes and the colours always blended delightfully.

"What do you want, Tamarisk?" I asked.

"To see you," she replied. "What you are doing?" She stared at Leah. "You're the gypsy," she added.

"Yes, I am."

"I know about you. Jenny and Mab told me."

"They told you?" I said sharply.

"No . . . not me . . . but I heard them. You live in the woods and tell fortunes."

Tamarisk approached and stood still, looking intently at Leah.

As for Leah herself she could not take her eyes off the child. I thought she was struck by her extraordinary beauty.

"Tell my fortune," said Tamarisk.

"Fortune telling is not for children," I said.

"Oh yes, it is. It's for everybody."

Leah had taken the small hand which had been thrust into hers. She said gently: "When you are young, there is nothing written in the palm. It comes when you grow older."

"Nothing written on it!" She seized my hand and studied it. "There's nothing written on Jessica's."

"It is not writing with a pen," explained Leah. "It's written by life."

"Who is Life?"

"What we are . . . what we are growing up to."

"I want Life to write on my hands."

"It will," said Leah with a smile. "I think it may have a great deal to write."

That pleased Tamarisk, but she was bored with fortunes if she was not to have one yet.

"There are four puppies. I like the big one. He squeals a lot and he is very greedy."

"Who took you down to show you the puppies?"

"Jenny."

"Where is she now?"

Tamarisk lifted her shoulders. "Do gypsies have puppies?" she asked.

"Oh yes," Leah told her. "We have our dogs and some of them have puppies."

"Where does Life write on them? They haven't got hands."

"It would find somewhere no doubt," said Amaryllis.

Tamarisk was quite taken with Leah. She put her hands on her knees and looked up at her searchingly.

"You've got gold rings in your ears."

"Yes," said Leah.

"I want gold rings in my ears."

"Tamarisk always wants everything everyone else may have," I said.

"I want gold in my ears," she repeated.

"Perhaps one day . . ." began Amaryllis.

"I want it now. They are always saying one day," she told Leah. "Do you live in a caravan?"

"Yes."

"Do you sleep there?"

"Yes. Sometimes if it is a very hot night we sleep out of doors . . . under the sky and when we wake in the night we can see the stars twinkling overhead. And sometimes there's a moon."

"I want to sleep under the stars."

"Perhaps you will . . . one day."

"*You* say it now. One day! I never want one day. I always want now."

I heard an agitated voice: "Miss Tamarisk. Miss Tamarisk. Where are you?"

Tamarisk buried her head in Leah's lap. I noticed how gently Leah's long brown fingers touched the dark straight hair.

I went to the door of the summer house and said: "She's here, Jenny. Did you think you had lost her?"

99

"She ran off and when I turned round she had gone, Miss Frenshaw."

"Well, she's here now. She ought to be put on a chain like a little dog."

Tamarisk lifted her head and put out her tongue at me.

"Oh, certainly she should be," I went on. "And taught how to behave."

"I know how to behave."

"Well, why not practise what you know?"

"Come along, Miss Tamarisk," said Jenny. "Jeanne is waiting to go."

She took Tamarisk firmly by the hand and led her away.

"She is a beautiful child," said Leah as the door of the summer house closed.

"And a very unmanageable one. They spoil her."

"She has a look of . . ."

"Romany Jake?" I said. "He is her father."

Leah nodded; her face was full of secrets and I did not know what she was thinking.

"Poor Tamarisk," said Amaryllis, "her mother is dead."

"She has her father . . ." began Leah.

"A father who does not know of her existence!" went on Amaryllis.

"She is his child," said Leah. "There could be no doubt of it."

She was quiet for a moment, then she said: "I am sorry I could not tell you more. That is how it is. I do not want to talk nonsense . . . as some of our people do . . . just while they are waiting for what is to come. Inspiration . . . truth . . . it flashes upon you . . . and you wait for it. But sometimes it does not come and then there is no fortune. But what can be done? Can one say, 'There is nothing. You do not inspire me. The powers are silent . . .' Or 'I do not wish to tell . . .' How could we say that? We can only wait . . . and sometimes it comes and sometimes not."

"I understand perfectly, don't you, Amaryllis?"

"Perfectly," she replied. "And you have given me such a lovely fortune. It's poor Jessica I'm sorry about . . . all those dark forces . . ."

"They are there surrounding us all. We must be like you and look neither up nor down. Then we shall not see them . . . and perhaps our good angel will guide our footsteps in the right direction."

I had brought money with which to pay her and I gave it to her. She accepted it gracefully with many thanks and we walked with her to the gates and then went back to the house.

Tamarisk and Jeanne had already left.

Guests were arriving for the party. Lord and Lady Pettigrew were there with Millicent and her son Jonathan.

Jonathan was a little younger than I, and Millicent, although my sister-in-law, was of an age with Amaryllis' mother, Claudine. My birth to my parents late in life had made some rather complicated relationshps for me.

I quite liked Jonathan. He had always been a high-spirited boy and was continually in some sort of scrape. He had a charming personality, and was always disarmingly sorry if he caused anyone any trouble. His mother said he was very like his father who had been killed nearly twenty years ago in a shooting affray with a French spy.

The Pettigrews were frequent visitors at Eversleigh and one day Jonathan would inherit the estate, and my father was quite interested in him, although he was often exasperated by him.

Lady Pettigrew was a very autocratic lady who thought she could manage everyone's affairs better than they could themselves, and unfortunately tried to do so. Lord Pettigrew was a very pleasant old man, gentle and resigned. As I said to Amaryllis, he had to be, living with Lady Pettigrew for years. Claudine said she was getting old now and we must bear with her. Amaryllis was a great favourite with her; I was not because I could not resist the temptation to contradict.

The Pettigrews had come several days before the birthday and we were all invited over to the Barringtons' to dine. I was next to Edward for dinner and I began to wonder whether we were being thrown together, for I always seemed to find myself close to him.

"I am very much looking forward to the party," he said.

"We all are."

"The eighteenth birthday! Rather a special one, isn't it? Eighteen is supposed to be one of the milestones of life."

"When one leaves childhood behind."

He looked at me seriously and nodded. I felt faintly uneasy. He was hinting at something. Could it really be that he was thinking of marriage?

I hoped not. I had always fretted to be grown up but when

one was an adult certain decisions had to be made. I did not want to be married yet. I liked Edward Barrington, of course. I also liked some of the other young men in the neighbourhood. Oh yes, I wanted to be grown up; but I did not want to leap straight out of girlhood into marriage. I wanted a little time to bask in the admiration of a number of people. I did not want to confine myself to the attentions of one, which I supposed I should have to do when I was married.

A faint gloom had been cast over the evening. Times change. Nothing remains the same for long. I looked along the table at my father and realized with a sudden anxiety that he was an old man. The great Dickon . . . old! I had always had a special relationship with him. I had been grateful from my earliest childhood when I discovered that I and my mother were the only ones who could soften him. I remembered Amaryllis' saying "Ask your father. He'll say yes . . . if you ask him." Miss Rennie had said, "Miss Jessica knows how to get round her father." It was especially wonderful because I did not have to know anything. I just had to *be*. I loved him dearly. For all his wickedness—and I believed he had been very wicked in his youth—I loved him more than I did anyone else—except perhaps my mother and that was equally. But they were both getting old and could not live forever. My father was fresh-faced; he looked healthy; but I realized with a pang that he was well into his sixties. The thought frightened me. And my mother was in her fifties. She was still beautiful, of course, because she had that kind of beauty which does not fade. There is a permanence about it. There was white in her hair now but it was still abundant; and her eyes, although they might be a little lined, were still of that arresting dark blue shade. But they were both getting old. Edward Barrington, by his insinuations . . . if insinuations they were . . . had reminded me of this.

"You look a little sad," Edward was saying.

I flashed a smile at him. "Sad? No, of course not."

I started to talk animatedly trying to dismiss those rather frightening thoughts.

When we returned home that night, my mother came to my room. It was a habit of hers. There were times, she said, when she was in need of a cosy chat. This was one of those occasions.

"A pleasant evening," she said. "It always is at the

Barringtons'. Nice neighbours. We were lucky when they came to Grasslands."

"A little different from the last inhabitants."

My mother frowned. "Yes, old Mrs. Trent was always something of a misfit and then that tragedy with Evie . . . and now poor Dolly . . . it seemed as though she were dogged by ill fortune."

"Edward is a little perturbed about the work people and the machines."

"Yes, I heard about that. I daresay Edward will overcome his difficulties. He's that sort of person. I like him, don't you?"

I looked sharply at her and burst out laughing.

"You know me well," she said. "Sometimes I believe you know what I'm thinking."

"For instance at the present moment?"

"Well, he's very earnest. Mrs. Barrington hinted to me . . . Now, you mustn't get on your high horse. Parents are like that. You'll know one day. It has occurred to me for some time that there might be a happy outcome."

"Why don't you say it outright. You want me to marry Edward Barrington. Well, Mother, I do not want to marry him or anybody."

"Don't look so fierce. Nobody is going to drag you to the altar against your wishes."

"I should think not!"

She laughed at me. "Just idle dreaming. I expect the idea is new to you. I'd like to see you happily married. It's nice to have children when you are young."

"As you did me?"

"That was a very special case."

"I don't want to think about marrying anyone. I want to be young for a while yet."

"Of course. But if you did decide on Edward Barrington we should all be rather pleased. You'd be near us, for one thing."

"He's in Nottingham a great deal of the time."

"Yes . . . but Grasslands would be a sort of root. I should hate it if you went far away."

"I have no intention of going far away . . . or marrying . . . for a very long time. I like it here. I can't imagine I should ever love anyone as much as I love you and my father."

She was deeply moved. "My dear, dear Jessica," she said. "What a comfort you have been to us both!"

"You don't need any comfort from me. You have each other."

"I'm so lucky."

"I think we all are."

She laughed. "We're getting quite maudlin."

"I felt a little sad at dinner because it suddenly occurred to me that you were getting old . . . you and my father . . . and it frightened me. I just could not bear it if you weren't there . . . either of you."

"We shall always be here until . . ."

"That's what I mean."

"My dearest child, all my joy has been in my husband and my daughters . . . you and Claudine. Charlot . . ."

"You rarely speak of him."

"I think of him often. He left us . . . on that day years ago and I have not seen him since. Perhaps I shall one day. He is after all my son, and when I think of him I thank God for my daughters."

I said: "Who is getting maudlin now? You are going to live forever and I'm going to be with you . . . your unmarried daughter who will always be there to look after you."

The door opened and my father came in.

"What on earth is going on here?" he demanded. He was looking at my mother. "I wondered what had happened to you."

"We got talking," she said.

"You look a bit . . . peculiar."

"Jessica was saying she was going to look after us for the rest of our days."

"Look after us! When did we need looking after?"

"She's worried because we're getting old, and so is she, and she is dead against marriage because she much prefers you to any suitor."

"Well, of course she does. She is going to find it impossible to discover someone who will match up with me."

"It's true," I said.

My mother slipped her arm through his. "It all came about because I mentioned . . . or did I hint? . . . that Edward Barrington looked as though he might have plans concerning her."

"I shouldn't object to him as a son-in-law."

"But it is *I* who have to accept or object, dear Father, not you."

"Parental approbation is usually necessary in the best regulated families."

"But this is not one of those. It's us. Please get out of your silly old heads that you have to find a husband for me. When I feel the need of one I'll choose him myself. At the moment, I am very content for everything to remain as it is."

"You've made that clear enough. And what's this about our getting old? I'll never be old."

"I don't believe you ever will."

"Well, come on, Lottie."

He took my face in his hand and looked at me. "Stop fretting," he said. "When have you not had your own way, eh? Nothing is going to change that . . . just because you have reached the mature age of eighteen. Stop thinking about age. That's the best way to ward it off. All will be well. You are like me . . . born lucky. Life works out for people like us. Look at me. A wicked old sinner and I have got the two best women in the world."

He kissed me swiftly.

"Good night," he went on briefly.

My mother kissed me and they were gone.

Nothing had changed. No one would attempt to force me, nor even persuade me, to do what I did not want to.

My fate was in my own hands.

It was the day of the party. In the morning Amaryllis and I rode over to Enderby. We did not think for a moment that Aunt Sophie would come, but we had to assure her that if she decided to, we should be very happy to see her.

I said to Amaryllis: "It is good to get away from the house. The servants seemed to be running round in circles like a lot of ants. They seem to be busy but they are not sure doing what."

"There is so much to be prepared and both our mothers want everything to go without a hitch. They'll be terribly hurt if it doesn't."

We had reached Enderby. Jeanne met us and told us that Aunt Sophie was not very well. She believed she had a cold coming.

"Would she not want to see us today?" I asked. "We only

came to enquire how she was, and to tell her that if she did decide to come to the party, we'd be delighted.''

"Oh, she wouldn't come to the party, but she will be glad to see you.''

We went into Aunt Sophie's room. Tamarisk was seated on a stool with a little table before her. She was painting in lurid reds and blues.

"I am sorry you are not well, Aunt Sophie,'' I said.

"Are we disturbing you?'' asked Amaryllis.

"No . . . no. Come in. I thought I'd have a day in bed. Jeanne thinks I should. Just a slight cold. Tamarisk is keeping me company.''

Tamarisk glanced up from her painting, looking very virtuous as though she were performing some act of mercy.

"What are you painting?'' Amaryllis asked Tamarisk.

"I'm painting gypsies.''

"Tamarisk saw the gypsies yesterday, didn't you, Tamarisk?'' said Aunt Sophie. "She came back and told us all about it. We wondered where she was. Jeanne went out and found her with the gypsies.''

"I like gypsies,'' said Tamarisk. "They have caravans. They sleep in them . . . and sometimes on the grass. There are horses and dogs and children without shoes and stockings. I don't want to wear shoes and stockings.''

"You'd hurt your feet if you didn't.''

"Gypsies don't hurt their feet.''

"They are used to it,'' I said, "and they would be thankful to have shoes.''

Tamarisk was thoughtful. Then she said: "They have fires on the ground and they cook the dinner on them.''

Amaryllis said to Aunt Sophie: "My mother would be so delighted if you came to the party tonight.''

"My dear child,'' said Aunt Sophie, "I am afraid I am not well enough.''

"I want to come to the party,'' cried Tamarisk. "It ought to be *my* party.''

"You always have a party for your birthday, *mon amour*,'' said Aunt Sophie.

"I want this party.''

"This is Jessica's and Amaryllis'.''

"I have a birthday, too.''

"We all have birthdays and this happens to be mine and Amaryllis','' I told her.

"Two of you! It ought to be mine, too. I want to come."

"My dearest," said Aunt Sophie, "it is not a children's party. It is for grown-ups."

"I don't want a children's party. I want a grown-ups' party. I want to come."

"When you are eighteen," I said.

Tamarisk glared at me and leaving her painting went over to Aunt Sophie. She looked at her appealingly. "Please, I want to go to the party."

"Now, Tamarisk my dear, you shall have a party of your own. This is not for little ones."

Tamarisk stamped her foot. "You don't love me," she said.

Aunt Sophie looked desolate. "Oh, my little one . . ."

"You don't. You don't," she cried. "I hate you. I hate you all." With that she ran from the room.

"Oh dear," said Aunt Sophie, almost in tears.

"She needs a very stern governess," I said, and even Amaryllis admitted that the child was getting out of hand.

"It's so sad for her, having no parents," said Aunt Sophie.

"Dear Aunt Sophie, you have done everything for her. She has not learned to be grateful. She must realize that she is not the only person in the world."

Jeanne came in and said that Tamarisk had gone to Miss Allen who was going to take her for a ride.

When we came out of the house we saw Tamarisk coming out of the stables with one of the grooms. She was on a leading rein and they were making for the paddock. She looked at us serenely, but I thought I saw a certain look of triumph in her eyes.

It was a beautiful night. There was a full moon which threw a romantic glow over the gardens and so after the buffet supper, which had been served in the hall, the guests strolled out to take the air. Through the open windows came the strains of music which was being played in the gallery for those who wished to dance.

I was with Edward who was very anxious to find a secluded spot as he wished to talk to me. I guessed of what he wanted to speak.

We sat on the wooden seat and he was silent for a few moments, then he said: "What a lovely evening!"

"Just what we hoped and prayed for," I replied.

"Jessica, I have wanted to talk to you for so long. I've been afraid to."

"You . . . afraid! I thought you were never afraid of anything."

He laughed. "I am . . . now. I am afraid that you will say No. I want to marry you."

I was silent, and he went on: "I fancied you knew. After all, it seems obvious to everyone else."

"I do know but . . . well, I haven't really thought about marriage. I don't believe I want to . . . just yet."

"You are eighteen now."

"I know that many girls are married at that age, but somehow . . . I don't feel ready."

"We could become engaged."

"That seems too . . . definite."

"My parents would be delighted."

"Mine would too. It seems that everyone would be. It is just that I am . . . well, uncertain. I am fond of you, Edward. It's been great fun since you came to Grasslands. We're all delighted to have you for neighbours." I thought then of our first meeting and when I did so there was one other figure who loomed large in my thoughts. But for Romany Jake I should never have known Edward. Then came the thought of what I should feel if instead of Edward sitting beside me on this moonlight night it was that other . . . he whom I had never been able to banish from my thoughts though it was so long since I had seen him. Something suggested to me that he might be at the root of my indecision. I dismissed that thought immediately as ridiculous. Then I thought of Leah . . . for whose sake he had been sent away. I thought of her large luminous eyes probing my mind. A choice, she had said. There were two paths. One would lead me to serenity, the other to danger. Surely this must be one of the choices and surely this life with Edward would lead me to peace. How could it be otherwise with a man like Edward? He was distinguished, of good family, comparatively wealthy, considerate and kind. He was all that my parents asked for in a son-in-law. But it should not be parents who made the choice.

As I sat there on that beautiful night with the scent of the flowers all about me and the strains of sweet music coming from the house, I felt it would be so simple to say Yes. Why should I think of a gypsy with the boldest eyes I had ever seen, a man who had danced round the bonfire with poor

Dolly and got her with child . . . it was quite ridiculous. I was foolish to hold back. But I seemed to see him there in the light of the bonfire looking at me, his eyes bold, wanting me to come down from my father's carriage and dance with him as he had danced with Dolly. What nonsense! He was a gypsy; he had killed a man; he was on the other side of the world and it was hardly likely that he would ever come back.

Edward was saying bleakly: "You are unsure, aren't you? Well, you have only just reached the great age of eighteen. There is time . . ."

"Yes," I said eagerly, "I must have time. Let me get used to the idea . . . Let me think about it. Will you?"

"I have no alternative, I'm afraid," he said with a sigh. "I can scarcely sling you across my saddle and ride off with you, can I?"

"Hardly. There would be nowhere to ride to."

"I might find somewhere. Alas, there will be no announcement tonight."

"That was what they wanted, was it?"

"My mother thought there might be."

"Oh dear, I feel I have let everyone down."

"I understand. But I'm going to make you change your mind soon."

"I'm glad. I hope you do. I'm afraid I'm being a little silly . . . a little young . . ."

"No, wise perhaps. One has to know one's own mind about these matters."

"Oh, Edward, I do love you. You're so understanding. It's just that marriage is such a big step. It's for life and I don't feel I've experienced enough of that to commit myself . . . for life."

"I have a feeling that it is going to be all right for us."

We sat in silence for some time.

It should have been exciting to receive a proposal of marriage on one's birthday, but I felt deflated. By refusing I was disappointing so many people.

He put his arm round me and kissed me gently on the cheek.

"Don't be sad about this, Jessica," he said. "I understand. That was why I was hesitating. I have spoken too soon."

How kind he was! How understanding! I was foolish to refuse such a man . . . and all because of some childish fantasy concerning a wild gypsy. Edward would be a good husband. But when one was eighteen one did not want a good husband so much as an exciting one; and although I liked Edward . . . loved him in a way . . . he did not set my pulses racing as I had heard lovers were supposed to.

I had seen the passionate devotion of my parents. Perhaps I wanted something like that to happen to me. I had also seen the love between Amaryllis' parents—strong, solid and true—but there was not that between them which there was between my parents; and it was that which I wanted.

Perhaps I was obsessed by foolish dreams. I was, when all was said, only eighteen. I did not seek the peaceful life; I wanted adventure, and deep within me was the conviction which had been planted there some years before, that there was someone who could give me what I wanted.

Clare Carson was coming across the lawn. I withdrew myself from Edward involuntarily. I had a feeling that Clare did not like me very much, and rather resented my intrusion into the family; and what she liked less than anything was Edward's feeling for me. I was certain that she was in love with Edward.

He was always charming to her, treating her like a sister; but that, I sensed, was not what she wanted and I had a feeling that often his brotherly attitude exasperated her.

"Jessica," she said, "your mother wants you to go to her as soon as you can. I told her I had an idea where you were and would look for you."

"What has happened?" I cried in alarm.

"She wants you to go quietly. Not make a fuss . . . not to disturb the party."

"I'll come with you," said Edward.

Clare put in quickly: "Mrs. Frenshaw did particularly say that she wanted no one else but Jessica."

Clare took the place I had vacated and I went quickly across the lawn and into the house. I went straight up to my mother's room. Tamarisk's governess, Miss Allen, was with her.

"Oh, Jessica," cried my mother. "I'm glad you've come. Amaryllis is looking for your father and David. Tamarisk is lost."

"Lost? How? Where?"

"Heaven knows. She is not in her room. She went to bed as normal and Miss Allen said she was asleep almost immediately, but when she looked in about half an hour ago the bed was empty."

"Oh, that child! She is always up to some mischief."

"Jeanne asked Miss Allen to come over. Jeanne is with Sophie who is almost frantic."

"I can imagine it. Why, it must be past eleven."

"Where *can* the child be at this hour?" said my mother. "Oh, here is your father. Dickon, something terrible has happened. Tamarisk is not in her bed. Where can she be? Sophie is in a demented state. What can we do?"

"I'll get over there and find out what I can. Where's David? He can come with me. Oh, here he is."

My mother quickly explained to David what had happened.

"We'll get over there with Miss Allen as quickly as we can," said my father. "Don't break up the party. No doubt she's hiding somewhere in the house. We'll be back soon, I daresay."

They slipped away and the rest of us joined the guests.

The party broke up at midnight. I think we were all relieved when the last guest departed. The family assembled in the hall—my mother, Claudine, Amaryllis and I. The men had not returned.

"What on earth are they doing!" cried my mother. "If she were hiding in the house they would have found her by now."

"It seems obvious that they haven't found her," I said.

"I think," continued my mother, "that we should go over there and see what is happening."

"I shall come with you," said Claudine.

Amaryllis suggested that we go too.

"There's no need for you girls to come," said my mother. "You go to bed."

But we insisted.

Aunt Sophie was in the hall with Jeanne, Miss Allen and some of the servants. Aunt Sophie, wrapped in a heavy dressing gown in spite of the fact that it was a warm night, looked very ill. Jeanne was hovering over her anxiously. The men were not there.

"No news?" asked my mother.

Aunt Sophie shook her head mournfully.

"Where are the men?" asked my mother.

"They are searching with some of our people," explained Jeanne.

"The house . . . the garden . . ."

"We've been over every inch of them," said Miss Allen. "I can't understand it. She was there, asleep in her bed . . ."

"Perhaps pretending to be asleep," I suggested.

"I don't know. She was there . . . I saw her when I looked in. It is terrible . . ."

"It was not your fault, Miss Allen."

She looked at me gratefully.

"How can we know what is happening to that poor child?" said Aunt Sophie.

"She will be found,"Jeanne said soothingly. "She will be safe. No harm will come to that one."

"Taken from me," mourned Aunt Sophie. "Why is it that I cannot keep anyone I love? Why is life always against me?"

No one answered. There was a faraway look in my mother's eyes and I knew she was thinking of the time when I was taken away by Dolly Mather. I had heard the story many times. And now Dolly's child had been taken. Or had she gone of her own accord? I could not imagine Tamarisk's being forcibly taken away. She would have screamed with all the strength of her lungs, which was considerable. But I could imagine her planning some devilment to teach us all a lesson, no doubt. She had been very angry about the party. She might have taken her revenge for not being allowed to attend.

My mother, who like me could not bear inaction, said: "Have the servants been questioned? Do any of them know anything?"

"They all know that she is not here," said Miss Allen.

"Well, let's do something," said my mother. "Let's have them in. Let's question them."

All those servants who were not out of doors searching for Tamarisk were commanded to come into the hall.

My mother said: "I want you all to think. Has anything strange happened in the last few days? Did the child say anything that might give us a clue as to where she may have gone?"

There was silence. Then one of the maids said: "She was always talking about being a witch."

"She told me yesterday that she would put a spell on me if she didn't get her own way," said another.

"Yes," I said. "She was always talking about being a witch. You don't think she has gone to Polly Crypton's place, do you?"

"Polly would have brought her home if she had. Polly's a witch but a white one. She would do no harm to anybody . . . not lest they'd done her wrong," said the cook.

"Perhaps we should send over to Polly's to see?"

Two of the girls said they would go at once.

When they had gone one of the housemaids said: "She was always talking about the gypsies."

"Oh yes," I said, remembering the occasion when Leah came to tell our fortunes. There had seemed to be a special affinity between them then. Of course the child's father was Romany Jake. "She wouldn't have gone to the gypsies, surely." I felt sure that if she had they would have brought her back.

"They say gypsies steal children," said the parlourmaid. "They sell their clothes. Miss Tamarisk always had of the best. Mademoiselle Sophie saw to that."

My mother cut in with: "Nonsense!" because she saw this talk was upsetting Aunt Sophie who had covered her face with her hands. Jeanne bent over her whispering in French that all would be well. Tamarisk would be coming through the door at any moment. She was sure of it.

My father and David came back with some of the men servants. One look at their faces showed us that the search had been unsuccessful.

Jeanne was telling Aunt Sophie that she would be more comfortable in bed and as soon as we had news it should be brought to her. If only she would go, Jeanne would make her comfortable. She could bring her something to soothe her throat.

Aunt Sophie shook her head. "How can I rest?" she asked. "How could I . . . until she is back?"

I went over to my father. I whispered to him: "I want to go to the gypsy encampment."

"What?" he said.

"Don't tell them here. It's just a feeling I have. Will you come with me? Just the two of us?"

"What's on your mind?"

"Something. I'm not sure. Please don't ask questions. Just come with me."

My mother looked at us questioningly.

My father said quietly: "Jessica has an idea."

We went out together.

"You're not dressed for the saddle," he said.

"No, let's walk. We may find her on the way. Please . . ."

"I know I have to obey orders, General."

"Father, I'm terribly afraid."

"Of what?"

"That the gypsies may have had something to do with this."

"You mean you think they have taken her. They wouldn't dare. Kidnapping! It could be a hanging offence."

"I don't think they would care about that. Besides, they would say she is one of them."

"Good God," he said.

And we walked on in silence.

The night air was still balmy as the day had been so hot. It seemed a very long time since I had been sitting in the garden listening to Edward's proposal.

At length we came to the clearing in the woods. There were no caravans there. My father went over to a pile of ashes. He knelt down and touched them. "They are still warm," he said. "They can't have gone long."

He stood up and we faced each other.

"Why?" he said.

"Leah," I said. "I may be wrong, but it did occur to me. She was very taken with the child . . . and the child with her. There was an affinity between them. I believe Leah loves the child's father, and because of that she wants his child."

"You're romancing, my dear."

"Maybe . . . and then maybe not."

"What do you propose we do now?"

"We could send after them. They've gone to the West Country. We'll see if Tamarisk is with them."

We went back to the house. I dreaded reaching it for something told me that when we did we should hear that there was no news of Tamarisk.

And it was significant that the gypsies should have left just at the time when Tamarisk disappeared.

Everyone was talking about Tamarisk's disappearance. It seemed a foregone conclusion that she had been stolen by the gypsies, or more likely gone of her own free will. One of the maids remembered that she had seen the gypsy woman talking to the child on the edge of the garden. Miss Allen confirmed that on the previous day she had insisted on walking to the camp, and when they were there she had talked to one of the gypsy women who had shown her inside a caravan.

It was too much of a coincidence that they should have gone at the very time Tamarisk disappeared.

Aunt Sophie was stricken with grief. She had been suffering from a cold before Tamarisk's disappearance: now that turned to bronchitis. She would not eat; she could not sleep. She just lay in bed crying for the child.

My mother and I went over with Amaryllis. We were deeply shocked. She just lay in her bed, her hood slightly awry so that we could see the beginnings of those sad scars which she had been so careful to hide; now she did not seem to care.

Two days had passed and there was no news of Tamarisk.

My father and David had gone in search of the gypsies but they had disappeared completely and left no trace. It seemed very clear that Leah had taken Tamarisk away.

It was difficult to believe that the gentle girl could be capable of such an act, but I remembered the knife in her belt and the way she had looked at Tamarisk. I was sure she had loved Romany Jake; it was natural; he was the man who had risked his life for her sake. I believed that she would be capable of deep emotions, passionate hatred, passionate love.

And she had wanted the child. So she had lured Tamarisk away from us. I was equally sure that Tamarisk had not been taken against her will.

I thought of Romany Jake sitting in Dolly's kitchen singing of the lady who had left her fine home for the gypsies.

That was what Tamarisk had done.

As the days dragged on and we had given up hope of finding Tamarisk, we became very concerned about Aunt Sophie.

We visited her every day. Jeanne was in despair.

"She cannot go on like this," she said.

Poor Aunt Sophie was sunk in melancholy. Someone from the family was there almost throughout the day. We would sit by her bed, saying nothing. She just lay there staring into space.

Jeanne was always trying to tempt her with some special dish. Poor Jeanne, she herself looked weary and older.

It was about four days after Tamarisk's disappearance. I

had gone over to Enderby to be met by Jeanne. She was pale and there were shadows under her eyes.

I said: "How is she?"

Jeanne shook her head.

"I used to say how much good the child did her. After she came she was happy as she had never been before. Now I would to God there had never been a child. Then we should be as we were before her coming."

"Do you think she will ever come back now?"

"She has gone with the gypsies. She is her father's child. Her mother was a strange and unhappy girl and with the gypsy her father, it is small wonder that she was rebellious. There is something wild about her. But we loved her and she was everything to Mademoiselle. Mademoiselle always wanted children. If she could have married and had them I think life would have been very different for us. Life is cruel. There she was . . . a young pretty girl. She goes out one night . . . one night only . . . and there is that terrible disaster and that is the end of the life she knew. A fresh one starts . . . a life of bitterness and regrets. Oh, it is so cruel. My poor, poor one. How I wish I could bear it for her."

"You have always been so wonderful to her, Jeanne. My mother always says you are one of the rare people, for people are rarely so good."

"She is my life, my child, you might say."

"How I wish that wicked girl would come back. She plagued us all with her presence, but never as she has now by her absence."

"Ah, if she would only come in at that door now. That would be enough for Mademoiselle. Then I could start feeding her . . . making her well again . . . make life good for her. But the child will not come."

"Shall I go and sit with Aunt Sophie for a while?"

Jeanne nodded. "She seems listless but perhaps she is happy to know that we are all so concerned for her."

So I went into that room and I sat there by the bed and I thought, There is something evil about this house. It was supposed to be haunted. Terrible things had happened here. My mother told me how surprised she had been when Sophie had decided to take it. They had said then that she had been bewitched by the melancholy of Enderby, the gloom which hung over it. The personality of the house was like that of Aunt Sophie.

But Jeanne had brought her impeccable French taste to the house. She had subtly changed the furnishings. She had made discoveries in the house and changed it a little. And Aunt Sophie had been happier here than she had since her disfigurement when she had lost her fiancé and the happy future to which she had looked forward.

But Aunt Sophie was doomed. Those she had loved, she said, were taken from her. Her fiancé was lost to her, although it was she who had refused to marry him, so my mother told me. He would have gone on with the wedding; but he had married my mother instead. Then there was Alberic, the French spy who had come into her life and whom she had loved—so Jeanne told me—as her son. He had died—murdered, said Aunt Sophie; meeting his just deserts, said my father; it was Jonathan, my father's own son, who had killed him and lost his own life in similar fashion.

So many tragedies! Yes, there was something about the house, I could feel it . . . in this very room.

A disembodied voice floated up to me.

"Is Mademoiselle all right?"

It was Jeanne speaking through the tube in the kitchen—a weird device, I had always thought it, connecting the two rooms. It always sounded odd to me, unnatural, even though I understood how it came through.

Aunt Sophie stirred a little.

"Am I all right?" she said. "I shall never be all right. Life is too cruel. Jessica, why do you sit there? Why don't you go away. Just leave me in my misery."

"Oh, Aunt Sophie, we are all so anxious about you. We all want you to be well."

"I lose all those I have loved. There is something fatal about my loving. I just have to love and they are taken from me."

"Oh no, it is not so, Aunt Sophie."

She raised herself a little. "Yes, yes," she cried vehemently. "There was Charles. He was so handsome. And he is long since dead. He married your mother. Charlot and Claudine were the result. I loved Charlot. Where is Charlot now?"

"He has his vineyard in Burgundy. My mother longs for the end of the war so that she can visit him . . . or perhaps he will soon come to us."

"Oh, the war will be over. Your mother will see her son. Everything works well for her . . . whereas for me . . ."

"Oh, Aunt Sophie, you are here with your family. You escaped with Jeanne. No one could have a more devoted friend than Jeanne. She at least is something to be grateful for."

"She is a good woman. I am devoted to her . . . but she is here with me in my prison. Charlot . . . Claudine . . . they might have been my children. But life is always against me. True, I escaped. I came here. I found this house. I thought life would be a little kinder to me . . . at last. Alberic came. He was a beautiful young man . . . always so eager to please me. And . . . they murdered him. I was fond of Dolly and she went with that gypsy and she died. But she gave me Tamarisk. I thought then I could be happy. I had this little girl to bring up as my own . . . mine at last. And now . . . she is gone. You see, whatever I do, whatever I touch, brings desolation. It is time I gave up the struggle, Jessica."

"You must not say such things. You have been so brave."

"Brave? I? Crouching in my prison . . . shutting myself away . . . afraid to see anyone . . . living like a hermit! You call that brave?"

I said: "It is brave in a way."

She laughed. "No, it is cowardice. I was always a coward. Afraid of life. I never grasped firmly as your mother did. Perhaps I should have married Charles. He would have married me. Gentleman's honour, you understand. I knew that he did not want me. I suspected even before the accident that it was your mother whom he wanted. I could have made him marry me. Perhaps I should have done so. I might have had children. After all, it was an obligation on his part. How different everything might have been if I had married him! Sometimes one has a choice in life. Two ways loom before one. Which should one take? And the decision makes all the difference to one's life."

I was thoughtful. Was that not what Leah, the gypsy, had said to me?

I sat there thinking of Aunt Sophie's decision. Which would I have taken had I been in her place?

There was silence for a while, then Aunt Sophie said: "Jessica, I sometimes feel there is no reason why I should go on. It would be so easy to let go . . ."

I said: "Tamarisk will come back. I feel it in my bones."

She shook her head. "I shall never see Tamarisk again."

There was nothing I could say or do to comfort her. I kissed her forehead and took my leave.

The weeks were passing. There was no news of Tamarisk. My father had done everything possible to trace the gypsies, but there was no sign of them. Enquiries were made and it was learned that they had not visited their usual haunts that year.

There were whole days when no one mentioned Tamarisk which was a sign that we were all beginning to accept the evidence that she had gone with the gypsies. She was not, after all, related to us. My father said: "The child is merely Dolly Mather's bastard by a wandering gypsy. If it wasn't for Sophie's preoccupation with her it would be no concern of ours that she is taken back to her father's people. It might be said that they have more right to her than Sophie."

I tried to explain to him what Tamarisk had meant to Sophie, but my father was apt to be impatient of the weaknesses of others. The only two people he cared about were my mother and myself. He had a certain pride in David who was a model son and as unlike Dickon as a son could be from his father. He regretted the death of Jonathan; he had a fondness for Claudine and for Amaryllis. But they were immediate family. Outside that he had little concern. So he shrugged his shoulders. Tamarisk had gone and that was the end of the matter for him.

How different was my mother. She was warm-hearted, making other people's troubles her concern; and particularly so in the case of Aunt Sophie, for whom she always had had this very special obligation to help.

Aunt Sophie was shrinking into a decline. She seemed to have shrivelled; she was constantly talking of Tamarisk, and Jeanne told me that she had gone into her room at midnight to find her at the window looking out because she had thought she heard someone in the garden and wondered if Tamarisk had come home.

The talk at Eversleigh now was all about Napoleon's advance on Russia. My mother always listened eagerly to news of the war. She was longing for the day when it would be over and she would be reunited with Charlot.

There was no fresh news about him but since she had heard that he and Louis Charles had a vineyard in Burgundy, she had been hopeful. She confided in me that it had been heartrending when she had believed he was fighting in Napoleon's army. "Fighting against us," she said. "It seemed so terrible. Now I can think of him in his vineyard. He will find that so interesting. And Louis Charles with him. He was always his shadow. I wonder what his wife is like. I might have grandchildren. It is maddening to be in the dark. But I must thank God that he is safe."

She did not try to bring a halt to the conversation at the table when it was about the war now as she had done in the past. She encouraged it, listening avidly for some indication that there might be peace.

My father watched events with great interest. He said that if Napoleon succeeded in conquering Russia the whole of Europe would be in his hands.

"Then," he went on, "he would turn his attention to us."

"But there is the sea to protect us," said my mother.

"If he could find a way of bringing his armies over . . ."

"The Navy would never allow it."

"If he does succeed in conquering Russia," said David, "he will believe he cannot fail."

"He failed at Trafalgar," pointed out Claudine.

"And by God, he is going to fail again," added my father. "But at the moment the Russians are in full retreat. Napoleon is after Moscow. If he succeeds in taking it the Russians will lose heart."

"Will that be the end of the war?" asked my mother.

"My dear Lottie, what do you think the mighty conqueror of Europe will do if he beats the Russians? He will have come to the conclusion that he is invincible. Nothing will deter him from an attack on our island."

My mother shivered. "It is all so stupid, so pointless. What does it matter to the people who is king or emperor?"

"Unfortunately, my love, it matters to the kings and most certainly to this particular emperor. Napoleon wants to see himself astride the world."

"He will never conquer us," said David firmly.

"Never!" agreed my father. "But there might be certain troubles to be faced first."

We visited Aunt Sophie regularly. Sometimes I went; sometimes Amaryllis did. Always Sophie talked of Tamarisk, her beauty, her charm. I said to Amaryllis: "She is fast turning the child into an angel of virtue." And she agreed.

Jeanne was very worried. "She eats scarcely anything; and

does not rest at night. Often I hear her moving about. I went in last night. She was sitting at the window looking out. She said she thought she had heard Tamarisk in the garden, calling to her. She was icily cold. I got her back to bed and although I covered her with several blankets she lay there shivering for a full hour. She can't go on like this.''

"I wish we could get some news of Tamarisk," I said.

It was a balmy September day when we heard that Napoleon had entered Moscow.

"This is the end," said David. "The effect of Moscow's surrender will be devastating for the Russian army. It will collapse."

David was a shrewd observer of the political field, I had always thought. He approached all subjects with logic. My father was apt to have preconceived notions and a certain amount of emotion crept into his judgements.

But for once David was wrong. We waited for news with the utmost eagerness. Moscow was burning. It was first thought that the French had set fire to it; but that would have been folly. Napoleon did not want a destroyed city. He had his army to house and feed. It was a last desperate manoeuvre by the Russians—an example of what they called the scorched earth policy. They had tried it out consistently during the war and Napoleon's advancing armies, far from home, found nothing ahead of them but burning towns.

"He has to make a decision now," said David. "To stay the winter in a burned-out city or to withdraw. He is hesitating. If he waits much longer it will be too late."

"What we must pray for now is his retreat from Moscow and an early Russian winter," said my father. "That will be better than an avenging army."

"Those poor soldiers," murmured my mother, and I knew she was giving up a prayer of thanksgiving because Charlot was no longer one of Napoleon's soldiers, but snug, she hoped, in his vineyard.

"Those poor soldiers, Lottie," retorted my father, "are the very gentlemen who would be over-running this land and bringing their accursed emperor here to rule over us."

"I know. I know. But it is always sad when men . . . whose quarrel it is not . . . have to risk their lives. I do hope it will be over soon. Oh, if only it could be."

"Then you should pray for a hard winter."

I have no doubt that the Russians prayed for the same—and

those prayers were answered. Napoleon's retreat from Moscow decimated his army. However well drilled, well disciplined those men, they could not stand up to the terrible climatic conditions.

There were many to rejoice—ourselves among them—when Napoleon returned to Paris, and of the army of six hundred thousand only one hundred thousand had survived.

We were dining with the Barringtons when the news came.

"Perhaps he will make peace now," said my mother hopefully.

"Not him," said my father.

"Nothing short of capture and the complete destruction of his armies will silence Napoleon," added Edward Barrington.

"You are right," added his father. "Nothing will subdue him but complete defeat."

"It will come, depend upon it," said my father. "And when it does we shall be free of this threat which has been hanging over us for so long. The French have a lot to answer for."

"Yes . . . all this unrest stems from them," added Mr. Barrington.

"You mean your trouble at the works?"

"It is really getting serious," Edward explained. "The mob is getting more and more violent. We have to have all-night guards on the machines."

"Idiots," said my father. "The law is not harsh enough."

"I think they are going to tighten it up," said Edward. "They'll have to. We can't go on like this."

Then they talked once more of Napoleon's retreat from Moscow and speculated as to what his next plans would be.

When we returned home one of the grooms from Enderby was waiting for us. He said that Mademoiselle Fougère was very anxious about Mademoiselle Sophie and she thought we should go over to see her as soon as possible.

My mother said we would go at once, so with my father, David, Claudine and Amaryllis, I went to Enderby.

I could never enter that house without a little shiver of expectation. I never knew what it was. Amaryllis did not feel it. She said it was my imagination; but I did really feel that so many strange events had taken place there that somehow they had been caught up, captured and become part of the house.

I was certain as soon as I entered it that night that I sensed the presence of Death.

Jeanne came down to the hall to greet us; her hair was awry which was unusual for Jeanne, who always believed that one's coiffure was of the utmost importance. Her face was white and the misery in her eyes was apparent.

"I am afraid," she said, "terribly afraid that she is slipping away from me."

We went up to Aunt Sophie's bedroom. We stood round her bed. I am not sure whether she recognized us. She lay with her eyes fixed on the ceiling.

"I wish I could have got a priest," said Jeanne.

My mother said: "Perhaps she will recover."

"No, Madame, not this time. This is the end."

As though to confirm this, Aunt Sophie's breathing became stertorous. After a while she was quiet.

"My poor Jeanne," said my mother, putting an arm about her.

"I knew," said Jeanne. "For the last days I have known. This last blow . . . It was too much."

My father said he would send one of the servants for the doctor.

"I have already done so," said Jeanne. "He will be here shortly. Ah . . . I believe now. But there is nothing he can do. Yesterday he told me. There is nothing, he said."

My mother gently led Jeanne out of the bedroom.

My father took the doctor into the bedroom and the rest of us went downstairs. As we sat in the hall with its high vaulted ceiling and its haunted minstrels' gallery I had the feeling that the house was listening, waiting. And I thought: Who will live here now?

Jeanne was saying that Aunt Sophie had never recovered from her grief over the loss of Tamarisk.

"It's a pity that child was ever born," said my mother.

"Poor Dolly," I said. "She would have loved her."

Claudine put her hand to her head and said irrelevantly: "I don't like this house. There's always trouble in it. I believe it is something to do with the house."

If I let my imagination stray I was sure I would have heard the house laughing, mockingly.

"She grieved for Tamarisk," mused Jeanne. "If only the child had not gone. She did so much for her. She was her life. She could see no wrong in her. To go like this without a word. The gypsy in her I suppose. And what it did to my poor lady!"

"What she would have done without you, Jeanne, I can't imagine," said my mother.

"She brooded on her misfortunes," said Jeanne. "She always did. I used to think she revelled in them. But not this one . . . not losing the child."

"I should like a little brandy," said my mother. "Something to warm us up. I think we all need something."

Jeanne went away to get it.

"It gives her something to do," said my mother. "Poor soul. This is a terrible grief for her."

When Jeanne came back the men joined us.

The doctor said Aunt Sophie had died of a congestion of the lungs.

"And a surfeit of sorrow," added my mother.

Claudine looked over her shoulder at the minstrels' gallery and shivered.

"Are you cold, Mamma?" asked Amaryllis. "Here. Have my shawl."

"No, my darling. I'm not cold." She looked with infinite fondness at her daughter.

The doctor was saying that Aunt Sophie had not wished to live. It sometimes happened when people had this death wish that death came to them. There was nothing which could have saved her—not all the devoted nursing possible. She was just tired of living, tired of fighting.

"She beckoned to death and it came," I said.

My father looked impatient and said it was getting late and there was nothing we could do tonight.

We went back to Eversleigh leaving Jeanne with her desolation.

On a dark and dismal day, Aunt Sophie was laid to rest. Tamarisk's disappearance had ceased to be a subject for contemplation among the servants.

There were a number of mourners at the graveside and even more spectators. Aunt Sophie had always been something of an oddity in the neighbourhood. Now she had died—or rather faded away—that was the end of her sad story.

The cortège had left Enderby and the mourners would come back to Eversleigh where they would be given food and drink; and after that the family would assemble for the reading of Aunt Sophie's will.

We had discussed the possibilities of what it might contain.

"Enderby would be a problem," said my father. He thought the wisest thing would be to sell. "The whole lot," he said. "Lock, stock and barrel. Get rid of the place. The problem would be to find a likely buyer."

"It's improved a lot since Sophie took over," said my mother. "Jeanne has stamped her impeccable taste on it and the blending of colours in some of the rooms is really exquisite."

"It's not everybody who is looking for fancy French taste," my father reminded her.

"Maybe not but people are impressed by a tastefully furnished house."

"We'll wait and see."

And now the waiting was over, and we were all assembled in my father's study for the reading of the will.

It was what might have been expected. Jeanne was amply provided for. She would have enough money to set up in a house of her own or return to France when the time was ripe. Aunt Sophie wrote most touchingly of their devotion to each other. There were small legacies to the servants and to us but the house itself was to go to Tamarisk "so that she would always have a home."

The will must have been made before Tamarisk's disappearance.

When the guests had all gone my father expressed his dissatisfaction about the will. "We shall have to find that girl now. I'm wondering what can be done about the house. I wonder what she will think to discover herself the owner of Enderby."

"She wouldn't realize what it is all about," said my mother. "She is only six years old."

"She's rather knowing," I said.

"But to own a house. What could Sophie have been thinking of!"

"Sophie did not think very clearly on the best of occasions," added my father. "We'll have to make an effort to find the child. The best thing would be to sell the house and bank the money for her till she comes of age. I'll see the solicitor and get his advice."

"I wonder who will buy it?" I murmured.

"Wait and see," said my father. "In any case I shall be glad to be shut of the place."

"Do you feel it is haunted and brings a curse on those who live in it?" I asked.

"I think it's a damned draughty inconvenient house, that's what I think of it. And nothing will please me more than to be rid of it . . . ghosts and all."

"Some people like that sort of thing," I said.

Claudine met my eyes and looked away. She felt very strongly about the house, almost as though she herself had had some uncanny experience there. So Enderby was going to pass out of the family.

I wondered who would come there next.

The Blind Girl

Further efforts were made to trace Tamarisk without success. It did emerge that the gypsies may have left and gone to Ireland which they had on other occasions.

My father shrugged his shoulders and after consulting with the solicitor, it was decided that for the time being Enderby was to be let as it was, if a tenant could be found to take it until a decision was reached.

Enderby was shut up; the servants were scattered; some of them came into our household and some went to Grasslands. Some of our servants went over once a week to keep the place in order—always in twos and threes I noticed. Not one of them cared to go alone. The house's reputation had become slightly more evil since the death of Aunt Sophie, and old rumours were revived.

"We had better put a stop to that," said my father, "otherwise we shall never find a tenant."

Jeanne herself often went to the house. She had moved to a cottage on the estate which happened to be empty. She was undecided about her future but I believed that one day she would return to France.

In the meantime the days were slipping past. My father said one day at dinner that he would have to pay a visit to London. He would be away for a week or so.

"You'll come with me, Lottie," he said.

"But of course," replied my mother.

He looked at me. "And I wonder if my darling daughter would deign to honour us with her presence."

"You know I should love to."

"Well, that's settled. We'll go as soon as you can get your fripperies together."

"A week," I said.

"Too long. We are leaving on Thursday."

"You always do these things in a great hurry," protested my mother.

"Procrastination is the thief of time."

"Slow and steady wins the race," I said.

My father turned appealingly to David. "The two of them line up against me. Did a man ever have such a wife and daughter!"

David and Claudine smiled benignly at us. His softness was all the more noticeable because it was for us alone.

How easily I could understand my parents. No inhibitions, no brooding grief such as Aunt Sophie had suffered. I was lucky. I never wanted to leave them. Edward Barrington was hoping that I would marry him. He did not actually ask me again but I could see the hope in his eyes.

It was a happy state of affairs. I was flattered to be so desired as a wife and I often thought I should accept his proposal; at the same time I did not want to leave my home. I liked to be there close to my parents all the time. I should have to feel very attracted by someone to want to leave them.

We left Eversleigh in the carriage, which was the most comfortable way of long distance travel.

"We should set out early and try to make the journey in two days," said my father.

We made good progress on the first day and did five miles more than we had believed possible, but as darkness was about an hour away my father said we had better look out for a good coaching inn, which we did and that was how we came to the Green Man.

It was a charming inn set back from the road, clearly displaying the sign which depicted a man clad in green.

"This looks a likely place," said my father. "Stop here, Jennings."

The postilion descended and went into the inn while we remained in the carriage.

"Let's hope they have rooms here," said my mother. "I am not eager to continue after dark."

The postilion emerged with the host who bowed obsequiously. Beside him was his wife, beaming a welcome.

"We are honoured," said the host. "It is Mr. Frenshaw and his lady wife and daughter. You shall have the best rooms in the inn, my lord. If we had known . . . As it is there is good roast beef and chicken pie only . . . If we had been warned of such nobility . . ."

My father held up a hand.

"Your good roast beef will suit us quite well," he said. "And we shall need two rooms—your best, of course."

I smiled fondly at my father. I supposed his fame had spread to every inn on the road from Eversleigh to London. Of course it was only necessary to look at him to sense his importance.

As we stepped inside the inn parlour, I noticed a man sitting there drinking from a flagon. He wore a stylish brown coat and there was a very white cravat at his throat. His brown beaver hat was on the table beside him. I judged him to be in his mid twenties; he was quite clearly interested in our arrival.

"First we will see the rooms," said my father. "And how soon can we sup?"

"When you wish, my lord, sir. Whenever is your wish. My wife will make sure that you are well served. You will wish to eat privately, will you not?"

"That would please me."

As we were being led towards the stairs I looked round and noticed that the man in the inn parlour continued to show interest. He caught my eye and half smiled. I looked away quickly.

The rooms were pleasant—a double one for my parents at the front of the inn, and a smaller one for me at the back. Their windows looked onto the road, mine over the stables to woods and fields.

My father said the rooms would be adequate and when the innkeeper retired, telling us that supper would be served in a small room leading from the inn parlour, my father added that we had been fortunate to find such a place.

"They seem to know you," said my mother.

"I have travelled this way for years and stayed at a number of inns. People talk. Now you two will want to wash the grime of the journey from your faces. When you've done so we'll eat. Then I think an early night and a good sleep. We'll travel on at daybreak."

Water was brought by a rosy-cheeked girl; and soon we were ready. As we were ushered into the private room I saw again the man who had been drinking in the parlour. He gave me a bow as though we were old acquaintances. I lightly inclined my head.

My mother whispered: "He looks as though he believes he has met us before."

My father replied in a rather audible voice which the man might have heard: "It's wise not to scrape up acquaintance in inns. One never knows what sort of rogue one can get saddled with." The door closed on us. We were in a small room where the table was laid for three and hot soup was being ladled into bowls.

"I do hope he didn't hear you," I said.

My father shrugged that aside. "It's true," he said. "Now let's see what the food is like at the Green Man."

It was quite good and after we had eaten we retired to our rooms.

"Don't forget," said my father. "An early start. I've explained to my host that we want a quick breakfast at daybreak. He has promised it shall be ready."

We said goodnight and went to our rooms.

I felt rather tired but disinclined to go to bed immediately. It was always difficult to sleep in strange beds and I did not want the night to seem too long.

I went to the window and sat there watching the activity in the stable yard. Our carriage was there being cleaned by our coachman and postilion. They were chatting idly together as they worked.

I yawned. It would be pleasant to get away from Eversleigh for a while. Aunt Sophie's death had cast a gloom over us all. I wished Amaryllis had come with us. She was not so fond of the London life as I was. I liked the shops and visits to the theatre; and there was almost certain to be a ball at one of our friends' houses while we were in town.

While I was thinking of this, the man who had been drinking in the inn parlour strolled out of the inn and paused by our coach. He talked to the men who were cleaning it. He examined the carriage, studying the family crest on the side.

He put his head inside the vehicle and touched the padded

seats. Our coachman was talking enthusiastically, pointing out the details of the upholstery and bodywork with obvious pride.

The man leaned against the side of the carriage and went on talking. I wished I could hear what they were saying. I saw him slip some money into the hands of the men and fearful that he might look up, I moved back from the window.

What was he talking about to our servants? And why had he thought it necessary to reward them? Gentlemen often tipped servants, of course—even other people's. Perhaps he was very generous and considered the details about the carriage which they were giving him were worth paying for.

I went to bed and in spite of its being a strange one, I was soon fast asleep, and the next thing I knew was that my mother was tapping on the door to tell me it was time to get up.

In the afternoon of the next day we arrived at the house in Albemarle Street, our London home. On the first day my father was away on business and my mother and I went shopping—a pursuit we both enjoyed. We bought materials, lace and ribbons and as we were returning home with our purchases I thought I saw the man who had been at the inn.

He was walking down our street and he seemed to pause for a second or so to look at our house. Then I thought I must have been mistaken. There were many men around dressed as he was dressed; and he had been tall—so was the man in the street.

I said to my mother: "Did you see that man?"

She looked round and said: "Yes."

"Is it the man we saw in the inn?"

"What man?" she asked.

And I did not pursue the matter. I wondered why I remembered him. Perhaps because he had talked to our servants, and I had seen money pass between them.

On the third day my father took my mother to visit some friends. I was not included. My mother said we would all go out in the afternoon. "I should like to take a ride in the Park then," she said. "Shall we do that?"

I said I should like it.

They had not been gone more than half an hour when the urge came to go out. There was some ribbon I had seen in one of the shops and I thought it would be a good idea if I went along to get it. My mother would not want to go back to the shops just for that.

There was no harm in my going out alone. My mother did not like me to, but then like all mothers she still saw me as a child. She had forgotten that I was grown up.

It would not take me long and I should be back before they returned.

I put on my hat and cloak and went out into the street.

There is an excitement about the London streets particularly when one is alone and accustomed to being chaperoned.

The air seemed to sparkle on that morning. There was a kind of frost in it. I decided I would go to Bond Street. Its elegance delighted me. The shops were all inviting with their windows divided into small panes with the displays of goods behind them. There were cravats, perfume, boots of every kind and all of the most fashionable; and the hats—they were a spectacle in themselves.

The carriages rattled by at great speed and I caught glimpses of the stylish occupants. Everywhere was noise and colour. I was fascinated.

I found the shop with the ribbon and bought it. I was in no great hurry to return to the house. I wanted to go on savouring the richness of this urban scene.

There was a moment when I had the feeling that I was being followed. I stopped short and looked round. There were several people about and they all seemed intent on their own business. Did I imagine it, or did I see a tall man in a brown beaver hat turn and suddenly become absorbed in one of the shop windows? No. I was becoming obsessed by the tall man in the brown beaver hat.

As I was about to cross the road I became aware of someone plucking at my sleeve. I turned sharply and looking down saw a young girl. She could not have been more than twelve or thirteen. She lifted her face to mine and murmured: "Please . . . could you help me cross the road?"

Something about the way she smiled into space told me at once that she was blind. She was neatly but by no means expensively dressed and she looked so helpless standing there that I was touched with pity. "Certainly I will," I said.

I took her arm.

"You are so kind," she said. "I was with my sister. I lost her. It was in the crowd. It is so bewildering when I am alone. When I am with her . . . or my mother . . . I think I can be all right, but it is different to be alone . . ."

"Of course," I said. "I think we could try it now. I'll hold your arm."

I took her across. It was certainly a little hazardous even for the sighted.

We had reached the other side. "Do you have far to go?" I asked.

"No," she said. "If you would just help me along to Greville Street . . ."

"It is just along here, I believe."

"Oh, thank you."

"Do you live in Greville Street?"

"In Grant Street. It is a turning off Greville."

"I am only too pleased to take you along there."

"You are so kind. My mother will be very grateful. I must tell her not to scold Sarah. It was not her fault. There were so many people, you see. It is rather bewildering to find oneself alone in the darkness . . . with noise all around one . . ."

"It must be. I am so glad you asked my help."

"People are so kind to those who are afflicted."

"Here is Greville Street."

"Would you really not mind taking me along to Grant Street?"

"Certainly I'll take you."

"I trust I am not taking you out of your way."

"That's of no importance. Oh, here it is."

"Would you mind taking me up to the door? It's number nineteen."

It was a biggish house of three storeys. There were balconies on the first floor and the windows were all discreetly curtained.

"I don't know how to thank you. Would you mind ringing the doorbell?"

I did so and was about to step back when she said: "Do wait a moment."

The door was opened by a big man who said: "Oh, there you are, Miss Mary. Miss Sarah's been back a full fifteen minutes. Your ma was getting worried."

"This kind lady brought me home."

"Come in a minute, Miss, will you?"

"There is no need to," I said. "Miss Mary is now safely home."

He looked at me appealingly. "The missus will be mad with me if you're not thanked properly," he said.

"I have done nothing . . ."

Mary had taken my hand firmly and pulled me into the hall. The door shut behind us. It had a hollow sound and I noticed there was no furniture in the hall.

"Who is there?" called a voice.

"Come on," said Mary. "That is my Mama. She'll want to thank you."

The big man threw open the door and Mary drew me into a room. It was very sparsely furnished. There was a table with two or three chairs and very little else. At the table sat a woman. I could not see her face very clearly because she had her back to the window but I was beginning to think there was something rather unusual about this household and I experienced the first twinges of apprehension.

On the table before the woman was a tea tray set with cups and saucers. She looked at me with curiosity as I came in.

"This is the lady who brought me home, Mama," said Mary.

"Oh, how good of you. It is not the first time a kind lady has brought Mary home. Thank you. Thank you. You'll have a cup of tea, won't you?"

"I won't stop now, thanks. I really should not have come in. It was nothing."

"It was a great deal and you must drink a cup of tea with me or I shall be a little put out."

"No thanks . . . please. I must get home."

"Oh, you are a very fine young lady. That is obvious. And here are we . . . about to leave our home. Our furniture has gone . . . or most of it . . . just a few sticks left. And we shall be going soon. I understand, of course, we are not the kind of people your sort would mix with . . ."

The big man appeared carrying a pot of tea.

I said: "Oh no . . . of course not . . ."

"Then a little cup, eh. Ah, I knew you would . . . Jacob, take this to the young lady . . ."

I felt there was something strange about this . . . something not quite natural . . .

The cup was put into my hands and my impulse was to gulp down the tea and get out as quickly as I could.

Mary and her mother were watching me; and it struck me that Mary no longer had the look of a blind girl.

As I was about to put the cup to my lips there was a violent ringing of the doorbell. Both Mary and her mother were clearly startled. We all seemed to be listening intently. I heard voices. There was a shout and what sounded like a scuffle . . . The door was flung open and to my astonishment, there stood the man in the brown beaver hat.

I rose to my feet spilling the tea. I heard myself stammer: "Who are you? What are you doing here?"

He was looking straight at me.

"What are *you* doing here?" he demanded.

"Get out. Get out of my house . . . whoever you are," shouted the woman. "What do you want here?"

"I want to know why you have brought this young lady here."

"How dare you! How dare you!"

He was looking straight at me.

"Let's go," he said.

I had set down the cup on the floor. I went to the man. The woman came towards us . . . so did Mary. They caught at my arm, but he flung them off and pulled me into the hall where the big man was lying on the floor moaning softly.

"Let's get out of this place," said the man in the beaver hat.

At the door he turned and shouted: "You'll be hearing more of this."

We came into the street. My first feeling was relief to have left behind that room which I now knew to have been evil.

My limbs started to shake. I did not realize until this moment how frightened I had begun to be. There had been an unreality about the entire proceedings—the girl pretending to be blind, the emptiness of the house, the strange almost theatrical atmosphere. I could not imagine what it had meant.

I looked at the man beside me. It was the first time I had been so close to him. He was quite handsome; his features were set in a classic mould; his light brown eyes could be humorous; but at the moment they were full of concern. I had been interested in him from the moment I had seen him. Now I was decidedly anxious to hear more about him.

"That," he said, "was a most unsavoury place for a young lady of good breeding to find herself in."

"I don't understand what it was all about. All I know is that I have to thank you for rescuing me."

"I was going to ask forgiveness for a certain curiosity, but it really served a good purpose in this instance. Would you like to come somewhere where we could have some refreshment? You need something.''

"Oh no . . . no . . . I want to go home.''

"You feel unsafe. I understand that . . . after what happened. Then I will escort you to your home.''

"Thank you.''

"The streets of London are not safe for attractive young ladies to wander in.''

"I cannot understand what that was all about. The blind girl . . .''

"Who was no more blind than you or I.''

"Then why . . .?''

"She was the decoy. They wanted to lure you to that house.''

"What for? Robbery?''

"I think . . . perhaps . . . for something even more serious. I was astonished when I saw you go in that house, Miss er . . .''

"Frenshaw.''

"That place, Miss Frenshaw, is what is called a house of ill fame. Forgive the term . . . a brothel.''

"Oh no!''

"Yes, indeed.''

"It was an empty house, I thought.''

"Nevertheless that was what it was. They lured you to it. It is not an unusual practice. They usually trap girls fresh from the country.''

"But . . .''

"They could not have known that you have an influential family. Forgive me . . . but I did see you when you were travelling in your family carriage. I was at the Green Man. I noticed you.'' He gave me a warm smile. "I saw the deference which was given to your parents. These people usually go for friendless girls.''

"I can't believe this.''

"They would have drugged you. When you awoke you might have found yourself on a ship going out of the country. These people are devilish . . . quite unscrupulous. They care for nothing but profit.''

"But this is terrible.''

"I see you are still shocked by the experience and find it difficult to believe me. But I assure you that something like this must have been planned. I thank God I was in Bond Street today. I saw you, recognized you and . . . forgive me . . . I did follow you. I think I must have been trying to find some pretext for speaking to you. I saw the girl approach you. I was suspicious because a moment or so before I had seen her darting through the crowds and as she could not so suddenly have lost her sight, I wondered what was afoot. I followed at some distance. I was turning the corner into Grant Street when I saw you enter that house. I was astounded. I sensed something sinister was going on. I am only sorry I hesitated so long. However, at length I decided to ring the bell and force my way in if necessary. You know the rest."

"Oh, thank you," I said faintly.

"It shall be my pleasure to restore you to your family. A charming family if I may say so. I did see you once in Albemarle Street. It was as though our paths were destined to cross. I was meant to save you from . . . whatever those people were planning for you."

I shivered. "It was miraculous."

"I think so, too."

"I had no idea that things like that went on or that such places existed."

"Of course you did not. I blame myself for hesitating those few minutes. I stood there asking myself what right I had to interfere. I could not understand why you should go into such a place. Then I threw discretion to the winds and rang the bell and demanded entrance. The man who answered it asked my business and I said I wanted to see the young lady who had just come in. He told me to get out. Then I heard voices coming from the room. He tried to detain me but I flung him aside for I was convinced then that you were being held against your will. I had heard that these people had strange ways of conducting their business. Well, that is the story. How glad I am that I happened to be on the spot."

"I don't know how to thank you."

"It was very little really."

"You did not know what you might have found in that place . . . how desperate they were. They are criminals. I think it was very brave of you to come after me."

"Thank you."

"My parents will want to thank *you*."

"I was rewarded enough when I was able to bring you to

safety." We had come to Albemarle Street and I insisted that he come in and meet my parents.

My father was not at home but my mother had returned. Her astonishment was great when she saw the stranger, and when she heard what had happened she was horrified.

"I don't know how to thank you, Mr.—er—"

"Peter Lansdon. I am delighted to make your acquaintance."

"You must come in. You must have some wine. Oh, Jessica, how could you! I have told you repeatedly that you should not go out alone."

"Oh, Mother, I am no longer a child."

"But not able to take care of yourself it seems. As for you, sir, we owe you our deepest thanks for rescuing our daughter and bringing her home to us. No protestations please. It was a brave thing to do. What is the address of that place—Nineteen Grant Street. My husband will have this looked into without delay. It is one thing to run these houses for people to go to of their own free will but when they start taking innocent young girls off the street, that is going to be looked into. Do tell us how you knew my daughter was there."

Peter Lansdon told her what he had told me.

"Insatiable curiosity, I have to admit. I saw you at the Green Man and remembered you. Then I happened to be in Bond Street this morning and recognized your daughter."

"Thank God you were!"

"I thought there was something suspicious about the blind girl."

"I was telling Mr. Lansdon how observant he is," I said.

My mother nodded.

"So . . . I have to admit, I followed at a distance. I saw your daughter go into the house."

"And you knew what sort of place it was?"

"I have heard mention of it. I believe at one of the clubs. I could not understand why your daughter should have been taken there by this girl . . . whose blindness seemed to have come on rather suddenly. Acting on impulse, I went in."

"You must dine with us tonight," said my mother. "That is if you are free."

"I shall be delighted."

He left us after half an hour.

"What a charming man!" said my mother.

When my father came in and heard what had happened he

was first of all astounded and then so angry that I thought he was going to have an apoplectic fit.

He turned on me. "How could you have been so foolish! You don't seem to have any notion of what can go on in a big city. The idea of going into a strange house . . ."

"The girl was blind . . . so I thought. She seemed so pathetic."

"Pathetic indeed! And you were an idiot."

I accepted his scorn meekly, feeling it was deserved and now that the ordeal was over I was beginning to feel rather excited. The tall man in the brown beaver hat had taken on a personality and it was a very interesting one. He was coming to dinner and I was sure that acquaintance with him could be stimulating.

My father said to my mother, "Keep the girl in. You never know what folly she'll be capable of. And, remember, Jessica. You are not to go out alone in any circumstances. Have I made that clear?"

"You have."

"Then give me your promise."

I did.

My father went out soon after that. He was bent on making enquiries about number nineteen Grant Street.

To my mother I had to repeat over and over again what had happened: how the blind girl had approached me, what had been said in the house. She kept saying: "Thank God for that young man. I must say he was charming . . . so self effacing. He really seemed as though he did not think he had done anything very wonderful. To go into a house like that . . . Goodness knows what might have happened to him. And for the sake of a stranger too . . . someone to whom he had not even spoken. I think he is wonderfully brave and gallant too. I am so glad he is coming to dinner."

My father came back some hours later. He had made enquiries about the house in Grant Street. It had been a brothel run by a woman calling herself Madame Delarge who was said to be French. There was no one there at the time. The place was about to be sold. Madame Delarge had what she called a reputable establishment in Piccadilly. She entertained gentleman callers it was true, but there was no enforcement of girls. Everyone came willingly. She had left the house in Grant Street and it had been vacated by her staff a week before. She could not imagine who the people were who had lured a young girl to the place. It was nothing whatever to do with her. She could only believe someone was playing some sort of joke.

More enquiries were made and it seemed that Madame Delarge was speaking the truth.

It was very mysterious, said my mother; and my father was baffled.

"A watch will be kept on the place," he said.

The adventure seemed to have become more curious than ever.

Peter Lansdon dined with us that evening.

My father's discoveries about the house in Grant Street had made him even more grateful towards my rescuer. He thought it was very odd that the house had been used by people unknown to Madame Delarge. He thought there was something very suspicious and sinister about the whole matter. He believed that there were organizations which abducted young women and took them out of the country to serve in houses of ill fame in foreign places and the thought that this could have happened to his own daughter roused his anger to such heights that my mother was afraid for him. He was having further investigations made.

"My dear Jessica," my mother kept insisting, "you must be more careful."

I promised that I would indeed and I felt very ashamed to have been so easily duped.

Peter Lansdon proved to be an interesting guest.

The dinner was just for the four of us. My parents had thought it better not to ask others. They did not want it known what a narrow escape I had had, and my father—who was by nature suspicious—wanted to know a little more about Peter Lansdon before he introduced him to our friends.

Peter Lansdon was willing—almost eager in fact—to talk about himself.

He had recently come to this country, he said. His family owned estates in Jamaica and had exported sugar and rum in large quantities. A year ago he had decided to sell out his holdings and settle in England.

"Such matters take longer than one at first anticipates," he explained.

My father agreed with this. "And what are you planning to do now that you are in England? I can see you are a young man who would not wish to remain idle . . . not one of those gentlemen about town who spend most of their time gambling in clubs.''

"You have assessed me accurately, sir. Indeed, that is not my wish. I had thought that I might buy an estate somewhere and settle here . . . somewhere in the south. Having been accustomed to a warm climate, I might find the north too invigorating.''

"Have you looked for anything yet?'' asked my mother.

"I have seen one or two . . . nothing which pleases me.''

"Have you a place in London?''

"Not yet. I have been travelling around. I am in a hotel at the moment. Exploring as it were.''

"My daughter tells me that you saw us at the Green Man.''

I smiled at him. "I remember you were in the parlour when we arrived.''

He nodded.

"And you recognized my daughter when you saw her in the street,'' said my father.

"Well,'' he smiled warmly, "she is rather noticeable. My interest was aroused when I noticed the girl who was pretending to be blind.''

"An extraordinary business,'' said my father. "The place was deserted when I called a few hours later. They must have left hastily. Madame Delarge who owns the place knew nothing of them.''

"She is a Frenchwoman?''

"I'm not sure. Posing as one perhaps. Why do they think the French are so much more expert at vice than we are?''

"Perhaps because they are,'' I suggested. "Vice must be rather like fashion. There has to be a special elegance . . . otherwise it becomes quite sordid.''

Peter Lansdon laughed. "There is something in that, I suppose,'' he said. "I have made enquiries too and I cannot believe that this Madame Delarge who seemed to be very desirous of keeping what she calls her reputation would stoop to such actions as these people did. It was so crude and so absurd.''

"You are making me feel that I was even more foolish than I have been led to believe to be taken in by it,'' I said.

"Oh no, no. Who would not be taken in? A poor blind girl asks to be helped. It would be a hardhearted person who would refuse.''

"But to go into the house . . ." I said.

"It all happened so naturally, I am sure."

"It certainly seemed very strange to me," said my father, and my mother added: "I shudder to think what might have happened if you had not been there, Mr. Lansdon."

"Don't think of it. All's well that ends well and this has ended very well for me, I do assure you. Coming from abroad I have few acquaintances here and it is a great pleasure for me to dine here with you. I sincerely hope this will not be the end of our acquaintance."

"There is no reason why it should be," said my mother.

"I was wondering if you could help me at all. You see, I know so little about this country. Although it is my native land I went to Jamaica as soon as I had finished with school and there I joined my father."

"Your father is there now?" began mine.

"He died two years ago. He was the victim of a virulent fever, endemic to Jamaica. He had suffered from it a few years before. That had a weakening effect . . ." He shook his head sadly.

"And you decided you would leave," I asked.

"One has a feeling for one's own country. One wants to be among one's own people . . . the same ideals . . . the same way of thinking . . . You know what I mean."

"I understand perfectly," said my mother. "I feel the same. I went to France when I was about twelve or thirteen. My first husband was French. But I always regarded England as my home."

Peter Lansdon was looking at me.

"No, no," said my mother. "This is Jessica's father. By my first marriage I have a daughter, Claudine, who is married to my husband's son. I also have a son who is in France."

"I see."

"A complicated relationship," she added.

"But you understand how I felt about coming home."

"Perfectly. One day you must meet my other daughter— Jessica's half sister."

"That would be a great pleasure. In what part of the country is your estate, if I may ask?"

"The south east. We are only a few miles from the sea. Our nearest big town is Dover."

"Oh, that part of the country? Is it fertile?"

"Yes. Our bane is the south east wind. That can be pretty

fierce. But as you know in the south of England we enjoy a fairly temperate climate. Farming is good. It's quite a reasonable spot.''

"I shall have to explore."

"I wonder . . ." began my mother; and I knew she was thinking about Enderby.

"Yes?" asked Peter Lansdon.

"There is a house which could be rented. It's quite close to us. It belongs to someone connected with the family and we are looking after it."

"Really?"

"It would be a good place to look round from, wouldn't it, Dickon?"

"I don't know of any estates up for sale in the area," said my father.

"What about the house itself?" asked Peter Lansdon eagerly.

"There isn't a lot of land attached to it."

"Could one acquire land?"

"It might be possible. Our estate covers most of the area round there, and there is another house, Grasslands. There are two farms attached to that."

"It seems promising. What is the name of this house?"

"Enderby," I said.

He smiled. "I wonder . . ." he said.

After the meal we went into the drawing room and Peter Lansdon talked to my father about Jamaica and the exporting of sugar and rum. My father was always interested in business projects and I think found Peter Lansdon's company entertaining. My mother had taken a great liking to him—largely I think because he had rescued me.

As for myself I was certainly intrigued. He had a special way of looking at me which told me that he admired me, and I guessed that the reason why he had been so interested was on my account.

He left us at ten thirty to go back to his hotel. My mother came up to my room and sat talking for a while.

"What an interesting young man! I am so glad he came to dinner."

"He seemed delighted to come."

"I daresay he hasn't many friends . . . coming so recently from Jamaica. My dear child, I thank God for that young man. When I think . . ."

"Oh, please, Mother, don't go over it all again! I was foolish. I was gullible. But I have learned my lesson."

"As long as you have . . ."

"Well, of course I have. It is experiences like that which make us wise. I'll never be caught like that again."

"You have to have your eyes open in a city like London."

"I know that now."

"Well, we have made the acquaintance of this interesting young man and your father is so grateful to him. Wouldn't it be amusing if he came to Enderby."

"Amusing?"

"I mean interesting. It's odd. But we met the Barringtons through a chance encounter and they came to Grasslands."

"I don't think he would want to live at Enderby. It's not a very enticing house."

"No, but other things might be . . . enticing."

"What do you mean?"

"I think he was rather taken by you."

"Mother! You are incurably romantic."

"Well, you are young and very attractive."

"In your maternal imagination perhaps."

"*I* think he is very interesting. I hope we see more of him."

I was thoughtful after she had gone. It had been a strange day. I went on reliving those terrifying moments in that room in Grant Street. It was very odd and I could believe I had dreamed the whole thing but for Peter Lansdon. I could not get the memory of him out of my mind.

It was small wonder that I found sleep evasive; and when I did sleep I dreamed of him vaguely.

And the first thing I thought when I awoke was: I wonder if I shall see him again.

How life had changed in our neighbourhood—and all within the space of a few years. One thing is altered and then another and another until it is an entirely different scene. It was not completely different because all remained more or less the same at Eversleigh. But Grasslands, where once the rather odd Mrs. Trent had lived with her granddaughter, was now the home of the somewhat conventional Barringtons; and Aunt Sophie was dead and we had Peter Lansdon at Enderby.

My parents had not thought for one moment that he would take the house. I had secretly held different views. I was beginning to think that he had fallen in love with me at first sight; and I found that exceedingly gratifying and romantic. From the moment he had seen me in the Green Man, he had been interested. He had questioned our coachman; he had seen where I lived in Albemarle Street and by great good luck he had followed me on my adventure to Grant Street.

This last had made a very special bond between us—and indeed with the family, who could never be grateful enough to him.

So I was not altogether surprised when he decided he would take Enderby for three months while he, as he said, "spied out the land"; and I was almost certain that he had come there to be near me.

I enjoyed his society very much and we saw a good deal of each other. My mother took him under her wing and procured servants for him. She invited him to our house frequently and he was now on very friendly terms with the family. Even my father enjoyed talking to him. Amaryllis thought him very charming—one of the most pleasant men she had ever met, she commented.

The Barringtons were slightly less enthusiastic; but I think that was because they felt he might be a rival to Edward.

I had thought a great deal about Edward since the arrival of Peter Lansdon. In Peter's company I felt stimulated; in Edward's interested and cosy, but not in the least excited.

At this time Edward was having a great deal of anxiety at his factory and this made him preoccupied; moreover he was away for long periods at a time. His parents were very worried about him and so was Clare Carson. I think she was rather pleased by the advent of Peter Lansdon, which confirmed my suspicions that she was in love with Edward.

Life had become very interesting since Peter was the tenant of Enderby. I was extremely gratified that he had gone to such lengths to be near me and I supposed this endeared me to him. I was still waiting for that great excitement which I connected with being in love. I had believed in it so fervently long ago when I had watched Romany Jake dancing round a bonfire. I had to grow up, I reminded myself. I would have to marry soon. It was expected of me. I thought I was fortunate to have two suitors and was rather sorry for Amaryllis who had no one.

It would be Peter, of course. Our meeting had been so romantic. Poor Edward, he would be heartbroken. I was very sorry because I was fond of him and the last thing I wanted was to hurt him. Perhaps he would marry Clare. That would be a satisfactory conclusion for everyone.

Peter had been so enthusiastic from the first and determined to take Enderby. He had travelled back to Eversleigh with us on that first occasion and my mother invited him to stay with us for a day or so.

He had been fulsome in his praise of our home. "A perfect example of Elizabethan architecture," he had called it; and he had wanted to know as much as he could about the family.

"It is what one misses when one makes one's home abroad," he said. "Oh, how I envy you!"

He studied the portraits in the gallery and asked questions about them. He rode round the estate with Amaryllis and me, and he was charmingly courteous to us both.

I was with my mother and Amaryllis when we took him to see Enderby. I wondered what he would think of it for it looked particularly gloomy as it did on winter days.

I studied him closely trying to see what his first impression was as we went into the hall—that gloomy old hall with the minstrels' gallery and high vaulted roof.

"It has an atmosphere," he said. "Not as grand as Eversleigh, but nevertheless splendid in its way."

We went up the stairs, through the bedrooms.

"Rather a large house for one gentleman," said my mother.

"It's a family house," he agreed.

"It's a house that needs people," said my mother. "My aunt, the last occupant, had just herself and her maid. Before that it stood empty for so long."

"You are not afraid of ghosts, I hope," said Amaryllis.

"I don't think Mr. Lansdon is afraid of anything," said my mother warmly.

"There might be something," he admitted. "But ghosts certainly not."

"It's interesting to look at the old house," said Amaryllis. "I must confess I never liked the place."

"Are you trying to discourage me?" he asked.

"Oh no . . . no . . . It's for you to say. I often think places have different effects on people. Some feel one thing, others another."

"Do you really think there is a possibility of your taking this place?"

"It could not be better situated for my purposes."

He smiled directly at me and Amaryllis.

I said: "You have decided to look round this area for a suitable place to buy then?"

"I think it might be an ideal spot."

"Of course," said my mother, "it is not like buying a place. I don't think you can get the feel of a neighbourhood until you have actually lived in it."

We went through the rooms.

"So many of them," he said.

"Yes, and there is an intriguing speaking tube from one of the bedrooms to the kitchen. I must show you that," I told him.

"It is a most exciting house. I should like to come and look at it again if I may."

"Whenever you like," said my mother. "The girls will come with you. Or perhaps you would prefer to be alone. I often do when I am going to make a decision."

We talked about Enderby constantly during that day.

"You are certainly letting me know the disadvantages," he said.

"There are not many advantages to tell you about really," I replied.

"There is one."

"And that is?"

"That I should have charming neighbours."

And before that visit was over he had decided to take Enderby for a short period; and I was sure he had done so, not because the house was suitable but because he was falling in love with me and wanted to be near the family.

He had moved in before Christmas. It was very easy because the place was furnished, just as Aunt Sophie had left it before she died. We seemed to spend a lot of time going back and forth to Enderby and he was often with us at Eversleigh. Amaryllis and I helped him decorate the place for Christmas and he insisted that he entertain us on Boxing Day as he came to us for Christmas Day.

My mother said it was rather touching to see Enderby in a festive mood. There had never been anything like that during Aunt Sophie's ownership, and before that the place had been empty and neglected. We brought in the yule log and hung a Christmas bush on the door; we stuck up holly and mistletoe in every conceivable place and we decorated the house with ivy.

The Barringtons were invited and I think Mrs. Barrington was a little put out because she wanted us all to go to them on the important days and it was she who had to have her Christmas party on Christmas Eve.

When I had danced with Edward at Grasslands he had once more asked me to marry him. I told him I was still undecided. He was rather sad—anxious about Peter Lansdon's coming into my life. I was sorry for him and should have liked to comfort him because he was going through such a difficult time; but I did not know how to, except by promising to marry him.

On that occasion I had a word or two with Clare Carson. She said: "What an attractive man your friend from London is."

I agreed with her.

"I wonder how long he will stay at Enderby."

"He is deciding what he will do now that he is going to settle in England. He has just sold his estates in Jamaica."

"How fascinating. I expect . . . you will marry him."

I flushed hotly. "Why do you say that?"

"I thought it was what he wanted . . . you too."

"You know more than I do."

She laughed and I realized that was something she rarely did. "I should be surprised if it didn't happen that way," she said.

I thought: Is it as obvious as that? Or was it a matter of wishful thinking on Clare's part.

The Pettigrews were spending Christmas at Eversleigh. My father liked Jonathan to come fairly frequently. He would, of course, be the eventual heir and my father was the sort of man to look ahead. He had a certain affection for Jonathan, a grudging admiration which I think meant that he saw in his grandson something of what he had been at his age.

Peter Lansdon was intrigued by the relationships in our family. He said: "It is so complicated that I have to keep reminding myself who is who. It seems odd that Jessica should be your aunt, Amaryllis."

"Oh yes," agreed Amaryllis. "It gave her such superiority when we were in the school room and you can be sure she took advantage of it."

"Jessica would always seize an advantage."

We were walking home from church at the time. It was Christmas morning and my head was ringing with the Christmas hymns which I loved. I felt so happy that I could have burst into song.

I said: "You make me sound grasping and scheming. Is that your opinion of me?"

He turned to me and took my hand. "I am sorry. I merely meant you are full of energy . . . full of the desire to enjoy life . . . which is what it is meant to be."

"It is true," Amaryllis confirmed. "Jessica is . . . how can I put it? . . . aware. I am far more gullible, more trusting, more stupid I suppose."

"I will not allow you to say such things." He had turned his attention to her. "Like Jessica, you are charming . . ."

"Although so different," she added.

"You are both . . . as you should be."

"You make us sound like paragons," I said, "which we are not . . . even Amaryllis."

"I shall insist on keeping my opinions."

"You will probably change them when you know us better."

"I know you very well already."

"People can never really know each other."

"You are thinking of the secret places of the heart. Well, perhaps that is what makes people so fascinating. Would you say that?"

"Perhaps."

"I am still a little at sea about these relatives of yours. Who is the lively young gentleman?"

"You mean Jonathan?"

"Yes, Jonathan. What exactly is his relationship?"

"My father in his first marriage had twin sons—David and Jonathan. Jonathan married Millicent Pettigrew and young Jonathan is their son. David married my mother's daughter by her first marriage, Claudine. And Amaryllis is the outcome of that marriage."

"So Amaryllis and Jonathan are cousins."

"Yes, and I am Jonathan's—as well as Amaryllis'—aunt."

"Isn't it strange what complicated relations we have managed to build up," said Amaryllis.

"My father likes Jonathan to come here," I said. "I daresay he'll have Eversleigh one day, after David has died of course."

"Don't speak of it," said Amaryllis quickly.

"It will be years and years and we all have to go some time," I retorted lightly.

"And haven't the Pettigrews got an estate for Jonathan somewhere?"

"They have a fine house but it is not exactly an estate," said Amaryllis.

"It will have to be Eversleigh for Jonathan," I put in. "My father will insist. It was lucky that his sons were so different. David was very good for the estate and I believe his brother Jonathan wasn't interested. He had all sorts of mysterious irons in the fire. He died violently . . . I think because of them. I am sure he would never have settled down to run the estate. It may be Jonathan will be like his father."

"My mother says he reminds her so much of him," said Amaryllis.

"Your father seems to be a man who knows exactly what he wants," said Peter to me. "And he'll make sure he gets it."

"That sums him up perfectly," I replied. "There will be trouble if Jonathan doesn't come up to expectations. He is always saying it is a pity David didn't have a son as well as you, Amaryllis. He is very fond of you but he would have preferred you to be a boy. He thinks David's son would have been . . . amenable."

"You see," said Amaryllis, "I have a reputation for being easily led."

"That's not exactly true," I replied. "Amaryllis can be firm, but she is inclined to believe the best of people."

"What a nice compliment for an aunt to pay her niece," said Peter lightly; he slipped his arms through mine and that of Amaryllis.

We had reached the house.

Peter said goodbye to us and went back to Enderby. He would be returning later for the evening festivities.

It was a very merry party which sat down for Christmas dinner, consisting of the Barringtons, with Clare Carson, Peter Lansdon, the Pettigrews and our own family. It also included the doctor and his wife and the solicitor from the nearby town, who looked after my father's domestic business at Eversleigh. For several years they had been our guests and the only newcomer was Peter Lansdon. He made a difference to the party. He had all the social graces to make him immediately popular. Clare Carson seemed to like him a great deal—but I think that was largely due to the fact that she believed he wanted to marry me and that I felt strongly about him.

I was thinking a great deal about Edward and it seemed to me that it would be an excellent idea if she married him. She would care for him, sympathize with him; and she knew something about the factory for she had lived with the family in Nottingham since she was a child.

How unfortunate life was! Why did people set their hearts on the wrong people?

I talked to Edward at dinner and asked how matters were faring at Nottingham.

He said: "No doubt you have heard that these people are getting more and more violent. It is not just confined to Nottingham now. It is spreading all over the country. This cursed French revolution has a lot to answer for."

"Indeed it has in France."

"Something like that can't happen without sending its reverberations all over the world."

"What will happen about these people who are breaking up the machines?"

"Penalties for the culprits must get harsher. It is the only way to stop it."

"You mean . . . transportation?"

"That . . . and hanging most likely. Only stupid men would not see that you can't stand still in industry. You have to go forward."

"Even if it means losing their jobs?"

"Then they must find other jobs. In time the industry will be more prosperous and that will mean more security for them." He looked at me apologetically. "Hardly the subject for the Christmas feast."

I put my hand over his. "Poor Edward," I said. "It is hard to forget it."

He pressed my hand. I think Peter saw the gesture and I thought with a little touch of excitement: He will be jealous.

I was young. I was frivolous. I was vain; and I could not help being excited because two men were in love with me. I liked Edward so much and I was very sorry for him. If Peter asked me to marry him . . . *when* Peter asked me to marry him . . . what should I say? I could not shilly-shally for ever. The circumstances of our meeting had been so unusual, so romantic. Of course I was going to marry Peter. I was not sure whether I was in love with him. I was very much a novice when it came to falling in love. I felt this was not quite how I ought to feel. But I *must* be in love with Peter.

My father was talking across the table to Lord Pettigrew who was seated opposite him. I heard my name mentioned and realized they were talking about the adventure and how Peter had rescued me.

Peter was alert, listening.

"I am still making enquiries," my father was saying. "I don't intend to let the matter drop. I am going to sift it out."

"Difficult to trace . . . The place is empty, you say."

"The Delarge woman is said to own the place. I don't believe that. I wonder if there is someone behind her. I'm keeping my eyes open."

Conversation buzzed round us and continued in a light vein until the meal was over and the hall cleared for dancing.

Peter was a good dancer. He danced with me and then with Amaryllis. That left me free for Edward, who danced rather laboriously—correctly but without inspiration.

"You ought to come for a visit to Nottingham," he said. "Your mother told me she would like to. She and my mother get on so well together."

"Yes, it would be interesting," I said.

"It is a very pleasant house really, lacking the antiquity of this one, of course. But it's a good family house . . . some way from the town and we are surrounded by green fields."

"Perhaps we can come in the spring," I said. "Edward, I do hope your troubles will be over by then."

"They must be. They can't go on. The law will be more stringent and then we shall see changes."

"Your parents are worried."

"Yes, about me . . . in the thick of it."

"Oh Edward . . . take care."

He pressed my hand. "Do you really care?"

"What a stupid question! Of course I do. I care about your whole family . . . your mother, father, you and Clare. Clare is very worried about you, I believe."

"Oh yes, she is one of the family."

I thought how pleased I should be if he and Clare married. I would cease to have a conscience about him then.

"You haven't made up your mind . . .?"

I wanted to say: Yes, I have. I think I shall marry Peter Lansdon, but how could I say that when he hadn't asked me? All I was aware of was that being with him was exciting, exhilarating, and the manner of our first meeting had seemed so unusual, so adventurous that it was significant.

I said hesitantly: "N-no, Edward. Not yet."

He sighed and I was very worried because I was going to hurt him. It seemed so sad in view of all his business problems.

I wished I could have made him happier. If I promised to marry him he would have forgotten his business troubles for a while at any rate. And how pleased his parents and mine would have been! At the same time I felt a little irritated with him. It is a sad commentary on human nature that when one could help and doesn't, one begins to dislike the person who arouses one's pity . . . largely because one hates feeling uncomfortable, I suppose.

I was glad to escape from Edward.

And there was Peter who, having danced with Amaryllis, was now coming towards me. His step was light. He took charge of the dance. I went where I was led and it was like dancing on air.

He said. "What a happy day it was when I stopped at the Green Man. Do you know I almost went to the Cat and Fiddle. Suppose I had? I should not have been in the street . . . I should never have noticed the girl pretending to be blind . . . never have rescued you . . . never have been here tonight dancing with you."

"And where should I be?"

"Don't think of that. I was just marvelling at the good fortune which has brought me here. Your father still thinks of it. I heard him talking to Lord Pettigrew."

"He won't let it rest. He has many concerns in London. If it is possible to find out who those people were . . . he will."

"They are probably out of the country now."

"Do you think so?"

"In that sort of criminal underworld you never know what is going on."

"My father is the sort of man who would never let any detail escape him. He doesn't go so much to London now that he is getting older, though. But he was in all sorts of things earlier . . . and so was his son, Jonathan. We hear whispers of it in the family. I think perhaps Jonathan would be more suited to that sort of work than running an estate . . . just like his father was. Some people have the temperament . . . others haven't. Amaryllis has quite a gift. She goes round the estate with her father. She has a gentle personality and the people like her. I have heard David say that you have to establish a relationship with the people on the estate. It is not merely a matter of keeping down rents and repairing homes. It's a sort of comradeship as well. Amaryllis has that gift, her father says. Her parents think she is quite perfect. Mind you, they are not far wrong. In our family there are the good and docile ones and the wild rebellious ones. Amaryllis and I are good examples of both types.''

"I think you are both enchanting.''

"But different.''

"Well, of course.''

"You dance well. Where did you learn?''

"I was sent to school in England and then I had a year in the North with some cousins where I was supposed to learn how to live in graceful society.''

"That was before you went out to help your father in Jamaica?''

"Exactly.''

"Well, they certainly taught you well.''

"Dancing or the social conduct required in English society?''

"Both.''

"It is amazing to remember that we have known each other such a short time.''

"Yes, but we have seen each other frequently since our first meeting.''

"I'm grateful to Enderby.''

"How are you liking it in that great barn of a house?''

"I like very much what is close to it.''

"How long shall you stay?''

"It depends.''

"You mean on what you find here? Have you discovered anything that might be suitable?''

"To tell the truth I've hardly had time to look—what with the Christmas festivities and the kind hospitality of my good neighbours. I like Enderby.''

"Do you? It's amazing how people become fascinated by it. There was my Aunt Sophie. She saw it and immediately wanted it.''

"It is a family house really.''

"Of course. Far too big for one.''

"It would change completely . . . with many children.''

"You are right. We should look for a married couple with a considerable brood.''

"The marriage need not be of long duration. The house could wait for the patter of little feet.''

I laughed. This was exciting. I thought he was going to ask me then. And what should I say? Could I say, It is too soon. I am not yet sure . . .

The dance was over and the servants were bringing round cooling drinks.

We sat for a while and then he said: "Excuse me. I am engaged to your niece for this one."

I watched him dancing with Amaryllis. She was laughing and talking quite animatedly. I was glad that she liked him too.

Edward came and sat beside me.

Peter was a gracious host at Enderby on Boxing Day. Amaryllis and I congratulated ourselves on the decorations which we had helped to put up; and I must say the old house seemed to have lost entirely that dour ghostliness which had been such a feature of it in the past.

Peter had devised a very clever treasure hunt through the house and this provided a great deal of merriment for he had wittily phrased the clues which led from one spot to another. It was rather uncanny to hear the old house echoing with laughter.

There was a good deal in what David always said, and Peter had seconded it, that with people in the house Enderby would be just like any other.

"I never thought we should have a jolly time in this house," said my mother.

"You've laid the ghost," my father told Peter.

It was two days later when Peter had been riding with Amaryllis and me and on the way home came into Eversleigh for a glass of wine before going on to Enderby.

We were in the hall. My parents were with us and so were Claudine and David—when one of the servants came in and said that Farmer Weston wanted to see my father—and added that Farmer Weston seemed rather upset.

"Bring him in," said my father, and Farmer Weston came into the hall. He certainly looked agitated.

"I want to have a word with you in private, sir," he said.

"You can say what you have to say here. Anything wrong at the farm?"

"No sir . . . not exactly. It's my Lizzie and . . . another. I'd rather talk in private."

"Come on in here then." My father led him into the room we called the winter parlour.

They were there for about ten minutes before they came out—Farmer Weston was very red in the face and my father looked quite angry, not with Farmer Weston though for he said to him quite gently: "Don't worry. I'll speak to him. Perhaps no harm's done. Young people . . ."

He went out with Farmer Weston and soon afterwards joined us. My mother looked at him interrogatively.

"That scamp Jonathan," he said.

"What is it this time?"

"Weston's Lizzie."

"She's only a child. What is she? Fourteen or so?"

"That makes it worse. Jonathan's not much older. That boy's got a few things to learn. If he's got to sow his wild oats he'd better choose somewhere else to do it—not on my land."

My mother looked at my father and then at Peter.

"I'm sorry about this," she said.

"Well," said my father. "Young people. Hot blood. These things happen. I had a job to calm down Weston."

Peter, showing a slight embarrassment as though he realized he had strayed into something which my father would have wished to be private, said he must be going and took his leave.

"He has impeccable manners," said my mother. "Dickon, need you have blurted that out in front of him?"

"You asked me and I told you. Nothing very unusual about it. I think we shall have some more of that sort of trouble from Jonathan. Or the Pettigrews will. I was wondering if I ought to speak to Millicent or her father."

My mother said: "You know Millicent. She can see no wrong in her boy. And Lord Pettigrew is too softly spoken. Now Lady Pettigrew . . . No, Dickon, you are the one who will strike fear into his wicked little heart. You'll have to do it."

"He's his father all over again."

"Well, Jonathan was a fine worker and he died nobly," said Claudine.

"Yes, but all this philandering doesn't go down well on the estate."

"You are quite content for him to do it elsewhere?" I said.

"My dear girl, you know nothing about these matters."

156

"Weston's a good man," said David. "His farm is a model for some of them."

"And now he's going to worry about his Lizzie," put in my father. "If she presents us with a baby in nine months' time, our Jonathan will be in trouble."

"I suppose that was why Weston came to see you at once," said David. "He wants you to know that Jonathan is responsible."

"The young can be a plaguey nuisance," said my father. "He's got to mend his ways. I'll not have Eversleigh going to someone who is going to play ducks and drakes with it . . . that's for certain. His father was no good on the estate."

"Well, you had David," said Claudine.

My father grunted.

"We'll see how the young scamp shapes up. I'll have to see him. I'm going to my study. Get the servants to find him and send him to me at once."

The incident had curbed the festive spirit. Everyone was a little subdued and I noticed that there was a certain defiance about Jonathan after his session with my father.

My mother had the full story from my father and she told it to me.

"Farmer Weston caught the pair of them in one of his barns. He was astounded. You know what a godfearing man he is . . . regular at church every day . . . and all the little Westons likewise. To find young Lizzie . . . flagrante delicto with Jonathan shocked him deeply. Well, I suppose it would most parents. Of course, your father understands . . . and isn't as hard on them as some would be. What annoys him is that it is Weston's daughter and on the estate. He was talking about bringing Jonathan over here to learn estate management . . . but I am not sure now. It's a pity there aren't more boys in the family."

"Why do they imagine a woman can't run an estate?"

"Largely because they can't."

"David is excellent. How lucky there were two of them."

"Dickon is always lucky. This will sort itself out. We shouldn't pay too much attention to this prank."

"Prank, you call it? Lizzie Weston loses her virtue and that is a prank?"

"That's what your father called it. He was thinking of Jonathan."

"Well, I can understand Farmer Weston's concern."

"So does your father. He says that if there are results it will be taken care of."

"Well, that doesn't really satisfy Farmer Weston."

"Hardly. But at least it helps. I wouldn't care to be in Lizzie's shoes for the next few weeks."

"And Jonathan will be let off with a caution. It doesn't seem fair."

"When was the world ever fair for women?"

"*You* seem to have made quite a success of things."

"So will you, my love," she answered.

"Perhaps," I said, thinking of Peter Lansdon.

January came in with a cold wind blowing from the southeast. Winter was with us. The trees stretched out their bare branches making a delicate lacy pattern against the grey skies; they seemed as beautiful as they ever did in the spring. People speculated as to whether there would be snow. The Pettigrews had left.

"Glad to be rid of them," mumbled my father. "Let Jonathan make trouble in their patch if he must and leave mine alone."

Peter had gone to London for a brief spell. He was not thinking of leaving Enderby yet, although his search for property was not proving very fruitful. But he had interests in London to attend to. He said he would soon be back.

Edward Barrington had gone back to Nottingham and Mrs. Barrington had caught a chill and had taken to her bed.

"You should go over to see her," said my mother. "She is especially fond of you."

So I went. I sat by her bed in the cosy room where a fire was burning in the grate.

"So good of you to come, Jessica. You've cheered me up a lot."

"How did you get this chill?" I asked.

"Run down I think. I worry a lot. I do wish Edward wasn't in the thick of all that in Nottingham."

"These people are becoming a real menace," I said.

"It's spreading, I'm afraid. It's a deadlock. Edward said that if they don't have the machines they can't compete with foreigners . . . and if they can't make profits the men will lose their jobs anyway."

"They can't see that, of course."

"They're shortsighted, Edward says. I am glad his father

158

has semi-retired. I do wish Edward could stay here for a while until it settles down."

"It is his business. He feels he must be there."

"Oh yes . . . but it worries me."

"It's a worry for us all."

She reached out and took my hand. "I wish . . . He's such a good young man."

"Yes," I said, "he is."

"There are very few like him, you know. He has always been so reliable. How I should love to see him settled."

Clare Carson came into the room. "I came to see if you wanted any more coal on the fire."

"I think it is all right, thank you, dear. I was talking to Jessica about those terrible riots."

"You mustn't fret," said Clare. "Edward knows how to take care of it."

"Oh, I know. But I do hate to think of it. I wish . . ."

"It can't last," I said. "I hear they are imposing more and more heavy sentences on those who create the disturbances."

"Sometimes that makes people more angry," said Mrs. Barrington. "Clare, do you think you could go and ask them to bring us some tea?"

Clare went out and left us.

"The fire will get rather fierce," I said. "Would you like me to put up the screen?"

She sighed. She would have liked to talk about marriage and she knew it was a subject which I wanted to avoid.

The tea came eventually. Clare took it with us and the talk was general—about the Christmas festivities, the weather and the prospects for the year.

On my way home I met Amaryllis with Peter. I was surprised. I had not known that he was back.

"I only arrived this morning," he said. "I called at Eversleigh this afternoon and learned you were out. Amaryllis and I decided to take a ride."

"We were just going back," said Amaryllis.

"So was I."

We all went back together.

During the next few days I noticed a change in Peter. He seemed preoccupied. I did not see him alone. I felt something must have happened while he was in London and I wondered whether some proposition had come up which meant that he was no longer interested in an estate near us.

Three days after his return he asked us over to Enderby to dine. The memory of that evening stayed with me for a long time. I don't think I had ever been more shocked in the whole of my life.

Amaryllis had been absent the whole of the afternoon. She had returned to Eversleigh to change for dinner and we had all gone together in the carriage.

Peter greeted us warmly and said how glad he was to be back, and very soon we were seated at the table. He talked about his visit to London, how glad he was to be back and what a pleasure it was to see us round his table. It was all very conventionally convivial.

Then came the blow.

He said: "I think it is time we let you into the secret. I do hope you will all share our joy. We are going to be married."

I stared at him. He had not asked me. Surely . . . I could not believe this was real. I must be dreaming.

He was smiling across the table at Amaryllis, who was blushing and looking extremely pretty.

"Yes," he said, "Amaryllis has promised to be my wife." He was looking at David and Claudine now. "My gratitude to Amaryllis' parents who have told me they are willing to accept me as their son-in-law. And I am hoping we shall have the approval of the rest of the family."

"Well, Amaryllis," cried my mother, "this is a surprise!"

I knew that she had thought I was the one in whom he was especially interested.

"As soon as we saw each other . . . we knew," Peter was saying.

Then everyone seemed to be speaking at once. Someone was talking of toasts. I felt myself behaving mechanically. There was a great lump in my throat. One thought was uppermost in my mind. No one must know.

I could not believe this was happening. I was so unsure of my feeling. I was not exactly in love with him. I had enjoyed his attentions. I had thought he was very seriously regarding our future. I was too shocked, too bewildered, to think clearly.

Amaryllis was smiling happily. She looked very beautiful. I lifted my glass with the rest. I noticed that Claudine was avoiding my eyes. She was sorry for me . . . Oh no, I could not bear it.

Had I betrayed my feelings? Was I betraying them now? I had to say something. I had to act normally. Did Peter know? Had he guessed? Amaryllis did not know. She would not be so happy if she did.

I heard myself say: "What a pity you didn't wait. Edward and I were going to announce our engagement when he came back to Grasslands."

Silence. Then exclamations of pleasure. This was what my parents had wanted. They had always wanted me to marry Edward Barrington.

"This is great news," cried my mother jubilantly.

My father said: "So it's to be two of them, is it? I didn't think our Jessica would allow Amaryllis to steal a march on her."

So they drank their toasts; and I sat there numb and thought: What have I done?

How like me to have acted on the spur of the moment. I should have been calm. But it had been the only way to cloak my feelings. I would not have them sorry for me—him too, knowing as he must have done that I had believed he was in love with me. And all the time it had been Amaryllis. I could not believe it even now.

Amaryllis was beside me. She put her arms round me and kissed me.

"I'm so pleased, Jessica. Edward is a fine man. Isn't it wonderful . . . both of us on the same day."

I said it was wonderful. I drank the toasts. And all the time I was longing to escape to my room.

I wanted to be alone to think about what I had done.

When we returned my mother came to my room. She knew me so well that I wondered if she had guessed.

She put her hands on my shoulders and drew me to her; she held me tightly for a few moments.

"My dear, you are happy, aren't you?"

"Yes, of course," I lied.

"Edward is such a good man. Your father and I have always liked him. We have always hoped . . ."

"Well, you are content now. But I shouldn't have blurted it out like that. I should have waited for Edward to be there."

"I understand," she said. "There was Amaryllis . . ."

"I wanted to share in it, I suppose. That was why . . ."

"Well, it is not important how and when the announcement was made. All that matters is that you and Edward . . ."

"I . . . I would rather it wasn't mentioned . . . not till Edward comes home. The Barringtons might be a little put out. After all, it should have been said when they were all present. I think it should be kept just in the family . . . until Edward comes back."

"Of course . . ." she said slowly. And she was looking at me intently. We had been very close all our lives. It had been something which had always comforted me, but at that moment I was wishing she did not know me quite so well.

She kissed me tenderly, said goodnight and left me alone with my thoughts.

I was too bewildered to sleep. I was hurt and angry. I felt I had been deceived but was not sure who had done the deceiving. Myself perhaps.

I was vain. Although I lacked Amaryllis' angelic looks I had thought myself to possess superior physical attractions. Now I had learned a lesson.

But I was sure in the beginning I had been the one. What had made him change? And what did I really feel? Was I brokenhearted to have been jilted . . . or something near it? My pride had been deeply wounded. It was not exactly that I was in love. I hardly knew this man. I had had romantic thoughts of him largely because of the romantic circumstances in which we had met. As for Amaryllis she knew him even less, yet she had had time to fall in love with him.

I could not really understand myself. And why . . . oh why had I been so recklessly foolish as to tell them that Edward and I were engaged? And I *was* engaged to Edward now. I had used him shamefully to extricate myself from an embarrassing position. Why had I not paused to think for a moment? How much more dignified, how much more honest it would have been to have sat there and taken the blow on the chin—as they say—and tried not to show how much I was flinching.

How typical of me to flounder in and put myself in an even more awkward situation.

I had a very restless night and the next day went over to Grasslands. Mrs. Barrington had recovered from her cold and was as brisk as ever.

I asked after Edward and learned that he was coming back the next day. I was determined to see him at the first possible moment.

Amaryllis was in a state of bliss. Not only was she in love but, being Amaryllis, at the same time she could spare a little pleasure because I appeared to be in a similar state.

I consoled myself that if I had not made the announcement Amaryllis' happiness would have been clouded because like my mother, and others perhaps, she had thought I was the target for Peter Lansdon's affections. It gave her great happiness to believe that I was in love with someone else because it left her free to enjoy her own bliss without the slightest twinge of remorse.

"Of course I always knew how Edward felt about you," she said, "but I thought you were undecided. You've been a long time making up your mind."

"I wanted to be sure," I told her.

She giggled happily. "Isn't it strange that you were the cautious one this time? Peter and I just fell in love at first sight. Isn't life wonderful? Just think . . . if that awful thing hadn't happened to you, I should not be engaged now. I do think Peter was so very brave to go into that house like that."

"Yes, he was."

She hugged me. "It's so wonderful. I'm so happy, Jessica. It will be marvellous to be married on the same day. We'll have to think about June. It seems a long time to wait."

"I think it would be a very good time," I said.

"Peter says it is far too long."

It was amazing to see Amaryllis thus and I almost reminded her that she hardly knew the man she was going to marry. A few weeks ago she had not even heard his name. But what was the use? She was in love and she was going to be married to the man of her choice. I should be married, too, but not to the man of mine.

Edward returned the following day. I went over to Grasslands in the early afternoon. He was delighted to see me.

I said to him: "I want to speak to you alone . . . soon."

"Now?"

"Yes, away from the house. Could we go for a ride? That would be easiest."

"Of course," he said.

He looked a little strained, I fancied. I guessed it was the usual trouble at the factory but he brightened at my suggestion and I warmed towards him. He was a very good man and I was sure he would do everything he could to help me now . . . and always. I was very lucky to be loved by such a man, how perverse of me it was not to return his deep feeling and to be so much more excited by the company of a man I did not really know. That was how I was beginning to think of Peter Lansdon. How was it that he had made me feel that he was exclusively interested in me and then suddenly I discovered it was Amaryllis whom he intended to marry? I would always be sure of Edward.

In a very short time we were riding together.

"Edward," I said, "I have a confession to make."

"A confession?" He was startled. We were walking our horses and he pulled up to look at me.

I went on: "You have often asked me to marry you. Do you still want to?"

"I shall always want you, Jessica."

Waves of relief swept over me.

I said: "My confession is that I have told them . . . told them that we are going to get married."

"Jessica!"

"Yes. It was most immodest of me. Amaryllis became engaged to Peter Lansdon . . ."

"Amaryllis? But I thought . . ."

"Things are not always as they seem. He saved me in London and when he came here he fell in love with Amaryllis and she with him. They announced their engagement at the dinner table and I thought, well . . . why shouldn't I tell them about Edward and myself . . ."

"Do you mean . . . ?"

"What I mean is that I thought we had hesitated long enough."

"We?"

"I. Oh, I've been silly . . . young and foolish I suppose, not being sure when I should have been. So I said, Well they are not the only ones who can be engaged. Edward and I have known each other for longer than they have and there are many more reasons why we should be married, so . . ."

He took my hand and kissed it. "What an odd place to hear this . . . on the back of a horse."

We laughed. His face was transformed. The lines of worry caused by the Nottingham rioters had disappeared. He looked young . . . and so happy.

"Well, Edward," I said, "it had to happen, hadn't it? It was inevitable. My parents are delighted. They have a great respect for you."

"Mine will be delighted too."

"Then there is delight all round."

"Oh, Jessica, this is wonderful. Let's ride back and tell them all about it."

So it was as easy as that.

I was sitting in the drawing room at Grasslands. Mr. Barrington had insisted on bringing one of his finest wines from his cellar. Mrs. Barrington was twittering round in a state of great excitement.

"There, Jessica. You're our daughter now. I can't tell you how happy you've made us all. Isn't that so, Father?"

Mr. Barrington said: "It is what we have always wanted. Why you had to be so long about it beats me."

"It was right and proper," said Mrs. Barrington, although I believed she had chafed at my procrastination more bitterly than her husband had. "One has to be sure about these things. That's so, isn't it, Jessica? What a wonderful day that was for us all when you picked up Father on the road and brought him home. I wonder what happened to that gypsy. He must have nearly served his time."

"It was seven years," I said. "He will have done six of them."

"How time flies! You were such an earnest little thing then, Jessica. You cared so much about that poor man. We all loved you for it didn't we?"

Barrington *Père* and *Fils* agreed.

My spirits were lifted in their company. I thought what a delightful family they were—simple in a way compared with my parents, and so lovable. My family for the future.

Edward said: "I want Jessica to come to Nottingham to have a look at the house. There might be certain things she'll want to alter."

"Yes, it's always nice for a bride to make changes. We furnished the house, didn't we, Father . . . how many years ago? Too many to remember. It would be a little old-fashioned now, I shouldn't wonder."

"But it will only be a second home," said Mr. Barrington. "You'll be back at Grasslands. Grasslands has become the family home, even though we haven't been here so long."

"We loved Grasslands from the moment we saw it," said Mrs. Barrington. "I've never regretted coming here and you know that is mainly because of the family at Eversleigh. And now this . . . I've wanted it for so long. By the way, where is Clare?''

"She'll want to be in on this," said Mr. Barrington.

"I remember. She said she was going into the town to do some shopping. She should be back soon. When is the wedding to be?''

"My mother thinks about June," I told them.

"June's a lovely month for a wedding."

"It seems a long way ahead," said Edward.

"Hark at the impatient bridegroom," laughed his mother. "We'll want a little time to get ready, won't we, Jessica?''

"Amaryllis is getting married too," I said.

"To that young man," said Mrs. Barrington, faintly disapproving. "Well, that was quick work. She hardly knows him.''

"I met him in the most dramatic circumstances," I said.

"I know . . . and brought him to Enderby. Well, it's funny how things work out. I think it is better when people have known each other some little time. There are all sorts of things you have to learn about people if you're going to live with them. Father and I were engaged . . . for how long was it, Father?''

"Two years," he said promptly.

"And then we'd known each other since we were children."

"It certainly turned out satisfactorily for you."

"Well, you see, we knew what we were getting."

"We knew what to be prepared for."

Mrs. Barrington laughed heartily and at that moment Clare came in.

"Oh, there you are, Clare," said Mrs. Barrington. "Come and hear the news. Get a glass for Clare, Father. It's happened at last. Edward and Jessica are engaged.''

She stood very still and I noticed that one of her hands which was hanging at her side was clenched.

"Oh," she said. "I thought . . .''

"We all thought they'd taken a long time about it," said Mrs. Barrington. "But at last all is well."

Clare turned to me. "Congratulations . . . And you, Edward.''

"We're drinking to their health and happiness," said Mr. Barrington. "Here you are, Clare.''

She took the glass and raised it. Her eyes, which were fixed on me, glittered oddly.

Did Edward know she was in love with him? Did the Barrington parents know?

I supposed not. She had been in the household since she was a little girl . . . an unwanted orphan taken in by distant relatives . . . treated as one of the family and yet feeling perhaps not quite one of them, although I was sure the Barringtons would have done everything possible to make her feel so. And she loved Edward . . . really loved him. It was not merely *her* vanity which was hurt.

She had taken her blow more gracefully than I had taken mine. I had a great admiration for Clare Carson and I believed, with a tremor of uneasiness, that she would figure largely in the life I had chosen for myself.

Riot

There was great activity throughout Eversleigh. Although we were three months from the weddings, my mother and Claudine threw themselves into the preparations with an abandonment I had never seen before.

This was to be a double wedding. We had had double birthdays in the past, but what were they compared with a double wedding. They thought it was most exciting and so appropriate that Amaryllis and I, who had shared our childhood, should both come to marriage on the same day.

"It is like a pattern," said Claudine.

I did detect a faint anxiety beneath my mother's gaity. I thought she was still a little worried about the sudden announcement of my engagement. I believe she thought there was more involved than a desire to be even with Amaryllis. She never lost an opportunity of extolling the virtues of Edward.

"Such a dear young man. Your father was saying only this morning how pleased he was that you had chosen Edward. After all, we have known the family well for some time now. They are delightful people, almost like our own family. Whereas . . ." I waited and she frowned. "Well, no matter . . ." But I knew she was implying that very little was known about Peter Lansdon.

On another occasion she said: "David is so trusting. He is not like your father. David is inclined to think everyone is as uncomplicated as himself."

"David is wise," I said.

"Wise in booklore. He can quote from the classics and has some literary comment on almost any subject. He's an expert on the past. He's an idealist. But I wonder how much he knows about the less agreeable side of human nature. Claudine has got more and more like him with the years."

"David," I said, "is a very good man"

"Yes. I am glad Claudine married him and not his brother. At one time I thought . . . But that's a long time ago. What was I saying . . . Your dress. We'll have to decide on the sleeves."

I wondered what was in her mind. She was comparing Edward with Peter Lansdon and was glad I had taken Edward.

Indeed there was such delight in my coming marriage from both my parents and parents-in-law-to-be that I began to feel that it was after all a very happy conclusion. There was only one person in whom I detected a faint animosity towards the coming event—and that was scarcely perceptible. But it was obvious to me that Clare was half in love with Edward. I could imagine her coming to the house and how Edward, the big cousin, would have been kind to her. Edward would always be kind, as indeed his parents would. There were some people who would feel like outsiders in such a situation and nurse a grievance against life for putting them in such a situation. Aunt Sophie had been such a one; perhaps Clare was another.

But I must confess I did not think a great deal about Clare, and as when I did she introduced a rather unpleasant flavour into the complacency which I was trying to keep going, I avoided her.

In March it was decided that I should go to Nottingham. Mother was to accompany Edward and me. Naturally Edward and I could not go alone and my mother said that if there were changes I wanted to make in the house I could discuss them with her.

We spent two nights in London on the way there and my mother and I did some shopping, and from there we set out on the one hundred and twenty-six mile journey north to Nottingham.

We rode in the carriage and stayed at some very pleasant

inns on the way where Edward was well known as he made the journey often.

It was quite exciting riding into the town—a very pleasant one situated on the River Trent. High on a precipitous rock, rising above the river, were the walls of Nottingham Castle, which had been dismantled by Cromwell's men during the Civil War. Edward was very proud of Nottingham, and told us little snatches of history as we went along. Of course it was the scene of the first of the battles between King Charles the First and the Parliament; he knew a great deal about its early history too, when the town had been overrun by the Danes.

The house was very attractive. It was just outside the town in fairly extensive grounds, built in the style which had become popular at the beginning of the previous century in the reign of Queen Anne. There was about it—as indeed there was about all houses built in the period—an air of dignity and restraint. It did not pretend to be a palace or a stately mansion. It was the home of gentlefolk of substance and good taste. It was built of the local stone which fitted well with the countryside.

My mother said it was a charming house. It made places like Eversleigh and Enderby look over-fussy.

I agreed with her, to Edward's delight, and it was clear that he felt an immense pleasure in showing us over the house. What he really wanted me to see was the factory, but he thought, in view of the situation, that he should take us there when work was not in progress; and as we had arrived on a Saturday, he suggested the following day.

It was an interesting experience. My mother was as fascinated as I was; and Edward talked with knowledge and great enthusiasm of lace, its history, its manufacture, its varieties and how it had changed through the ages.

He showed us some exquisite patterns—specimens of Venetian, Italian and English needlepoint, and Flemish, Russian and German Pillow Lace. He pointed out the old-fashioned bobbins which were being used to placate the workers, and then he took us into a room where new machines were being installed.

There was a man on duty there, a young boy with him. He touched his forelock as we entered.

"All well, Fellows?" asked Edward.

"Yes, sir," answered the man.

Edward introduced him as Fellows and his son Tom who was just coming in to the works. He explained to us that it was necessary to have someone guarding the machines night and day. If any of the Luddites broke in Fellows would be there to give the alarm.

I shivered. I could understand Edward's deep concern. I realized that he must have the machines and on the other hand I could see why there was anxiety in the workers' minds.

Edward explained the intricacies of the machines.

"This is the Leavers Lace machine," he said. "Let me show you. The number of threads brought into operation is regulated by the pattern to be made. See. The threads are of two sorts, beam or warp and bobbin or weft."

"It looks very complicated."

"It's easy enough to work. One man can control it and sixty pieces of lace can be made simultaneously."

"So it can do at once what sixty men would take much longer to do."

"That is how it is."

"No wonder they are afraid of losing their jobs."

"It's progress," said Edward.

Interested as I was I wanted to leave that room which contained the machines.

We left Fellows and his son on guard and returned to the house. I was feeling rather sober. Edward slipped his arm through mine.

"You're feeling sad, aren't you? You mustn't. We'll ride the storm."

My mother said: "It is such an insoluble problem. I suppose you must have the machines."

"Certainly we must—or give up. We can't face competition without them."

"And yet those poor men . . ."

"You realize the difficulties. But this is the sort of situation which will arise throughout the history of industry. We have to move with the times."

"Which means that some must suffer on the way."

"It is progress," said Edward.

I turned my attention to the beautiful house. I think we were all trying to forget the problem of the machines.

The days began to pass pleasantly as I threw myself wholeheartedly in to discussions with my mother about furnishings.

"Actually," I said, "there is very little I want to change."

"It is all very tasteful," agreed my mother. "I love the simplicity which disguises its elegant comfort."

"It is a charming house," I said.

"Don't get too fond of it. We shall want to see you often at Grasslands."

As the week progressed my mother, as always, showed a little nostalgia for home. She hated to leave Eversleigh too long and decided to return home in the middle of the following week.

Edward was away most of the day. I loved to walk through the town gardens and all the time I was grappling with myself, deciding that this was the life I had chosen and I must prepare myself to like it.

Why should I not? I was getting more and more fond of Edward. He was kind and gentle and would make the best of husbands. Young girls were foolish to seek exciting adventures, dreaming of knights on horseback performing valiant feats; they did not exist outside a girl's imagination. I was too old for fancies. I had to grow up and face facts. It was not as though I had been in love with Peter Lansdon. I had just been flattered because in the first place he had noticed me and followed me in the street, taking such risks to rescue me. It had seemed like a romantic adventure, whereas my relationship with Edward was staid, steady and very comfortable.

Peter was fickle. He must have been to transfer his attentions from me to Amaryllis so quickly. What were my feelings? Pique. Jealousy? Had I always been a little jealous of Amaryllis—her superior beauty, her charm, serene nature, her unselfishness? She was indeed the finer character and presented with the two of us a man would be a fool not to prefer her. Then Edward was foolish for he had always loved me. What was it one of the maids had once said? Men were fools when it came to women . . . And she had been talking about Amaryllis and me. I was the one they looked twice at . . . all except Peter Lansdon.

No, I was not in love with him. Flattered at first . . . finding his company stimulating . . . a little mysterious. Edward, of course, had never been mysterious.

I must learn to love Edward. I had accepted him in a rash moment, and he had supported me. Sometimes I wondered whether he knew that I had spoken out of pique, just as I wondered whether my mother did. She did mention Edward's virtues continually as though stressing that I had made the wisest possible choice.

Yes, I must love Edward. I must prepare myself to be contented with the life which lay before me. I had chosen it and Edward had supported me magnificently . . . as he always would.

I must remember. I was the lucky one.

It was I who said I should like to visit the factory during working hours. I was eager to see the lace-making in progress. Edward did hesitate for a moment but I went on: "It would be so interesting . . ." And he was delighted in my interest and gave way, though I fancied with some reluctance. However, it was arranged that he would take me there.

I arrived with him in mid-morning, and as I went through the doors into that huge room which was full of people all engaged on the business of lace-making, I felt a sense of excitement.

I was aware of eyes following me as Edward conducted me through, here and there pausing to explain some little technicality. I spoke to one or two of the people. They answered me with restraint and I wondered whether there was a certain sullenness about them. Perhaps I felt a tremor of uneasiness or did I imagine that afterwards? I cannot be sure now I look back. I had become suddenly aware of my appearance in my dark blue wool jacket trimmed with sable at the neck and sleeves; my little hat with the scarlet feather and my scarlet gown. The contrast between my clothes and theirs must have been noticeable.

I was glad to leave the work room for a smaller one where a woman was sorting out specimens of lace and putting labels on them.

"This is Mrs. Fellows," said Edward. "She is an expert. She can detect a flaw which is hardly visible to the naked eye."

Mrs. Fellows, whom I guessed to be in her early forties, looked rather gratified.

I said: "Was it your husband I met the other day?"

"Oh yes, he's on duty with the machines."

"We've got more than two Fellows in the factory," explained Edward.

"There's my son Tom," said Mrs. Fellows. "He's here learning the trade . . . and I've another son who'll be coming along in a year or two."

"We like to keep it in families," said Edward.

Just at that moment a man came in and said something to Edward which I did not hear. Edward turned to me and said: "I'll leave you for a moment. Stay with Mrs. Fellows. She'll show you some of our finest patterns."

I smiled at Mrs. Fellows. "I suppose lace has been made in this town for years and years."

"That's about right," she said.

"It must be gratifying to be able to make something which is so beautiful."

"For how long, M'am, that's what we all say?"

I felt embarrassed. "Why . . . why not?"

A sullen look came over her face. "These cursed machines . . . they're going to take away our living."

"I have heard that it will be better for the prosperity of the town if . . ."

I could not go on. She gave me a scornful look. I noticed the darn in her worsted gown and I was very conscious of my fur trimmed coat and my shoes made of the best leather. I felt ashamed to speak so glibly of a matter which was of such importance to her. I wanted to tell her of my sympathy and understanding but I did not know how to.

And just at that moment I heard strange noises. There was a thumping sound as though some very heavy article was being dragged across a floor. There was a scream . . . followed by shouting.

I looked at Mrs. Fellows in alarm. She had turned very pale. "God help us," she murmured. "It's come. I knew it would . . . and now it's come."

I clutched her arm. "What's happening?"

"It's the men . . . It's been brewing, and now it's come. It's the mob . . . breaking in . . . And God help us . . . the men will be with them."

I turned to the door.

She held on to me. "I wouldn't. It's rough . . . No place for a lady."

"Mr. Barrington . . ."

"He brought 'em in, didn't he? He shouldn't have brought them in. It's his fault if harm comes . . ."

I wrenched myself free and opened the door. The big room was deserted. I could hear shouts from above and I thought Edward is up there. They are destroying the machines . . . and what will they do to Edward?

Several people were rushing down the stairs as though eager to be gone. They ignored me. They were wild looking men with fanaticism written in their faces. As I ran up the stairs more came out of that room and I was almost knocked off my feet. But they did not look at me, nor did they attempt to impede my progress.

And there I was in the room where a few days ago Edward had proudly showed me his machines. I stared in dismay at the sight of so much destruction. The machines were smashed. Several men were still attacking them with hammers and pieces of iron. I saw the man Fellows whom I recognized and I saw Edward too.

"Stop it," Edward was shouting. "Stop it, Fellows, stop it. You've joined them have you, Fellows? You've joined the wreckers."

He had gone towards Fellows who picked up an iron bar. I caught my breath. Edward advanced; then Fellows struck. Edward reeled and then fell among the remains of what had been his precious machines.

I ran to him and knelt beside him. He was unconscious. I thought he was dead, and sorrow and remorse swept over me. He had been reluctant to bring me; it was I who had wanted to come. It was my fault. I had brought him here.

I just knelt beside him looking at him in anguish.

I was suddenly aware of Fellows standing there.

I cried: "You've killed him."

"Oh no . . . no."

"Get help," I cried. "Get help at once. Get a doctor. Bring him here without delay."

Fellows ran away. I did not know whether he would do my bidding or not.

There was silence now . . . terrible silence. These men had done their work . . .

They had come to break the machines and they had killed Edward.

I do not know how long I stayed in that room among the crippled machines with Edward lying there among them . . . white and still. Some parts of a machine had fallen across his legs. I tried to move them but I could not do so. It was eerie. I dared not leave him and yet I knew I must get help. I kept thinking of Fellows. When I had first met him he had seemed gentle, respectful. But how different he had been in that room when he had lifted the iron bar and struck. The light of fanaticism was in his eyes. The mob, I thought. The mob does not reason. It is caught up in the desire to destroy everything and everybody in its way. Their fury had far outgrown fear of poverty and starvation, it had changed them from law-abiding citizens to destroyers. "Progress," Edward had said.

"Oh Edward," I whispered, "you must not die. I will love you. I *will* love you. I will make myself into a good wife. I will never let you know that it was because Peter Lansdon preferred Amaryllis to me that I wanted to show them I did not care. I will be loving and tender always. You must live so that I can show you that I am not entirely selfish, Edward . . ."

He opened his eyes. "Jessica," he said.

"I'm here. I'm staying with you . . . always . . ."

He smiled and closed his eyes again.

How silent it was! How long had I been there? Somebody must come soon.

It was like an evil dream. It seemed so unreal. And yet it was true, startlingly true. I thought of the first time I had heard Edward speak of the trouble over the installation of the machinery. I had listened with mild interest and it had led to this, and I was involved . . . deeply involved.

After what seemed like hours and when I was asking myself if I should leave Edward and go in search of help, to my great joy I heard the sound of voices.

Someone was coming. I called out: "Here. In here."

It was Fellows. He had a man with him.

"I'm Dr. Lee," said the man; and I almost cried in relief.

The debris which was imprisoning Edward's legs was removed.

I said: "He's not . . . dead, is he?"

The doctor shook his head.

"We'll have to move him," he said. "We'll have to get him back to the house."

I said: "The carriage is downstairs. Unless they have broken that up, too."

"I think not," said the doctor. "Fellows, can you help me. We'll make a stretcher of something. That's the only way to carry him. I'll give him something to ease the pain first."

I watched them in a daze.

"We'll get him home," said the doctor to me. "You're Mr. Barrington's fiancée, I believe."

I told him I was.

"He'll need looking after for some time, I think," he said.

And so we brought Edward home.

There were visits of several doctors. Edward lived but he was very seriously hurt. His spine had been injured and he had lost the use of his legs.

"Will this be cured?" I asked.

The doctor lifted his shoulders. He implied that it was not very likely.

My parents and Edward's come to Nottingham. My father was incensed by the damage which had been caused, not only to Edward but to the machinery as well. Thousands of pounds' worth of equipment had been destroyed.

Mr. Barrington took over the management of the factory and said it was the only way to show these people that they would not be intimidated by mob rule. They would in due course install new machines.

Our main concern was Edward.

He bore his affliction with extreme fortitude; and that was another admirable side to his nature which I discovered. How would an able-bodied person react, suddenly during the course of one day, finding himself reduced to being an invalid in a bath chair, dependent on others?

He was very quiet. He did not rail against fate—at least not openly. He was so grateful to me because I insisted on staying with him. Mr. Barrington engaged James Moore, a male nurse, to attend to all his needs and he appeared to be a very efficient and interesting man. I was with Edward for the greater part of the day and his gratitude moved me deeply.

"You must get out," he was constantly telling me. "You must not spend so much of your time in my room."

"But this is where I want to be. Don't you understand that?"

He was too moved to speak and I sat there with the tears flowing down my cheeks.

There was a great deal of talk about the arrests which had been made. The leader of the mob was caught and was standing on trial with Fellows.

Fellows was the man who had struck the blow and Fellows was an employee of the Barringtons.

It was time an example was made of these wreckers, said the judge. And when people were injured during a fracas that was a very serious matter. Hitherto the Luddites had been treated too leniently. They thought they were given licence to destroy and attempt to kill those who stood in their way.

Both the leader of the mob and Fellows were sentenced to hanging.

We did not tell Edward this at the time. His father said it would upset him because he had thought highly of Fellows. Fellows had always been a good man and his wife and son were in the business. What had come over Fellows he could not imagine. But it was only justice which was meted out and the Luddites had to be pulled up sharply. We could not have the mob ruling the country and deciding what was and what was not to be done.

It was a black day when Fellows was hanged. Many people crowded to the place of execution to witness the grisly spectacle. I sat alone in my room brooding on what must be happening in the Fellows' home. I thought of the woman to whom I had spoken. She had lost her husband. I thought of the boy named Tom Fellows. He would be fatherless. Yes, a black day for the Fellows and a black day for Nottingham. And for us, too, with Edward lying there in his bed, his active life over . . . perhaps for ever.

Edward said to me as I sat beside his bed: "Jessica, I don't know what is going to happen to me. I'll probably stay here. You must go back to Eversleigh."

"You will go to Grasslands. It will be better for you there . . . away from all this."

"I was thinking about you. You are so good. You have been wonderful to me. You mustn't feel bound in any way."

"What do you mean? Bound?"

"Engaged to me. That is over. I accept that."

"Do you want it to be over?"

"I rather think that is a matter for you to decide. Jessica, you are wonderful. You are bold and brave, I know. Don't make too hasty a decision. Don't think you have to do the noble thing."

"I have thought this matter out very fully. What I propose to do is to go back to Grasslands and manage you . . . the house . . . everything."

"It wouldn't work."

"Why not? Have you turned against me?"

"Please don't joke. I love you. I've always loved you and

always will. But that is no reason why you should sacrifice yourself for me.''

"Who's talking of sacrifice?"

"I am."

"Well, I am not. I've made it a habit of my life to do what I want, and what I want is to marry you. I intend to be mistress of Grasslands. Mrs. Jessica Barrington. No, Mrs. Edward Barrington. Doesn't that sound fine? I shall bully you, rather as Lady Pettigrew does his lordship. Have you noticed? It's better you don't. You might jilt me, if you did.''

"You're joking about a very serious matter.''

"It's very serious to me, and I am going to marry you, Edward . . . just as we arranged before this happened.''

"Jessica . . . no. Think.''

"I have thought and I know what I want. You will be jilting me if you refuse to marry me and I shall be wretched.''

"How can it be a real marriage? You are so young . . . you don't understand.''

"Edward Barrington, since I was ten years old, I hated to be told how young I was. When I am forty I might like it, but I have not yet reached that stage. And until I do, no more talk about youth, please. I know what I want and I am going to have it.''

"I beg of you not to rush into this.''

"I'm not rushing. I have given the matter serious thought, and this is the unshakable decision I have come to.''

He took my hand and kissed it. "I trust you will never regret it. I shall do my best to make sure you never do. And if at any time you find the situation intolerable . . .''

I put my hand over his mouth. I was deeply moved. I loved him far more as a broken man than I ever had when he was strong and well.

When the Barringtons knew that I was determined on marriage with Edward, Mrs. Barrington embraced me and wept. She told me how she admired me, how happy I had made her, and how much she thanked God that Edward had won the love of a good woman. I was embarrassed to hear myself described thus, but Mr. Barrington also embraced me and called me his brave and beloved little daughter.

My own parents were less enthusiastic. They both came to my room to talk seriously to me.

"You're being rash," said my father.

"Darling Jessica," said my mother, "do you realize what

this entails? You'll be married to an invalid. Edward's injuries are such . . .''

"I know. I know," I replied. "You mean no normal . . . what you call family life. No children."

"Yes, my dear, that's what I mean."

"I shall be happy looking after Edward."

"At first perhaps . . .''

"You've got some idea about nobility and that sort of thing," said my father. "Believe me, life is not like that."

"It may not be for some," I insisted, "but I intend it shall be for me."

"You are young and inexperienced of the world . . .'' began my mother.

"If anyone else calls me young again I shall . . .''

My father grinned at me. "What will you do, eh?"

"I really do know what I want to do."

He took me by the shoulders. "Yes. You know what you are doing today . . . tomorrow and perhaps for a little while. But there will come a day. Someone will come along . . .''

I said angrily: "We are not all like you."

"Human nature does not vary so very much, dear child," he said. "Some of us go more in one direction than others . . . but we are all frail at heart."

"I can see she has made up her mind," said my mother.

"And she is like you, my dear wife. Once she has, she is inclined to be obstinate."

"I think we shall have to accept this," went on my mother. "Dearest Jessica, if at any time you are in doubt . . . or trouble of any sort, you know your father and I will understand and help."

I looked at them both—the two people I loved most in the world. I embraced them both.

"I know," I said. "But I have to do this. I would never be happy again if I did not marry Edward now."

They accepted that, but they were very uneasy, I knew. There was a great deal of discussion as to what arrangements should be made. Mr. Barrington said he would go back to Nottingham and take over the management of the factory. Edward should return to Grasslands.

Clare Carson, who had been deeply shocked by what had happened to Edward, was to stay with the family in Nottingham. Edward and I should be married almost immediately.

There would be no grand double wedding now. Amaryllis would have the great day all to herself.

And so we went back to Eversleigh and at the beginning of May, in spite of further attempts by my parents to dissuade me, I became Mrs. Edward Barrington.

In those first weeks following our wedding I was very happy. I lived in a rarefied atmosphere of self sacrifice. I felt ennobled. I had honoured my obligations and I reminded myself that if I had not married Edward I should have despised myself. I had used him in the first place out of pique; well now I was ready to keep my part of the bargain.

And how easy it was! James Moore, the male nurse who looked after Edward, had turned out to be exceptionally efficient and was fast becoming a good friend of myself as well as Edward. He was there when he was needed and could be remarkably self effacing when the moment required he should be. We had been fortunate in finding him.

Moreover, Edward was not the sort of man to nurse his grievances. I was beginning to understand what a fine character he had. He had great courage and belittled that courage. He even said on one occasion that he could not help feeling relieved to have escaped the burdens which had been created by the Luddites and was only sorry his father had to shoulder them.

"Here I live . . . in luxury, with an angelic wife to take great care of me, with James who is the soul of patience . . . and all I have to do is let them fuss over me."

I kissed him. But sometimes I saw the pain in his eyes, the frustration, the contemplation of the years ahead during which he could not hope to live normally.

I used to read to him a great deal. He enjoyed that. We played piquet and he taught me chess. The days slipped by and I lived in a state of euphoria, feeling that I had done something very noble. I often thought that that was how nuns must feel when they take their vows. In a way I had made similar vows.

I rejoiced in the moment. I lived in a world of adoration. It was quite clear that Edward looked on me as something of a saint.

The Barrington parents came from Nottingham to visit Grasslands, and Mrs. Barrington told me how she would never forget what I was doing for her beloved son, and she thanked God nightly for having brought me to them. It was very gratifying to find myself suddenly playing such a noble part.

Then came Amaryllis' wedding day—that day which was to have been mine too.

She was married in the chapel at Eversleigh and she and Peter were going to London for the honeymoon. The continent was out of bounds because of the Napoleonic wars. Since the retreat from Moscow, Napoleon's good fortune had dimmed a little but he was still formidable. Wellington had invaded France and now and then we heard of his successes.

Amaryllis was a beautiful bride; white suited her and in her silk and lace gown she looked like an angel. She was radiant and David and Claudine were so proud of her.

My mother said that we did not really know a great deal about Peter Lansdon, but I think she was a little jealous on my behalf and when she saw Amaryllis with her handsome bridegroom she could not help thinking of her own beloved daughter who had rashly committed herself to a marriage which was not fully one.

There were festivities at Eversleigh and Edward was brought in a wheelchair to join them. There were the usual speeches and toasts and after the bride and groom had left, Edward and I stayed on with the other guests.

The wedding had its effect on me.

After James had got Edward to bed I went in to say goodnight and sit with him for a chat before retiring to my own room.

I hoped I did not show the slight depression which had come to me. Edward had become very sensitive. It was almost as though he had developed an extra sense.

He said rather wistfully: "It was a beautiful wedding."

"Yes. Amaryllis is a very beautiful girl."

"She looked so happy."

"She is," I said.

He was silent for a while, then he said: "This was to have been our wedding day. How different it might have been."

"It is very good now," I said.

"Are you happy?"

"Completely," I lied.

"Jessica, you can't be."

"What do you mean by doubting my word?" I cried with a touch of annoyance.

"It should have been so different."

"It is as it is . . . and I am happy."

"Jessica?"

"Yes."

"It can't always be so. You will miss so much. Seeing Amaryllis so happy . . . so contented . . ."

"I, too, am contented."

"You are wonderful, Jessica."

I smiled complacently. I had to admit I did enjoy playing the role of saintly woman who had given up so much for the man she had promised to marry when he was in the prime of life. I had always seen myself in dramatic situations in which I had shone. Now I was living in one of these youthful fantasies. But today, at Amaryllis' wedding, I had realized how easy it had been to escape from my wild dreams when they no longer appealed. This was real life; it could not be shooed away when it began to pall.

But I could feel a certain happiness when Edward looked at me with that adoring devotion.

I kissed him.

"No more of this talk," I said. "Shall we play a game of piquet before I say goodnight? Or are you too tired?"

"I should so much enjoy it, my dearest."

So we played, but when I went to my room the vague depression was still with me.

I had passed out of a phase. Seeing those two going off together on their honeymoon had awakened me to my situation.

Suppose I had been going off on *my* honeymoon with my bridegroom, how should I be feeling? Wildly excited, expectant, gloriously in love?

I pictured it—and the bridegroom was not Edward. It was not Peter either. It was some vague shadowy figure . . . someone I had known years ago when I had been a young girl . . . a child no more . . . Dark, glowing, full of life, dancing round a bonfire.

How foolish to indulge in fantasies. I was the noble wife who had made the ultimate sacrifice for the sake of honour. That was the role I was playing. I wanted to play it. It made me feel good so that I could forget all the little peccadilloes of the past . . . all the selfishness, the waywardness which had dogged me before I had married Edward.

In the last few weeks for the first time in my life I had felt satisfied with myself.

And now I was having disturbing thoughts.

That night I dreamed that I was being married. I was standing at the altar at Eversleigh waiting for my bridegroom. He came out of the shadows and waves of emotion swept over me. I was in love . . . passionately in love.

He was beside me. I turned, but his face was in shadow. I cried out to him to come to me.

Then I awoke.

The Debt

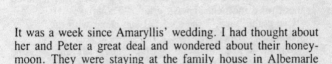

It was a week since Amaryllis' wedding. I had thought about her and Peter a great deal and wondered about their honeymoon. They were staying at the family house in Albemarle Street, so I could picture them clearly.

I thought of their visiting the theatre, taking trips up the river, riding through the surrounding districts, calling at interesting inns—all the exciting excursions one could take in London.

I found myself imagining the intimate moments between them. Beautiful Amaryllis; handsome Peter Lansdon. I wondered about Amaryllis. She had always seemed uncertain and reserved; but she had been like a flower opening to the sun since her engagement to Peter Lansdon.

I felt restless and uneasy. I had a vision of myself living this life for years and years to come.

During those hours I would always take a horse and ride out. I liked to gallop along the sand and feel the wind in my hair. It gave me a sense of freedom. I was always thinking of freedom nowadays. It occurred to me that I was beginning to feel shackled. I always dismissed that thought as soon as it came. The last thing I must do was feel sorry for myself.

If anyone should feel self pity surely that must be Edward. He was an example to me. If he could accept what had happened to him, surely I could.

Another thought came to me. I had willingly accepted this life; he had had it forced upon him.

But these thoughts did not come often . . . as yet. I was still pleased with my role of self-sacrificing wife.

That afternoon when I came in from my ride I was confronted by one of the servants who said that someone had come over from Enderby and wanted to see me urgently.

"Is something wrong? Mr. and Mrs. Lansdon . . .?"

Images were crowding into my mind. There had been an accident. Amaryllis? Peter?

"No, no, Mrs. Barrington. It is nothing to do with the master and mistress. It's someone who has come. She is asking for Mademoiselle Sophie . . . I didn't know what to do."

"I'll come," I said. "Who is it?"

"It's a woman and child."

I went back with the maid.

In the hall was a woman and with her a young girl. I stared at them for a moment. Then I cried: "Tamarisk."

"I've come back," she said. "Leah came with me."

"But . . ." I began.

"Where is Mademoiselle Sophie? They say she is gone . . . Gone? Where has she gone?"

"She died," I said.

Her face crumpled. "Where is Jeanne?"

"She lives in a cottage on the estate."

"But . . . I don't understand."

Leah spoke then. She said: "The child is distraught. She has talked so much of Mademoiselle Sophie and Jeanne. She missed them sadly. She would not rest until she came back to them."

"It is a pity she walked out without saying a word."

"I've come back," said Tamarisk.

I felt angry with her, remembering the suffering she had caused.

I said: "She was so sad when you went away without telling her even. She pined and didn't take care of herself. Then she became ill . . . and had no wish to live."

Tamarisk's great dark eyes were fixed on me.

"You mean . . . I did that?"

I shrugged my shoulders. I said: "What is this? A brief visit?"

"I've come back," she said.

Leah laid a hand on my arm. "Please . . . be kind," she said. "The poor child . . . she has suffered."

"Everything has changed now," I said.

Tamarisk covered her face with her hands and began to sob.

"I do not want her to be dead. She loved me. Nobody ever loved me like Mademoiselle Sophie did. As soon as I had gone I wanted to come back."

"It's true," said Leah. She was looking at me appealingly.

I said: "I don't know what can be done now. The house is let." I suddenly remembered that the house belonged to Tamarisk. She did not know this, of course, and it was not for me to tell her now.

I thought the best thing I could do was take her and Leah to Eversleigh. My parents would know what should be done.

I suggested this. Leah nodded and with the weeping Tamarisk we walked the short distance across the fields.

My mother was astounded at the sight of them. She noticed at once that they looked weary and travel-stained and that what they were most in need of was hot water to wash, clean clothes and some food. She arranged that this should be provided and her brisk, practical approach seemed a great help.

While this was in progress there was a family conference including David, Claudine, my parents and myself.

"The child has grown tired of the nomad life," said my father, "and I don't wonder. My impulse is to send her back to it. She was pampered at Enderby by Sophie and light-heartedly she decided to try it with the raggle-taggle gypsies. Then when the novelty of that wore off she says, I'll go back now. She should be taught a lesson. However, we have to remember that Enderby belongs to her now."

"She doesn't know it yet," said David.

"No, and perhaps it would be wise not to tell her just yet. She might decide to take up residence immediately and banish the honeymooners when they return. She should be a little older before she learns of her inheritance."

"The question is the immediate future," put in my mother. "Where is she going to stay? We'll have them here, of course. They can't go to Enderby with Amaryllis and Peter away."

"I wonder where the gypsies were," said David. "We did make extensive searches at the time she disappeared."

"Gypsies know how to stay away when it is expedient to do so," said my father.

Claudine said. "How would you feel about having her at Grasslands, Jessica?"

"Jessica has enough to do," said my mother quickly.

I hesitated. The days were a little monotonous. They could hardly be that with Tamarisk around. She interested me. Romany Jake was her father. He, too, had fascinated me when he appeared briefly in my life.

"I will take her to Grasslands if you like," I said.

"But Edward?"

"Edward would not object. He never does to anything I want. I think she might amuse him. Yes, I'll take her until we decide what is to be done."

"That's a problem," said my father. "The house is hers. I'm a trustee and she couldn't do anything without my approval and that of the solicitor fellow, Harward, who acts jointly with me. We have to think of her interest, of course. I am of the opinion that we should go on letting the house for a few years."

"I wonder if Peter and Amaryllis will stay?"

"I hope so," said Claudine fervently.

"Peter doesn't seem in a hurry to buy that estate he was talking about."

"No, he has interests in London now," said my father. "I think becoming a landowner doesn't appeal any more."

"This isn't settling the problem of Tamarisk," said my mother. "Let them stay here tonight. You can talk it over with Edward, Jessica, and if he is agreeable I don't see why they shouldn't go to Grasslands for a while. We've got to look after Tamarisk for Dolly's sake . . . and in any case we wouldn't want to turn the child away."

"She was desperately upset when she heard about Sophie," I said.

"So she should be," retorted my father. "Little minx! Going off like that . . . and then calmly coming back and expecting to have the fatted calf killed for her."

"We'll have to wait and see how things work out," my mother insisted. "Anyway, let them stay here for the night. Then we'll see."

That was how Tamarisk came back to Eversleigh.

It was almost a year since Amaryllis' wedding and the return of Tamarisk.

I had taken the child and Leah into Grasslands. When I had discussed the matter with Edward, he, suspecting that it was what I wished, had said it would be a good idea to have her come to us. My mother was secretly pleased. Tamarisk was not the most lovable of children and my father certainly not the most patient of men. He was already irritated because Sophie had left Enderby to Tamarisk and so created problems. He said that if he had had his wish he would have sent the child back to the gypsies. So my mother, the soul of tact as ever, thought it would be a good idea if she came to us.

I suppose I really got along with Tamarisk as well as any. I never attempted to show too much affection to her. I was sharply critical and oddly enough that seemed to inspire a certain respect in the child. One thing in her favour was that she was genuinely sorry for the pain she had caused Sophie, but whether this was due to the fact that she missed Sophie's blatant adoration or to true remorse, I was not sure. Whenever Sophie was mentioned her eyes would grow dark with sorrow and I had often seen her fighting to keep back her tears. One night I heard her sobbing in her bedroom and went in.

"You are thinking of Mademoiselle Sophie," I said.

"She's dead," she muttered. "I killed her."

"That's not exactly true," I said.

"She died because I went away."

"She was very grieved when you disappeared. We searched everywhere."

"I know. We went to Ireland. We went straight across the water. It was horrid. I wanted to come back. I wanted to be with Aunt Sophie again."

"I expect it was uncomfortable living in a caravan after your lovely bedroom at Enderby."

She nodded.

"And it was only then that you realized all the care you had had."

"Leah loves me."

"But she could not give you a warm feather bed, a pony of your own to ride."

"I had a horse to ride."

"Silk dresses . . . delicious food."

"It wasn't that . . . only."

"Poor Tamarisk. You made a mistake. You walked thoughtlessly away from Mademoiselle Sophie who had done everything for you."

"I remembered after."

"Yes. When it was too late."

"I wanted to come back. I did really."

"I daresay you did."

"I couldn't get home . . . because of the water. And they wouldn't let me go."

"You chose them. You hurt Mademoiselle Sophie deeply by deserting her for them."

She was crying gently. I was unsympathetic but I felt that was what she needed. Any attempt to smooth over what she had done would not have pleased her. She was, at heart, an extremely logical person. She was more impressed if one spoke the truth. She had brought great sorrow to Sophie who had given her nothing but kindness, and any attempt to deny it would strike her as extremely false.

"When something is done it's done," I said. "There is no going back. You have to accept it and go on from there. That's the best way."

"But she's dead."

"Yes. But that is past. You have learned a lesson."

"What lesson?"

"To think of others besides yourself."

"Do you think of others?"

"Sometimes."

"Not always?"

"We're none of us perfect."

"So you do wrong things."

"Of course I do."

She smiled and the tears stopped flowing.

"Listen, Tamarisk," I said. "You're a lucky girl. You did a wicked thing. You walked out on someone who had been kind to you and loved you dearly."

"I killed her."

"No, you didn't. If she had been stronger she wouldn't have died. She caught a cold and became ill. It was some time after you left. You caused her great suffering, that's true. But most of us act badly at some time. The great lesson to learn is that it is done and you must try to atone for it."

"What is that?"

"Being better in the future. Think of others. Go and visit Jeanne more often. Let her see you love her and that you are grateful to her for all the love she gave you. Try to be thoughtful and kind and then Mademoiselle Sophie will look down from Heaven and say, 'It was not in vain.' There! Here endeth the first lesson. Now go to sleep.''

I tucked her in and wiped the tears from her cheeks.

"Goodnight," I said.

I tiptoed out and shut the door.

I wish I could say she changed after that night. She did not. But I think she began to grieve less. She was as headstrong as ever.

Leah was her constant companion and she was a great help in looking after her. I engaged a governess for her. She was eight years old now and in need of tuition. She was bright and eager to learn and very quickly made up for a lack of schooling during the time she had been with the gypsies.

I was seeing a great deal of Amaryllis and every time I came back from Enderby I would fight a battle with myself, for I was becoming more and more aware of what I was missing in life. What I wanted more than anything was a child. I learned that Amaryllis was expecting one. She was in a seventh heaven of delight. She was so much in love with her husband. It could not be anything but a happy house with Amaryllis in it. She was in constant conclave with Claudine; they went to London to buy materials for the baby's clothes; the nurseries which had been quiet for so long were opened.

David had been wrong when he had said that if the bushes were cut down and more light let in it would take away the eerie brooding atmosphere. The bushes were of no account. Amaryllis, her happy marriage and her coming baby were enough to change that house.

Oh yes, I was envious. Not of her husband. That had passed. It was the baby I wanted.

So much was happening abroad. Napoleon was no longer having one success after another and Wellington was making progress. He was the hero of the hour and when he with his allies marched into Paris and Napoleon was forced to abdicate, we believed that really was the end of him. Napoleon had been banished to Elba and there was once more a king on the throne of France. Louis XVIII now reigned over them.

My mother's comment was: "All the misery might never have taken place. Here they are just as they were before the storming of the Bastille."

"Wiser, let's hope," said my father.

But the great topic was the coming baby.

Peter was often in London. He had great interests there. He

had abandoned the idea of buying an estate. He said he did not think he was meant to be a squire. Moreover he had gone into several flourishing concerns and it was these, apparently, which took him so frequently to London. He talked a little about his affairs with my father and David. David, of course, did not pretend to understand the sort of business in which Peter was engaged. My father admitted that it was a little obscure and something with which he had never had any connection. Peter talked a great deal about his interests in Jamaica and I gathered that he was concerned in the importing of sugar and rum. He discussed Jamaica at length; but since my father was not entirely sure about what he was doing, it was hardly likely that the rest of us would be.

It was of little importance. He was clearly a man of substance; Amaryllis was very happy; and he was the father of the newcomer for whom such a welcome was being prepared.

At the end of April Amaryllis' baby was born, and there was great rejoicing throughout the family although my father said: "Another girl. When is this family going to produce a boy?"

My mother chided him and said she had not noticed that he had an aversion to her sex.

The baby was christened Helena. I saw her when she was a few hours old, looking rather like a wrinkled and irritable old gentleman; but as the days passed the wrinkles disappeared, her skin developed the texture of a peach and her startlingly blue eyes delighted us all. We were all very soon Helena's slaves; and the ache within me grew stronger every day.

I took to calling frequently. Amaryllis used to watch me with the child, for I always held her, if that were permitted, and I did fancy she had a special feeling for me. I caught Amaryllis' eyes on me and they were full of pity. I felt resentful against her then . . . against life, I suppose. I began to ask myself whether I should have listened to my parents' warning.

Then I went home to Edward and sat by his bed desperately trying to checkmate him and failing miserably. I thought: No. I have done the right thing, the only thing. I should never have been happy if I had rejected him because of what had happened to him. But however right an action may be at the time it can be hard to live with. One quick act of self sacrifice is easy; but to go on practising it for years—perhaps for life—that is a very different matter.

I noticed that Peter was spending more and more time in London; and I wondered if this hurt Amaryllis. I mentioned it tentatively one day.

She said: "Oh, Peter is very busy. He has all sorts of commitments in London. He is very much the businessman."

"All that sugar and rum," I said.

"Yes. He knows so much about it, having been brought up where they produce it. He has opened several new warehouses."

"Does he store the stuff then?"

"I suppose he must do if he is opening these places."

"Have you seen any of them?"

"Me? Oh no. They are near the docks, I think. He has never taken me there. He said they were no place for me. He is so happy about it because he says it has turned out so well."

"Does he talk to you about his business?"

"Very little. But he does give me money now and then saying that is a dividend."

"You mean you have money in his ventures?"

"Of course."

"I see."

We had both received large sums of money on our marriages. It was all part of some settlement. I think the sums had been equal. Mine was invested and Edward never suggested touching it. The interest came to me and remained mine.

"All I have to do is sign the documents when they come along," said Amaryllis.

"What documents?"

"I don't know. Papers about money and all that. You see, I'm a shareholder. Peter manages all that."

"So your fortune is in his business?"

"It's a joint affair . . . only Peter does all the work."

"And you supply the money?"

"My dear Jessica, Peter did not become rich only when he married me. He was far more wealthy than I before that. He is just allowing me to share in what he has. I do nothing. I don't understand it. Really, Jessica, what should *I* know about importing rum and sugar and distributing it to people who want to buy it?"

"Nothing at all, I should imagine."

She changed the subject, but it set me thinking. He was using her money for this big business in London. Was that why he had married her—so that he could use her money?

I suppose I was really trying to find an excuse for his turning to her. But it did not make sense. I was equally well endowed. There was absolutely no reason why he should have switched his attentions to her except that he found her more attractive.

It was natural. She was sweet and gentle and very pretty. I was abrasive, questioning everything, asserting myself, rather conceited. There was every reason why he should have preferred her.

She was more amenable, of course. Had I been involved in this business with rum and sugar, I should have wanted to know more about it. I should have wanted to see the warehouses; I should have wanted to see the accounts. Not that I was particularly interested in money; I just liked to be aware of all that was happening.

Why should I seek reasons? It did not matter. He had chosen her. I had not been in love with him . . . just flattered by his attentions and perhaps finding in him a certain sensuality which kindled something in myself. No, I had not been in love with Peter Lansdon, but sometimes I think I might have begun to be . . . a little.

I would stop thinking about him. The real source of my envy was the baby. She had brought home to me that while I remained Edward's wife I could not have a child.

There was a sense of euphoria across the whole country now that the ogre who had haunted our lives for so long was in exile. We could go about our peaceful existences without fears of invasion.

"The French should never allow such a man to arise again," commented my father.

"I think," replied my mother, "that the French nation adored that man. They looked upon him as a sort of god."

"What I meant was that we must never allow the French to produce such a man again."

"Or any nation for that matter," added my mother. "Why can't people see how much happier we should all be living peacefully with our families . . . not hankering after great conquests."

"Unfortunately," said David, "it is not the people who decide. It is the so-called great men."

"They may gain glory for themselves but they certainly bring misery to millions. I wonder what he is thinking of grinding his teeth on Elba."

"Thinking of escape no doubt," said my father.

"That must never happen," added my mother.

Napoleon was finished, everyone said. He was not the first man who had dreamed of conquering the world and doubtless would not be the last. But eventually he had been brought to defeat and we could sleep in peace.

It was a lovely May afternoon when we had visitors. I was at Eversleigh sitting in the garden with my mother, Claudine and Amaryllis, when one of the maids came out to say that two gentlemen had called to see my mother. "Foreigners," she added.

"Did they give their names?" asked my mother.

"No, Madam. They just said to see you."

"Bring them out," said my mother.

And they came.

My mother stared; then she grew pale and I thought she was going to faint. Claudine had risen; she gave a little cry.

Then my mother said faintly: "Is it really . . . ?" And with a little cry she flung herself into the arms of the elder of the men. The younger stood by, looking on in a bewilderment which was shared by Amaryllis and myself.

"Charlot . . . Charlot . . ." cried my mother.

Claudine stammered: "Oh, Charlot, is it really you?"

And she embraced him too.

Charlot! My mother's son—my half brother, who had left England before I was born.

"My dear dear son," my mother kept murmuring. "To think . . . after all these years . . ."

"I came as soon as it was possible," he said. "It seems so long . . . You recognized me."

"My dear boy, as if I should fail to do so."

"This is Pierre, my son."

My mother took the hands of the younger one and stared at him. Then she kissed him on both cheeks. "Just think, you are my grandson. And this is your Aunt Claudine . . . Charlot, Jessica is my daughter . . . your half sister . . . and Amaryllis, she is David and Claudine's daughter."

"Much has happened since I left."

"All those years . . ." said my mother. "It has been a long time to wait. Now tell me . . . You will stay with us for a while. This is not to be a brief visit. There is so much to talk of. All those years to account for . . ."

"I should have been here before only travelling was out of the question."

"Thank God it is over and the tyrant is in exile."

"We have a king on the throne of France now, Maman."

There were tears in her eyes as she said: "You were always such a royalist, dear Charlot." She went on briskly: "Amaryllis, will you go and tell them to prepare rooms. See what's going on in the kitchens. Tell them my son and grandson have come home!"

My mother had eyes only for him. I realized how saddened she had been by his departure. It must have been more than twenty years since she had seen him. Wars! Revolutions! They did not only ruin states, they brought havoc into the lives of countless families. How we had suffered through them!

Now there was rejoicing. The prodigal had come home.

When my mother had recovered from her emotion a little, we sat in the garden and Charlot told us about his vineyard in Burgundy. Louis Charles would have liked to come with him but they had thought it would be unwise for the two of them to be away together.

Pierre was his eldest son. He was sixteen years of age and was learning about the production of wine. There were two other sons, Jacques and Jean-Christophe; and two daughters, Monique and Andrée.

"What a family man you have become!"

My father came to join us. He expressed amazement to see Charlot. He liked the look of young Pierre and was quite interested in the talk about the vineyards; and in any case, he was pleased to see my mother so happy.

I had never seen her so completely content. All through the years she must have felt this nagging sense of loss, as I suppose one must if one lost a son. The thought that he was there just across the water must have been with her for a long time. Death is irrevocable and one can do no good by remembering, but when a loved one is alive, and separated by a devastating war there must always be the fear, the longing for reunion, the continual doubts, the question as to whether one will see that loved one again.

I said goodbye and left them on the lawn. I went back and told Edward all about it.

There would be great rejoicing at Eversleigh that night. I wished I could have been there to share in it.

Charlot stayed at Eversleigh for two weeks and when he left it was with assurances that he would come back, bringing other members of his family with him; and Louis Charles would come with his two sons.

"As for you, Maman," he said, "you must visit us in Burgundy. We have a fine old house which somehow managed to survive the vandals. Louis Charles and I have had a great deal of pleasure repairing it. Pierre helped, didn't you, my son? And Louis Charles eldest is quite a carpenter. We have plenty of room. You ought to come for the vendange."

"I will. I will," cried my mother. "And you too, Dickon. You'd be interested."

"You'd be welcome, sir," said Charlot.

And my father said he would be very interested to see everything. It added to my mother's joy in the reunion that my father welcomed Charlot so warmly.

Amaryllis told me that her mother had said that when Charlot lived at Eversleigh there had been a certain antagonism between the two.

"In those days," said Amaryllis, "your father had not long been married to your mother and he resented her having been married before and having two children. My mother said he tolerated her but could not bear Charlot. They were always sparring. Now he seems to have changed."

"It is living with people that is so difficult," I observed. "Visitors are quite another matter."

So Charlot returned to France with promises of meetings in the near future.

My mother said excitedly: "It will be wonderful to visit France again. It is wonderful that all the troubles are over."

My father commented that it was early days yet and while Napoleon lived, we must not hope for too much. But my mother refused to believe anything but good. She had recovered her son whom she had thought to be lost to her for ever. She was happy.

I noticed my father was a little preoccupied and one day, soon after Charlot's departure, when I was alone with him, I asked him if anything was wrong.

"You're a very observant girl, Jessica," he said.

"I think we are all aware when those who mean a great deal to us are anxious."

He put out a hand and gripped mine. He was not one to

give way to demonstrations of affection so I guessed he had something really on his mind which was causing him concern.

"You'd better tell me, I said. I know something is bothering you."

"Old age, daughter."

"Old age? You? You'll never be old."

"What is the span? Three score years and ten? I'm approaching it, Jessica. With the best will in the world I can't expect to be here much longer. Do you know how old I am?"

"Years have little to do with it."

"It would be comforting if that were true. Alas, we wear out."

"Not you. You never did what other people did. You'll go when you want to and that will be never."

"What a charming daughter I have."

"I am glad you realize it."

"My greatest regret in life is that I was prevented from marrying your mother when we were young. If we had not been stopped, we should have had ten children . . . sons and daughters like my own Jessica."

"No use regretting that now. You have a wonderful son in David."

"He's a good son, yes. But what has he produced? One daughter. And now she has produced a daughter."

"Oh, I see, it is this masculine yearning for men in the house."

"I have the best daughter in the world and I wouldn't change her, but it would have been a help if you had been born a boy!"

"I'm sorry, dear father, I would do anything I could for you but I cannot change my sex."

"Oh, I wouldn't have my Jessica changed . . . not even for a son."

"I am flattered. But is this all that is wrong? No boys in the family?"

"David and Claudine won't have any more. David won't live forever."

"I hate talk about death. It's morbid."

"I'm just planning for the future. Seeing that boy, Charlot, with his Pierre growing up in the business, teaching him everything . . . and the other boys as well. It made me think. What about us? David . . . and then what? Jessica, I am sixty-nine years of age."

"And you are as well and vigorous as someone twenty years younger."

"Even I cannot defy nature forever, my dear. There is going to be a day when I go, and then David will follow me. And what of Eversleigh? Do you realize that for centuries this family have lived in this house?"

"Yes, I did know. They were Eversleighs at one time and then the name changed."

"I want Frenshaws to be here for another four hundred years. You see, you have made this marriage. It was your choice. But I had hopes of you. If you had brought me even a girl I would have said Jessica's girl would be as good as anyone else's boy. Now what? Amaryllis has had this girl. If she had had a boy it would have been different. What I am getting at is that there is only one thing for me to do— Jonathan."

"I see. You are going to bring him to Eversleigh."

"That is what I am going to do, and without delay. But he's wild. That worries me. He's like his father. His father would never have been any good for the estate."

"You were lucky to have twin boys. Just like you. Not content with one you had to have two."

"That was indeed good luck. Jonathan was a fine fellow. Adventurous, brave . . . none braver . . . full of vitality and charm. But he would never have been any good on the estate. David stepped into the breach and I have to say he is a natural squire. I have been lucky. I had hoped David would have had sons, but all he gets is Amaryllis. That leaves Jonathan who I am afraid is going to turn out just like his father."

"He is young yet."

"But he already shows tendencies. I would never have attempted to put his father on the estate. Fortunately there were other interests, and he excelled in those. The estate would have gone to rack and ruin under him and that is what I want to avoid."

"So you are going to train Jonathan?"

"That's about it. But I must say I am uneasy. I know his sort. That affair with the farmer's daughter. Fortunately there were no results, but there might have been and then he would have been saddled with keeping a child begotten in a few moments in a hayloft."

"Quite a number of people recover from a misspent youth."

"That's what I want him to do. But one has to have a

talent for managing an estate. I had it . . . in spite of being somewhat like Jonathan in my youth. I was in and out of trouble but it was always the estate which was of the utmost importance. Not only the estate . . . other business too. I have to make Jonathan realize this. That is why I am bringing him into the household.''

''And that is what is putting furrows on your brow?''

''Your mother is in such a state of excitement about Charlot's return that I can't get a sensible word out of her.''

''So you turn to your offspring who was so inconsiderate as to be born of the wrong sex.''

''She's clever enough to know she couldn't have meant so much to me if she had been a boy.''

''But how much more convenient.''

''And not half so charming.''

''You are a flatterer, dear sixty-nine-year-old Papa.''

''Jessica, my dear child, I don't often mention this to you, but you and your mother are the most important things in my life.''

''Dear Father, do you know, you rank rather high in ours.''

There was a brief silence when I think both of us were too moved to speak.

Then he said briskly: ''So you think it is a good idea to send for Jonathan?''

''I do. But what of the Pettigrews?''

''What of them?''

''They might not want to let their darling boy go.''

''He's a Frenshaw. His duty is to his father's family. Of course, it will mean having Millicent here too. Anyway, we'll see.''

I kissed him on the forehead and left. I was touched that he had confided in me. But I was at the same time worried about him. It was disturbing to have brought home to me the fact that this man who had dominated my childhood, who was held in such awe throughout the estate—and the country it seemed—who had always harboured such a deep love for me, should be an old man.

There were several meetings between Eversleigh and Petti-grew Hall and at length it was agreed that Jonathan should come to Eversleigh. He was to work with David, establish a relationship with the tenants, learn about estate management— all with a view to eventual inheritance.

David had thought it was an excellent idea. Amaryllis and I were the natural heirs after him, of course, but as we were both of the female gender, it was not easy to decide who should have come first between us two. Eversleigh would naturally pass to David on my father's death; true I was my father's daughter but Amaryllis was the direct descendant of the man who, on my father's death, would own the place, so I supposed she would come before me.

It was all too complicated and neither of us would know how to manage an estate. Jonathan came before either of us, and he had the additional qualification of being masculine.

The solution clearly lay in him and my father's real anxiety was that he should be worthy.

"There is a great danger," my father told me during one of our talks, "of getting a gambling squire. That's the worst thing possible for an estate. A frolic in the hay . . . well . . . that's to be deplored if it is someone on the estate . . ."

"Outside is quite permissible?" I asked.

"Oh quite," he answered. "One must not be too puritanical or attach too much blame to a young man for indulging in a little frolic now and then. It's all in the nature of the animal."

"And for young women?"

"An entirely different matter."

"It is a great advantage in this day to be born a man," I commented with a degree of bitterness.

"I am not sure of that. Women have their advantages if they know how to use them."

"It is so unfair. These little frolics, which are so natural for a young man and so disastrous to a woman."

"Because, my dear, these little episodes can have results and it is the woman in the case who is saddled with them. It is very logical when you look at it. A young woman has to bear her husband's children. It is, to say the least, awkward, when she bears someone else's."

"People should remember when they condemn her . . ."

"When did people ever do what they should? And we are straying from the point. I am talking about young Jonathan. He is the sort of young man who will have his fun. All I ask is that he chooses partners who are not on my estate, that's all. It's the gaming tables I won't have. I have seen good estates dwindle away . . . and all because their owners had a fancy for a gamble . . . I suppose there are some who have success at the tables, but that is rare and for one success there are a thousand failures. Yes, I want young Jonathan trained before I go. David is too gentle. He needs a firmer hand than David will give."

Soon after that conversation Jonathan arrived. His mother had decided she would stay with her family. Jonathan, of course, would visit her frequently, and the Pettigrews would be coming to Eversleigh. They were not so very far away.

It was a week or so after Jonathan was installed at Eversleigh that I noticed a certain relationship growing up between him and Tamarisk. He visited us often and Tamarisk would go to Eversleigh which she regarded as her home as much as she did Grasslands and Enderby.

This relationship showed itself in a certain antagonism. Jonathan teased her; and she told him she hated him. He called her Little Gypsy which infuriated her. I remonstrated with him for it and he retorted: "Well, she is, isn't she? She knows it and I don't think she minds, after all. In fact I think she likes it. She's proud of her connections."

She was sharp witted and I began to realize that she enjoyed his taunts and tried hard to give him as good as he gave her. There was no doubt that if he did not come to Grasslands to see her she grew moody.

Leah said he was good for her and she should know. Miss Allen was only too glad to have the care of her taken from her shoulders however briefly. So Jonathan and Tamarisk were often together.

It was a strange attraction because their temperaments were in complete contrast. For all his faults Jonathan was very lovable. Tamarisk was scarcely that. She was rebellious, contradictory for no reason but that she wanted to disagree; she was a great trial to her governess, who was only mildly placated by her thirst for knowledge. Tamarisk could be interested in a subject, and then she was almost docile, asking many questions and listening intently to the answers. But if there was something she did not like, she would put up a stubborn resistance and refuse to learn. Arithmetic was one of those subjects which she was set against and she nearly drove Miss Allen to despair. I had to console the young woman again and again. I was afraid she would leave and that it would be impossible to find another governess who would stay.

Tamarisk was passionately interested in geography; she

liked history only slightly less; but botany and literature were favourites. I suggested to Miss Allen that perhaps it would be best to concentrate on these subjects, although of course she must be taught everything she should know.

She was given to passionate loves and passionate hatreds. Passion was the keynote of her character. If she did not feel hatred or love she was indifferent—and that was how she was with most of us.

But she had a real affection for Jeanne, whom she visited often, and for Leah too. I was glad that Leah had come back with her for she seemed to be the only one who could control her. But she was certainly not indifferent to Jonathan. Her feeling for him seemed to be a passionate hatred—but I was not sure that that described it exactly.

She was eight years old at this time; he was ten years older, so the difference in their ages was great, and I wondered why there should be that sort of awareness between them. He was—so they told me—exactly like his father, undoubtedly good looking, though not in a conventional way. It was his manner which was so charming, his rather musical voice, and a certain insouciant attitude to life which quite a number of people—particularly women—found irresistible. His was a kind of careless good nature. Whatever outrageous thing he did would never be done out of malice. There was a certain lack of involvement in his attitude which seemed to set people at ease. I think the impression he gave was that he would never be critical and one felt he could charm his way out of any difficult situation. And that there might be plenty of those was evident. I was not surprised that my father felt a little apprehensive about him, and had secretly told me that an eye would be kept on him.

His coming into the immediate family circle had certainly added a spice of interest to our lives.

I was often at Eversleigh. Whenever possible I would take Edward over there to dine. My mother always welcomed this. James would wheel him out to the carriage, lift him in, fold up the chair, and when we arrived at our destination, wheel him into the house.

Much as I wanted to go, I could not allow it to be too frequent an occurrence because it tired Edward a good deal, but on the other hand he did enjoy mingling with the family and during the course of the evening he often forgot his disability.

It was the beginning of June and we were at the dinner table at Eversleigh with my parents, Amaryllis and Peter, Claudine, David, and Jonathan. David and Jonathan had spent the day at a nearby sale and were describing what they had bought.

This gave my father an opportunity to expound one of his favourite themes.

"Just think of it," he was saying, "Oaklands Farm used to be one of the finest in these parts. That was when old Gabriel was alive. He would turn in his grave if he could see this day."

"It's terrible for Tom Gabriel . . . his home gone like that."

"Don't waste your sympathy on Tom Gabriel," snorted my father. "He brought it all on himself."

"What was his particular sin?" asked Peter.

"That which has been the ruin of many a man," said my father. "Could never resist a gamble, Tom Gabriel couldn't. When he was a boy he would be gambling with conkers and marbles. It was in his blood. God knows, old Gabriel had a good head on his shoulders. It was a fever with Tom Gabriel and it destroyed him and his farm. It is by no means an unusual story, I can tell you. There are some who never learn. I have seen gambling ruin more homes than anything I know."

"You have never been a gambler, sir?" asked Peter.

"Only when I'm certain of winning."

"That is not a gamble, Father," I said.

"I'm telling you it's a fool's game," retorted my father. He banged his fist on the table. "I would never have it in my house."

"I don't think any of us is likely to take it up," said Claudine lightly. "You wouldn't, would you, David?"

My mother laughed. "I doubt David would know one card from another."

"As a matter of fact," said David, "I know the whole pack. But I agree with my father. Risks should never be taken with anything that is important."

"Well, Jonathan," went on my father, "you've seen today what can happen to a man who gets caught up in all that foolishness."

"Of course," replied Jonathan, who could never resist taking the opposite view, "he might have won at the tables and instead of seeing his farm sold might have bought several others."

My father's fist once more came down on the table and this time the glasses rattled.

"Careful, Dickon," murmured my mother.

"I tell you, young fellow, it's a fool's game. The chances of coming out on top are one in a million. Any sign of anyone here taking to gambling and they'd be out . . . like a shot."

I noticed Peter was watching Jonathan intently and there was a glitter of amusement in his eyes. Jonathan was silent. He realized, as we all did, that my father's vehemence on this matter was not to be treated lightly.

My mother, as she often did on such occasions, changed the subject, and the first thing she could think of was Napoleon's defeat. It was a subject which had not yet grown stale and there was excitement over Wellington's return to London.

"There will be galas and celebrations," said my father. "It was like that with Nelson. Wellington has taken his place. He's a Duke now. Well, it is good to see honours bestowed where they are deserved."

"It will be a great homecoming for him," said my mother. "I heard that he had been out of the country for five years."

"A long time to be away," said Peter. "I know how I feel when I make my periodic trips to London." He smiled at Amaryllis and she smiled back while Claudine looked at them fondly.

"They say," went on my mother, "that he is not exactly enamoured of his Duchess."

"But his marriage was most romantic," said Claudine. "It is true I believe that he fell in love with Lady Wellington . . . I suppose one must say the Duchess now . . . when he was a very young man. I heard that Lord Longford, her brother, at that time refused to accept Wellington as his brother-in-law because he had only his army pay."

"I daresay he would feel differently about it now," I put in.

"Well, there was no marriage and Wellington went to India and when he came back he found Catherine Pakenham unmarried—it was said because she had remained faithful to him, and he felt in honour bound to marry her, even after all those years."

"Are you suggesting that he did not want to?" asked Peter.

"That's the story. He is supposed to have certain lady friends."

My father rapped the table. "This is a hero. He has just defeated the menace of the world. Let him have his relaxation in whatever way he wishes. It is his reward."

"I'd rather have a faithful husband than a hero," said Amaryllis looking at Peter.

"Well, let's hope that everyone will be satisfied," said my father. "Now what I was saying was that there will be fine doings in London when the Duke arrives. I think it would be a good idea to take a little trip, a party of us."

"Oh, it would be lovely!" I cried; then I saw Edward glance at me and I wished I had not spoken.

David said he could not go. "Estate matters," he murmured.

My father nodded and Claudine said: "I shall stay at home, too."

"You, my dear, will no doubt be one of the party." My father smiled at my mother who replied: "Yes, indeed."

Edward said: "You must go, Jessica."

"Oh, I'm not sure."

"Yes, you must. You are too much at home. I want you to go."

"I'll see," I said.

"Amaryllis?" said my mother.

"Well, there is Helena."

"Oh nonsense," said my mother. The nanny is excellent and your mother will be at home. You could leave for a few days."

"Yes, do come," said Peter.

She smiled and said: "Well, perhaps I could."

"Well, that's settled," said my father. "Lottie and I, Amaryllis and Peter and Jessica. Jonathan?"

"Certainly," said Jonathan. "I can't wait to be in the big city."

"It will make a pleasant party," said my mother.

"I think the Duke will be there on the twenty-third," said my father. "Suppose we went two days earlier?"

"So be it," replied my mother.

When Tamarisk heard we were going to London she begged to come with us. I had not at first thought of taking her. To tell the truth I was a little afraid of having charge of her. At Grasslands I felt relieved by the presence of Leah and Miss Allen—and to have the entire responsibility thrust onto my shoulders was daunting.

"I want to go . . . so much," she said. "Why can't I go? What difference does it make to you?"

"If I could be sure that you would behave . . ."

"Oh, I will, I will. Only let me come. I long to see London and the great Duke."

"There wouldn't be room for Leah or Miss Allen in the carriage."

"They won't mind staying behind."

I sighed. "If you will promise me to be good . . ."

"I will be good . . . I will."

So it was arranged.

My mother was dubious. "The child can be such a responsibility. And, after all, she is no relation of ours."

"She is Dolly's child," Claudine reminded her.

"Yes, and of a wandering gypsy," added my mother.

"She is mixed up with the family because Aunt Sophie adopted her," I reminded them. "And she does own Enderby. She really is in a way a member of the family."

"I wish she were more like the rest of us."

"She'll change perhaps. And she has promised to be good."

It was a lovely summer's morning when we set out—my mother, Tamarisk, Amaryllis and I in the carriage with my father, Jonathan and Peter on horseback.

And so we came to London.

Tamarisk watched our approach in silent wonderment. She sat quietly demure, her hands folded in her lap. How lovely she is I thought, when she is peaceful like that particularly! I could be very fond of her if she were always thus.

We arrived at the house and the following day Peter, Amaryllis, Jonathan and I took Tamarisk sightseeing. We sailed up the river as far as Greenwich. Later we walked in the park. Tamarisk was true to her promise and was on her best behaviour.

My mother, Amaryllis and I took advantage of being in town to shop; Peter disappeared, as he said, on business and my father was likewise engaged. Jonathan once more took Tamarisk on the river and gave her a whitebait supper. She came back with shining eyes and I think it was the first time I had seen her look completely happy.

The twenty-third, the great day, dawned. London was *en fête*. The great Duke was coming home victorious. Because of his efforts the bogey, Napoleon, was on Elba where he could do no harm. We could sleep happily in our beds again and all because of the mighty Duke.

There was no doubt about it, he was going to be given a great welcome.

People were in the streets early.

"We could get near Westminster Bridge where he will alight," said Jonathan.

"There'll be crowds there," warned Peter.

"Maybe, but it will be the best spot."

My parents were going to watch from a window and my father advised us to do the same.

"Oh, let's go into the streets," begged Tamarisk. "It can't be the same from a window. I want to be down there with all those people."

"You come with me," said Jonathan.

"Oh yes." She was jumping up and down with joy.

"Well, if you want to get into the crush, do," said my father.

In the end, Amaryllis and I went out with Tamarisk, Jonathan and Peter.

"Not too near Westminster Bridge," warned my father.

"I know the very spot," said Jonathan.

I had to agree with Tamarisk that there was nothing like the excitement of being in the streets. Traders were selling flags and effigies of the great Duke. There were mugs with his image on them. "Not very flattering," commented Jonathan.

Everyone seemed to be shouting. A band was playing *Rule, Britannia*. The crowds were greater as we came near the Bridge.

"We'll stay here," said Jonathan.

"It's a little close," pointed out Peter.

"We want to be close. We want to see the great man," pointed out Jonathan.

"There'll be a scuffle when his carriage moves away."

"The great point is to see him," said Jonathan. "Tamarisk has told me that she insists, haven't you, Gypsy?"

"I want to see the Duke," she replied firmly.

"It is all right now," admitted Peter. "And it is the best spot we can hope for. I was thinking of when the crowd begins to move."

"All keep together," said Jonathan. "No straying, Gypsy. Do you hear me?"

"Of course I heard you."

"Well, remember it."

The tumult had increased and there, in person, was the great Duke. Tamarisk cried desperately: "I can't see. There are too many big people." Jonathan picked her up and, to her intense delight, set her on his shoulder holding her high above the crowd.

The Duke was stepping into the carriage, acknowledging the cheers. He was neither tall nor short—about five feet nine inches, I guessed. He was handsome in his uniform, which was glittering with medals—spare figure, muscular looking as though he were in perfect health; and his features were aquiline and I was close enough to see his grey penetrating eyes.

"God bless the great Duke," cried the crowd and the cheers went up.

Then the crowd took over. The horses were removed from the carriage and the people crowded round for the honour of pulling his carriage to the Duchess's house in Hamilton Place. It was an extraordinary sight.

"There," said Jonathan. "It wouldn't have been nearly so good from a window, would it?"

"More comfortable," I commented.

"It *is* comfortable," said Tamarisk.

"We don't all have the privilege of being held aloft by a gallant gentleman," I reminded her.

She looked blissfully happy then.

The carriage was moving slowly away and the crowd started to follow. Jonathan put Tamarisk down and said: "Keep close."

The crowds were pressing round. This was what Peter had warned us against. The shouting throng was pressing round the Duke's carriage.

"We'll get away from the crowd," said Peter. He took Amaryllis' arm and mine. "Come on," he added.

Tamarisk said: "I want to follow the coach."

And with that she edged away in the opposite direction.

"Tamarisk," I shouted.

But she had pushed herself farther away. I caught sight of her standing alone trapped by the surging mass of people and I imagined her being trampled underfoot for people were converging on her from all sides and she was so small and light. I was numb with horror.

Jonathan had seen what was happening. I heard him murmur: "She'll be crushed to death."

He pushed his way through the crowd. He was just in time to reach her before she was swept off her feet. He snatched her up and held her in his arms. He was attempting to force his way through the crowd to where we were standing. It was not easy. The crowd surged round him making its way towards the carriage. Amaryllis was clinging to Peter's arm. I felt sick with fear. I had myself experienced that terrifying feeling of crowds surging round me . . . enveloping me . . . forcing me down, trampling over me. That would have been Tamarisk's fate if Jonathan had not snatched her up.

He reached us. He was obviously shaken but I do not think Tamarisk realized the danger she had faced.

Jonathan did not set her down until we were on the edge of the crowd.

"What I need," he said, "is a drink. A draught of good ale or cider, possibly wine. Something. I'm as dry as a bone."

"I'm thirsty, too," said Tamarisk.

"As for you," said Jonathan, "you deserve a spanking. You were told to stay where you were. That should be your refreshment and I would like to be the one to administer it."

"Don't treat me like a child," she said, her black eyes flashing.

"When you behave like one, Gypsy, that is how I shall treat you."

I said: "We told you not to leave us, Tamarisk."

"I wasn't far off."

"Thank God for that," said Peter.

"You're all against me," cried Tamarisk. "I hate you all."

"Extraordinary gratitude towards one who has just saved your life," I said.

"Here's the Westminster Tavern," said Peter. "It's a reasonably good inn."

"Let's go in," said Jonathan.

There were several people there, all presumably with the same idea of escaping the crowds.

We seated ourselves round a table and ordered cider.

"Did you really save my life?" asked Tamarisk.

"It's difficult to say," mused Jonathan. "You might merely have been scarred for life or suffered a few broken limbs. It might not have been death."

She stared at him in horror. "Like Aunt Sophie," she said. "I didn't think . . ."

"That is the trouble," I said, governess-fashion, "you don't think as much as you should . . . of other people."

"I *was* thinking of other people. I was thinking of the Duke."

Jonathan wagged a finger at her. "You were told not to stray and you promptly did so."

"And if Jonathan hadn't rescued you . . ." I began.

"Oh." She looked at him with wondering eyes.

"That's better," he said smiling at her.

"Thank you, Jonathan, for saving my life."

"It was an honour," he said, taking her hand and kissing it.

I thought what a beautiful child she was when she was soft and affectionate. She was now looking at Jonathan with far more admiration than she had bestowed on the Duke himself.

We sat in silence drinking our cider. I was thinking of the great Duke being drawn in his carriage by the people who wanted to show him how they honoured him; and I wondered about the meeting between him and his Duchess when the carriage arrived at Hamilton Place. There he was at the height of his triumph, honours heaped upon him, the people wanting to show their gratitude. He must be a happy man. Was he?

There was Amaryllis sitting close to Peter. She was happy. There were Jonathan and Tamarisk; she was looking at him with something like adoration. I hoped she was not going to care too much for him, for something told me that when Tamarisk loved, it would be most passionately. And Jonathan . . . he was lightly bantering, mocking her, calling her Gypsy. I felt that nothing would ever touch him deeply. Yet a few moments before he had rushed in to save her. And there was I, bound to a man who, loving as he was, could never give me that which I was beginning to feel would become an ever-increasing need in my life.

Refreshed we went home. My parents were not yet in. They came later. They had had an excellent view of the carriage being drawn by the people. Did not the Duke look magnificent? asked my mother. And hadn't it been a day to remember?

I retired early. It had become a habit with me. We entertained scarcely at all at Grasslands and Edward should not be up late, said James.

I could not sleep though. I kept thinking of that fearful moment in the crowd when I had thought Tamarisk was going to be trampled underfoot and how Jonathan had snatched her up just in time and brought her back to us.

I went to the window and looked out. I could see the firework displays over the Park and the light of bonfires. And as I stood there, two figures emerged from the house—Peter and Jonathan. I watched them walk down the street together.

It was ten o'clock. I wondered where they were going. But I was tired and soon forgot them. Their nightly outings were no concern of mine.

I went to bed and was soon fast asleep.

I thought Jonathan looked a little disturbed the next morning. This was so unlike his usual nonchalant self that I noticed it immediately.

I asked if he had had a pleasant evening, remembering that I had seen him leave the house in Peter's company.

He said: "Yes, thanks, Jessica." But without a great deal of conviction.

I wondered vaguely where he and Peter had been.

I was to discover a few days later.

We were still in Albemarle Street for, although immediately after his ride from Westminster to Hamilton Place the Duke had gone to join the Prince Regent at Portsmouth, he would shortly return to London to take his place in the House of Lords and the celebrations were still going on.

My mother always found a great deal to do in London and she was ready to stay a little longer than we had planned. I was the same, though Amaryllis found it very hard to tear herself away from her baby, but she was happy to be with Peter, whose business detained him here.

I was in the house when a man called asking to see Mr. Jonathan Frenshaw. I saw him arrive. He was a rather seedy looking individual with a somewhat truculent manner, and I wondered what his business could be with Jonathan. They were closeted together for about half an hour before he left, and as he was taking his leave I heard him say: "It must be settled by the fourth of July, Mr. Frenshaw. Not a day later."

Then I knew that Jonathan was in trouble.

Although I was only two years his senior, I was a married woman and I felt that gave me some authority. I was very fond of Jonathan—it was difficult not to be—but I had always realized that he was the type of young man who could easily slip into trouble. There had already been the affair of the farmer's daughter. He had skipped out of that by good luck. The girl had merely lost her reputation and he had enhanced his as a rake. That was the only outcome.

It looked to me as though he might be in financial difficulty. Since I had married and had come into a certain inheritance I was by no means poor and might possibly help him.

I called him into the room and said: "Jonathan, are you in difficulties?"

He looked at me in surprise.

"I saw your caller," I admitted. "I heard what he said about the fourth of July."

"Oh that," he said. "A little debt."

"Are you in difficulties?"

"Not really. It is just a matter of laying my hands on the ready cash."

"Can I help?"

"You're a dear girl, Jessica," he said, "and I love you. But it won't be necessary. I can raise it in time."

"How much?"

"Five hundred pounds."

"Five hundred!"

"Yes . . . rather a lot. That's why I can't get it at once. I can't understand why there is this rush. Usually people know one has to have time."

"Was it . . . ?" I began.

He looked at me shamefacedly. "Gambling," he said. "I don't know what my grandfather would say."

"He'd be horrified."

"Cut me right out, I reckon. Send me packing . . . right back to Pettigrew Hall."

"Sometimes I don't think you would care."

"It's odd. I've got fond of the old place. I know you think I'm a waster and all the rest of it . . . but I believe I should be a tolerably good squire."

"I think you would, too."

"But I won't be if Grandpapa hears of this."

"How could you lose so much money?"

"How indeed? The stakes get higher. One is carried away. A sense of bravado . . . and one believes one's luck will turn."

"You're a gambler."

"Do you know, I haven't touched it before. Just the odd bet or two. Nothing really."

"I guess you were tempted because your grandfather is so set against it."

"Is that it, do you think?"

"I know how your mind works."

"Then you are cleverer than I."

"Oh, Jonathan," I said, "he mustn't hear of this. You've got to find that money and that has to be the end of it."

"It will be. I have suddenly realized how I should feel if I had to leave Eversleigh. And the chances are that I shall be sent packing if the news of my misconduct reached the old man's ears."

"He can be very firm," I said.

"Don't I know it."

"Did you go . . . with Peter?"

"Yes. Peter knows London. He took me to this place. He left me there."

"Didn't he gamble?"

"I don't think he's the gambling sort."

"Yet he took you there!"

"Oh, he knows about the London haunts. He's a club man. We got talking about it and he said if I wanted to look in at any time he'd show me. He's too wise to gamble himself, I suppose. Of course I thought I was going to make a pile. Peter . . . he's the businessman. Finger in all pies and when he draws it out, profits are clinging to that probing finger. I bet if *he* sat down at the tables Lady Luck would come to him."

"We've got to think what you're going to do," I said. "Five hundred is rather a lot. It was a pity you didn't stop before you lost so much."

"How often have those wise words been used?"

"Well, we have to find that money, pay the debt and prevent this reaching my father's ears."

"First find the money."

"If only it wasn't quite so much."

The door burst open and Tamarisk stood there, her cheeks scarlet, her eyes blazing.

"I'll sell Enderby," she said. "I can. It's mine."

"What are you talking about?" I demanded.

"The money," she said.

"You've been listening at the door."

"Of course."

"Tamarisk, that's a very unpleasant habit."

"It's the way to get to know."

"You should never do it."

"I always do it." She ran to Jonathan and seized the lapels of his coat. "Don't worry. You shall have the money. Enderby's worth more than five hundred pounds and there is all the furniture in it. That's worth a lot."

He lifted her up in his arms. "You're an angel, Gypsy, and I love you."

She smiled. Then she said angrily, "You're a stupid man. Don't you know it's silly to gamble?"

"You are right, Little Gypsy. I am and I do. I have learned my lesson. It shall never happen again."

"This is our secret," she said. "Nobody must know."

"How are you going to sell Enderby without anyone's knowing?" I asked.

That puzzled her and Jonathan put an arm round her and held her against him.

"Don't worry, Gypsy. I can get the money easily."

"Don't ever do it again," she begged.

"I won't. But I'm glad I did this once because it has shown me what good friends I have."

"I only offered to sell Enderby because you saved my life."

"Of course. *Quid pro quo.* One good turn deserves another."

"Five hundred pounds is a lot of money," she said severely.

"A life is worth a little more," he told her. "So you still owe me."

She was very solemn.

I said: "It's all right, Tamarisk. Don't say anything about selling Enderby. Don't say anything at all."

"Of course I won't. It's a secret."

"We shall pay the money and that will be an end of it. No one shall know except us three."

She smiled slowly. Secrecy appealed to her devious nature.

The incident revealed to me her feelings for Jonathan, and that gave me a few twinges of uneasiness.

That should have been an end of the matter. Jonathan could raise the money. The Pettigrews were a very rich family and the debt itself, though large, would not have given Jonathan major anxiety if it had not been for the time limit for payment and my father's somewhat fanatical views about gambling.

The matter would have passed off smoothly—and I believe

it had provided a good lesson for Jonathan—but for one thing. Someone was determined to make mischief.

When my father was breakfasting a day or so later, a letter was brought to him. I was with him at the time. He liked someone to breakfast with him and as I was an early riser and believed that he would rather have it with me than anyone else—except my mother—I usually contrived to be with him.

He did not pick up the letter immediately but after talking to me about the celebrations and when we should return to Eversleigh he opened it. His face turned puce with fury.

"What's wrong?" I asked.

"The young scoundrel!" he cried.

I took the letter from him. It was headed Frinton's Club, St. James's.

> Dear Mr. Frenshaw,
> I think it is my duty to bring to your notice the fact that your grandson, Mr. Jonathan Frenshaw, visited this club on the night of the 24th June and lost the sum of £500 in play. Knowing your feelings regarding this pastime—which I share—I thought it only right to let you know so that you may—if possible—turn the young man from this foolhardy practice.
>
> A Friend

I cried: "What a beastly hypocritical letter. I think the person who wrote it is loathsome."

"It's true, I suppose."

I was silent.

"My God," he said, "and this is the young idiot we are harbouring at Eversleigh! Tell them to send him to me . . . at once . . . this minute."

"He probably isn't up yet."

"No. Late night, I daresay. At the tables till the early hours of the morning!"

"Aren't you accusing him before you know?" I said, with sinking heart.

"Second thoughts . . . I'll go to see *him*."

He strode out of the room clutching the letter. I followed him up the stairs. He threw open the door of Jonathan's room. Jonathan was in bed fast asleep.

"Wake up," roared my father.

Jonathan slowly opened his eyes and stared at us in astonishment.

"What are you doing in bed at this hour? Why aren't you up and about? Late last night, were you? At the gaming tables were you? I'll tell you this, young man, you're out. You'll not be coming back to Eversleigh. You can go straight back to your mother. I shall speak to your grandfather about you, you lazy good-for-nothing."

Jonathan was the sort of young man who would always be at his best in a crisis.

"Am I dreaming?" he asked. "Are you figures in a dream? You look real enough to me. Is that you, Jessica?"

"Yes," I said, and thinking it best to put him in the picture as soon as possible added: "Someone has sent a letter about your gambling debt."

That startled him. "How tiresome," he said.

My father went to him and taking him by the shoulders shook him. Jonathan's head went back and forth, his hair flopping over his face. He looked so comical that I would have laughed if the situation had not been so serious and I was feeling so upset because I liked having him around at Eversleigh.

"You had better not try to hide anything from me," said my father.

"I had no intention of doing so," said Jonathan. "I incurred the debt in a rash moment and oddly enough without having any desire to."

"Stop talking like an idiot."

"It's true, sir. I went to the club and was persuaded to sit down and before I knew what was happening I had lost five hundred pounds."

"Do you think I say what I don't mean?"

"Certainly not."

"Haven't I told you that I won't have gamblers on my estate?"

"Many times."

"And you deliberately defy me?"

"Defiance was not really in my mind."

My father would have struck him but with a graceful gesture Jonathan evaded the blow.

"I can only admit that this accusation is true," said Jonathan, "and add that it shall never happen again."

The door was flung open and Tamarisk came in.

"What do you want?" I cried.

"Get that child out of here," said my father.

"You mustn't blame Jonathan," said Tamarisk. She ran to my father and hung on his arm. "It was my fault. I gambled. I lost the money. I was the one. It was five hundred pounds and I am going to sell Enderby to pay for it."

It was so nonsensical that it stemmed my father's anger.

"The girl's gone mad," he said.

"Yes, it was madness," went on Tamarisk. "It was the gambler's fever. You get it . . . and you are mad. You go in . . . the stakes get higher and you go on, saying I'll go higher . . . I'll go five hundred pounds."

She was so beautiful in her charming innocence and determination to save Jonathan that I almost loved her in that moment. Her wonderful dark eyes were blazing and the colour in her cheeks made a charming contrast to her dark hair. No one could have watched her unmoved—not even my father, angry as he was, could be anything but susceptible to a beautiful woman. She was scarcely a woman but her innocence and passionate devotion gave her a certain maturity.

Jonathan was looking at her with great tenderness. I understood his feeling. This selfish rebellious girl was capable of love and when she loved it would be a fierce emotion which matched her temperament.

My father said gruffly: "You're talking nonsense, child."

"No . . . no. It's true. I was there."

"When?"

"When I lost the money."

My father took her by the shoulders and looked into her face. "Don't lie to me," he said.

"It's not lies. It's true. Jonathan was pretending . . . to save me."

"As you are pretending . . . to save him?"

"You'll be sorry if you send him away."

"Do you mean," said my father and I saw his lips beginning to twitch in the way I remembered he had often looked at me when some precocity of mine had amused him during my childhood, "that *you* will be sorry if he goes?"

"Yes . . . yes . . . and so will you. He's very good on the estate. The people all love him . . . more than they do—"

"More than they do me?"

"Yes. And people on the estate should love the squire. It's all part of it."

"He doesn't deserve such an advocate."

"A what?" she asked.

"He doesn't deserve your confidence in him."

"I don't like Enderby much. It can be sold."

Jonathan had risen from his bed and wrapped a dressing gown about him while this conversation had been going on.

"Tamarisk," he said, "thank you for trying to save me. I can repay the money and if I have to go I shall come back and see you."

She stamped her foot. "It won't be the same."

My father was a little disconcerted.

"I'll see you later, Jonathan," he said, and went out.

I sat on the bed and looked at Jonathan.

"It's a letter he had. Anonymous. Signed 'A Friend.' "

"I wonder who that dear friend could be."

"It was a miserable thing to do."

"It was rather. I'd have had the whole thing cleared up in no time and saved all this fuss."

Tamarisk was looking from one of us to the other.

She said: "He's very angry. He'll send you away. I know."

"He always sounds more angry than he is," I reminded them.

"It just happens to be the cardinal sin," said Jonathan.

"What's that?" asked Tamarisk.

"The worst possible thing you can do, Gypsy."

"I hope he doesn't send you away."

"If he does, I'll come over to see you. We'll have secret meetings."

"I'd rather you were there all the time."

He came over to her and taking her hands looked into her eyes solemnly. He said: "Everything is worthwhile to know I have such a good and loyal little friend."

Then he kissed her gently on the forehead.

I felt very moved.

I said: "I'll try to talk him out of it."

"Do you think you can?" asked Jonathan.

"If anyone can, I can . . . or my mother. I'll get her help."

We did talk him out of it, but it was not easy.

I said that people who wrote anonymous letters were the worst possible and to give them the satisfaction of achieving their ends, was to pander to them.

I insisted that Jonathan had learned his lesson. He would never be so foolish again.

My mother and I both agreed that if he were found guilty of gambling again we would stand firmly beside my father and make no attempts to persuade him to act other than his inclinations advised him to.

And at last he gave way with a bad grace.

"When Eversleigh is bankrupt, you'll be the ones to blame . . . just as much as that young jackanapes," he growled.

We said meekly that we would accept the blame, hugged him and told him that he was not really such a fierce old curmudgeon as he made himself out to be—and even if he were, we still adored him.

Jonathan paid back the five hundred pounds and came back with us to Eversleigh.

But I did wonder who had written that anonymous letter and as the weeks passed I saw that Tamarisk's feeling for Jonathan was growing stronger.

After Waterloo

The months passed quickly. One day was so like another. I seemed to be caught in the monotony of the days. Sometimes when I awoke in the mornings, I would say to myself: Another day. Is it going to be like this all my life?

Mr. and Mrs. Barrington were frequently at Grasslands. There was less trouble with the Luddites now. They may have been sobered by the terrible events of the day when Edward had been hurt and the fact that two of them had gone to the gallows for it.

New machines had been installed in the factory and the workers seemed to be reconciled to that necessary evil. Mr. Barrington would talk to Edward for hours and I would see the light in Edward's eyes which would afterwards be replaced by a look of helplessness. I often thought how frustrating he must find it to be reduced to his state.

He was, on rare occasions, mildly irritable and afterwards suffered great remorse. I used to tell him that it was nothing and I marvelled at his good humour. He suffered a great deal—not only physically.

Try as we might we could not make ours a really happy household.

Amaryllis was pregnant again. When I heard this a great depression seized me. I congratulated her and pretended to be pleased, and I despised myself but I could not control the jealousy which beset me.

I had been rash. I could have remained Edward's friend. I could have devoted a great deal of time to him, visiting him, playing chess and piquet with him. Why had I married him? It had been a quixotic gesture, which was certain to bring frustration. My parents had tried to make me see this but as usual I had been obstinate and gone my own way.

There were days when I felt shackled, when I looked ahead to the years to come and saw myself growing older in this house, rising in the morning, taking solitary rides and walks, sitting with Edward, playing endless games with him, retiring at night. That was my life.

I would get old, lined and wrinkled, beyond the age of childbearing.

I was becoming obsessed by the desire for a child. And now that Amaryllis was going to have another, this desire in me was stronger than ever.

My mother guessed at my feelings. I would often find her eyes on me, a little sad and sometimes, I thought, with a hint of fear. She knew me well, perhaps better than anyone, even myself. I think that in her mind was the thought that somewhere, sometime my resolution would break. I was a woman of natural impulses. I was not meant to live unfulfilled.

She and my father had paid a visit to France that autumn and she had come home very happy. They had been present for the vendange, and how exciting that had been! Charlot and Louis Charles lived with their families in a small *château* which, although it had been vandalized to some extent during the revolution, they had been able to restore, and there they lived with their growing families in perfect harmony it seemed.

Louis Charles and Charlot had always been like brothers. They were actually half brothers for Louis Charles had been my mother's first husband's bastard. There was a great bond between the two and it seemed such a happy solution that they should share a flourishing vineyard.

My mother gloried in long descriptions of how they brought in the grapes, the pressing, the bottling, and the great rejoicing when everything was brought to a satisfactory conclusion.

My father grudgingly admitted that they were making a success of it and that their wines were excellent.

I saw him looking at Jonathan and drawing comparisons. He was still suspicious of Jonathan. He would never forget that episode, and every now and then would expound on the pitfalls of gambling.

I teased him a little about it. "Obviously," I said, "it is one of the few vices in which *you* have not indulged at some time or other."

He replied that he had always been intent on making a success of what he had and, thank God, had had the sense to realize that he would not jeopardize one acre of land to chance. "Certainty was what I was after," he added. "I was not staking my future on the drop of the dice or the place of a card in the pack."

I think he was anxious about me and I guessed he and my mother had long talks in the privacy of their bedroom.

In the meantime life went on as before. Jonathan was doing well . . . at least he was avoiding trouble. I think he really was interested in the estate, but that nonchalant air, that easy charm which gave him an air of indifference, was something my father found irritating.

There were occasional explosions of temper on his part which my mother usually managed to soothe without too much trouble.

Tamarisk was often at Eversleigh and there was a very special friendship between her and Jonathan. My mother did comment on this once and betrayed a certain apprehension. "She is young yet. Not nine until the summer. But she is a precocious girl. No doubt her feelings will abate a little as she gets older."

"Jonathan is very fond of her," I pointed out. "She will be quite safe with him."

"I hope so. I haven't said anything to your father about it. He's very critical of Jonathan and I don't want to make him worse. He would come to all sorts of conclusions."

"You worry too much," I told her and added: "About everything."

Which brought us back to the position in which I found myself. There was an uneasiness in the air—faint but present.

I had never been perfectly at home with Peter since his announcement of the engagement between himself and Amaryllis; and I often felt that he was a little wary of me. He must have known that I had believed his interest to be in me. I often thought of our dramatic meeting and how he had followed me in the street. He had seemed so attentive, so eager to know me, and then suddenly he had fallen in love with Amaryllis.

I suppose it was natural, but it did seem a little odd. He must have been aware of this and it made for restraint between us.

When I looked back I realized that I had scarcely been alone with him since the announcement. He was always busy—making frequent visits to London. He was a highly successful businessman. He was doing well with his rum and sugar and seemed to have many interests. He was still renting Enderby, which seemed an ideal arrangement; the money was banked for Tamarisk for when she came of age, so the house was an investment for her; and the fact that Amaryllis and Peter continued to live there shelved the problem of what was to be done with it. I sometimes wondered about his business and would have liked to see those warehouses of his. I still marvelled at Amaryllis' lack of interest, particularly as she had money invested in the company. Once or twice I tried to discover something about this but she was vague. All she could tell me was that they were very successful and Peter's business was growing so rapidly that he had to be more and more in London.

There was one occasion when I found myself alone with him. I had been to Eversleigh from Grasslands when I came face to face with him. We said good morning but could hardly pass on without a word.

He added that it was a fine morning and after that we exchanged a few trivialities. Then he said: "I hardly ever see you, Jessica, without a lot of people being present."

"I suppose that is inevitable. We are a large family."

"Are you . . . happy?"

I was startled: "Why yes, of course . . . very happy."

He was frowning slightly, looking over my head, back to Grasslands.

"I'm glad," he said.

"And I hear from Amaryllis that you are going from strength to strength with your new warehouses and so on. Business, I gather, flourishes."

"She talks to you about the warehouses?"

"Yes. I expect you will be proudly showing her round them one day."

Something in his manner attracted my attention. He seemed a little watchful.

"She wouldn't really be interested. Business is not for ladies."

"I should have thought anyone would be interested. I am. And Amaryllis particularly, since she has a share in them."

"Oh, when I am here I like to forget all about that."

"So you are not one of those businessmen who is obsessed by work?"

"Only when I am engaged in it."

"I suppose you have time when you are in London for enjoyment?"

He looked startled.

"I mean clubs . . . and all that. Jonathan said you knew such places. After all it was you who introduced him to Frinton's."

"Oh." He laughed. "That was disastrous, wasn't it? I wish I had known he was going to make a fool of himself. He just asked me about a few clubs and I mentioned that one. I didn't realize he would go to the tables."

"I think he has learned his lesson."

"Your father does not forget it, I'm afraid."

"Poor Jonathan! It just happens to be something my father feels very strongly about."

"I see his point, don't you?"

"Of course. But I think Jonathan will do very well. We're all very fond of him."

"He's a charming fellow . . . if a little weak."

"Just that one incident! We mustn't judge him on that. How is Amaryllis?"

"Very well."

"Will you tell her I will come over to see her tomorrow?"

"She'll be delighted."

"Well, I must go now."

He took my hand and held it lingeringly. There was an expression in his eyes which I could not understand.

I was glad to get away. He made me feel a little uneasy. I suppose it was because of the past and because once I had thought I might be on the verge of falling in love with him. He was attractive and that touch of mystery added to his charm. I had been young and romantic then. I wondered how many girls fell in love not exactly with a person but because the time seemed ripe and someone appears at that moment. Falling in love with love, was what it was commonly called; and what an everyday occurrence it must be! I had been ready to do just that with Peter Lansdon. The romantic circumstances of our meeting, his immediate interest and what I thought of as the beginning of a courtship . . . oh yes, that was the trappings of romance and I was ready to fall in love as most girls did.

Now I had had time for reflection and I realized that I should never have truly loved Peter Lansdon; there was something about him which repelled me, some element of secrecy. That might be intriguing in a way but it seemed now a little sinister. Perhaps I compared him with Edward, who was so open, so frank, so honest that beside him all other men seemed devious.

The next day I called on Amaryllis. She was showing the first signs of pregnancy. Her baby was due in August and Helena at this time was only nine months old.

"How are you, my fruitful vine?" I asked.

She kissed me and said she was feeling better than she had in the last weeks. "The first three months are the worst," she added.

"You should know," I said. "You seem to be making a practice of this sort of thing."

"Well, one has to endure the discomfort but it is wonderful when the baby arrives."

"Yes, I can imagine it."

She looked at me wistfully. "I think of you a lot," she said.

"Now you will have more interesting things to think of."

"I worry . . . a little."

"About me?"

"Well, I know Edward is a dear, but the life . . . My mother was saying . . ."

"I really must stop this," I said. "I'm perfectly all right. I'm living my life the way I want it. I saw Peter yesterday."

"Oh?" She looked at me covertly.

"Yes, we had a little chat."

"He told me. Jessica . . ." I sensed she was going to say something apologetic because she felt uneasy about marrying Peter. She had thought—as many had—that I was the one in whom he was interested and I daresay it was a surprise for her when he proposed. I had had enough of people's speculations about my feelings and all their anxiety because I had married an invalid.

I said quickly: "Peter is delighted about the child, I suppose."

"Oh yes. He wants a boy."

"Men always want boys. They think they are so much more important. I wonder they don't put girls out on the bleak mountainside and let them freeze to death. Poor, unwanted little thing."

"Oh, Jessica, what nonsense you talk! He loves Helena. We all do. The idea of any harm coming to her . . ." She shivered.

"It is just this obsession with boys which irritates me. My father is just the same, and when you think how he has always enjoyed the company of women . . . far more than that of men, you can't help laughing."

"You were always very serious about things like that. Edward is serious, too. I think you are very well suited."

"We understand each other. And you and Peter . . . you are not much alike."

"Ours is the attraction of opposites."

"I see." And as I looked at her frank open face it was borne home to me that this must be the case.

It was later, when I was in Edward's room and James was putting extra logs on the fire. The wind had turned cold.

"We must expect it," said Edward. "March is still with us and we have to endure more wintry weather before the spring."

The fire blazed up and James turned to me.

"Shall I get the chess board for you?" he asked. "That was an interesting game you left yesterday."

Edward said: "I think, my dear, I have cornered you. I see mate in the next two moves unless . . ."

"Unless!" said James. "That's the point. Mrs. Barrington always fights best when she is in difficulties."

"I think you are right," agreed Edward. "How many times have I anticipated victory and had it in my grasp only to be outwitted at the very last move."

"It's a great quality," said James, "to be able to do your best when your back is against the wall."

"Thank you, James," I said. "I am glad you both appreciate my indomitable nature."

James set out the table and carried the chess board to it.

"There," he said. "Not a piece but where it was during the heat of yesterday's battle."

We concentrated on the board and after watching us for a while James went off.

It must have been about ten minutes later when he came

227

back. He dashed into the room and it was obvious that he had exciting news which he was eager to tell us.

"What is it?" cried Edward.

"Mr. Jonathan has just come from Eversleigh with the news. He's on his way up. Napoleon has escaped from Elba."

So the euphoria of the last months was wiped out in a single moment. We were back to the fears of the past. The lion had escaped from bondage. He was on the rampage again.

Peace was shattered. Everyone was talking about the escape and asking what it meant. Was it all going to start again? Were we going to be plunged into war?

My mother was particularly bitter. The visit to Burgundy was still fresh in her mind; she was making plans for Charlot to bring his family to visit us and our going over to Burgundy in the summer. And now this miserable wretch had escaped and was preparing to start it all up again.

Edward and I were often at Eversleigh. There was much to talk about, and the conversation was all about Napoleon and the future which concerned us all so much.

David took a calmer view than the others. My father was apt to be choleric and his hatred of the French clouded his opinions. Jonathan was not sufficiently involved. Peter was more concerned with what effect it was going to have on business; so it was David to whom I listened with the greatest attention. We used to sit over dinner talking long after the meal was finished.

David said: "Napoleon is the idol of France and temporary defeat cannot alter that. They have never taken kindly to the King and it is to be expected that they will turn him out now that their hero has returned."

"I heard they were welcoming him throughout France," said my father. "The fools! Do they want war? Do they want conquests?"

"Of course they do," said Jonathan. "Who does not want conquests?"

"Those conquests bring no good to the people," went on my father.

"They enjoy the return of the victorious armies. They like to think of Europe under the control of Napoleon."

"He's certainly made kings and rulers of the members of

his family," said my mother. "And irrespective of their merits."

"That is a weakness," agreed David. "And one most human beings are guilty of. But let us face facts. The return of the Bourbons was unpopular. Louis had turned the army against him by appointing émigrés to high posts when a short while ago they were fighting with the allies against France."

"They were fighting for the restoration of the monarchy," said my father hotly.

"That was against France," pointed out David. "Now Napoleon has appeared as the liberator of France, the army is rallying to him."

"And now," added my mother wearily, "it is all going to start again."

"I heard," said Peter, "that he has become fat. And part of his success was due to his physical fitness."

"But he was an epileptic, wasn't he?" asked Claudine.

"Well, he had been in his youth," replied David. "But that has not prevented his being the most outstanding man in Europe. Whatever you think of him, you have to admit that."

"We'll find his match," said my father. "I'd like to hear what the Duke is doing about this."

"It is a blessing that he remained close at hand," added David.

"Yes," agreed my father. "That idiot Liverpool wanted to send him to America. Thank God the Duke refused to go. Perhaps he saw something like this coming. In any case he did not want to move far away while Napoleon was alive even though he was in exile."

"What will happen now?" asked Amaryllis.

Her husband smiled at her. "For that, my dear, we have to wait and see."

We did not have to wait long. Wellington took command of the army and left for Belgium at the beginning of April. Napoleon was going from strength to strength. He was proclaimed Liberator of France. Louis had fled to Ghent and in the streets of Paris people were dancing in transports of joy.

The conquering hero had returned to them.

Each day we awoke to a feeling of expectancy mingled with dread. He had been so victorious in the past. He was back. He was a legend and legends are hard to defeat. But we had a mighty Duke and he was such another hero to us.

Defeat seemed as impossible for him as the French saw it for Napoleon.

The Duke was in Flanders where he would join up with Blucher and our Prussian allies. Feelings ran high. "This time," said the people, "we are going to see the end of Old Boney for all time."

Through May this mood continued. Napoleon, brilliant general that he was, was doing everything he could to prevent the union of Wellington and Blucher.

June had come—hot, uneasy days. Napoleon had defeated the Prussians at Ligny and that news was received with great gloom which lifted considerably when we heard that the Prussian army had managed to escape.

Wellington was at the village of Waterloo where, said my father, he could keep an eye on Brussels while he awaited the arrival of Blucher's army.

We knew how important this battle was. It was going to decide the fate of Europe. On it rested Napoleon's Empire and our own future well-being and safety.

The French had Napoleon but we must never forget, my father told us, that we had Wellington.

And so to the great battle which will never be forgotten in our history.

Forever I shall remember the day when news came of Wellington's victory at Waterloo, bringing with it the knowledge that Napoleon had been defeated for ever. From now on we should be able to sleep peacefully in our beds at night.

What days they were following that historic battle. There was rejoicing everywhere. Bonfires, dancing in the streets . . . Waterloo! It was a word which was written in glittering letters on our country's history and the man who had made that victory possible was everybody's hero. I thought of how people had dragged his carriage from Westminster Bridge to Hamilton Place. That would be nothing compared with the welcome he would receive now.

He was the mighty Duke, England's great son, the saviour of the world who had freed Europe from the tyrants. His praises were sung in stately mansions and in cottages; men fought out the battle on their table cloths after dinner and we were no exception. How many times had I seen the pepper and salt and cutlery laid out on a table Waterloo. "Here is Napoleon . . . Here is Wellington. Napoleon wanted to finish off the English before the arrival of Blucher. Wellington's idea was to hold the ground . . . here . . . until they came. And hold the ground they did against all attacks. Now in the afternoon the Prussians were sighted. Here they are approaching. It is the end for Napoleon. He knows it. Ney knows it. They're beaten. Napoleon flees to Paris. He's finished. The end of a dream . . ."

Never, never must he be allowed to come back. That must be the end of Napoleon. The wars he had created were over.

"Long live Peace," was the universal cry. "Glory to the Victor. Blessings on the great Duke!"

This was a wonderful day for England.

The entire country was rejoicing. Celebration balls were given. There was one at Eversleigh to which the whole neighbourhood and friends from farther afield were invited.

Napoleon had tried to escape from France, but finding this impossible had surrendered to Captain Maitland of the Bellerophon at Rochefort about a month after his defeat at Waterloo. He must be given no opportunities to escape again; and this time he was banished to St. Helena.

This must be the end of him.

And so the celebrations continued. Later people would be counting the enormous cost of the war and complaining about the taxes that had had to be imposed to pay for it. While the war was in progress these had been accepted; it was only when it was over that voices would be raised in protest.

But in the meantime there was little thought beyond the euphoria of victory, and everyone was determined to make the most of it.

We went to London where we received invitations to the Inskips' ball.

The Inskips were associates of my father, and Lord Inskip was a very important and influential gentleman. This would be one of the most splendid balls of that season of rejoicing.

We needed very special ball gowns for the occasion and my mother said they could not be trusted to our seamstresses. We must go to the Court dressmakers and give ourselves a little time beforehand, because naturally on such an occasion we must be suitably garbed.

Amaryllis was not with us in London, being in no condition to travel and therefore Claudine preferred to stay at home with her. David naturally did not come. He, after all, had not been concerned in the London side of my father's involvements. So it was just Jonathan, my parents and myself.

My mother and I had a busy time shopping and attending the dressmakers. I had never had such a dress. It was of flame-coloured chiffon, narrow at the waist and a skirt which billowed out in flounce after flounce. It was slightly off my shoulders and my mother said I should wear my hair dressed high with a gold ornament in it. About my neck I was to wear a gold necklace and there were to be gold earrings in my ears.

My mother's maid spent hours with us both, dressing our hair and making sure that our gowns set as they should and we wore the right accessories.

My mother was beautiful in her favourite shade of peacock blue. Jonathan was his jaunty self and my father looked distinguished and handsome, but I noticed how white his hair had become and that gave me a tremor of alarm. Even he could not live forever, I thought uneasily.

However, those were not reflections for such a day.

We set out in the carriage for the Inskips' mansion which was close to the Park. There Lord and Lady Inskip received us most graciously and as we mingled with the glittering guests our magnificent dresses seemed suddenly to become commonplace among that throng.

Dancing was in progress in the ballroom and I danced with Jonathan. My mother and father danced together. When it was over a young man approached. He knew Jonathan who introduced us and he and I went into the next dance.

There followed the cotillion and the quadrille. Conversation was light and meaningless as it is on these occasions for one cannot very well talk of anything of moment when one is being whirled round the ballroom.

It was when the quadrille was over that I looked up suddenly and saw a man coming towards me. There was something familiar about him. He was very tall and so lean that he looked even taller than he actually was; his hair was dark, his eyes a lively brown; and there was something in his face which suggested that he found life very amusing—in fact something of a joke. I wondered vaguely why I should notice so much in such a short time. It might have been because I had seen it all before.

I must have stared at him, showing some interest.

"I believe," he said, "that we have met before."

He stood before me, smiling. "You don't remember me evidently."

"I . . . am not sure."

"Perhaps it is a long time ago. Would you care to dance?"

"Yes," I replied.

He took my hands and excitement gripped me. He was very like . . . He couldn't be, of course. That would be impossible.

"When I caught sight of you," he said, "I was taken back . . . years ago. I thought we had met before."

"I had the same feeling. Do you live in London?"

"I have a place here . . . a small house. My home is in Cornwall."

"I don't think we can possibly have met before. But you are so like someone I knew once . . . when I was a child . . . briefly. He was . . . a gypsy."

I saw his mouth twitch. "Don't be afraid to tell me. He was a wicked character, was he? Someone it was not right that a well-brought-up young lady should know? And I resemble him?"

"Well, in a way you do. But there is a difference."

"How long ago was this?"

"Nine years."

"You remember so promptly."

"Yes, I remember."

"Tell me how different I am from him?"

"Your skin is more brown."

"That's the Australian sun."

My heart began to beat very fast. "You have been in Australia?"

"As a matter of fact I have but recently returned. I have been in England some six months. You have changed . . . more than I have. After all you were only a little girl. I was at least grown up. But nine years can do something to a man, especially when they are nine such as I have had."

"You can't be . . ."

"Yes, I am."

"What a strange coincidence."

"We should have met sooner or later. I was planning to come down your way to see what had happened after all those years."

"Are you really Romany Jake?"

"I confess I am."

"They sent you away . . ."

"For seven years."

"And now you are free."

He nodded. "There is one thing I never forget," he said. "I should not be here but for a certain young lady."

"You know that I didn't betray you then?"

"I never thought that you did. Well, perhaps for just a little while when I came out of that house and they were there with you."

"I suffered agonies. Then I made my father help you."

"It would have been the end of me if you hadn't."

"I can't tell you how glad I was when I knew your life was spared. There is so much I want to know. It is difficult to talk here."

"There is a garden. We'll slip away and find a corner down there where it is quieter. I have much to tell you."

He took my hand and we went out of the ballroom and down the stairs. The Inskip garden faced the Park and beyond the wall it stretched out before us—the trees reaching out to the midnight blue sky, the stars shining there and the light of a crescent moon turning the Serpentine to silver. It was a perfect night but I was hardly aware of it. I was not aware of anything much but the man at my side.

There were one or two couples there who had sought the quiet of the garden, but they were well away from us.

We sat down together.

"I can't believe you are Romany Jake," I said.

"That is well in the past."

"Tell me . . ."

"Let me tell you how Romany Jake managed to get an invitation to such an exclusive ball. I am a man of substance now. Sir Jake Cadorson. Jake to his friends. The Romany no longer applies."

"But the last time I heard of you you were on a convict ship going out to Australia."

"Seven years' transportation. Those seven years were up two years ago. I am a free man."

"So you came back to England."

"At first I did not intend to. I was put into the service of a grazier in New South Wales some miles north of Sydney. He wasn't a bad fellow. He was just and fair if one worked well. I was glad to work. There was so much to forget. So I worked and I was soon in favour with him. When my years of servitude were up he gave me a patch of land. I was going into wool myself, and I did for a year. I didn't do too badly. It is easier in a new country. All one has to contend with is the elements, the plagues of this and that and other blessings of nature. It can be pretty grim, I can tell you; but there was a challenge in it and it appealed to me.''

"But you decided not to stay?"

He looked at me intently. "Life is strange," he said. "You know I left home to wander with the gypsies. I never got on with my brother. He was considerably older than I, and very serious . . . without imagination. But that's my side of the question. When I went he was glad to be rid of me and washed his hands of me. The family estates are in South Cornwall. Well, my brother died and then everything, including the title, has come to me. You see I have come a long way from the gypsy and felon I was when you last knew me.''

"I am so glad it has turned out very well for you."

"And you?"

"I married."

There was a brief silence and then he said: "I suppose that was inevitable. Is your husband here tonight?"

"No. I am here with my parents."

Again that silence.

"My husband is an invalid," I said slowly. "He was injured during the Luddite riots."

"I'm . . . sorry."

His manner had changed.

I said coolly: "I think I ought to tell you that you have a daughter."

He stared at me.

"Dolly . . . of course," he said. "Poor Dolly."

"Poor Dolly indeed. She died giving birth to your child."

"What?"

"Of course you wouldn't remember anything about it. You had your little . . . frolic. Do you remember the bonfire? Trafalgar Day? Your daughter in fact lives with me now."

"But this is incredible."

"Of course you had forgotten. It is amazing, is it not? These things seem so trivial to some who partake in them, but they can have devastating results, and one of the partners is left to deal with them."

"A daughter, you say?"

"Her name is Tamarisk. She is a rather wild, rebellious girl, as perhaps might have been expected."

"You are hostile suddenly. A few moments ago . . ."

"Hostile? Indeed not. I was just stating the facts. When Dolly discovered she was to have a child, her grandmother was so upset she died."

"Died! Because her granddaughter was going to have a child?"

"Some people care about these things. She had a similar trouble with another granddaughter. She just seemed to give up. She went out one cold winter's night to consult someone and she froze to death. Dolly was taken under the wing of my Aunt Sophie and she died when the child was born. My aunt brought up the child who showed her gratitude by running away with the gypsies. You remember Leah."

"Leah? Certainly I remember Leah."

"It was because of Leah that you almost lost your life."

"One does not forget such things. Poor Dolly . . . and the child."

"She came back to us. She had tired of the gypsy way of life. She wanted her warm bed, the comforts of that other life she had experienced. But when she returned my aunt had died of a broken heart. You see what a trail of havoc one little frolic round a bonfire can bring?"

He closed his eyes and suddenly I felt sorry for him. He must have suffered a great deal.

I said more gently: "Well, now Tamarisk is with us. I don't think she will want to go wandering again."

"I must see the child," he said.

"She is at Grasslands. Do you remember Grasslands? It was Dolly's home."

"The house in which I was hiding when they took me?"

"Yes," I said. It was all coming back to me so vividly— that moment when he had opened the door and I had suddenly become aware that I was not alone, and that he would think I had betrayed him.

"I live at Grasslands now," I went on. "It is my home. It was bought by my husband's family before he was injured."

"So much happens as the years pass," he said. "I must see the child. I wonder what she will think of me. Perhaps I should take her back to Cornwall with me."

"She will be excited to know she has a father."

He was silent for a while. Then he said: "Forgive me. I am

overwhelmed. I feel that sitting here I have lived through years. I have been thinking ever since I came back to England that I must come and look for you. How foolish one is! I let myself believe that I should find you just as I left you . . . a young girl . . . nine years ago . . . as if nothing would change.''

"And you? You married?"

He shook his head. 'I always knew I should come back to England.''

We heard a distant bell ringing through the house.

"I think that means they are serving supper," I said.

The other people left the garden and we were alone.

"Isn't it beautiful?" he said. "I can't tell you how often I dreamed of coming home when I was away.''

"I suppose one would.''

He stood up and taking my hand drew me up to stand beside him.

"I used to say to myself, I'll go back. I'll ride through the country. I'll visit the places we used to see when we trundled through in our caravans. I'll go down to Eversleigh. I remembered it well. That cosy corner of England. Isn't it called the Garden of England?''

"Yes, because of the apples and cherries and plums that grow there better than anywhere else in the country.''

"Eversleigh . . . Grasslands and the young girl with the dark expressive eyes who had a spirit like mine and would fight for what she believed was right. Do you know, I thought you were the most enchanting little girl I had ever seen.''

"And Dolly?" I could not resist saying.

"She was a tragic little thing. Life had been unkind to her.''

"You mean people, don't you?"

"I was thoughtless . . . careless . . .''

"You betrayed her.''

"I betrayed myself.''

"What does that mean?"

"That I thought nothing of it. We were dancing round the bonfire. Dolly was eager to be loved . . . even fleetingly.''

"Oh I see. Just worthy of your attention for a very short time.''

"It wasn't like that, you know.''

"But you honoured her briefly with a little of your attention.''

"You are angry suddenly.''

"I hate this attitude towards women, as though they are here to pander to the temporary needs of men, little playthings to be picked up, amusing for a while, and then cast aside."

"You are talking in well worn clichés."

"Clichés come about because they are a neat way of stating a truth."

"I have never before heard them so described and I repeat that it was not like that with Dolly. She was not forced, you know."

"I think we should go to supper," I said.

He took my arm and pressed it.

"This has been a most exciting evening. Meeting you . . . like this. I meant to come to see you within a few days. This is the first opportunity I have had of getting to London. My brother was an old friend of Lord Inskip so naturally I, the heir, was invited to the ball."

"Do they know that you served several years . . . as a convict?"

"In Australia, yes. It doesn't count. People are sent to Australia for their politics. There is not the same smear as serving a term of imprisonment here. I shall not attempt to hide my past, I assure you. People must take me as they find me."

I had turned away and we went into the supper room. My emotions were in a whirl. I had been so taken off my guard. It had taken me some time before I could believe that he had come back.

For some reason I did not want to see him again. He disturbed me. I realized that over the last nine years I had thought about him quite often. He had intruded into my thoughts and now that he was back he seemed more disturbing than ever.

I saw my parents seated at one of the tables and leaving him I hurriedly joined them.

My mother said: "What a distinguished looking man you came in with. Had you been in the garden?"

"Yes. It was rather hot in the ballroom."

"Who is he?"

"Sir Jake Somebody."

"Your father said he thought he knew him but couldn't quite place him."

I was not surprised.

The salmon was delicious; so were the meat patties; there was champagne in plenty. I ate and drank without tasting. I could not forget him.

I saw him across the supper room. He was seated at the Inskips' table, talking vivaciously and there seemed to be a good deal of merriment around him.

He caught my eye across the room and smiled.

"He is very attractive," said my mother, following my gaze. "He seems to have his eyes on you."

"I daresay he has his eyes on quite a number of people."

"Was he flirtatious?" asked my mother. "He looks as if he might be something of an adventurer."

"Hardly that."

"But interesting."

"Oh yes, very interesting."

She sighed and I knew she was once more wishing that I had not hurried into marriage.

After supper he asked me to dance. I rose, trying to assume an air of reluctance which I was far from feeling.

"It is good of you to do me the honour," he said.

We joined the dancers.

"I must come down and see my daughter."

"Perhaps it would be better if she were brought to London."

"Would you bring her?"

"Perhaps my mother would. Or her governess. Leah is with us."

"Leah!"

"When she returned from her sojourn with the gypsies she brought Leah with her. Leah has stayed with us ever since."

"Leah . . ." he said softly and I felt a ridiculous stab of jealousy. That should have been warning enough in itself. I was a staid married woman; he was a one-time gypsy, a convict, a seducer of an innocent girl, and he had killed a man. Why should I feel jealous of Leah? Why should I feel so emotional to be near him? Why should this ball be the most exciting one I had ever attended?

Because of him? Oh yes, I should have recognized the warning signals.

"I would rather you brought her," he said.

"I should have to consider it. I do not care to leave my husband too frequently."

"And he is too ill to travel?"

"Yes."

239

I thought of Jake at Grasslands, a guest in our house. That would be very disturbing. It was such an extraordinary situation. I imagined myself explaining to Tamarisk: "You have a father. He has just appeared. Here he is." And Edward? What would Edward think of this man? He was very perceptive, and where I was concerned particularly so. He was always conscious of the sacrifice I had made in marrying him. Constantly he said that I should never have done it and as constantly I tried to show him a hundred reasons why I should. I loved Edward. I loved him more than I had when I married him. My admiration for him had grown. I was resigned to my life with him and never until this night had I realized how much I gave up to marry him.

Briefly I imagined myself free. Suppose I had not married Edward and tonight I had met Jake . . . we should have been together after all those years.

I felt angry with life, with myself, with this man who had come back almost casually into my life and talked so lightly of his relationship with poor Dolly. But I was forcing myself to see him in a certain light. I remembered Dolly as she had looked dancing round the bonfire, sitting at the kitchen table in Grasslands while he sang and played on his guitar. Dolly had adored him. Dolly had loved him. Dolly had wanted that moment of passion between them. It was the only time she had felt herself to be loved . . . well, desired. And that had resulted in Tamarisk. Dolly had wanted the child. Flashes of memory came back to me. I remembered how she had talked of her child. Dolly had regretted nothing . . . so why should he?

At least he had brought colour into her life, a joy which she had never before known, and if it had not meant so much to him as it had to her, he was not to blame.

"How long have you been married?" he asked.

"It is nearly two years."

"So if I had come back . . . ."

He stopped. I knew what he meant. If he had come back earlier he might have been able to prevent my marriage.

It was a confession. He must feel as drawn to me as I did to him. The thought made me blissfully happy . . . for a moment. Then I realized how absurd this was. I had never thought to see this man again. When I had known him I had been a child with a child's emotions. Why should I feel this exhilaration one moment, this despair the next . . . just because he had come back into my life.

I said to him: "I was engaged to him. He was injured . . . badly . . . in his factory. I could not break my promise to marry him." I hesitated. "Nor did I want to," I added almost defiantly. "He is a good man . . . a very good man."

"I understand. And may I come to Grasslands to see my daughter?"

"Yes, of course."

He came close to me as we danced. "You have not changed very much," he said. "I believe you would do again all those wonderful things you did then . . . for me."

"I was sorry for you. You had done nothing criminal. You saved Leah."

"Perhaps you will again take pity on me."

I laughed as lightly as I could: "I doubt you are in need of that now, Sir Jake."

"I may well be. And then you will be . . . just as you were all those years ago."

The dance was over. My mother was sitting with Lady Inskip and he returned me to her, bowed and was introduced by Lady Inskip. My mother expressed her pleasure in meeting him and after a few words he departed.

"Charming man," said Lady Inskip. "His brother was a good friend of mine. He has come into quite a large estate and I hope to be seeing a good deal of him if he can tear himself away from Cornwall. Yes, very large estates there and a nice little house in London just off Park Lane. John Cadorson did not use it a great deal."

"I thought I had met him before," said my mother.

"He is very attractive. I shall take him under my wing. I can see he will be a prey to all the rapacious mamas in London. He's had a very romantic past, too, and he makes no secret of it. Why should he? It was to his credit really. He killed a man who was trying to assault a young girl. They tried to bring in murder. That was absurd. He was sent to Australia for seven years."

"Oh," said my mother blankly. "I am beginning to understand."

"There was quite a stir at the time in Nottingham or somewhere like that. Jake went off and did the seven years and now he is back . . . one of the biggest catches in Town."

My mother looked at me anxiously. Perhaps she noticed the shine in my eyes.

When we arrived home she came to my room for one of those talks of which she was so fond and made a habit.

She came straight to the point.

"Do you realize who that man was?"

"Yes. Romany Jake."

"That's right. I was trying to think of his name. You danced with him quite a lot."

"Oh, yes."

"Did he talk about the past?"

"Yes. Quite freely. As a matter of fact I told him about Tamarisk."

"Good heavens, yes. Of course he's her father . . . if Dolly was telling the truth."

"Dolly would not have lied. He is the father. I can see something of him in her."

"What a situation. Who would have believed it?"

"He's making no secret of his past. Lady Inskip mentioned it, didn't she?"

"Oh, it adds a sort of glamour. The man who lived as a gypsy, killed a man to save a woman's honour and served seven years in a penal settlement because of it. Lady Inskip is right. It's so romantic—particularly when there's a fortune and a title to go with it."

"Yes," I said. "He will be much sought after. He will have a wide choice."

"He seems to have a very pleasant manner. Not much of the wandering gypsy there tonight."

"I thought he was very much the same."

"You had a long session with him, of course. Oh, here's your father. He must have guessed where I am. Hello, Dickon. You were right. We were gossiping again."

"I'm always glad when these affairs are over," he said, sitting down in my easy chair. "You were the two most beautiful women at the ball."

"Isn't he a good faithful old husband and father?" said my mother. "There were more glittering figures than we were."

"I wasn't talking about glitter. I was talking about beauty."

"Dickon, did you see who was there?"

"Half of fashionable London, I imagine."

"Anyone in particular?"

"I had eyes only for my beautiful wife and daughter."

"Dickon, you are really old enough now not to be so maudlin."

"You ungrateful creature!"

"What I meant was did you see the young man who was dancing with Jessica quite a lot?"

"Dark fellow."

"That's right. Did you notice anything about him?"

"Good looking, well set-up sort of fellow."

"Dickon, you are so unobservant. He's a figure from the past. Do you remember Romany Jake?"

"God bless my soul! Well, yes . . . I can't believe it."

"It's true," I said. "He made himself known to me."

"Lady Inskip told us," said my mother. "They are making no secret of it."

"What was he doing at a ball like that?"

"Invited," I replied. "And he was an honoured guest."

"Introduced to me by Lady Inskip herself," put in my mother.

"He's inherited a fortune and a title. That's why he has come home from Australia. His estate is in Cornwall but he has a house in London."

"You certainly found out all the details."

"Isn't it a romantic story?" said my mother.

"He's a romantic sort of fellow."

"He's coming to Grasslands," I said.

They both looked rather startled.

"He has a right to see his own daughter."

"Tamarisk, of course," said my mother.

"Best thing to do would have been to keep quiet about that," added my father.

"He doesn't seem to want to keep quiet. He wants to see his daughter."

"So he'll be staying at Grasslands?" said my mother. "Would you prefer us to have him at Eversleigh?"

"Why?" I asked.

"Oh," said my mother quickly. "I thought you might have preferred it."

"Tamarisk is at Grasslands. He would want to be where she is."

"Quite so," said my father.

"I hope people are not going to harp on about his sentence," I said.

"What does it matter? He's served his term. It's over."

"He has a daughter," my mother reminded him.

"Lots of men have daughters."

"Illegitimate ones?" asked my mother.

"Scores of them!" he retorted. "Let him come. He might even take her off your hands, Jessica. That wouldn't be such a bad thing." He yawned. "Come on. I'm not so fond of these late nights as I used to be. Goodnight, daughter. Sleep well."

My mother kissed me tenderly. I had a notion that she was aware of the effect Romany Jake had had upon me.

The next morning he called at the house and asked for me. I received him in the drawing room, pleased that he had come and yet uncertain of myself.

"Good morning," he said, taking both my hands and smiling at me. "I hope you will forgive such an early call. We left each other last night without making arrangements."

"Arrangements?" I repeated.

"You kindly said I might visit you at Grasslands to see my daughter."

"Yes, of course. I think I had better consult my mother. When would it be convenient for you?"

"As soon as possible. I feel that having suddenly learned that I possess a daughter I should lose no time in making her acquaintance. I was going to ask you if you would care to take luncheon with me. I know one or two very good inns hereabouts."

I hesitated and he went on: "There is so much I want to know about . . . my daughter."

"I understand that, of course."

I felt foolish, awkward . . . wanting so much to go with him and at the same time feeling it was unseemly to do so with so much enthusiasm. But why not? I was no longer a young girl, I was a married woman. They deserved certain privileges, certain freedoms. To refuse to go with him alone would have suggested that I suspected him of intending to make advances. Or would it? Sensing my hesitation he pressed home the point.

"What about a trip on the river? Some of the riverside inns are of the best. We could sit in the gardens and watch the world sail by. I always find that pleasant."

I said I should be ready in ten minutes. I went to my mother's room but her maid told me she had just gone out with my father. I was rather glad as I did not want her speculating.

I put on my cloak and came down.

He looked very elegant in his dark blue coat and light waistcoat and his hessian boots. In my dreams I had seen him in his brown breeches and orange-coloured shirt. Even then he had had a certain style—gypsy fashion it was true, but he had been outstanding as he always would be.

I was beginning to feel happy for no reason at all except that I was in his company.

He took my arm as we walked through the streets towards the river. It was a lovely morning: the sun was warm and that ambience of victory still hung about the streets. Everyone seemed full of joy.

"I am so pleased I found you," he was saying. He pressed my arm. "Of course I should have done so in due course. I was planning to come down to find you when I left London. How much more interesting this is! I little knew when I set out for the Inskips' ball how much I was going to enjoy it."

"Surprises are always appreciated."

"Pleasant surprises, yes. Do you know, I have often thought of something like this, sauntering through the streets of London, a beautiful young lady on my arm, and the strange thing was that it was with one particular young lady . . . and here I am. In my mind's eye I have seen it many times. Is that precognition, would you say?"

"Certainly not. Once you were in London you could easily have found a young lady to stroll with you. You must have been homesick during your stay abroad."

"Homesick for a morning like this."

"It is certainly a beautiful one and I suppose however far one roams one never forgets one's native land."

"The longing to return is always there."

He turned his head to look at me. "I had a very special reason," he said.

"Because you were a prisoner and you knew you could only walk again in the streets of London as a free man."

"It was more than that."

We had reached the river. He hired a boat and helped me in; then he picked up the oars and we were speeding past the banks, past the Tower of London and all the other craft on the river. There were people in boats, bent on enjoying themselves, laughing, shouting to each other, some singing, some swaying to the strains of violins.

"It will be quieter by Greenwich," he said. "That is where

I propose to take you. The White Hart. I went there long ago and was impressed. Of course, I was young then. Do you think it is wise to go back to the haunts of one's youth?''

"Hardly ever. They become beautiful in retrospect. Then when you see them again they are less than you expected, because they remain the same as they always were.''

"I have an idea that the White Hart is going to be more delightful today than it ever was.''

"Don't set your hopes too high. I should hate them to be disappointed.''

"That will not happen.''

"You're tempting fate.''

"I have always tempted fate. Do you know, I have a sneaking feeling that fate likes to be tempted.''

"I don't think that is the general opinion.''

"I was never one who went in for general opinions. I was always an individualist.''

"You must have been to leave home and live with the gypsies. How long were you with them?''

"About two years.''

"That's quite a time.''

It was a gesture of defiance. They were camping on our land. My brother and I were engaged in one of our quarrels. It would have been unusual if we had not been. These quarrels were part of our daily lives. He said, 'You're no better than those gypsies. It would suit you roaming about, getting nowhere, living aimlessly . . .' I said to him, 'Maybe you're right. At least they live naturally.' And then I went off and joined them. It was a stupid thing to do. I was eighteen at the time. One can do stupid things at eighteen.''

"Yes,'' I said quietly, "one can.''

"Not you. You never would.''

"You do not know me.''

The boat had drawn up at some stairs. We alighted and he tied it up. "Here is the inn,'' he said. "Right on the river. There are the gardens. We could sit out there and watch the craft on the river while we eat. It's just as I remembered it.''

We climbed the slight incline to the inn and seated ourselves. A buxom girl in a mob cap and a low-cut bodice came out to attend to us. There were fish fritters, whitebait, cold beef and pigeon pie, she told us, with ale, home-brewed cider or real French wine to go with it.

"I wonder if it is Charlot's burgundy," I said. "That is my half brother who lives in France."

"Let's have it in honour of your half brother."

"I must tell you about him," I said.

We decided on the cold beef and it was served with hot potatoes in their jackets. The food was plain but delicious. I quickly told him about Charlot's vineyard and how now the war was over and Napoleon finally defeated, I expected we should be visiting him now and then.

He listened attentively, then he said: "It is so good to be here with you."

I flushed a little and gave my attention to the beef.

"I want to talk to you about my experiences. Do you know, I have never talked about them much."

"Won't that bring back to your mind something you would rather forget?"

"Once I have told you I shall begin to forget. Can you imagine my feelings in that courtroom?"

"It is difficult to imagine something which has never happened to one, but I have a fair idea what it must have been like. Horrifying!"

"I trust you will never come so close to death as I did."

"We all have to come close to it some day."

"When we are old it is inevitable, yes, but not when it is decided by others that it is time you left the Earth. I used to lie in my cell and wonder. The uncertainty was hard to bear. I used to say to myself, This time next year, where shall I be? Shall I be on Earth or in the realms of the unknown?"

"Don't speak of it."

"I shall tell you once and then never again refer to it. There I was in the courtroom. I believed I was going to be condemned to death. To be hanged by the neck is so ignoble . . . so undignified. No man should be subjected to that humiliation. That was what I cared about . . . the degradation . . . not losing my life. I've risked that often enough."

"You must put it out of your mind."

"I will, so I'll go back to the moment when I knew I was going to live. I had not realized before how very sweet life is. To live . . . but as a slave . . . seven years of servitude in a foreign land. But for a time I rejoiced. As I said, life is sweet."

"Tell me about Australia," I said.

"I shall never forget my first glimpse of Sydney Harbour.

We had been battened down in the hold for the voyage. We did not know whether it was night or day. There were the terrible hours at sea when the ship pitched and tossed. People were ill and some died. The sea was beautiful but we only saw it when we were taken up on deck for an hour's exercise each day. There we were roped together . . . thieves, vagabonds, murderers, men who had been guilty of poaching a pheasant, stealing a handkerchief or writing something which was not approved of. All of us together . . . the seven year men, the fourteen year men and the lifers. There were times when I wished your good father had not intervened on my behalf and I was sure it was more comfortable dangling from a rope than living in that hell.''

I put my hand across the table and touched his. The response was immediate. He grasped my hand.

I said: ''I am very sorry. I wish I could have helped you escape from Grasslands that day.''

''If I had I should have been a hunted man for the rest of my days. Now you see me free. I have served my sentence. I am at liberty. I was fortunate. I could have been in a chain gang.''

I shivered.

''Imagine that. Guarded by troops when at work, never having the chains removed from one's legs . . . living in a stockade with a hundred other wretches. But why am I telling you this? This was to be a happy day.''

I said: ''I think you want to talk of it . . . just once. Relieve your mind and then try to forget. Have you talked of it often?''

''No. There is no one to whom I wish to speak. It is different with you. You were my friend . . . right from the day when you came upon me in that house.''

''I thought it was so unfair. You had killed that man who deserved to be killed. You had saved Leah . . . and for that you were hunted . . . called a criminal.''

''Now let me tell you of my good fortune. We came up and there before us was that wonderful harbour. How can I describe it to you . . . all those inlets, the sandy beaches fringed with foliage. It was quite splendid and one's spirits rose to contemplate it . . . The hot sun, the fragrance in the air, the magnificent birds . . . cockatoos, parrots . . . of the most dazzling colours. It must have looked a little different from when Cook first saw it for now buildings were visible, little houses which had been built by the settlers, low hills, gullies and the bush in some parts coming to the water's edge. When one has been cooped up for months it is a glorious feeling to look at all that beauty, to take deep breaths of that wonderful air and suddenly to feel how good it is to be alive.

"We were in the ship a few days before we were chosen by those who would be our masters for the term of our sentence. An advertisement would have appeared in the newspapers to say that a cargo of prisoners had arrived for selection. We were taken on deck and there we stood while our prospective owners came and inspected us. I can tell you that was one of the most humiliating moments of my life. We were like cattle. But I distress you again and I want to tell you of my good fortune. I was selected by a grazier who had a small station some miles out of New South Wales. He was not a bad man. He wanted a good worker. I was young and strong and I was to serve a seven years' term, which was an indication that I was not a hardened criminal.

"Joe Cleaver selected me and from that moment I began to feel a little more like a human being. It was not an easy life. I began to realize how comfortably I had lived during my twenty years. But I was not averse to work. In fact I welcomed it. I was given blankets and I slept in a hut which I shared with two others. There we prepared our food and boiled our water in billy cans. Eight pounds of beef a week, ten pounds of flour; and a quart of milk a day—that was our ration. And we laboured from dawn to sunset. It was a hard life but I began to like it. Joe Cleaver noticed me because I had introduced him to one or two methods of work which produced good results. Within a year I was sleeping in the house. He consulted me now and then."

I nodded. I could well imagine it. He would be noticed wherever he was.

"The months passed . . . the years passed . . . all seven of them and I was free. Joe didn't want me to go. He gave me a strip of land and helped me. I had a few sheep. Then I had more sheep. Joe said I would be a lucky grazier. He reckoned in no time I would have a station of my own. Then the news came. They had traced me. My brother had died and I had inherited my family's estate and title."

"So you left what you were building up and came home."

"Yes, I came home."

"You will go back to Australia?"

"I think I may one day. You would be interested to see the place?"

"I am always interested to see new places."

"It changes all the time. It grows. I saw it grow in the years I was there. Joe used to take me into Sydney with him. He said I had a way of bargaining which he lacked. I supposed I was more articulate, more shrewd perhaps. Joe and I became very good friends. What was I saying . . . Yes, a growing town. There are streets where once there were cart tracks. There are so many natural assets. Yes, I should like to go back."

"What of the land you have there?"

"I put a man in charge of it, so I must go back one day."

"Not to stay."

"No. My home is in England . . . in Cornwall. Do you know Cornwall?"

I shook my head.

"You would like it. It is different from the rest of England. It's closer to nature. It isn't that only. The Cornish are a superstitious race. There is something there . . . something fey. You who are so practical, so full of good sense would be sceptical perhaps."

"I fear I am not so full of common sense as you appear to think."

"I am sure you are."

"How could you be sure? You hardly know me."

"I know a good deal about you."

"You met me when I was a child more or less . . . and then nothing more until last night."

"You have never been far from my thoughts since our first meeting."

I laughed lightly. "Gallantry, I suppose," I said. "The sort of thing men feel they must say to women."

"The truth," he insisted. "Do you know, when I was battened down in that loathsome place I could soothe my fury against fate by thinking of that bright-eyed little girl who was so earnest, so eager and who had saved my life. One never forgets someone who saved one's life."

"You exaggerate."

"Indeed not."

"*I* didn't save your life. My father did what he could."

"Because you insisted. Penfold told me everything. He came to the docks to see me off before I left."

"I felt responsible."

"Because you were followed to the house. Yes, you sustained me during those days. And then afterwards when I was living in my hut I would think of you. I used to say to myself, One day I am going to be free and I shall go back and find her. She will be grown up then . . ."

"Did you ever think of Dolly?"

"Now and then. Poor Dolly."

"I should have thought she might have been the one in your thoughts."

"Dolly? She was there . . . and she was gone. I think she felt like that of me."

"Do you think a girl like Dolly would indulge in a light relationship, a sensation of an hour and then think no more of it? Dolly never knew a man before you, nor after you. Dolly was no light o' love to be picked up and thrown aside."

"It happened. She understood. She knew I was going away. It was that sort of relationship. There was never intended to be anything permanent . . . on either side."

"I find that difficult to understand."

"Of course you do. But for the child it would have been of very little moment."

"I do not think it was for Dolly, but then of course she is a member of that sex which is born to serve the other."

He smiled at me. "How fierce you are in defence of women. You are just as I knew you would be. But I never thought I should come back and find you . . . married."

"Why not? I am not a child any more. I shall soon be twenty-one."

"Seven years . . . eight years . . . it's a long time out of a life. Tell me about your marriage. Are you happy?"

"I am happy."

"But not completely so?"

"Why do you say that?"

"Because I sense it."

"I could not have a kinder husband."

"You have told me very little about him. He had an accident. That is all I know."

"Before that accident I was engaged to marry him."

"Were you very much in love?"

I hesitated. I did not know why I had to be entirely frank with him.

"You weren't," he said. "Then why did you marry him?"

"Amaryllis had become engaged, and I suppose I thought it was time I did. They all wanted me to marry Edward . . . his family and mine."

"Rich, I suppose? Of good family," he said ironically.

"Not particularly rich. Comfortable, with a business in Nottingham . . . good solid people, honourable. My family liked them. As a matter of fact, but for you we should never have known them."

He looked surprised.

"It was when we went to Nottingham . . . when you stood on trial . . . that we met them. They became friendly and they bought Grasslands when Dolly died. They became our neighbours as well as friends."

"So you became engaged because Amaryllis did?"

"It was something like that. Then there was this terrible accident. Edward was so brave . . . so wonderful. He wanted to free me but I wouldn't have it. So we were married."

"It is no life for you," he said.

"It is the life I have chosen."

"You were not meant to live a nun's life. You are a vibrant person, full of life."

"Were you meant to be treated like a slave? What do you mean when you say it is not what I was meant for? Clearly we are meant for what befalls us."

"I could not help what happened to me. Could I have stood by and seen Leah ravished?"

"Could I stand by, having given my promise, and leave Edward because he had been crippled?"

"You do the most quixotic things. The idea of tying yourself for life because of a gesture!"

"And what of you? The idea of coming near to death and then suffering seven years of servitude . . . just for a young girl."

"Would you say we were a pair of fools?"

"I can only say that what I did I had to do. And I believe the same applies to you."

He took my hand and held it. "What a serious meeting this has been. I meant it to be so happy, so full of fun . . . meeting after all these years. We should be enjoying our reunion." He filled my glass with the burgundy. He lifted his. "Come, laugh and be merry."

I was surprised at the manner in which he could throw off his melancholy. Now he was very much like the laughing gypsy I had known long ago.

He told me about his estates in Cornwall and so vividly did he talk that I could picture the old grey stone mansion with the battlemented towers, with its long gallery—"haunted, you know. No house in Cornwall is worthy of the term ancient unless it has its ghost. We're not far from the moors and we have the sea as well. I hope you will visit it one day."

I let myself believe I would. He had that effect on me. He transported me into a world of make-believe. He made me feel young and carefree. I could temporarily forget that I had duties and responsibilities. I saw myself going through that house in Cornwall, marvelling in the long gallery, the solarium, the crown post, the priest's hole, the great hall and the garden full of azaleas and rhododendrons with hydrangeas, pink, blue and white, growing in profusion.

He was a vivid talker and brought it all to life for me; moreover he made me long to be there to see it for myself.

I was brought back to reality by the realization that time was passing. My family would wonder where I was and I must go back.

Reluctantly we returned to the boat and I was a little sad as we rowed back. I had been indulging in dreams and as I came out of them I realized as never before, what a rash act it had been to marry Edward. When I looked at this man, pulling at the oars, smiling at me in a significant manner, all the melancholy I had seen in his face when he had talked of his trials disappeared. I was stirred as I never had been before. I wanted to go on being with him. I wanted to see that joy in living which he could display and which seemed particularly exciting when I heard of all he had endured during his years of servitude which would have been so hard to bear for a man of his nature.

In those moments on the river I said to myself: This must be falling in love. I had thought it would never happen to me, and now it had . . . too late.

We alighted from the boat and began the walk to the house. I realized it must be nearly three o'clock. I felt faintly irritated, frustrated. I had forgotten how anxious they would be about me, so completely absorbed had I been.

We came out into Piccadilly. I must have increased my pace a little, and he said: "You are anxious to get on."

"I didn't realize it was so late."

"Let's take this street. It's a short cut."

That was how I saw her. Recognition was instantaneous—after all she had made a great impression on me. It was the girl who had pretended to be blind.

How different she looked now! There was no doubt that she could see. She was fashionably dressed in rather a gaudy manner; her cheeks were startlingly red, the rest of her face very white; those eyes which had seemed so pathetically sightless were rimmed with kohl. She had crossed the road and gone into a building.

I said: "What place is that?"

Jake said: "It's Frinton's Club."

"Frinton's! I've heard of that. That was where Jonathan lost so much money. What sort of place is it?"

"It has rather a shady reputation, I believe."

It was very strange. What was that girl doing in Frinton's Club? Something should be done. I did not know what.

"Do you know who owns it?"

"It is said to be a Madame Delarge."

"I've heard of her."

"There are a chain of clubs like Frinton's. I've heard all sorts of things go on in them. Not gambling only. They are the haunts of prostitutes and idle young men—and perhaps older ones—who have more money than sense."

"I see."

"There are a number of them in London. Madame Delarge is the accepted owner, but I have heard that she is just a name, and there is some big organization behind her. Frinton's is just one of a chain of such clubs. Madame Delarge is the one behind whom the real owners cower. At least so I've heard."

"Why should there be this need for anonymity?"

"It is rather an unsavoury business. It wouldn't surprise me if the real owners are posing as pillars of society."

I felt shaken. After my idyllic experience I had seen that young woman who for some time had haunted my dreams. To say the least, it was disconcerting.

When I told my parents I had seen the girl who had pretended to be blind and that she had gone into Frinton's Club, my father said: "She's obviously a loose woman. Many of them frequent those clubs. There's nothing much we could do even if we approached the girl. It's too long ago."

"There is a woman who is said to own the place. A Madame Delarge."

"Oh yes. She's just a figurehead, I believe."

"It was a great shock to see that girl. I should have known her anywhere although she was so dressed up and quite different. And her face . . ."

"Let's hope she sticks to her trade," said my father, "and doesn't attempt any more to kidnap young innocent girls."

"I think something ought to be done," said my mother.

My father said to me: "Don't you attempt to follow her if you see her again. Don't do anything like that."

"As if I should!"

My mother was more concerned about my going out with Jake Cadorson.

"I wondered where you were," she said, mildly reproving.

"I came to tell you I was going but you were out. He wants to come down to see Tamarisk. I am not sure how Tamarisk will feel having a father suddenly presented to her."

"She's an unpredictable girl," said my mother.

"I think," I mused, "it will be best to break it to her gently. Then when she knows, I'll ask him to come down."

"We'll have him at Eversleigh."

"Why should you? Tamarisk is at Grasslands."

My mother looked faintly embarrassed.

"I wondered . . ." she said.

She betrayed to me that she, who was very perceptive where I was concerned, had guessed that my feelings for this man were perhaps a little more intense than was desirable.

I said calmly: "I will ask him in due course."

He called next day and my father asked him to dine with us. He accepted with alacrity. It was quite clear that my parents liked him. He had a special gratitude towards my father and quite openly they discussed the trial and the state of the country after this most devastating and prolonged war which had been going on.

"Twenty years one might say," said my father. "The people are in a merry mood at the moment . . . singing the praises of the great Duke, but wait till the taxes are enforced. It will be a different story then."

"You expect trouble?" asked Jonathan.

"I know there'll be murmuring." He turned to Jake. "I don't know how things are in Cornwall."

"Very much the same as in the rest of the country, I fear," replied Jake. "And of course the people there are considerably poorer to start with."

"We've had an example of what the mob can do," said my mother. "Jessica's husband has been a victim of that."

"Yes, so I heard."

"We are better off on our estates," put in my father. "We manage to weather these storms. It's townsfolk who suffer most."

"In addition to the poverty engendered by the war, the people have another complaint," said Jake. "They are demanding representation. They want universal suffrage."

"It will be some time before we get that," said my father. "Do we want every Tom, Dick and Harry who can't read or write making the laws of this country?"

"They are not asking to make the laws," I pointed out. "They are merely asking to have a voice in which man they send to Parliament to represent them."

"Nonsense," said my father. "The people have to learn. They have to accept what is. They have to march with the times."

"I would say that is just what they are attempting to do," I said.

"My daughter is a very contentious woman," my father remarked to Jake. "Raise a point and she is bound to come up with the very opposite."

"It makes life interesting," said Jake.

I was glad they liked him. I was glad he fitted in so well.

After he had gone my father said: "Interesting fellow. Fancy entertaining an ex-convict at your table, Lottie. I'm surprised at you."

"I found him better company than quite a number I could name."

"Such experiences are bound to leave their mark. I'm glad things worked out the way they did. It would have been a tragedy to hang a man like that. He was only in that position because he'd saved a young girl from a drunken bully. Silly young idiot."

"Why silly?" I said. "It was just the sort of thing you would have done in your youth."

256

"My dear daughter, you flatter me. I never did much which was not going to bring me good."

"Why do you always make yourself out to be so much worse than you are? You're bad enough without that."

We grinned at each other. I felt so happy because they all liked Jake Cadorson.

I did not think it could happen so soon.

We should be leaving London at the end of the week and it was a Wednesday. It was arranged that Jake should visit Grasslands one week after our return. That would give me time to break the news to Tamarisk that she had a father.

He had said there was so much he wanted to know about Tamarisk, and he confessed that he was a little nervous about meeting her.

It was afternoon. I wanted to go out and make a few purchases and when I left the house I met him. I believe he had been waiting for me.

"It seems so long since we have met," he said.

I looked at him in astonishment. "It was yesterday."

"I said it seemed a long time . . . not that it was." He went on: "I want to talk to you. I have so much to say to you."

"Still? I thought we had talked a lot."

"Not enough. Let's find somewhere quiet. I know. You have not seen my house yet. It isn't very far."

"I was going shopping."

"Couldn't that wait?"

"I suppose so. It wasn't really important in any case."

"I should like to show you my house. It is small by the standards of your family home. My brother used it as a pied à terre, and as he was a confirmed bachelor I suppose it sufficed."

He took my arm and I felt as though I danced along those streets. The house was in a quiet little cul de sac. There was a row of Georgian houses with a garden opposite.

"It's charming," I said.

"Yes. My brother had elegant tastes and liked to indulge in the comforts of life."

"Who looks after the house for you? Have you servants?"

"There is a basement in which live Mr. and Mrs. Evers. They as they say 'do' for me. It's an excellent arrangement. Everything is looked after. Mrs. Evers is a good cook and their great virtue is that they don't intrude. My brother taught them that. They appear like Aladdin's genie when called on. Otherwise they remain tucked away with their lamp, which is of course in their basement apartment.''

"How fortunate you are. I often think we are plagued by our servants. They note everything we do, embellish it, garnish it and serve it up as salacious titbits.''

"I am free of such observation. It can be very comforting.''

He opened the door with a key and we stepped into the hall. There was a grandfather clock and an oak chest on which stood a big brass bowl, very highly polished. The silence was broken only by the ticking of the clock. I thought to myself: I ought not to have come.

He turned and faced me.

"It is a wonderful moment for me," he said, "to have you here . . . in this house.''

"I'm longing to see it.''

"Here is the dining room and the kitchen, and on the next floor a drawing room and study, on the next two bedrooms. It is quite small, you see, but enough for my needs.''

"And you have the estate in Cornwall. I take it you will be living there most of the time.''

He took me up to the drawing room. It had big windows, reaching from floor to ceiling. The apple green drapes were trimmed with gold braid and the furnishings were a deeper shade of green. The furniture was elegant in the extreme.

"Let me take your cloak," he said, and did so, throwing it over the back of a chair. We stood facing each other and suddenly he put his arms round me and kissed me.

For a moment I did not resist. I had forgotten everything in the acute pleasure such as I had never experienced before.

Then I withdrew myself trying to give the impression that what had passed between us was nothing more than a friendly greeting. It was a poor pretence.

He said: "It is no use trying to pretend this does not exist, is it?''

"What?'' I retorted sharply.

"This—between us—you and me. It's there, isn't it? Wasn't it there right from the beginning? You were only a child but I knew. Of course it seemed ridiculous then. You a little girl . . . Myself a man who had abandoned everything to go off with the gypsies. I can't tell you how I regretted that when I saw you. Do you remember?''

"Well . . . vaguely. You were sitting under a tree wearing an orange shirt. You had a guitar. Do you still play it?"

"Now and then. I was playing a part, playing at being a gypsy."

"You had gold rings in your ears."

"Yes. I worked hard at it. When I saw you I thought I had never seen anyone quite like you."

"I certainly had never seen anyone like you. But then I knew little of gypsies."

"I thought: I shouldn't be meeting her like this. It should be at a ball and she should be older. She should be seventeen, her first ball, and she should have the first dance with me. I realized then what I had done by throwing away my old way of life, my background, everything . . . just for a whim."

"I don't believe that."

"It's true, I swear."

"But you did not go back to your home."

"You know the pride of the young. They take a step and refuse to see that it is folly. I was determined to go on with what I had begun, but I never forgot you. And then . . . there I was in danger of losing my life and you came to save it. Doesn't that show that you and I were meant to be a great deal to each other?"

"I don't know about such things. Perhaps I don't believe that anything is *meant*. Things are what we make them."

He said slowly: "I am not going to let you go now I have found you."

"I daresay you will visit us. You are Tamarisk's father. You will want to see her and she will probably want to see you."

"I was not thinking of that. I love you. I always have. I used to think of you on that fearful ship and later in my hut. I used to come out at night and look at the stars overhead. I used to imagine that you, too, would be looking at the stars and they would be different from the ones I saw. We were on opposite sides of the world. We should be together always."

"I think I should go," I said. "Show me the house quickly and I will get on with my shopping."

He rose, took my hands, and pulled me up beside him. For a moment we stood very close. I felt an extraordinary lassitude creeping over me. I was unsure what it meant except that it was a warning. I ought to get out of this house as quickly as possible.

We mounted the stairs, he leading the way.

"Small, as I told you," he was saying. "But compact."

We had reached a landing and he threw open a door. There was a large bedroom with a four-poster bed. The curtains were of green velvet; they matched the drapes at the window and there were touches of green in the carpet.

"Your brother was very fond of green," I said.

"His favourite colour obviously. Do you like it?"

"Enchanting. It's so fresh."

He shut the door and I said: "Show me the next room. Then I must go."

He put his arms round me and pulled me down to sit on the bed. "What are you doing with your life?" he said.

I laughed on a rather high note. "I believe," I answered, "that I am doing what most people do with their lives. I am living it."

"You are living in a half world, Jessica. You have shut yourself away from reality."

"My life is real enough."

"You are merely existing. Why did you do it?"

I turned rather angrily to him. "I had to do it. Why did you leave your home and become a gypsy? Why did you kill a man for the sake of a girl and almost lose your life for it?"

"Why do we do these things? But having done them should we suffer for them for ever?"

"You won't. You have cast your misfortunes aside admirably. I shall never forget how you looked at the Inskips' ball. No one would have guessed."

"One doesn't have to live for ever with one's mistakes. You cannot shut yourself away. You can't just wither away in that place."

"I'm not withering away. I am living a very useful life."

"Now that I have found you, you don't imagine that I am going to let you go."

I was shaken. I wanted to hear him say that. I should have gone then . . . but I could not. More than anything I wanted to stay.

I replied: "I have made my bed, as they say, and I must lie on it."

He shook his head. "You and I will find happiness together."

"How can that be?"

He drew me to him and kissed me over and over again.

No, said my conscience. But something else said: Stay. Why shouldn't you? What harm is it doing?

Harm! But I was married to Edward.

Edward would not know.

That was the danger signal. I was actually telling myself that Edward need never know. I felt quite depraved and with it a sensation of great excitement. I knew in that moment that I was going to succumb to temptation.

He went on kissing me.

"It had to be," he said.

I made no effort to break away.

"Please, Jessica," he said, "I have dreamed of this for so many years. It has sustained me . . . brought me through. One day I shall find her, I told myself. And now I have, I shall never let you go."

I was in love with him. How different this was from the mild attraction I had once felt for Peter Lansdon. This was overwhelming, an intense longing to be with him. I thought, I shall never be happy when he is not there.

"I know you love me," he said.

"I can't. I must not."

"You cannot say you can't when you do."

"Jake," I said pleadingly. "Jake, I must remember my obligations. I never knew until now what a terrible mistake I have made, but it is done, and it is my mistake. I must live with it."

As I was speaking he was slipping my gown from my shoulders; and I knew I could not resist.

So it had happened. I felt bewildered and exhilarated by the experience. I felt as though I were dreaming. But there he was beside me and I knew that I loved him, had always loved him, and would love him for ever.

He kissed me tenderly. "You must not be sad," he said. "It had to be. You could not go on in that way . . . not when I was near you. You must not be afraid."

I could only say: "I have done this . . . to Edward."

"Edward would understand."

I shook my head. "He must never know."

"He won't."

"I would die rather. He has been so good. That terrible accident . . . to happen to such a man. I have to care for him for the rest of our lives."

"It will not always be like this," he said. "We will think what it is best to do."

"We must never meet again."

"That is quite out of the question. My dearest Jessica, this is not such an unusual occurrence as you think."

"I know wives are unfaithful to their husbands, husbands to wives. But that does not help me. This is not any husband and wife. This is Edward. It is myself."

"My dear sweet Jessica, life is not meant to be a penance. It is to be lived to the full . . . to be enjoyed. As soon as we met again this was inevitable. In view of what your marriage has been no one would blame you."

"I blame myself."

"I will teach you differently."

Then he took me into his arms and made love to me again . . . this time less urgently, tenderly.

And I made no attempt to restrain him.

I knew that I had changed the course of my life then. I knew that this was a beginning and that I should not be able to resist him. I was about to embark on a double life.

Blackmail

If that had been the end perhaps there would have been an excuse for me. But it was not. I was as though intoxicated. I made excuses for myself. I was a woman with natural desires. Edward could never help me fulfil these. I had taken a lover. That sounded casual. I loved deeply and was loved in return. I believed now that I had always loved Jake. Something had passed between us when we first met and I had only to see him again to realize that he was the man for me.

I went on explaining to myself. Edward would understand. He had always been worried because he knew that this was not a natural life we were living. I would make up to him for what I had done. I would be even more solicitous, even more caring.

I told myself that I must never go to that house again; but I could not keep away. We had planned to spend four more days in London. Four more days! I could not help it. I sought every opportunity to be with Jake.

I was shameless, I supposed. I realized that I had been starved of love. I was wildly happy in some moments, filled with remorse in others. I would experience a deep sadness when I contemplated Amaryllis who had made such a success of her life—the happy wife and mother. I often thought how happy I could have been if I were married to Jake.

As for him, he was less burdened by guilt than I. Indeed I believe he felt none. But then I was deceiving my husband. He had no such matrimonial burdens to consider. He constantly tried to lift my spirits. Mine was no ordinary marriage, he insisted. It was understandable that this should happen some day. Edward would understand if he ever knew.

"He must never know," I cried vehemently. "He has suffered enough."

"He would realize . . ."

I shook my head. "He would be kind, understanding, forgiving, but he would be wounded . . . deeply wounded." Then I added: "I must not come here again."

I said that often, but I did go . . . again . . . and again, and I waited through the days for the opportunities, so that I could slip into that house in Blore Street.

They were such strange days—days of exultation, days of shame. The hours flew by as they never had before and yet those four days seemed like a year. I had experienced so much; grown up, I supposed. I had ceased to be an innocent girl. I was a vital woman, scheming for meetings with her lover—eager, passionate . . . and then suddenly remembering what I was doing.

I felt my guilt must be written on my face for them all to see. But no one noticed. Not even my mother.

One day I had been to the house and Jake was escorting me back to Albemarle Street, and as we walked along we came face to face with Peter Lansdon.

Hastily I withdrew my arm from Jake's. I think I flushed a little.

"Peter!" I cried. "I didn't expect to see you. I didn't know you were in London."

He smiled at me. "Business," he said. "Trouble at one of the warehouses."

"This is Sir Jake Cadorson. Sir Jake, this is Peter Lansdon —my niece's husband."

The two men acknowledged each other.

"I was just returning to the house," I floundered. "I had been out . . . and I met Sir Jake."

"You will be going back to Eversleigh soon, I believe."

"Have you been to Albemarle Street?"

"No. I have just arrived. I went straight to the warehouse."

"Peter is a very busy man," I said to Jake.

"Trouble has a habit of cropping up," said Peter. "I must

be going. More business to attend to. I'll be coming on to Albemarle Street later."

We said goodbye.

"Do you think he knew?" I asked. "Was it obvious that we had been together?"

"I think he had one thought in mind . . . his own affairs."

"He is very absorbed in them," I replied with relief. "I am afraid it might seem a little obvious."

"You must silence that uneasy conscience of yours, my dearest," he said. "Everything will be all right."

But Peter Lansdon had put a blight on the day. He had brought home to me more forcibly the wrong I was doing.

Edward was pleased to see me. "It has seemed so long," he said.

"It was not really very long."

"How were the celebrations?"

"Very enthusiastic."

"I wonder how long the mood will last."

"We are at peace. People are going to remember that for a long time."

"People have short memories."

"Edward, how pessimistic you have become!"

He laughed. "Well, it is nice to have you back."

"James has showed his usual efficiency?"

"Oh yes, we played a lot of piquet and I'm teaching him chess. I think he'll be quite a good player."

"That's wonderful."

"Jessica . . . you look different."

I felt my voice falter. "Different? How different?"

He looked at me with his head on one side. "You look . . . radiant. It was obviously a good holiday."

"Yes, I think it was. All the excitement . . . There was such adulation for the Duke. One gets caught up in all that."

"It's a very happy state of affairs. We should all enjoy it while we can."

After a while I said: "Oh, an interesting thing happened. It was at the Inskips' ball."

"That was a grand affair, I imagine."

"Very grand. We met a Sir Jake Cadorson. Guess who he turned out to be. I'll give you three guesses." I gave a nervous little laugh, trying to be merry. Did it sound artificial?

"Some businessman?"

"No . . . not exactly."

"I was going to say a friend of Peter."

"No, I'd better tell you. Do you remember Romany Jake?"

"The gypsy, yes. I'll never forget him. It was through him that we met each other."

"Well, he has become *Sir* Jake."

"How did he manage that?"

"He was no real gypsy. He ran away to join them. He comes from an old Cornish family. He went to Australia and served his seven years and then heard he was heir to estates in Cornwall. There was a title too. And there he was at the Inskips' ball—quite an honoured guest."

"I never saw him. Did you recognize him?"

"After a while, yes. We had a talk together . . . several talks. My father asked him to the house."

"That must have been interesting."

I was glad I was sitting with my back to the light.

"You know he is Tamarisk's father," I said.

"Good Lord, yes. Dolly, of course."

"I have had to ask him to come down here for a short visit. He wants to see his daughter."

"That's natural enough."

"I am wondering how to break the news to Tamarisk. What will her feelings be, do you think?"

"She can be unpredictable."

"I want to get her used to the idea before he comes."

"Of course. What sort of man is he . . . this gypsy cum baronet?"

"Well, I suppose he is in his late twenties . . . maybe thirty. He's dark . . ."

"I didn't mean his appearance so much."

"He . . . er . . . fitted very well into the Inskips' circle."

"That's just about top notch, isn't it?" he said with a laugh.

"I suppose so. He told me that he had run away from home to join the gypsies because of family disagreements."

"And now he has apparently stepped back into his rightful niche."

"I suppose you could say that."

"Tamarisk ought to be pleased to have such a father. I wonder if he will want to take her away."

"I wonder if she would want to go."

"With Tamarisk, one never knows. One thing I know is that you will do what is right . . . and for the best."

He smiled at me lovingly and in that moment I felt the burden of my guilt was almost unbearable.

Tentatively I approached the matter with Tamarisk.

"Tamarisk," I said, "have you ever missed not having a father?"

She looked surprised and thought for a moment. Then she said: "No."

"What would you say if you suddenly found you had one?"

"I don't want one," she said.

"Why not?"

"He'd tell me what to do. Old Mr. Frenshaw still tells young Mr. Frenshaw what to do and he's quite old."

I laughed. "Old Mr. Frenshaw tells everybody what to do. You might like your father."

"I don't think I need one."

"It's nice to have one."

"What for?"

"Well, everybody had a father at some time."

"I haven't."

"You couldn't be born without one. There has to be a mother and father."

She looked puzzled, and feeling I was getting into difficult ground, I started again. "As a matter of fact you have a father."

"Where?"

"In London. He wants to meet you."

She stared at me in amazement. "How can he, when he doesn't know me?"

"He knows *of* you."

"Why isn't he here then . . . like other fathers?"

"It's rather complicated. He had to go away. He's been away for a long time, right to the other side of the world. Now he's back and he wants to meet you."

"When?"

"Next week?"

"Oh," she said. There was a pause before she went on. "Brownie had to have a bran mash this morning. Stubbs is giving it to her. Jonathan is coming over this afternoon and we're going to ride together."

Brownie was her very own horse and the joy of her life. Stubbs was one of the grooms.

I could see that she was not greatly impressed by the prospect of seeing her father, and that her mind was on other matters far more interesting in her opinion. Riding with Jonathan was far more important to her—so much so that she did not want to consider anything else.

I felt excited and apprehensive at the thought of having Jake at Grasslands. I was very much afraid that we might betray our feelings for each other.

I introduced him to Edward and watched them together . . . my husband and my lover. Edward was courteous and as Jake was quite frank about his life as a gypsy and on the convict settlement there were none of those uneasy moments which occur when there are subjects which must be avoided.

Edward's verdict when we were alone was: "What an interesting man! I suppose all that happening to one would give one a certain . . . what shall I say . . . an aura of fascination perhaps. Then running off with the gypsies. He's an individualist. There is no doubt about that. He will liven us up, I daresay. You'll want to take him over to Eversleigh, I imagine."

I said they would invite us and we should also go to Enderby, although Amaryllis was scarcely in a condition to entertain.

"Oh, Eversleigh will do the honours. But the main problem is Tamarisk."

It was a strange meeting. She came into the room and he stood up and went to her. She looked up at him with curiosity.

"So you are my daughter," he said.

"They say that," she said almost disbelievingly.

"Well, then it is time we got to know each other."

She shrugged her shoulders and turned away.

"Tamarisk," I cried indignantly. "Your father has come a long way to see you."

"You've been to the other side of the world." She turned to him and there was a certain interest in her eyes.

"Yes," he said. "It's very different there."

"With kangaroos?"

He nodded.

"Did you ever see one?"

"Yes."

"With a baby in its pouch?"

"Yes, and I've eaten kangaroo soup."

"You killed it."

"Somebody must have killed it to make the soup. You can't make soup out of live things."

"Did you have a boomerang?"

"Yes, I had that. I hear you are riding and that you are a good rider."

"Do you like horses?"

"Very much. Perhaps we can go for a ride together and have a good talk."

"All right," she said. "I'll put on my riding habit. I've got a new one."

"That's splendid. You can show me the country."

"All right," she said. "Wait there. I won't be long."

I smiled at him when she had gone. "I think," I said, "you have taken the first step."

We were alone in the room.

"Jessica," he said. "I have missed you so much."

"Please . . . not here . . . not in this house."

"You will come to London."

"Oh Jake, it can't go on. Now I am back here with Edward I see that."

"He will never know. And we need each other."

"I could not bear for him to know."

"You can't be expected to live like a nun . . . not you, Jessica. You couldn't."

I said: "I have already shown that I am no nun. I have already broken my marriage vows."

"I love you."

"And I love you . . . but it is all impossible. We have to see that. This is the way I have chosen. I could not ever hurt Edward. He has suffered so much already. What do you think it is like for him, lying there, day after day . . . a man and yet not a man."

"What is it like for us . . . being denied each other?"

"You will find someone."

"There is only one I want."

"That can't be so. If we had not met at the Inskips' . . ."

"I should have come down here and found you. It was inevitable . . . from the moment we met all those years ago. It had to be."

"We must be strong. *I* am going to be. It was a madness

269

which came to me in London. Now that I am home . . . with Edward . . . I know that.''

Tamarisk burst into the room wearing her new riding habit and looking pleased.

"I'm ready," she announced.

"Well, let us away," said Jake.

He opened the door for her and she went through. Then he turned to look back at me. He put his fingers to his lips and threw them towards me.

I should be pleased. The meeting had gone off better than I had hoped. Tamarisk was wary but he would soon win her with his charm. I could see that.

It might be that she would have another hero to set beside Jonathan.

I went to Edward.

"I can see all went well," he said. "You look very pleased with yourself."

"They've gone riding. I think she is going to take to him."

"Well, he's a likeable fellow. I wonder if he will want to take her away from us."

"That will be for him and her to decide."

"She might like the idea of that place in Cornwall."

"There is one person you have forgotten. Jonathan. She has quite a passion for him."

"Oh yes. It would take a great deal to get her to leave him."

"I wouldn't be sorry to see her go to Cornwall."

"She is something of a liability."

"I wasn't thinking of that. She is old for her years and I am a little perturbed about this obsession with Jonathan. Jonathan himself has quite a reputation."

"I am sure Jonathan would never misbehave at home."

"I hope not. I fear that violent passion of hers might tempt him."

"No, no. It is true he has been rather free with the girls. Tamarisk is different. Whatever his inclinations he would curb them where she is concerned."

"The feeling might come over him. After all she is there, his willing slave. She is old for her years . . . precocious . . . growing up fast."

Edward shook his head. "Jonathan would show restraint, I am sure. He is a decent fellow at heart."

Oh Edward, I thought, you believe the best of everyone.

What would you say if you knew your wife had thrown restraint to the winds in a house in Blore Street, that she has betrayed you not once but several times with this man who is now a guest in your house?

There was an innocence about Edward. He was like Amaryllis in a way. He believed in the goodness of people. Such as they were aroused a protective instinct. I never wanted Edward to know the truth about me. I vowed that he never should. I remembered fleetingly the occasion when Peter had come across us arm in arm in Blore Street. Peter might not be very observant, having other matters on his mind, but everyone might not be the same.

There was only one way to ensure Edward's never finding out that he had an unfaithful wife. So far we had been undetected. We must never let there be a chance of our betraying our guilty secret.

I remembered what a big part Leah had played in our story. She had come into our household and now seemed like one of the ordinary servants. She was an excellent nurse for Tamarisk and I often wondered what I should have done without her. She was quiet, they said below stairs, and kept herself to herself. She was not interested in the young men although many would be ready to take notice of her with a little encouragement. It was whispered that she was afraid of them because of an "experience" she had once had.

We knew what that experience was for it had nearly cost her saviour his life and he had paid for his part in the affair with seven years in a penal settlement.

And now she would come face to face with him.

She was there when they returned from their ride. I had prepared her for I thought that was wise. She had turned very pale and then flushed.

She said: "It was a long time ago."

"Yes," I agreed.

"I never forgot what he did for me."

"Of course you wouldn't."

And there they were. He was rather flushed from the ride; his eyes were alight with pleasure. I think he was rather intrigued by his daughter. Tamarisk looked like a handsome boy in her riding clothes; she was a daughter of whom he could be proud.

"We had a lovely ride, Leah," said Tamarisk. "We raced. He beat me . . . but only just."

"Leah," he said. "Little Leah."

He went to her and took both her hands. She lifted her eyes to his and I saw the adoration there. It moved me deeply.

"So you are looking after my daughter?"

She nodded. There were tears in her eyes. She said: "I have thought of you."

"I've thought of you too, Leah," he answered gently.

"What you did for me . . ."

"It was long . . . long ago."

"And they blamed you. They were going to hang you . . ."

"But here I am . . . hale and hearty."

"You're gentry now," she said. "You were never one of us."

"It wasn't for lack of trying."

I thought I ought to go and leave them together. I felt as though I were prying on Leah's emotion.

"Come, Tamarisk," I said. Strangely enough she obeyed me.

She ran off to see that her horse was all right. I went into the garden . . . out to the shrubbery. I felt I wanted to get away from the scene of reunion.

I wondered if Leah loved him. She had made a hero of him, that much I knew. She had lured his child away from her home because she must have wanted something which was part of him. She loved Tamarisk devotedly.

And what were his feelings for Leah? He had spoken to her very tenderly. He had cared for the innocent young girl in the days when he had first gone to the gypsies. He had been overcome with fury when he had come upon that brute intent on rape. He had lashed out in that fury and it had nearly cost him his life.

How would he feel about Leah now? I was aware of the stirrings of jealousy.

He was susceptible to women, I was sure. I remembered Dolly dancing round the bonfire. Dolly had loved him, and how had he felt about her? He pitied her, I think, but there must have been some desire; and he had lightheartedly given way to it. How lighthearted had he been such a little while ago in a house in Blore Street?

And Leah? When she had been a gypsy girl and he had come among them, had she thought it possible that one day there might have been a match between them? It could have happened. Now, of course, everything was different with him. He was a country gentleman and Leah could have no place in his life. Or could she?

And in any case, what part could I have? Nothing but a secret one.

He must have seen me go into the shrubbery for he found me there.

"At last," he said, "we are alone."

I had sat down on the wooden seat there and he was beside me, very close. I was deeply stirred as I always was by his proximity.

I said: "Poor Leah was deeply moved."

"Yes, she was. It brought it all back to her. When I saw her again I was glad I killed that devil. She was such a gentle girl."

"She still is and she has been wonderful with Tamarisk. If Tamarisk went to live with you in Cornwall, Leah would have to go with her."

"Tamarisk won't leave you. I'm a newcomer. She's not sure of me yet. Jessica, couldn't we be alone . . . somewhere . . . together . . ."

"Here?" I cried. "In this house? Oh, no . . . no."

"It is hard for me to see you here . . . so near and yet so remote."

"That is how it has to be."

"You'll come to London?"

"Yes . . . no . . ."

He smiled at me teasingly. "You'll come. You must, Jessica, we'll work out something. We can't just go on like this."

"I cannot see any other way of going on."

"There are ways. There are always ways . . ."

"You mean secret meetings. Clandestine . . . furtive meetings . . ."

"We must take what we can."

"It should never have gone so far."

"It was inevitable."

"Tell me about Leah."

"What of her?"

"How was she . . . coming face to face with you like that?"

"Deeply moved, I think."

"*I* think she loves you."

"She is grateful to me."

"And you?"

"I am fond of her."

"Do you love her? She is a beautiful girl."

"She is. But I love one only . . . now and for ever."

For a moment I lay against him and then I remembered that I was near the house and that at any moment someone might come out. I stood up and he was beside me, his arms round me. He kissed me tenderly and then with passion.

"Not here . . ." I said, which was an admission that it could be somewhere else.

"When will you come to London?"

"As soon as it is possible," I said.

"Perhaps you could bring Tamarisk. She ought to be with her father."

"She is very sharp. What if she saw . . ."

"We'd be careful."

I said: "It must stop."

I withdrew myself and came out of the shrubbery with him beside me. He was holding my arm tightly.

I looked towards the house and wondered if anyone was watching.

Jake's visit was declared to have been a great success.

"I like him," said my father. "He's lively."

My mother liked him too, but she was a little reserved when speaking of him and I wondered if she guessed that my feelings for him went deeper than was wise.

He had suggested that Tamarisk visit him in London. There was so much there that he wanted to show her. Then he thought it would be a good idea if she went to Cornwall.

She must remember that he was her father and that his home could be hers if she wished, I told her.

She said: "I like it here." And she was looking at Jonathan who happened to be there.

The great concern now was Amaryllis. Her time was getting near and Claudine was fussing, as Dickon said, like an old hen.

"Amaryllis is a healthy girl, and women were meant to have children. Why all this fuss?"

"There speaks the arrogant man," said my mother. "Naturally Claudine is fussing. All mothers do. I'm fussing and we shall continue to fuss until we have the baby. As for you, I remember you fussed a little when Jessica was born.''

"I must have known that she would not be content to make a quiet and ordinary appearance.''

"Well, you were wrong. She did. Jessica, you were such an adorable baby . . . right from the first.''

"A squalling brat as far as I remember,'' said my father.

"Whom you adored from the moment she was born.''

That was how they always were, sparring in a way which betrayed their love for each other.

How fortunate they were! I thought. Aunt Sophie had always said my mother had been one of the lucky ones. Yet she had at first been denied the man of her choice and made a not entirely satisfactory marriage; and she had passed through a horrifying experience coming close to death in a most frightening manner during the revolution in France . . . and only finally to this happy state at Eversleigh.

Poor Aunt Sophie, who had always pitied herself and never learned that one has to make the most of what one has.

I was always telling myself that—particularly now. I had married Edward—good kind Edward—and it was my duty to care for him and shield him from all hurt.

I must learn to like this way of life, to stop dreaming of the impossible, to forget that I had stepped over the bounds of morality and convention . . . and never, never stray again.

I was with Amaryllis a great deal during those days when she was awaiting the birth of her child, wishing that I could have one. I must not wish for that—for if I did it could not be my husband's.

I could only sit with Amaryllis and play with Helena.

Poor Amaryllis. She was rather long in labour but the great moment came and I could imagine her joy when she was coming out of her exhaustion and heard the cry of her child. And this one was a boy.

There was great rejoicing throughout the household. I had never seen Peter so delighted. What a store these men set by boys! I felt a little annoyed though I joined in the general rejoicing.

Amaryllis was so proud. She lay in her bed, pale, looking fragile, but beautiful with that radiance on her which I had seen at the time of her marriage.

It was mean of me to feel those twinges of envy. Yet I could not help myself.

She has so much, I said to myself. And what have I? Guilty memories.

I must pull myself together. I must never become like Aunt Sophie . . . bitter because life had passed me by. I had chosen the way I should go. Of course it was not always one's fault that life took a certain turn. Was it Sophie's fault that she had been disfigured in that fireworks disaster? Was it Edward's fault that he had been cruelly injured? But we must not nurse our misfortunes. Someone had said never take them out and teach them to swim. Take them out and drown them. I must remember that.

I kissed Amaryllis.

"I feel I am the luckiest woman on earth," she said.

"What are you going to call him?"

"Peter," she said promptly. "After his father."

"Does Peter want that?"

"Yes. And I do too."

So the child was called Peter and because it was a little confusing to have two Peters in the household, he was soon known as Peterkin.

My father was undoubtedly delighted with the boy.

"At last," he said. "A man in this household of women!"

"Don't you call David and Jonathan men?" I asked.

"David will never have a son. As for Jonathan . . . well, I'm uncertain about him."

"You're unfair to him," said my mother.

"Unfair? In what way?"

"Just because of that gambling business and Farmer Weston's girl."

"He's got to behave himself if he takes on Eversleigh."

"All young men sow wild oats."

"Not on their own patch of land."

"Well, the gambling took place in London."

"That could affect the estate more than anything. It's the first step on the downward path."

"Dickon, please, not another lecture on the dangers of gambling."

"Too much can't be said about it."

"You have already made that plain. Well, now you have your great-grandson and you are very pleased. You should be grateful to Amaryllis . . ."

"I wish Jessica . . ."

She silenced him. "Let's go and have a look at Peterkin."

It was amusing to see my father marching round the nursery with Peterkin in his arms.

"The master just dotes on that child," they said throughout the household.

And they were right.

The christening of little Peterkin caused the usual flutter in the household. Christening robes were brought out and examined; and there was a great deal of discussion as to the guests who would be invited.

The Barringtons came from Nottingham, Clare with them. I always felt uneasy in Clare's presence and often thought how much wiser Edward would have been if he had married her. I was sure she would have been a faithful wife; and there was no doubt in my mind that she loved him. Men so often chose the wrong women . . . as a servant had once told me.

Jake had prolonged his visit but he could not stay with us indefinitely. He had departed most reluctantly after extorting a promise from me to go to London as soon as the christening was over.

"Bring Tamarisk," he said. "I should get to know my own daughter. Or . . . I shall come back here. Bless the child. She gives me the excuse I need for visiting you."

He took our affair more lightheartedly than I did. Well he might. He was not deceiving anyone . . . as I was.

I loved his dominating nature while I deplored it. I kept telling myself that it was one lapse on my part and it must never happen again.

The ceremony went off very well. Peterkin behaved with unusual decorum and was duly christened. I don't know who was more proud of him—his father or mine.

They had their precious boy.

Amaryllis looked beautiful. She was radiantly happy. Lucky Amaryllis, for whom life ran so smoothly.

There was a reception in the great hall at Eversleigh and the usual toasts were drunk. Peterkin, by this time, was sleeping in his cot and several of the guests were taken up to admire him. I was with them. The old Eversleigh nursery had new life in it. Helena was there seated on the floor building a castle with bricks. The perfect domestic scene, I thought enviously.

Mrs. Barrington noticed my looks, I think. She took my hand and pressed it.

"I want to have a talk with you, dear," she said. "When we are alone."

Alarm shot through me which was due to the sensitivity of a guilty conscience. Whenever anyone spoke to me in that way, I imagined that something had been discovered.

The moment came.

She said: "Sit down, dear. I'm a little worried."

"Oh? What about?"

"About you, my dear. You look a little drawn."

"Drawn?"

"Not quite yourself. I think you must be very tired."

"Oh no, I'm not in the least tired."

She patted my hand.

"You've been wonderful. We never cease to talk about you and all you have done for Edward. I know how fond of him you are . . . but I think you are getting a little tired."

"You mean . . ."

"I just mean that you are here all the time . . . and you must get really worn out."

"Oh no . . . no. I've been to London. I went for the Waterloo celebrations. Edward insisted that I did and so I went."

"I understand, dear. But I think you need help. That is why we have decided that Clare shall stay here . . . to help you."

"Clare?"

"Why not? She is like a sister to Edward. They are fond of each other."

"I know she has always been fond of Edward."

"And he of her. But it is you I am thinking of, my dear. It will give you a little respite."

"It is not necessary."

The last thing I wanted was for Clare to come here. I always felt she had been resentful of me. I thought: She will be watchful. And I could not afford to be closely watched. She would try to find fault with me. Heaven knew that should not be difficult.

I protested again, but Mrs. Barrington had made up her mind.

"Do you know," she went on, "being forced to go back to Nottingham has put new life into us both. Father didn't really want to retire. It was those mobs that upset him. Well, that's quietened down now. The punishment was getting so severe that they thought better of making all that trouble."

"Yes," I said, thinking of the man, Fellows, who had been hanged for what he had done.

"So you see, we can do without Clare quite easily. She will help with Edward."

"It is so kind of you, but I really can manage quite well."

"I know you can, dear. But Clare will stay and I'll send on what she needs."

There was only one thing to do and that was thank her graciously.

There were letters from Jake—one for me, one for Tamarisk.

He had written what could only be called a love letter, telling me how lonely it was in London without me. He would have to go to Cornwall, he supposed, and he would hate to be so far away. Suppose he asked me to bring Tamarisk for a visit? Since I had given him such irrefutable proof of my love, he could not do without me. He lived over and over again those hours we had spent in Blore Street and separation was unendurable.

I read the letter and put it away. I knew I should want to read it again and again.

Tamarisk was pleased with her letter, and although she assumed an indifference I believed she was really delighted to find herself with a father. I think she was a little fascinated by him.

"Would you like to go to London?" I asked her, trying to keep the lilt out of my voice.

"I don't mind," she said, coolly but with her eyes sparkling at the prospect.

"Your father thinks it would be a good idea if I took you. You would like that, wouldn't you?"

"I don't mind," she repeated.

I decided I would talk the matter over with my mother. The prospect of a visit to London always excited her. She said she thought it was a good idea and Tamarisk ought to see more of her father.

"It might well be that he will want to take her," said my mother.

"You mean to live with him?"

"Why not? It would be natural."

"I wonder if Tamarisk would want to go."

"She could take Leah with her."

The thought of Leah in Cornwall and myself miles away at Grasslands tormented me. Beautiful Leah who, I was sure, was either in love with Jake or ready to be.

"I don't think she would want to leave Jonathan," went on my mother, "although it might be a good idea if she did."

"You're a little worried about her penchant for Jonathan."

"I would call it more than a penchant. A grand passion, more likely. She's an intense little thing and Jonathan . . . well, let's face it . . . he's not the most stable of young men. He seems to enjoy that adoration she gives him."

"We all like to be admired."

"She's growing up fast."

"Oh, she's a child."

"Some girls don't remain children long. Your father has misgivings about Jonathan."

"Because of that gambling incident."

"That was the start. No . . . I suppose the farmer's daughter was that. But he has got off to a bad start. Your father thinks a great deal about the estate nowadays . . . more than he used to."

"David looks after it magnificently."

"Yes . . . but David hasn't a son. Now there is little Peterkin, bless him."

"Dear Mother, is Father planning to teach him estate management in his cradle?"

"No. But it has made a lot of difference. He feels if Jonathan is unsatisfactory there is little Peterkin to follow."

"I think Jonathan will be all right."

"He is so like his father."

"A very fascinating gentleman, by all accounts."

"Supposed to be. David is the solid one . . . and that's what your father wants."

"I gather he himself was not unlike his son, Jonathan, and that must mean that his grandson Jonathan is a little like him too."

"Your father is unique. He could live recklessly and at the same time get to the top of whatever he undertook. I do wish he and Jonathan got on better. However, what about this trip to London? It should be easier for you now that Clare is with you."

I found it hard to hide my eagerness.

"I could go quite soon," I said.

"I think your father wants to go. He wants Jonathan to meet someone up there. So we might all go again. Amaryllis wouldn't want to. I wonder she doesn't take a trip with Peter now and then. He is always up and down."

"It's all those business interests, but of course she hates to leave the children."

So it was arranged.

When I told Clare I was planning to go, she said I need not worry about leaving Edward so soon after my last visit. She would see that everything went well. I said I was grateful to her and she replied that that was what she had come for—to give me a change now and then.

"A respite," she said, and there was a little curl to her lips which I tried not to notice.

The outcome was that we set out once more for London—my mother, my father, Tamarisk and myself in the carriage and Jonathan following us on horseback.

When we arrived at the house in Albemarle Street I noticed the new maid at once. Servants were apt to come and go in London. The housekeeper engaged them. Young girls often married after a short stay in the house and disappeared. In the country, if they married, it was usually someone on the estate and often meant that they continued working for us.

Prue Parker was the sort of girl one noticed because she was pretty in a rather gentle way. She had a demure manner. The housekeeper said that she was exceedingly shy, but she thought in time she would "shape up."

I noticed Jonathan give her a second glance. He was like that with all young women. Weighing up their accessibility I called it.

Jake visited us on the day of our arrival.

"So eager to see your daughter?" said my mother.

"And delighted to see you . . . all," he added.

He dined with us. He said he had paid a quick visit to Cornwall since he had last seen us and would have to go back there soon, but he would be in London for some little while yet; and he hoped during that time to get to know his daughter better.

He took her out the next day. He invited me to accompany them but I declined, saying that I must shop with my mother. But the following day Jonathan took Tamarisk for a trip on the river and there was our opportunity.

Of course I should have resisted it. I meant to, but my

resistance crumbled and there I was as I had been before in that house in Blore Street, quite abandoned to my love.

He said that our separation had been unbearable. He made all sorts of wild plans and I let myself imagine that there might be possibilities of their coming to pass.

But how could there be? I was married to Edward. There was no way out for me.

I wondered how long he would wait. He was a very impatient man. He chafed against frustration more than I did. At least I had my guilt to hold me back.

When I looked ahead I saw years of secret meetings like this, years of frustrated longing and even when those longings were satisfied they were accompanied by the heavy weight of guilt.

"How I wish we need never leave here," he said. "If we could stay here for ever . . . just the two of us . . ."

I reminded him: "You are forgetting this visit was arranged so that you could see your daughter."

"And Jonathan has obligingly taken her off our hands."

A thought struck me then. Obligingly? Could it possibly be that Jonathan *knew*? Was he helping us to be together? That was just the sort of thing he would do. Jonathan, at least, would understand.

But the very thought of anyone's sharing our secret alarmed me.

I was restless . . . even in moments of intense passion. Then I thought of Amaryllis so secure in her domestic happiness. Oh happy Amaryllis!

I said: "We can't go on like this."

But he just looked at me and smiled. He knew—as I knew—that we would whenever the opportunity offered itself. More than that, he being the man he was would make those opportunities.

As we came out of the house I saw a man standing on the street corner. He turned and started to walk away in the opposite direction. I fancied I had seen him in this street before. It could have been on my last visit to London. I did not give him a second thought then.

We walked slowly back to the house.

We had retired for the night. I was very tired and went to sleep almost immediately to be awakened suddenly by the sound of shouts and footsteps. I hurriedly put on a dressing gown and slippers and went into the corridor. I could hear someone crying. It sounded like a woman's voice; and the noise was coming from my parents' room.

I ran to it and there I stopped short. My father was red faced and angry. Jonathan was there in a state of undress as though he had just got out of bed hurriedly; and with her bodice torn and a scratch on her neck was Prue the new parlourmaid. Great sobs shook her body and she was trying to cover her breast with her hands.

Jonathan was shouting: "It's a pack of lies. I did not send for her. She came."

"Oh sir . . . oh sir . . ." moaned Prue. "Nobody will believe me."

"Be silent," cried my father. "Do you want to wake the house?"

"Oh sir . . . he sent for me . . . he did . . . on my honour he did . . . and when I come he just got hold of me . . . and tore my bodice. I was frightened."

My father said: "All go to your rooms. We'll talk about this in the morning."

"You won't believe me," wailed Prue. "You'll all say I'm a bad girl . . . I'm not. I'm a good girl. I never done nothing . . ."

"You won't be condemned without reason," said my father, glaring at Jonathan. "But this is not the time."

My mother got out of bed and put on her dressing gown.

"Come with me, Prue," she said. "You should go to bed. We'll hear all about it in the morning."

"The girl's a brazen liar," said Jonathan.

"Hold your tongue!" cried my father. "And get out. Lottie, can you do something about this girl?"

I went over to her. "Come on, Prue," I said. "You can tell me all about it."

She lifted her face to mine. "I never . . . I swear I never."

"All right," I said, "all right. Which is your room?"

"I share with Dot and Emily."

"Well, first of all we'll tidy you up a little."

My mother looked relieved. "Will you see to it, Jessica?"

"Yes," I said.

Jonathan caught my arm.

"I swear, Jessica, she came to me."

"Look, Jonathan," I said. "It's late. We don't want to

wake all the servants. Go to your room. It can all be sorted out in the morning.''

"It was a trick."

"All right. But go now."

I could see my father was getting more and more angry and that his anger was directed at Jonathan, and I felt I must put an end to the scene as soon as possible.

I managed to get Jonathan and the girl outside. Then I saw Tamarisk.

"What's happened?" she cried.

"Nothing," I said. "Go back to bed."

She looked at Jonathan. "Are you all right?" she asked.

He nodded, smiling at her.

She ran to him and caught his arm. "You look funny."

"Angry," he said.

"Not with me?"

"Of course not."

"With Jessica?"

He shook his head.

"Why is Prue's blouse torn? Why is she crying?"

"Never mind now."

She clung to his arm. "Are they trying to hurt you?"

"Yes, they are."

"I won't let them."

"No, of course you won't."

"Jonathan," I said. "Go to your room. You, too, Tamarisk. We'll meet in the morning. Come along with me, Prue."

I took her into my room and firmly shut the door.

I said: "We'll wash your face and tidy you up a bit. Tell me exactly what happened."

"It was my turn for late duty. I was just going to bed when the bell rang for Mr. Jonathan's room."

"Yes?"

"So I went up, Mrs. Barrington."

"And what happened then?"

"He said, 'Come in.' He was in bed. He said, 'Come over here, Prue.' So I went to the bed. Then he got hold of me and pulled me down. I knew that I had to get away. I started screaming and fighting. He was very angry. But I got away and ran to Mr. and Mrs. Frenshaw's room because I reckoned that was where I could be safe from him. They won't believe me, Mrs. Barrington. They'll believe him.''

"They'll want to know the truth and that is what they'll believe."

"But I'm only the maid and he . . . and he . . . Oh, they won't believe me. They'll say I'm a bad girl . . . They'll send me away and I won't get a reference . . ."

"Now listen to me, Prue. In the morning there'll be questions. If you answer up truthfully you will be believed."

She shook her head. "They won't . . ."

"Oh yes, they will. Now let us bathe your face."

She stood still, her face full of misery. I bathed her eyes.

"There," I said briskly. "That's better. How badly torn your bodice is. Do you think you could slip into your room without the others noticing?"

She nodded.

"Well, do that. Go quietly. They'll probably be asleep. And in the morning we'll sort it all out."

"It's no good. What's my voice against his . . . He's one of the family . . ."

"That won't make any difference with Mr. Frenshaw. He will find out the truth and see that justice is done."

"Thank you, Mrs. Barrington," she said quietly.

I took her to the corridor and watched her go upstairs.

Oh, Jonathan, I thought, how foolish you are!

Next morning there was consternation in the house. Prue had left.

Dot came to tell me, her eyes wide with that excited horror which some people betray when they are the bearers of bad news.

"She's gone, Mrs. Barrington. Clean gone. Took all her things, she has. We never heard nothing . . . me and Emily. Her bed wasn't slept in. I reckon she crept out like . . . so's we shouldn't hear."

Poor Prue, I thought. She couldn't face the shame of it. She was so convinced that she would not be believed.

My father was furious when he heard. "I've just about had enough of that young man," he said.

"You haven't heard the whole story yet," I reminded him. "You're jumping to conclusions."

"A pretty clear conclusion, I would say."

"On the face of it."

"You're standing up for him. Can't you see he has been caught redhanded this time?"

The scene between him and Jonathan was violent. I thought they might have come to blows. Then my mother went in to intervene.

When Jonathan came out he looked quite unlike himself.

He said to me: "I suppose you share the general view?"

"What's that?"

"That I tried to rape the girl."

"Did you?"

"I swear I didn't."

"What was she doing in your bedroom?"

"Ask her. She came in. I didn't send for her."

"She said you did."

"Then she's a liar."

"Do you mean she just walked in?"

"That's it. I was half asleep."

"And . . . she offered herself?"

"I suppose it was like that. I didn't have time to think. I was half asleep, I tell you. Jessica, like the rest you won't believe me, but I'm innocent of this."

"If you tell me so I'll believe you, Jonathan."

"Well, I am telling you."

"What did she do it for?"

"Ask me something simple."

"A victim to your fatal charm? She seemed a quiet girl. Shy, they said."

"They are sometimes the worst . . . or the best . . . it depends which way you look at it."

"Jonathan, this is terrible. You know what my father is like."

"Not my most devoted admirer at the best of times."

"The trouble is you are too like him."

"You would think that would make for understanding. I am sure he was not exactly a paragon of virtue in his young days. What is so maddening, Jessica, is to be blamed for something you haven't done when I suppose there are so many things for which one could be blamed."

"This will pass."

"The wretched girl has gone. I wanted to have it out with her face to face."

"I wonder why she ran away."

"Too shy to face the enquiry, they said. Guilty, that's what."

"I don't think they'll see it like that."

"You can bet they won't. I shall be branded yet again."

"Never mind. It will blow over. These things often do."

"If I don't get sent packing in the meantime."

"Oh no . . ."

"The old man is in a fury. Just another little nail in the coffin of the heir of Eversleigh. I seem to have some evil spirit dogging me. When you think of that letter some snake sent about my gambling spree . . . it makes me wonder. And now this."

"That girl can't have anything to do with your gambling. And I daresay there are little peccadilloes which don't always come to light."

I had managed to produce a smile.

Tamarisk came running up. She seized Jonathan's arm.

"What are they going to do to you?" she asked.

"Hound me."

"What's that?"

"Lining up against me."

"Who? Jessica?"

"No. Jessica is a pal, I believe."

"I'm your pal."

"I know that, Gypsy."

"I'll always be your friend and I'll hate anyone who isn't."

"What could be fairer than that!"

"Is it that girl, Prue?"

"She's gone away," I said.

"Where to?"

"That is a mystery," I told her. "Jonathan, go for a ride. There's nothing like a gallop to take your mind off these things."

"I'll come with you," said Tamarisk.

"All right," replied Jonathan. "Come on."

We left London. The affair of Jonathan and Prue had ruined the visit. My father was in a black mood and neither my mother nor I could charm him out of it.

Amaryllis rode over to Grasslands and Peter came with her. It was rarely that I saw them together and rarer still that he had time to pay visits.

Edward was with us in his chair.

James had, some time before, suggested that he occupy a bedroom on the ground floor, so that it would be easy for him to get into the garden if he wished to do so. This had proved to be an excellent idea and it gave Edward opportunities of getting about more easily.

We sat in the drawing room drinking tea.

It was a warm October day and the French windows were wide open. The smell of burning leaves floated in to us and every now and then I saw a man pass to and fro, a long fork in his hand, picking up leaves and conveying them to the bonfire.

This was Toby Mann—a newcomer to the gardening staff. Old Robert, whom the Barringtons had brought with them from Nottingham, had died and Toby had come along at the right moment and taken the job. I had heard he was a very good worker. He did a little boxing and was known as the Champion by the servants. I was thinking of Jake, as I often did, and wondering if he was thinking of me. Was he planning to go to Cornwall? How I wished I could go with him! Should I take Tamarisk for a visit? How could I? It was too far away. If Tamarisk went Leah would have to go with her. That thought filled me with misgivings. Leah had been very fond of Jake. I expected she still was. She was a very beautiful woman and would be single-minded in her devotion.

Amaryllis was talking animatedly about her children and I fancied Peter listened with a kind of indulgent impatience. Perhaps he had heard accounts of their extraordinary prowess before.

He said suddenly: "Poor Jonathan seems a little melancholy these days."

"It was that affair in London," said Amaryllis. "You were there, weren't you, Jessica?"

"Yes," I said.

"Do you think your father will send him back to Pettigrew Hall?" asked Peter.

"I don't think so. It will blow over."

"There is little sign of it at the moment," said Amaryllis. "Oh, I do wish they did not have to have all these quarrels."

"A little discord I suppose is inevitable in the best regulated families," said Peter. "What was the girl like, Jessica? I don't remember ever seeing her at the house."

"*You* wouldn't notice her," said Amaryllis almost teasingly.

"I confess I never did."

"She hadn't been there long. I thought she looked quiet and rather shy," I said.

"And young Jonathan took advantage of that, eh?"

"He swears he didn't."

"Well, I suppose he would, wouldn't he?"

"Not Jonathan. He's amazingly frank. He told me seriously that she had come into his room of her own accord."

"Why should she do that?" asked Amaryllis.

"Because, my dear, Jonathan is a very personable young man," Peter explained. "That's so, is it not, Jessica?"

"I don't know much about these matters. If you say so, I suppose it is."

"Well, his allure got him into serious trouble this time. I somehow don't think it is going to blow over."

"He is the heir, after David," I said.

"Don't forget we have our little Peterkin now. That has undermined the dashing Jonathan's claim to the throne somewhat."

Edward said: "It's a sad business. From what I understand on the face of it, it would seem that he summoned the girl . . . but things are often not what they seem."

He was looking ahead of him and I felt a twinge of alarm. I was beginning to look for double meanings in all his remarks.

"It wouldn't surprise me," put in Peter, "and perhaps it would be a good thing, if Jonathan was asked to slip gracefully out."

"I agree with Jessica. He is the heir. After all his father would presumably have had a share in Eversleigh had he lived. Jonathan could become quite steady once he has his responsibilities."

I smiled at Edward. He was so balanced in his judgments, and he always had a special word for the oppressed. It was hard to think of Jonathan in that category, but in this instance he was generally looked upon as the one to blame.

I said: "My mother and I are rather concerned about the girl. We have been wondering where she went when she left the house."

"Poor child," said Peter. "I do think this will set his grandfather against Jonathan more than ever."

Tea was brought. I served our guests and then took Edward's over to him. He smiled at me tenderly.

There was a little shelf which could be placed across the chair and which we found very useful. This had been set up and I placed the cup on it. But as I turned away my sleeve must have caught in the shelf and the cup went over; the shelf was dragged off the chair. Edward made an effort to save it and fell from the chair to the floor.

I cried out in dismay. Peter dashed over. Edward lay on the floor, looking very pale and I guessed he was in pain.

I said: "Call James. He knows the right way to lift Edward."

Peter was trying to help Edward to rise and I could see we needed James' expert hands.

He came to us and his face was creased in consternation when he saw Edward. He half lifted him and then gave a little cry. Edward was back on the floor and James was writhing in agony.

"What's happened, James?" I asked.

"I've strained something. It's my back. I can't move without excruciating pain."

"Let me help," said Peter.

"It needs two," said James.

"Toby is outside," I cried. "I'll get him." I ran to the window where I could see Toby wreathed in the smoke from the bonfire.

"Toby," I cried, "come quickly."

He came running and, taking one look at Edward, he saw at once what was required of him.

"We want to get Mr. Barrington into his chair, Toby," said James.

"Right," said Toby. Peter stood by. "Best manage on my own, sir," added Toby and, with the greatest of ease it seemed, he picked up Edward and sat him gently in his chair.

"Edward," I said, "are you all right?"

"Yes, quite. It's poor James I'm thinking of."

James face was white and I saw the sweat glistening on his skin. He said: "It'll pass."

He was about to wheel Edward's chair across the room. I said: "I am sure Toby would do that. You're going to find it difficult, James. Do you know what's happened?"

"I've done it before. It can come suddenly. But it will pass. All I need is a little rest."

"Then for heaven's sake take it. What about Toby's coming to give you a hand?"

Toby smiled: "I'd like that, Mrs. Barrington."

"I thought you were so fond of your work in the garden?"

"I am . . . but if I could be of more use . . ."

"You could, I believe. The others can weed and make bonfires. James, you ought to rest I'm sure. And Edward, you've had a shock. You go along and help with Mr. Barrington, Toby.''

James looked relieved, though a little ashamed of himself for being so weak as to have an ailment. He was the sort of man who would pretend it didn't exist.

Peter said: ''Let me help.''

''We can manage, sir,'' said Toby, his expression showing the delight he felt to be of such use.

''I'll come with you, Edward,'' I said. And to the others: ''Excuse me.''

Edward said. ''No. You stay. Don't fuss, Jessica. I'll be perfectly all right.''

I nodded. I always obeyed Edward on such occasions.

The door closed on them.

''Poor Edward,'' said Peter.

''It is so sad,'' murmured Amaryllis, no doubt comparing my barren life with her fruitful one.

''It was good that the bonfire man appeared so fortuitously,'' said Peter.

''He seemed very eager to help,'' added Amaryllis.

And as I sat there, the smell of burning leaves permeating the air, and talked in a desultory way, I thought how fortunate they were to have met, loved and married and to have two beautiful children to prove the success of their union.

Then I looked ahead to my own future. As far as I could see it would go on like this for ever.

Edward was none the worse for his fall. He said he was pleased that it had happened because it had brought Toby in to help James. He had been anxious about James for some time.

''I knew I was too heavy for him to lift,'' he said.

''Toby seems a very pleasant young man.''

''Yes. Very eager to help. I feel a great burden. There are you, James, and Clare . . . and now Toby all waiting on one useless cripple. But you are the one I worry about most. Sometimes I feel it is too much for you.''

''What nonsense is all this?''

''You . . . young . . . beautiful . . . tied to me. It seems so wrong.''

''Please, Edward, you promised me not to talk like this. I chose this, didn't I?''

''Sometimes people make rash choices and then they are

stuck with them. It's no life for you, Jessica. I was thinking of Amaryllis. There she is a happy wife and mother."

"I wouldn't change places."

"You are so good, Jessica."

I thought: If only he knew! I was almost on the point of telling him, of trying to explain. I love you, Edward, but I love Jake in a different way. It isn't anything to do with your being crippled. I love Jake as I can never love anyone else. I'm not the same person when I am with him. Everything becomes exciting and wonderful.

How could I tell him that?

He was right. I had chosen this way. In a moment of pique I had chosen it. And now it was my life.

His next words startled me. "What about that man . . . Tamarisk's father?"

"What . . . what of him?" I asked faintly.

"What is going to happen about him?"

"What do you mean?"

"Is Tamarisk going to live with him?"

"I think she ought to be given time to decide."

"Is he agreeable to that? Did you see much of him when you were in London?"

"Oh yes. He came to dine with us, and Tamarisk was with him quite a few times."

"Do you think she will want to go with him?"

"I think she is getting fond of him but she is so devoted to Jonathan."

"Yes. That's almost a love affair, isn't it? It's surprising that the young can have these fierce feelings."

"Tamarisk is fierce in her emotions."

"I expect it's a phase."

"I think it is what will make her want to stay here. She wants to be where Jonathan is."

"Time is the answer."

"You mean . . . don't rush into anything."

"Exactly. Let her see as much of her father as she can. I suppose he would like to be asked down here."

"He might find it difficult to leave London. I believe he has business there, and he also has that estate in Cornwall. Perhaps something will be decided soon."

"In the meantime all you can do is take her to London to see him."

"Y-yes. I shall want to go up before Christmas. Will you be all right?"

"Certainly. I have all these people to take care of me."

"You don't mind my going?"

"I miss you, of course. I miss you very much, but on the other hand I get a comfortable sort of feeling that at least you are getting a little respite. I know how much you enjoy those visits to London. You always come back rejuvenated."

My deceit weighed heavily on me. But at the same time I was thrilled at the prospect of another visit to London.

I asked Tamarisk if she would like to go again. She wanted to know if Jonathan was going. I said I did not know. I thought he might not be eager to after the last disastrous visit.

"What happened about that girl?" asked Tamarisk.

"What girl?"

"Prue, of course. What was Jonathan supposed to have done to her?"

"Jonathan says he did nothing."

"Then he didn't. So why was there all that fuss?"

"Oh . . . it's all over now."

She stamped her foot. "It's not over. Great-Grandpapa Frenshaw is very cross with Jonathan and he might not leave him Eversleigh."

Where did she learn such things? Listening at doors, I supposed, slyly questioning the servants. I knew she would be adept at that.

She went on: "That girl came into his bedroom. He didn't send for her."

"Who told you that?"

"Never mind," she said severely. "It's not the point. She came in and he didn't send for her. Then she blamed him and said he tore her clothes. She was lying."

"It's all over now," I said. "We don't want to worry about it any more."

"I want to know the truth. I'm going to make Prue Parker tell the truth."

"Prue Parker has gone. We shall never see her again."

"She must be somewhere."

"Listen," I said, "do you want to go up to London to see your father?"

"Yes."

"Very well, then. We'll go."

* * *

David and Claudine came with us this time. Neither of them really wished to leave Eversleigh, but there were some products which David had to buy. Peter was already in London. He had left some days before—on urgent business, he said.

When we arrived at the house in Albemarle Street he was there.

I could not stem the exuberance which was rising in me. I should see Jake. It would be difficult to be alone with him because there was Tamarisk to be looked after. It had been different when Jonathan was there to take her off my hands.

Jake was delighted to see us. Tamarisk asked a good many questions about his home in Cornwall which made me think she might be considering going there. There was no doubt that she was rather fascinated by him. Who would not be by Jake?

There was an occasion when Tamarisk was out of the room and we had a few words together.

"When?" he asked.

"It's difficult," I replied. "There is Tamarisk . . ."

"If you could come one evening."

"I can hardly do that."

"We could say we were at a concert . . . a theatre . . . Who is with you?"

"David and Claudine."

"They would not be as watchful as your mother. I fancied sometimes she was . . . aware."

"She may well have been. She is aware of a good deal . . . particularly when it concerns me."

"This is too frustrating," he said. "We shall be together. I can't stay here just waiting for you to come to me. I'll find some reason why you have to be here."

"No . . . not in this house. It seems too great a betrayal."

"We'll stay in an inn . . . I'll rent a house . . ."

I shook my head.

"What are we going to do, Jessica?"

"The wise thing would be to say goodbye. If Tamarisk would go with you to Cornwall that would be a solution."

"And never see you . . . or rarely!"

"There isn't anything for us, Jake."

"Nonsense. You love me. I love you."

"It's too late. Someone once said that life was a matter of

being in a certain place when the time was right. The time was wrong for us."

"My dear Jessica, we have to make it right."

I shook my head. "It is impossible. I couldn't hurt Edward. He relies on me. He has suffered. I can't just use people like that."

"He would understand."

"Yes, he would understand. But understanding doesn't make the hurt less. He would understand too well. I will never leave him."

"And what of me? What of us?"

"We are two strong and healthy people. We have to live our own lives in the best possible way."

"You are condemning us to a life of emptiness."

"You have your daughter. She is an interesting girl. You could find great joy in her, and if she gives you her affection she can be fiercely loyal."

"As she is to Jonathan. Who else?"

I shrugged my shoulders and he went on: "To you? To the people who did so much for her? I agree she is interesting. I should be happy to have her affection . . . if she deigned to give it. But it is not a daughter I crave for. It is you . . . my own love, my Jessica."

"I can't see a way out then. Perhaps in time it will be easier to bear."

"I don't intend to stand aside and let life use me."

"What will you do?"

"I'll find a way."

"You frighten me a little when you talk like that. I think you could be rather ruthless."

"I am sure you are right," he said.

"There is no way . . . except by telling Edward, and I will never do that."

"If he knew he would understand. It is unnatural for you to be condemned to such a life."

"He is my first duty."

"Your duty is stronger than your love?"

"In this case it has to be."

He shook his head. "I will find a way," he repeated.

Tamarisk came into the room.

"Are you talking about me?" she demanded.

"You always imagine people are talking about you. Do you think you are such a fascinating subject?"

"Yes," she said and we all laughed.

When it was time to leave Jake said he would come back with us.

"That is not necessary," I said. "I want to call in at one of the shops and we have not far to go."

He stood at the door waving to us. I was deep in thought remembering his words. He had looked so determined when he had said he would find a way. What could he do? There was only one way: To go to Edward and ask him to release me.

I knew I could never be completely happy again if I did that. Edward would haunt me all the days of my life.

We had turned out of Blore Street when I saw a young woman, some yards ahead of us, hurriedly start to cross the road.

In a second Tamarisk was after her. The woman disappeared round a corner. Tamarisk followed.

What was she doing? I started to run. I did not want her to be alone in the streets of London. She knew her way to Albemarle Street, of course, but how inconsiderate of her to run off suddenly without a word.

I turned the corner. The woman was going into a building. Tamarisk went after her.

I ran as fast as I could.

Then I recognized the building. It was Frinton's Club, that place of ill omen where Jonathan had lost five hundred pounds on his visit.

"Tamarisk!" I shouted. "Where are you going?"

I pushed open the door and went in. There was a hall carpeted in glowing red. The walls were plain white. A man was seated at a desk, staring after Tamarisk's flying figure.

"Where are you . . . ?" he was beginning when he saw me . . . I ignored him. My eyes were on Tamarisk who was disappearing through a door which led from the hall. I followed.

There were people in the room—two men and several women. I stared in bewildered amazement. One of those women was our one-time parlourmaid, Prue Parker. But what a different Prue Parker! Her face was delicately painted and she was smartly dressed in a light navy coat trimmed with fur; her gloves were a delicate grey which matched her shoes. I realized that she was the woman whom Tamarisk had been following.

That was not all. The girl beside her was not unknown to

me. On the other occasion when I had seen her she had been pretending to be blind. Yes, there with Prue Parker was the girl who had led me to that empty house.

But the greatest shock of all was the sight of the man who had risen from his chair and was staring at us as though he could not believe his eyes.

It was Peter Lansdon.

There was a silence, which seemed to go on for a long time. It was as though neither of us could believe what we saw and were trying to come to understanding in our bewildered minds.

He spoke first. "Jessica?" he murmured.

I did not answer. I looked from him to those two women.

"How . . . how did you get in here?" he stammered.

"We walked in," I said.

"It's no place for you."

"No. I daresay not."

"There are explanations I must give you."

"Indeed . . . yes."

He came towards me, quite calm now. Everyone else in the room was silent.

"I'll take you and Tamarisk home," he said.

Tamarisk cried: "I want to take her back." She pointed at Prue. "She lied. She was the one . . . not Jonathan."

"Yes, yes," said Peter soothingly. "I've discovered everything. I'll take you back and tell you all about it. Come along, both of you."

I was summing up the situation. He was involved in this. He knew the blind girl; he knew Prue; he knew these clubs. They were not ordinary clubs, after all. Strange things went on in them. What had I stumbled on?

He took Tamarisk and me by our arms.

Tamarisk was shouting; "You've got to tell them. You've got to tell Grandpa Frenshaw. It wasn't Jonathan. It was Prue. She ought to come back with us. She ought to confess."

"Leave it to me," said Peter. "I'll explain everything. Jonathan shall be cleared."

That satisfied Tamarisk.

I was silent, bewildered and incredulous.

We came out into the street.

He said: "I found the girl. I was trying to help her. She planned the whole thing . . . to compromise Jonathan. She had blackmail in mind of course."

"It's all right now," said Tamarisk. "I wish Jonathan were here. When can we go home and tell him, and tell them all. *I* found her. Wasn't it clever of me? I recognized her by the way she walked . . . because she looked different, didn't she? But I knew her."

We came to the house. Tamarisk ran in at once to tell David and Claudine what had happened.

They listened in a somewhat bewildered fashion while Peter explained calmly that he had discovered Prue Parker and confronted her. She admitted she was trying to compromise Jonathan so that she could extract money from him. Then she became frightened and had run away. Peter said he believed he was going to save her from a shameful existence. He had already found a post for her in a respectable household and had arranged to meet her at the club where she worked to tell her of her good fortune. He was there for this purpose when we burst in on them.

"I saw her," repeated Tamarisk. "I recognized her, Jessica, didn't I?"

"You were very sharp, Tamarisk."

After they had marvelled at the story Claudine said she and David had to call on the Mattons, who particularly wanted to meet Tamarisk. "Will you come with us, Jessica?" asked Claudine.

I said I would prefer to stay at home.

So they went off and as soon as they had gone Peter came to my room.

He stood looking at me almost slyly and then said: "Well?"

"Are there any warehouses?" I asked. "Is there any importation of rum and sugar?"

"There are as a matter of fact."

"And your main business, I believe, is in another kind of house. Not exactly a warehouse. Do they call them whorehouses?"

"An unpleasant term I always thought."

"Why did you want to see me?"

"I have to discover to what conclusions you have come."

"I have been thinking a great deal . . . over our acquaintance, and certain things seem to be becoming clear to me. I hope you have not prepared some intricate fabrication for I shall not believe it."

"I know that. You are very shrewd. I soon became aware of that. I can see the intricate fabrication would soon be

298

pierced by your astuteness, so therefore it would be a waste of time to manufacture it.''

''I believe you are a scheming adventurer.''

''There is no point in denying it.''

''You came into my family because you knew there was money there.''

He nodded.

''I suppose the inn meeting was a chance one?''

''Yes. There I learned who your father was, and also a great deal about the family from the innkeeper.''

''I see, and you decided that his daughter would be a worthy wife. How could you make your entry? My father is a rather suspicious man with many interests in London. Is that how you figured it out?''

''But of course.''

''So we had the little blind girl episode. One of your girls from your warehouses?''

''We were moving out of the premises. That gave us the venue, you might say.''

''What a convenient coincidence that you were there that day with your decoy.''

''Oh, we had waylaid you several times. We were waiting for the opportunity.''

''It was an unusual beginning, designed of course to earn our gratitude. Having succeeded in that you started to pay court.''

''It was very agreeable. I have always found you attractive.''

''Thank you. But you turned to Amaryllis.''

''You were too lively . . too inquisitive. I thought you would very quickly start to pry.''

''And Amaryllis was docile so you chose her.''

''And in pique you turned to the gentleman who is now your husband. Hard luck you should go on with the game after he was injured. But that was your own fault.''

''And having charge of Amaryllis' fortune, you are increasing your holdings in your apparently very prosperous business?''

''It is indeed profitable. Amaryllis has increased her fortune since marrying me.''

''It is still her fortune, is it?''

''I have been very careful about that. I have used her money, but not taken it. If your father . . . or any of the family . . . decided they would look into my affairs they could not default me. I am in the clear.''

"How worthy of you! I wonder what Amaryllis would say if she knew for what purpose her money is being used.''

"She will never know. She is a completely contented wife and mother. It is better she remains so.''

"I think I would rather know what is going on around me. I know why Jonathan was led to Frinton's. I know where the anonymous letter came from. And then you staged that little affair with Prue Parker. You are determined to discredit Jonathan in my father's eyes.''

"Well, we have Peterkin now. A male heir right in line. I'll see that he makes a better job of Eversleigh than Jonathan would.''

I cried: "It's monstrous! And to think Tamarisk was the one to expose you!''

"That child is a nuisance. She always has been. Let's hope she goes off with her father.''

"You amaze me,'' I said. "You are so indifferent. You don't mind being exposed.''

"Not by you.''

"What do you mean? You wouldn't want my father to know the manner in which you make your fortune. You are a procurer. I always thought that was one of the worst things to be. You won't want my father to know about those tricks you played on Jonathan.''

"I certainly would not.''

"And yet . . . you seem to think your secrets are safe with me!''

"They are.''

"What do you think my father will say when he knows you deliberately brought Prue into the house, sent her to Jonathan's room and made her feign that attempted rape scene?''

"He would be horrified of course, but he won't hear of it, will he? He will be told that by one of those queer quirks of coincidence—which happen more in life than people realize—I discovered Prue Parker walking the streets. I was horrified, for after all she had such a short time ago been a servant in the family house. I questioned her; she confessed that she had attempted to compromise Jonathan and demand money. She knew that he was already in his grandfather's bad books and had a great deal to lose. It went wrong. Jonathan wouldn't play, so she pretended he had attacked her. She became frightened by what she had done and fearing exposure ran away. She was without work and there was nothing for her but the streets. She was attached to that club where you discovered us, and when I had found a post of parlourmaid in a respectable household I went along to the club to find her. Then you and Tamarisk burst in.''

"And you think I will allow you to get away with this?"

"You must, mustn't you?"

"Why should I? How do I know what other schemes you have. I think Amaryllis should know how her money is being used. I think my family should know. After all, you are a member of that family now.''

"But nobody must be allowed to bring disgrace on the family.''

"You already have. It was an ill day when you came into it.''

"We all have our weaknesses. You too, Jessica. This is going to be our little secret.''

"You presume too much.''

"I have justification. Let the one who is without sin cast the first stone.''

I was silent. A terrible fear was beginning to grip me.

"You certainly, my dear Jessica, are not without sin. What of this passionate love affair with the fascinating Sir Jake?''

I felt myself flushing hotly. I stammered: "What . . . what do you mean?''

"I have been frank with you. You must be with me. Do you think I don't know what is going on? You and the handsome gentleman are lovers, are you not? You visit his house . . . alone. You spend several hours there. You see, Jessica, it ill behooves any of us to pass judgment on the rest of us.''

I could see his smiling face through a haze of wretchedness. My secret was in the hands of this evil man.

"Sit down," he said. "You've had a shock. I was aware some time ago of the feeling between you. You couldn't disguise it from me. You have the glow of love upon you, Jessica. Oh, I thought, I must be watchful of this. I am always eager for scraps of information. One never knows how useful they will be. And now here is this. One of my people has been set to watch you.''

"You mean I've been followed!"

"To and from the little love nest. Naughty Jessica! But

understandable, of course. I'm not blaming you and I shall keep your secret . . . as long as you keep mine."

"And if I don't?"

"It would be rather sad for that kind husband of yours to know that when his wife comes to London it is to be with her lover. You would not want that?"

I was silent. I felt as though the walls of the room were closing in on me. I wanted to shout out to him to go away. He terrified me. He had changed a little. His face had become evil. He was like someone who had removed the mask he had been wearing and now showed himself for what he really was.

He was smiling at me cynically, sardonically, horribly.

"That's our little bargain," he said. "You don't tell on me and I don't tell on you."

He came close to me, took my arm and brought his face near to mine. "Remember," he said. "One word from you and I shall go straight to your husband and tell him of those jolly little occasions in Blore Street. Do you understand, Jessica?"

I nodded dumbly. Then I wrenched myself away and ran from the room.

Suicide or Murder?

I was back at Grasslands. I had not had a moment's peace since that interview with Peter Lansdon. I saw Jake only once before we returned. I dared not tell him what had happened for fear of what action he would take. It was blackmail of a sort. I was as guilty as Peter himself. If he were blackmailing me I was blackmailing him.

I had a notion that Jake might welcome the exposure. Jake was the sort of man who hated inaction. Patience was not one of his virtues. I knew that he was capable of reckless action as he had shown when he had run off and joined the gypsies, when he had dashed in and killed the man who would have ravished Leah. He would have said: "Let him talk. He should be exposed for what he is—and we'll take the consequences."

Those consequences, he would believe, might well result in our being together. *I* wanted to be with Jake forever. I wanted a permanent union. I wanted a home with him; I wanted his children. But I could not hurt Edward. I could not disturb his world in which I knew I was more important than anything. He would have his comforts, the attentions of James, Toby and Clare. But it was my presence which made it possible for him to endure the life into which misfortune had thrust him.

I could never be completely happy if I hurt Edward.

So I could not tell Jake. But what had happened could not

fail to have an effect on me; and he knew that something was wrong.

I left him frustrated and uneasy.

Peter Lansdon had returned to Enderby before we arrived home. He had already told his story and I had to admit he made it sound plausible enough. He mentioned what a great pleasure it was to him to be able to put right this little difference between my father and Jonathan.

The great topic at Eversleigh was Peter's discovery of Prue Parker. My father was a little shamefaced, trying to be more gracious to Jonathan. Jonathan was delighted that his innocence had been proved.

When we returned Tamarisk's pleasure in seeing Jonathan again was overwhelming. She kept telling him how she had seen Prue in the street and, recognizing her, had followed her because she was determined to prove him right and Prue wrong. "And then we went there," she cried, "and Peter was there . . ."

Nobody thought it strange that we should have seen her when she was on her way to meet Peter and that he had chosen that questionable club as a rendezvous. It was a coincidence, but they were so interested in the story that they did not probe too deeply into the details.

Peter dismissed any doubts they might have had. "It was a place she knew; she was attached to it in some way. It seemed reasonable to meet her there."

He modestly accepted the gratitude of all for having solved the mystery.

I wanted to shout at them that it would have remained a mystery if Tamarisk hadn't seen the girl in the street and we had caught him there redhanded.

But how could I? I had to be silent.

I did not want to go to London again. I did not feel I could go to Jake. How would I know whether or not I was being watched? Peter had spoiled everything for me. He had made me feel unclean . . . wicked . . . as bad as he was. He did not mind; he revelled in his wickedness; he called it shrewdness.

When he caught my eye he would smile at me in a very special way. I had the horrible feeling that he was assessing me. What had he said: "I always found you attractive . . ." He was implying "More so than Amaryllis." But he had chosen her because she was docile. I told myself I would never have married him. I admit I had at first been attracted,

304

but not by him as much as the glamour of romance . . . being rescued, as I had thought he had rescued me.

The horrible thought came to me that he might make another suggestion as a price of silence. I was thankful that I had enough against him to balance our evil doings.

There was something cold about him, snakelike. I wondered at Amaryllis who was so much in love with him still. He was clever. He could slip in and out of his masks, changing his personality, shedding a skin. Yes, snakelike.

He began to haunt my dreams as a nightmare figure.

Sometimes in the night I felt I would go to Edward and confess. I would tell him that I would stay with him for ever and never see Jake again. Jake must take Tamarisk away. They could go to Cornwall, on the other side of England, a long way from us.

Only confession could free me from Peter Lansdon.

My mother said: "Are you all right? You haven't looked well since you came back from London."

"I'm quite well, thanks."

If only I could tell her! She would understand. But I dared not.

"It will soon be Christmas," she went on. "It is amazing how time creeps up on one. We'll have to start planning for it soon."

I agreed.

She was not the only one who noticed. Clare said to me: "Are you well?"

"Why do you ask?"

"You seem different . . . since you came back from London. A little nervous . . . Did anything happen during your trip?"

"No . . . no."

I had always had an uneasy feeling about Clare. She was useful in the house. She would sit and read to Edward and play piquet with him. She was a great help but I always felt she resented me.

Leah was useful too. While Tamarisk was in London she turned her attention to the sick room.

"I have two handmaidens now," said Edward. "Clare and Leah. And with James and Toby I am really cosseted."

"You have me . . . another handmaiden," I reminded him.

"You are not a handmaiden. You are my queen."

I laughed, but my heart was heavy. He must never know, I told myself.

Meanwhile Jake was getting restive. He had been to Cornwall, for it was necessary for him to return, but his stay there was brief and he was soon back in London.

He wrote to me again. His letter was an impassioned plea to come to London. If I did not, he said, he would come to Grasslands. He had plans. He could not wait forever. We were wasting our lives. We belonged together.

The letter alarmed me while it delighted me.

I told myself I should destroy it but I could not bring myself to do so. For a day I carried it with me, tucked into my bodice but I thought that might be detected so I hid it at the back of one of my drawers with that other letter. I read them again and again. They comforted me; they set me dreaming of the impossible.

When I was talking to my mother about Christmas I said: "What about Tamarisk's father?"

"Perhaps he will want her to go to him in Cornwall?"

"She never would. She is more devoted to Jonathan than ever."

"I suppose we should ask him here."

I hesitated.

"Is it difficult? We could have him at Eversleigh."

"No . . . no. He should be where Tamarisk is."

"He doesn't seem in any hurry to take action about the child."

"I think he would. It rests with Tamarisk."

"It's an unfortunate business. One sees why convention and regularity in family life is so sought after."

"I agree," I said.

"We shall have a full house as usual at Eversleigh, I daresay. The Pettigrews will be here . . . and others, I suppose."

"Oh . . . I have room at Grasslands."

The idea of having him in the house excited me while it filled me with apprehension.

Peter would be at Enderby. He would certainly be home for Christmas. The three houses would be united in the festive celebrations and I should see a great deal of him. I wondered how I should feel being with Jake, while Peter looked on. I could imagine his bland looks and secret amusement.

I wrote asking Jake to come for Christmas.

After I had done so I went up to my room and, as I did in moments of solitude, I wanted to read the letters again.

Reading them brought him back to me, made me relive those magic moments, made the longing for him so intense that I forgot everything else but him.

I opened the drawer and felt behind the gloves and handkerchiefs for the letters.

They were not there.

But I remembered putting them away. I had been most careful. I turned out the drawer. I rummaged through the one immediately below it. I went through all the drawers. There was no sign of the letters.

Panic set in. Someone had taken them.

The idea of someone else reading those letters horrified me. Peter! I thought. It must be Peter.

I must find him at once. I must retrieve the letters. What price would he ask for them? I should never have allowed myself to be blackmailed. Blackmailers were known for not stopping in their demands. They wanted more and more. Oh, I should never have entered into this diabolical pact. I felt frantic with anxiety.

I met Clare on the way down.

I said: "Did Peter call yesterday?"

"Yes . . . I believe he did. He was with Amaryllis. They looked in while you were out. They must have forgotten to tell you."

"I must see him at once."

I went to Enderby. Peter was not there.

"He's gone into town," said Amaryllis. "He's leaving for London tomorrow."

"What . . . again?"

"He's so involved in business," she said with pride.

I pondered whether I should go and look for him. No, I thought. It will make me appear too anxious. If he threatened to use those letters I should go at once to my father and expose him for what he is. He would not want that. I was safe because I knew so much about him.

I must have been away an hour. The house was quiet when I returned. Soon it would be time for me to go to Edward. I would tell him that my mother was full of Christmas plans and had suggested that we invite Tamarisk's father for the holiday.

I kept thinking about the letters and imagining their falling into Edward's hands. It would be better for me to tell him myself. I would make him understand how it had happened. It should never happen again, I would assure him. I would pledge myself to that.

How devious I was! And with the worst kind of deviousness, because I deceived myself. I was longing for Jake to come and I knew that when he did, nothing would matter to me but that we were together again.

I went up to my room, took off my riding clothes and changed into a house dress.

I saw Leah and the thought struck me that she would have ample opportunities for taking the letters. She had loved Jake and had lured Tamarisk away from her home because she was his daughter. Since she had joined our household she had seemed to be gentle, law-abiding, but at heart she might well still be the fierce gypsy. Did she still love Jake? Had she, with that special perception which gypsies possess, divined that Jake and I were lovers? Why should *she* take my letters? And having read them what would she think of them? Clare? Could it be Clare? Clare loved Edward. She would believe that she should have been the one who should look after him. What would she think of one who had taken the position which should have been hers and then showed contempt for it?

If Clare had found the letters would she show them to Edward? Would she expose me for the adulteress I was?

My uneasiness had increased. Each morning when I awoke it was with a fearful dread of what the day would bring.

Christmas was almost upon us. The following day Jake would be here.

The weather had turned cold and I was anxiously watching the sky, fearful that there might be snow which would impede his journey.

I yearned to see him and yet I was fearful of his coming.

I went up to see the room which had been prepared for him. It was on the first floor. I opened the door and looked in. There was the red-curtained four-poster bed; the rich red curtains and the carpet with the touch of flame colour in it. I had changed the furnishings when I had come here. This had been Mrs. Trent's room. It had been rather sombre then. She had been a strange woman who had had a reputation for being a witch and I had wanted to eliminate all traces of her.

A fire was now burning in the grate. Rooms grew cold in a house like this when they were not used.

I touched the bed. The warming pan was already there. They would renew it when it grew cold.

I thought of his arrival. He would try to lure me into this room, but I must be strong.

I sat down by the window and watched the firelight throwing flickering shadows on the walls.

The door began to open cautiously.

It was Leah.

She jumped when she saw me—as startled to see me as I was her.

"I . . . just came in to look at the fire," she said. "They can be dangerous . . . even with the guard up."

"Oh yes. Sparks on the carpet."

"Yes," said Leah and prepared to go out.

I said: "Just a moment, Leah." She paused and I went on: "Sit down."

"This room looks cosy in firelight, doesn't it?" I said. "It's really a very pleasant room."

Leah said that it did look cosy and it was a pleasant room.

Edward had used it before he had gone to the one downstairs and many times had I sat by the red-curtained bed reading to him. I had been content enough then . . . living in the glory of self sacrifice. But making sacrifices, so ennobling in the initial stages, becomes wearying. A quick sharp sacrifice is all very well, but when it goes on and on one becomes angry—not so much with oneself who has made the decision in the first place, but with the one for whom the sacrifice is being made.

I must never show the faintest irritation which I sometimes felt towards Edward. How perverse people are! They are irritated by the goodness in others. If Edward had been a little tetchy more often, a little less patient, I could have let my anger flare up, I could have released my pent-up feelings. But because he was so good, I must feel this bitter remorse.

"Leah," I said suddenly, "do you ever think of the old days?"

"Oh yes, Mrs. Barrington."

"Do you ever wish yourself back with the caravans and the free and easy life of the roads?"

She shook her head. "I'm content here. It was bitterly cold

at night. The sun was too hot or the wind blew too cold. I've got used to living in a house.''

''And of course Tamarisk is here. You will go to Cornwall with her when . . . and if . . . she goes.''

''Is she going, Mrs. Barrington?''

''I suppose she will eventually.''

''She won't want to leave here. That I know.''

''She will, I daresay, go with her father.''

''She didn't know she had a father until a little while ago.''

''Well, now she does and her place is with him.''

''Oh, I don't know,'' said Leah. ''Her place is where she is happy.''

''She's a strange child. You know her well, Leah. It is hard to get close to her.''

''Oh, she's fond of you . . . in her way, Mrs. Barrington. And she's fond of me . . . in the same way.''

''She has her likes and dislikes. Yet she ran away from us, remember. Can you understand her running away from a comfortable home to live in the open?''

''Sir Jake did it, Mrs. Barrington.''

''So he did and became Romany Jake for a while. Those days seem long ago, Leah.''

''Yet they live clear in the memory. They might have been yesterday.''

I looked at her across the darkening room. There was an expression of terror flitting across her face and I knew that she was living through those moments when that man had seized her and Jake had come to her rescue. That was something she would never forget.

She had lured Jake's daughter away from us, yet how gentle she looked now as she sat there with her hands in her lap, remembering.

Did she love Jake? Was she aware that he was my lover? Was it Leah who had taken the letters from my drawer?

We were both startled by the opening of the door.

Clare looked in.

''Oh,'' she said, ''sitting in the dark?''

''I came in to see if the fire was all right. Leah did the same. Then we started to talk.''

Clare looked from one to the other of us. ''Shall I light a candle?'' she asked. ''It looks a little eerie in the firelight.''

She did so and turned to look at us, her eyes gazing steadily into mine.

I could not read her expression, but it seemed to be hiding something.

What is she thinking? I wondered. What does she know?

She was right. It did suddenly seem very eerie in that room.

Jake arrived two days before Christmas and my joy on seeing him was intense. I thought the manner in which we looked at each other must surely betray our feelings. I took him up to the red room myself. As soon as we were there he turned to me and held me fast against him.

"The waiting has been maddening," he said.

"But now you are here, Jake," I answered. "Yes . . . it has seemed very long."

"I've made up my mind," he went on. "We are not going on like this. Something shall be done."

He would not release me and as I clung to him I shivered. "Not here, Jake. Not here in this house."

"Something has to be done . . . and soon."

"Yes," I said. "But wait. Be patient. We'll talk." Then I tried to behave like a hostess. "I hope you have everything you want. If you don't, one of the maids . . ."

He laughed. It was rather wild, reckless laughter which I had heard so often. "There is only one thing I want," he said. "You know what that is."

I replied: "I must go down. People are watchful in this house, I believe."

"Watchful?"

"Leah . . . because I believe she is in love with you and Clare because she is in love with my husband." I drew myself away. "We shall be dining at seven. Could you be down just before."

And I was gone.

It was a pleasant evening. I was amazed how Jake could behave with such detached calm towards Edward. No one would have guessed that he was indulging in a love affair with Edward's wife.

As her father's presence made it a special occasion, Tamarisk dined with us. I was delighted when she asked him questions not only about London but about Cornwall too.

He discussed the differences between farming in England and Australia and talked so entertainingly that Tamarisk said:

"I should like to go to Australia." And he replied: "Perhaps I will take you one day."

Much later when I went to say goodnight to Edward I sat down and we talked for a while.

He said: "I think that man is beginning to charm Tamarisk a little."

"I thought so too."

"I daresay the day will come when she will go to him."

"We shall have to wait and see. I have a feeling that she will always prefer to be where Jonathan is."

"She's a faithful creature. I like that in her."

I said a hasty goodnight. Talk of faithfulness was a little disturbing to such a guilty conscience as mine.

The next day with Tamarisk and Jake I rode over to Eversleigh to help my mother with the arrangements for Christmas.

The house was in turmoil. The gardeners were bringing in plants from the greenhouses and festooning holly and ivy round the pictures in the gallery and on the walls of the great hall: mistletoe was placed in such places as would allow people to stand beneath them and give and receive the traditional kisses. From the kitchen quarters came the smell of baking.

My mother was in a state of delight and exasperation. She loved these occasions at Eversleigh when everything must be done in accordance with the old traditions. Jonathan had gone with some of the gardeners to bring in the yule log and Tamarisk immediately declared her intention of going to help them.

"The Pettigrews will be arriving today," said my mother. "You know how house-proud her ladyship is. She's prying into everything to see if there is a speck of dust anywhere."

"I daresay the servants at Pettigrew Hall are glad to be rid of her for a short while," I said.

Tamarisk had gone off and after a little conversation during which my mother told me that everything was under control and there was nothing I could do to help, Jake and I left. I could see that this was one of the rare occasions when my mother wished to be on her own.

As we rode off together, Jake said: "How good it is to be alone . . . for a while."

I broke into a gallop and he was soon pounding along beside me.

"Where are we going?" he asked.

"To the sea," I shouted.

I could smell the sea . . . that mixture of seaweed and wet wood and the indefinable odour of the ocean. I filled my lungs with it and I was happy for a moment . . . putting aside all fears and doubts and giving myself up to the sheer joy of being with Jake.

We pulled up as we came to the cliff and I walked my horse through the gully onto the shore, Jake following me.

The sea was slate grey on that morning; the waves came in delicately swishing the shore, showing a lacy froth on the edge of their frills.

"It is always magnificent . . . whatever mood it is in," I said.

"Admittedly the sea is very grand," said Jake. "But, Jessica, what about *us?*"

"What can there be? You've been to the house. You've talked with Edward. Surely you can see there is nothing I can do. I could never tell him that I was going away from him."

"You could spend the rest of your life . . . just like this?"

"I have accepted it."

"You accepted it before you realized what it meant."

"You mean . . . before you came back?"

"That has changed it, hasn t it?"

I was silent.

Then he said: "Jessica, what *are* we going to do?"

"Nothing. There is nothing we can do. The wisest thing would be for you to go away from here . . . for us to forget each other."

"Do you think I should ever forget you?"

"I don't know. In time I suppose you would."

"Never," he said. "You can't believe I shall allow this state of affairs to continue."

"It is not a matter of whether you will allow it or not. It is as it is. We have made it as it is and that is how it must remain."

"You will give me up . . . for Edward?"

"I have no alternative. I shall never be happy, I know, for I shall be thinking of you every minute of the days. But if I left Edward I should be thinking of him. I have resigned myself to living this life which leads nowhere . . . except to the end. That is how it must be. I made it that way and now I must endure it.''

"I shall not let it be like that.''

"Dear Jake, how will you prevent it?''

"I shall find a way. I shall not rest until I find a way.''

"Let's gallop along the beach,'' I said. "It's exhilarating. I always love to do it. Come on.''

I went forward and he followed me. The wind caught at my hair and for a few moments I could forget everything but the joy of the ride, forget all the problems which had to be faced; I could forget trusting Edward and demanding Jake; I could forget that I had betrayed my husband and that I was being blackmailed by Peter Lansdon and that someone else had seen the impassioned letters which Jake had written to me and in which was an unmistakable admission of our relationship. All that could be set aside during those few moments of a reckless gallop along a shore with the grey quiet sea on one side and the white cliffs rising on the other.

But as we walked our horses, single file, through the gully which led from the beach to the road, I kept thinking of Jake's words: "I shall not rest until I have found a way.''

Christmas Day dawned mild and damp.

We had all been to the midnight service on Christmas Eve and had gone back to Eversleigh to drink hot punch and eat mince pies afterwards. Then Jake and I, with Tamarisk—who had pleaded to be a member of the party—all rode back to Grasslands while Amaryllis and Peter went back to Enderby.

There were several guests staying at Eversleigh—including Millicent and Lord and Lady Pettigrew. So we were a very merry party.

"You must come over in the morning, Jessica'' said my mother. "You must be here when the carol singers arrive.''

"I'll be here,'' I told her. "But I'll go home for luncheon and come back again with everyone about six o'clock.''

My mother nodded, well pleased.

There was a great deal to do and this was one of the occasions when my help was needed.

I awoke on Christmas morning with that strange mingling of excitement and alarm which was often with me now.

I went to see Edward, taking my gift with me . . . a silk dressing gown, the kind of garment which he used frequently now, for often he would not get dressed but would sit in his dressing gown all day.

He received it with great pleasure and he produced his gift for me. It was an eternity ring, one of those with diamonds all round. It was very beautiful and I exclaimed in delight.

His next words disturbed me slightly. He said: "I asked Clare to choose for me what she thought would suit you best."

So Clare had chosen the ring! An eternity ring! Was that to remind me that I was bound to Edward for as long as I should live? What was going on in Clare's mind? I was convinced now that she was the one who had found the letters.

I slipped the ring on my finger.

"It's beautiful," I said.

"It is to remind you that I shall love you for ever. I don't say enough. I'm too reticent, but there are things which I feel so deeply and words are inadequate to express. I could never tell you what I feel about all you have done for me. When I knew I was never going to be whole again I was in despair. Willingly I would have ended my life. Then you came and said you were going to marry me."

"You tried to dissuade me, Edward."

"I had to. I couldn't condemn you to a life that was really no life for a healthy young woman. And when you insisted I was coward enough to let you do it. But that gave me the courage to go on. I knew I could . . . with you. And that is how it is. While you are with me, showing me your loving care, I can bear it all. You are wonderful."

"Oh Edward," I said, "you make me feel so ashamed."

"Ashamed! Why should you? You have made life happy for me. When I see you in the mornings I feel glad to be alive. I would do anything within my power for you, Jessica."

"You do," I replied. I kissed him and he held me tightly. I felt very emotional. I loved him. It is possible for a woman to love two men at the same time. I loved Edward for his gentleness, his unselfishness, his kindliness, and for the depth of his love for me. I loved Jake because he was vital, exciting, the man with whom I could know complete happiness if in taking it I was not hurting Edward.

I released myself and he kissed the ring on my finger. I made a vow within myself then. I said: "Edward, I shall always be here . . . as long as you want me."

We went to church on Christmas morning and after that we

all went back to Eversleigh. The carol singers came and I helped my mother serve them with hot punch and Christmas cake which was the traditional offering.

Then I returned to Grasslands for luncheon. In the afternoon I went for a ride with Tamarisk and Jake. Clare joined us.

There was little opportunity to talk to Jake. He sought to elude the others but I did not encourage him in this. That tender scene with Edward was still very much in my mind and I was conscious of my eternity ring and all it implied.

Clare seemed to be always beside me. There was a set smile about her lips. I fancied she was reminding me of the duty I owed to Edward.

The evening was like many Christmases I remembered at Eversleigh. The table in the great hall was beautifully decorated with several silver candelabra which were only used on such occasions; and there were sprigs of holly by every place.

We had the usual fare and dinner went on for a long time after which we retired to the solarium where games were played until the hall was cleared for dancing.

I was sitting beside Edward when Jake came along and asked me to dance with him.

I said: "No. I would like to sit beside my husband."

But Edward would have none of it. "You must dance," he said. "I like to see you dancing."

"I don't think I will, thanks."

Jake took my hands. "She should, shouldn't she?" he said to Edward.

Edward replied most emphatically that I should. "I'll watch you," he added.

"I'll take great care of her," replied Jake.

"I'm sure you will," said Edward.

I felt uneasy with Jake and a little angry. I was very emotional on that night and Jake seemed almost lighthearted. He did not seem to understand how I felt about Edward.

I knew that Edward's eyes were on us as we danced. I could imagine that he was thinking how cruel life was to rob him of his strength and manhood, of his ability to lead a natural life so that he must sit there and watch his wife dance with another man.

I don't know what was the greater in that moment—the desire to abandon myself to this emotion which Jake alone could arouse in me, or my love for Edward and my determination never to let him know that I had swerved from the vows I had taken on our marriage.

Jake said: "You *must* tell him some time, Jessica."

"How could I?"

"Just tell him."

"You've seen how he is."

"I believe he would understand."

"He would certainly understand. But how could I leave him?"

"You have a choice to make. So has he. So have I. Yours to take which way of life is more important to you; his to keep you and suffer infinite remorse because of what he has deprived you. Mine is how much longer I shall allow this state to prevail."

"It is not in your hands, Jake."

"It could be," he said.

"It is for me to make the choice, and I have known for a long time that I cannot leave Edward."

"You love him more?"

"Of course I don't. I could love you completely . . . if Edward were not there. But he is there. I married him and I know for certain now that I can never leave him."

"And what of us?"

"You will go back to Cornwall. You will forget me."

"I must certainly go to Cornwall. Forget you, I never will. Nor shall I lose you. I am going to find a way, Jessica. Believe me . . . we are going to be together . . . somehow."

"No, Jake. It can't be. I knew today . . . if ever I knew, that I have to stay with Edward as long as he needs me."

Clare passed. She was dancing with Lord Pettigrew who performed rather ponderously. They were close to us and I saw that Clare's eyes were watchful. What was she thinking? She knew that Jake and I were lovers. The letters had betrayed that. I believed she hated me because I had married Edward. I had taken him from her and now it seemed I did not want him.

Of course he ought to have married Clare. She would have been a devoted nurse. That would have been enough for her. She had always loved him. I guessed she would have looked up to him as a small child when he would have seemed so much older than she was, and so powerful. He would have been kind to the poor orphan girl, the poor relation who had been taken into the household because there was nowhere else for her to go. He would have been kindly sympathetic, sensing her loneliness. And of course she had given her absolute devotion to him. She was the faithful sort who would love him for ever. She must have hoped to marry him. That would have been the perfect culmination for her. Then I had come along, taken him from her, and having secured the prize indulged in a passionate love affair with someone else.

I could see Clare's point of view and why her antagonism was aroused against me.

I was glad when it was midnight and I told my mother we must leave. We had to get Edward home and for that reason we had the carriage, so we would all go home in it with Edward: Jake, Clare, myself and Tamarisk who had been allowed to sit up as it was Christmas.

Toby came too for he was needed to help Edward into the carriage. James was still suffering from his strained back and Toby was very useful.

We said goodnight to my mother and other guests and set out for home.

"What a wonderful Christmas Day it has been!" said Jake. "There is nothing like the old traditions."

We all agreed and Edward told us about Christmases in Nottingham and we all joined in until we arrived at Grasslands.

Toby—with Jake's help—took Edward to his room; Clare said goodnight and took a somewhat subdued Tamarisk off with her. She would soon be asleep. Indeed she was half way to that state already.

I met Jake coming out of Edward's room. "All is well," he said. "That Toby is a strong young man."

"Goodnight, Jake."

He took my hand and kissed it. "Come with me," he whispered.

I shook my head.

"Just see me up and say goodnight."

I went up the stairs with him to the bedroom. It looked very cosy. There was a fire in the grate and it threw its flickering light on the red curtains which had been drawn across the windows.

He closed the door and put his arms round me. "Stay with me," he said.

"No. I am going to sit with Edward. I always do when they have got him to bed."

"Afterwards . . . come back."

"No, Jake. Not here."

"Does it matter where?"

"Yes, I think so."

"What strange ideas you have, Jessica. Place and time . . . they are unimportant. What matters is that we are together."

"Edward is so near."

He looked at me in tender exasperation. "You will stay with me here . . . through the night . . . please."

"I couldn't. It would seem to me as though Edward were here . . . in this room. It would seem like the ultimate betrayal."

"If you are going to think along those lines the ultimate betrayal has already taken place."

"I don't think you see it as I do. Perhaps infidelity comes more naturally to men. It is condoned by society . . . unless it is discovered. What I have done is so wrong. It would be wrong for any woman . . . but because of Edward it is dastardly. I hate myself."

"For loving and being loved by me?"

"Oh no . . . not for that. That is something which will always sustain me. I shall always love you, Jake. But I have made up my mind very definitely that I cannot leave Edward. I shall be with him as long as he needs me. I have given him my word and that is how it shall be. He has suffered so much. I would never add to that suffering if I could help it."

"Do you mean that I must go away . . . I must leave you . . . that all I have to hope for is the snatched moment?"

"You will go away knowing that I love you as you love me."

"I love you exclusively. I would never allow anything to stand in my way. I should consider no one but you . . . us . . . being together always."

"You have seen how it is."

"I have seen, of course, that Edward relies on you. He would be very sad if you went away. But he is not a man who would demand a sacrifice."

"He is the most unselfish of men."

"Yes. He has qualities which I do not possess. Yet you love me, remember. You loved me enough to break those marriage vows by which you set such store."

"I do. I do. But you must understand. I must be here. I must stay with Edward while he needs me. I married him. I must remember that. It is too late for us, Jake."

"It is never too late."

And now, I thought, someone knows about us. Someone took the letters you wrote to me. Clare? Leah? I wanted to tell him to make him understand how careful we must be. But I hesitated. He would brush it aside. It was unimportant, he would say. Some day everyone would know that we were lovers because he did not intend to allow matters to remain as they were.

I withdrew myself.

"I must go and sit a while with Edward. I always chat with him for a few minutes before I say goodnight. He looks forward to it."

"Come back," he said.

I did not answer but came out of the room, and as I did I heard a door quietly shut. It could have been Clare's room or that of Tamarisk. Tamarisk was adept at listening at doors. I thought Clare might not be guiltless either.

I went down to Edward's room. He was in bed waiting for me. And his face lit up with pleasure as I came in.

I sat down beside the bed. On the top of the small cabinet which served as a table was the sleeping draught he took most nights, for he often found it difficult to sleep and the doctor said he must get the rest he needed.

On this night he looked tired. It had been a strenuous day for him.

I said: "You must be tired. It has been a heavy day."

"Christmas is rather special, isn't it?"

"Did you enjoy it?"

"Very much. Has our guest retired?"

"Oh yes. He's probably fast asleep by now."

"So should you be."

"I shall go after our chat."

"I loved to see you dancing. How I wish . . ."

I sighed and he went on: "Sorry, self pity."

"You're entitled to a little. Heaven knows you don't indulge in it often."

"I should not be sorry for myself . . . having you."

I kissed him.

"Sleep well," I said.

"I'm not really tired. It must be the excitement of Christmas."

"So you will have your draught tonight?"

"Yes. I asked James to leave it ready for me. It's effective."

I picked up the glass and gave it to him.

He drank it and grimaced.

"Unpleasant?"

"A little bitter."

"Well, I shall say goodnight." I stooped over and kissed him. He returned my kiss lingeringly.

"God bless you, dearest Jessica, for all you have given me."

"God bless you, Edward, for all you have given me."

He smiled at me ironically and I shook my head at him.

"Always remember, Jessica, I want to do what is best for you."

I kissed him hurriedly once more and went out of the room. I felt as I always did when he revealed his devotion to me . . . unclean and ashamed.

I came up the stairs. The door of Jake's room was slightly open. I stood still for a few seconds looking at it. Then I took a step towards it.

I hesitated. I had a feeling I was being watched.

I turned away and went deliberately to my own room. I shut the door firmly, all the time fighting the urge to go to him to give way to my longing, to abandon the principles to which I was trying so desperately to cling.

I went to bed, but not to sleep. I lay awake for a long time thinking of Jake in his room, waiting for me in vain.

It was symbolic of the future.

I must never go to him. I must give my life to looking after Edward. I felt very apprehensive, waiting, fearful that Jake would come to me, for if he did I knew I should have no power to resist.

Finally I slept.

I was awakened early next morning by a knocking on my door.

I called: "Come in." It was Jenny, one of the maids. She looked white-faced, disbelieving and scared.

"What's wrong?" I asked, starting up.

"Oh, Madam, will you come . . . at once. It's the master. James said to tell you he wanted to see you."

"Where is he?"

"In the master's bedroom."

I leaped out of bed snatching my dressing gown. I ran

downstairs to Edward's room. He was lying back in bed, unnaturally white and very still.

I felt myself turn cold and I started to shiver.

I murmured: "Oh God, please don't let it be . . ." I went to the bed and took his hand. It was cold and fell limply from my grasp.

"James?" I cried.

James came to me and shook his head. "I'm afraid . . ." he began.

I murmured: "Dead. Oh no, James . . . not dead."

"I've sent Toby for the doctor."

"When . . . ?"

"I came in this morning to see about breakfast as usual. I did not notice at first. I drew back the curtains and said good morning. There was no answer. Then I came to the bed and I saw . . . I couldn't believe it. Then I sent Jenny for you."

"James . . . how . . . ?"

James looked at the glass which was on the top of the cabinet—the very one which I had handed to Edward on the previous night.

"Oh . . . no," I said.

"We won't know until the doctor comes."

"But there was nothing wrong with him . . . apart from his injuries . . . nothing that would be fatal?"

James shook his head. "Sit down, Mrs. Barrington. You look faint."

"It can't have been . . ." I went on.

"He was worried about himself . . . being so incapacitated. We'll have to see what the doctor says."

Clare came running in. "What is it? They are saying . . ."

She looked from Edward to me. "Oh no. It can't be true . . ." Her eyes came to rest on me. They were dark with misery and suspicion.

"How I wish the doctor would come," I said.

There was a terrible silence in that room. The tick of the clock seemed unusually loud. I thought: I'm dreaming. This can't be. Edward . . . dead!

At last the doctor was with us. We left him alone with Edward and when he came out he was very grave.

"Mrs. Barrington," he said, "this is most distressing."

"I cannot believe it," I said. "Why . . . Doctor . . . what . . ."

"I am certain it is the sleeping dose. How much did he take?"

"James always prepares it for him."

James said quickly: "It was the usual dose, doctor."

"I think it was more than that last night."

"So it *was* that," I murmured.

I thought of our last meeting when I had sat by his bed and he had kissed the eternity ring. He had wanted the best for me. A horrible thought struck me. Had he deliberately taken that dose . . . to make me free? Oh no, he would not do that. I had never allowed him to think for a moment that I wanted to be free. But did he know?

Clare was looking at me with horror in her eyes.

The doctor said: "Was the bottle within his grasp?"

I knew that question was fraught with meaning. Had Edward taken the strong dose himself or had it been given to him?

James hesitated. "It was in the cupboard beside his bed. I suppose he could just have managed to get the door open and take out the bottle."

The doctor nodded. "There will have to be an autopsy, of course."

A terrible fear had started to race round and round in my mind. I was trying to remember all that had happened last night. Jake had helped Toby carry Edward in. The glass had been beside his bed when I entered the room. I had actually given it to him.

How much of the drug had been dissolved in that water? One small dose was all that must be taken. It was dangerous to take more. That was clearly stated and the doctor had warned us many times that more than the prescribed dose could be fatal.

Jake had been there. He had helped Toby to bring Edward in. He had killed a man once and he had said only this night: "I will find a way."

I was desperately afraid.

The doctor had just left and we were seated together in the drawing room—myself, Clare and Jake with James. A terrible silence had fallen on us. I dared not look at Clare; I could see the accusation in her eyes. I dared not look at Jake. I was terribly afraid of what I might read in his eyes.

At length James spoke: "How could it have happened? I

did not think he would ever attempt it. He was a man who believed that life had to be lived to the end no matter what tribulations had to be faced. It would have been all against his nature . . . as I knew it.''

Jake said: "Where was the stuff? Could he have reached it?''

"Yes . . . just," said James. "The little cabinet served as a table. It wouldn't have been easy for him to reach the bottle but he could have done so.''

"He would never have done it," burst out Clare. "I know he would never have done it.''

"What alternative is there?" asked Jake in a curiously quiet voice.

There was silence and I felt Clare's eyes on me accusingly. I raised mine and looked at Jake. For a few moments his gaze held mine. I did not know what I read there. But the thought would come to me. He killed a man once. He had done that in the heat of anger. If one had killed once did it come easily to do it a second time?

No, I thought. Not that. There had been a barrier between us before. That would be an unsurmountable one. I must know the truth. I should not have a moment's peace until I did.

I heard myself saying: "What actually happened last night? When could it have been put in the glass? Was Edward alone for any time?''

James said: "Sir Jake and Toby helped him out of the chair. We got him into bed between us. I poured out the water and put in the sleeping draught. I put it on top of the cabinet. We talked as we always did. He was in good spirits but of course he always did hide his feelings. What happened then? I think we all went out.''

"I believe I lingered to say a few words to him," said Jake.

My heart began to beat very fast. Oh, Jake, I thought, were you alone with him . . . even for a few minutes?

"Well, Mr. Barrington was by himself until you came in, Mrs. Barrington.''

"Had he taken the sleeping draught then?" asked Jake.

"No. He usually took it while I was there . . . just as I was leaving actually. He didn't want to feel sleepy while we were talking. I stayed a while. We talked as usual. He drank it while I was there. Then I took the glass from him and put it on top of the cabinet."

"I can't understand it," said James. "And on Christmas night! If he had contemplated doing it he would surely not have chosen Christmas night."

"You think the time is important?" said Clare harshly.

"Well," explained James, "he would think of people enjoying Christmas. He was always one to think of other people. No. It was a mistake. He would never have killed himself in the first place . . . and certainly not on Christmas night."

"Then," said Clare, and I noticed how her eyes glittered, "someone else must have done it."

There was silence with none of us daring to look at each other.

Suddenly I knew I could endure no more. I stood up and said: "There will be things to do."

And I went out of the room.

I cannot remember much of the rest of that day, except that it was like a bad dream. Messages were sent to Mr. and Mrs. Barrington. My father and mother came to Grasslands. They were deeply shocked. Amaryllis came over with Peter.

Amaryllis was deeply moved; she embraced me with great affection. "Dear, dear Jessica, this is terrible. Poor Edward! But it is those who are left who suffer. He was such a good man, and he loved you so much."

I knew that whatever happened I would always have Amaryllis' support and affection. I noticed Peter watching me rather sardonically. I dared not think what was going on in his mind.

My mother said: "Would you like to come back with us to Eversleigh? Your father says you are not to worry. He is going to take charge of everything. There'll have to be an inquest. Perhaps it would be better for you to stay with us until that is over."

I said I would stay at Grasslands.

"What about Tamarisk? Perhaps I'll take her back with me. Jonathan can come over and persuade her if she is difficult."

"Yes," I said. "I should be glad of that. It is no place for her."

"I expect the Barringtons will be here soon. What a terrible blow to them! They are such a devoted family and Edward was the apple of their eyes . . . particularly I think since his infirmity.''

The long day dragged into evening and I was glad when it was time to retire. I had avoided Jake all day. There was so much I wanted to say to him and so much I was afraid to say. I thought that if I asked him outright he would tell me the truth.

But did I want to know the truth? In my heart I was terrified of it.

I went to bed but I knew I should not sleep. I lay there, my eyes shut, thinking of the previous night and trying to recall every second, what Edward had said, what I had said. Had he seemed different? I was trying to read something in his words, something significant. I was trying to make myself believe that there was a possibility that Edward had taken his own life. If he had, then it was what he wished. I remembered how he had persuaded me to dance with Jake. I had looked over my shoulder and seen his eyes following me wistfully.

If Edward had taken his life it must have been what he wished. He had a right to leave this world if it had become intolerable to him. But no one else had a right to banish him from it. Only if I could be sure that Edward had wished to die and had taken the action himself, could I begin to grow away from the tragedy. No one . . . not even Jake . . . could make me truly happy again if that were not so.

How could I know?

The door of my bedroom opened quietly. For a moment I thought it was Jake and sat up ready to protest. It was not Jake. It was Clare.

She stood at the end of my bed. ''Edward is dead,'' she said, as though I did not know it. ''He had to die, didn't he? Otherwise how could you marry your lover?''

''What are you saying?''

''Surely you know. I loved Edward as you could never love anyone. When I came to them I was only seven years old, the poor relation. Oh, they were kind, but he gave me a special sort of kindness. He made me feel as though I were a person . . . not just a poor relation taken in because I had nowhere else to go. He was different. He was fond of me. I believe he would have been very fond of me. But you had to come along and spoil it.''

"I'm sorry, Clare."

"Sorry? I don't suppose you ever thought of him . . . or me . . . or anyone but yourself. You wouldn't have him for a long time and then you decided you would. After that you made the grand gesture, didn't you? He was crippled. He would never walk again, so you would show everyone how noble you were."

"It wasn't like that."

"I know how it was. You thought Peter Lansdon wanted you. You thought every man must want you. And when he turned to Amaryllis it was a great shock, so you thought, All right, I'll take Edward. So you did. That was why you became engaged to him. And then you got tired of it, didn't you? I would have given my whole life to nursing him. But you took a lover, didn't you . . . the dashing Sir Jake."

"You don't understand, Clare."

"I understand everything. Do you think I am blind? I know what is going on. And I have proof."

I stared at her and she laughed at me. "It's all rather clear. He set it down, didn't he? I have two letters he wrote to you. Don't think you are going to brush me aside again. It's evidence, you know. I will show them the letters. You were both with him that night. Sir Jake was there. Did he put in the extra dose or did you? Perhaps when you went in to say goodnight to him? You actually handed it to him, didn't you? You said you did. Which one put in the fatal dose is anyone's guess. But it was you who handed it to him."

"Clare, Clare, what are you saying?"

"That you and your lover between you killed Edward."

"It's not true. I wouldn't have hurt him for . . ."

"Wouldn't you? When you had your lover staying in this very house?"

"There is so much that you don't know."

"And so much I do, eh? Don't imagine I shall stand by and let you get away with this. I am going to show them at the inquest. I am going to give them proof."

"It is no proof."

"It is proof that two people in this house wanted Edward dead, and both of those people were with him on the night. They both had an opportunity of putting the dose into the water."

"Clare, this is madness."

"It sounds like common sense to me."

327

With that she went out and left me.

I lay down. So she had the letters and she would show them. Jake and I would be exposed as having had a motive for murder. I would never have hurt Edward willingly. But Jake?

There was no sleep for me all through the night.

I rose early next morning. I went to the stables and saddled a horse. I had to get out of the house. I had to be alone to think. I rode down to the sea and galloped along the shore. There was no joy in the exercise on that morning. One thought was hammering in my mind; Clare had the letters. She it was who had stolen them. I had guessed correctly.

I could not face Jake yet. I was too much afraid of what I would discover.

There was one to whom I had turned during the whole of my life when I was in trouble: My mother.

I left the shore and rode to Eversleigh.

She expressed no surprise to see me. I said: "I have to talk to you at once . . . alone."

"Of course," she said.

She took me into the little sitting room which led from the hall. She shut the door and said: "No one will come here."

I told her everything—that Jake and I were lovers. I told her of my remorse and my determination not to hurt Edward.

She nodded, understanding.

She said: "It was natural, Jessica. You cannot be blamed."

But when I told her of the letters which had been written by Jake and stolen by Clare, she was very grave.

"It was clear from what he had written that we had been lovers," I told her, "that he was impatient and wanted me to go away with him. She threatens to produce them and use them against me."

My mother was silent. I could see that she was very disturbed.

"I'm afraid," I concluded. "It will appear that either Jake or I . . . or the two of us together . . . planned to kill Edward."

"Those letters must not be seen by anyone else," she said.

"Clare has always hated me. She loved Edward and hoped to marry him. Perhaps if it were not for me she might have done so. She will never forgive me, and now she sees this chance . . ."

"It's got to be stopped."

"She is determined."

"We must get hold of those letters before the inquest," said my mother firmly.

"She will never give them up."

She said then what she had always said in the past and which I had often laughed at: "I'll talk to your father."

I did not laugh now.

She went on: "My dear, you should go back to Grasslands now. I am going to suggest that Jake comes over to Eversleigh. It would be better that he is not in the house with you. We'll explain that as things are it is better for him to be with us. Tamarisk is here, and Jonathan is being very good and giving her a lot of attention. It is not right for children to know too much of these things. The Barringtons will be here soon. Clare will be in the house of course. I hope she will not give too much trouble."

I clung to her. She kissed me and said: "Everything will be all right. Your father and I will see to that."

Jake saw the point of staying at Eversleigh. I did not have a chance to speak to him alone before he went. I did not seek it. If I had been alone with him I should have had to ask him outright if he had killed Edward, and I was afraid of the answer.

Mr. and Mrs. Barrington arrived. Their daughter Irene and her husband came with them. They had left the children with their paternal grandparents. They were heartbroken. Mrs. Barrington clung to me and wept.

Later we talked together. She said: "He was so noble, my dear Edward. He was always such a good boy, so thoughtful to others . . . always. When you married him he could not believe his good fortune. Poor dear boy! That he should be the one to suffer from those wicked men! But then you showed your love for him as few would have done, and I shall never forget it. You made him so happy. I blessed the day when you came into his life."

I thought: Clare will talk to her. Clare will produce the letters. What will she think of me then? What would she say had she known that I had broken my marriage vows? She would have a different opinion of me then.

My parents came to Grasslands. They did not talk a great deal about the tragedy. In fact my father scarcely mentioned it except once when he said: "Poor Edward, he could see no future for himself. I would have been the same. Better to get out than the way it was."

He had made up his mind that Edward had killed himself and he was the sort of man who would make sure that everyone agreed with him.

It would be different at the inquest. I had never been to an inquest and was unsure of the procedure, but I did know that the verdict was all-important, and it would be decided whether or not this was a case of suicide, accidental death or a case of murder against some person or persons unknown. And if the latter a trial would follow.

It was the day before that fixed for the inquest. My mother sent a message to Grasslands asking me to come over to Eversleigh.

I went immediately.

It was late afternoon and the house was quiet. She was waiting for me in the hall. She said: "Jonathan has taken Tamarisk for a ride. Jake has gone with them."

"What has happened?"

"Come up to our bedroom," she said. "Your father is there."

"Something has happened. Do tell me."

"Yes. You can trust your father to act."

He was there in the bedroom and to my surprise Mrs. Barrington was with him. She kissed me warmly. "I expect you are surprised to see me here," she said.

My father put his arms round me and kissed me.

"Sit down," he said. "Everything is going to be all right. The inquest is tomorrow and there is going to be a verdict of suicide."

"How?" I stammered.

"I've talked to Jake. I know he had no hand in Edward's death."

"How can you know?"

"Because he said so. I know men. I know he would not have been such a fool as to do a thing like that. He was confident of getting Edward's understanding and you your freedom."

"He had not spoken to Edward!"

"No, but he intended to."

"Then how do you know . . . ?"

"Toby has told me that Edward spoke to him two nights before his death. He said he thought there was little point in his going on living. He said, 'I am sometimes tempted to slip in an extra dose. That would finish the job and I'd slip quietly away.' That will be important evidence and Toby will give it. There will be no one who had the slightest reason for wanting Edward's death."

I said: "What of the letters?"

My father put his hand in his pocket and drew out two sheets of paper. I snatched them from him.

"Where did you get them?"

"I have them. That's the important part. I wanted you to be here . . . to be sure. These are the letters?"

"Why yes. But I don't understand . . ."

There was a lighted candle on the dressing table. I had vaguely wondered why it was there as it was not dark. He took the letters from me and held them out to the flame. We watched them burn.

"There!" said my mother, blowing out the candle. "That is an end of that."

"Did Clare give them up?" I asked.

My mother shook her head. "I took Mrs. Barrington into my confidence. When I explained everything to her she understood . . ."

She smiled at Mrs. Barrington who said: "Yes, Jessica my dear, I understood. You brought great happiness to my son. He was never so happy as he was through you. I am for ever grateful. Your mother made me see that you loved this man, and he you . . . and I love you all the more for not leaving Edward but staying by his side. I want to help you. Clare can be of a jealous nature. She was always a difficult child, always looking for slights. Edward could manage her better than the rest of us, and she was very fond of him. I did think at one time that they might have married . . . but it turned out otherwise, and he was so happy with you. I wanted to help, so when I knew there were incriminating letters I was determined to find them.

"Clare has a very special box which Edward once gave her. It was on her fourteenth birthday. It was very precious to her. In it she kept her treasures. Clare is a creature of habit. She always kept the key to that box on a key-ring—another present of Edward's—and it was kept in the third drawer of her dressing table. I guessed that the letters would be in that box and I knew where the key was. Poor Clare, she has always been an unhappy girl. She came to us when she was seven. She was a distant cousin's child. Her parents had been poor. Her mother had died and her father had very little time for her. He was glad when we offered to take her. She was an envious child. Perhaps if her life had been different, she would have been. She always had to remember misfortunes and thought other people should suffer as she had. The only time she was really happy was when she was with Edward. It might well be that he would have married her if you hadn't come along. People drift into these things. I think she would have been a different girl if he had. Well, I knew of the box and I knew of the key. I chose an opportunity when she was out. It was quite simple. I went into her room. I took the key and opened the box and, as I expected, there were the letters. I brought them to your mother.''

''You have done this . . . for me?'' I cried.

''How can we ever thank you,'' said my mother warmly.

''I knew in my heart that it was what Edward would have wanted. The last thing he would have wished would have been for you, Jessica, to be unhappy. So I am doing this for Edward as well as for you.''

My father said: ''This will make all the difference. There will be no accusation now.''

My relief was so intense that I could not speak.

My father took my arm and led me to a chair. I sat down beside my mother and she put an arm round me.

''This will pass, my darling,'' she said. ''Soon it will be like some hazy nightmare . . . best forgotten.''

I went back to Grasslands. I should have been easier in my mind but the gloom had returned to hang over me. I felt as though I were groping in the dark and at any moment would come upon a terrible discovery.

I wanted to see Jake . . . desperately I wanted to. I wanted to talk to him . . . to ask him questions, to beg him to tell me the truth. I did not think he would lie to me. Did he hold life cheaply? Once he had killed a man and felt no remorse for that. What sort of life had he led on that convict ship? He must have seen death and horror in various forms. Did that harden a man? Make him hold life cheap? Make him determined to get what he wanted no matter the cost?

Yes, I wanted to see him and I dared not see him.

As I approached the house I noticed a rider coming towards me. It was Peter Lansdon, one of the last people I wanted to see at that moment.

"Jessica!" he cried.

"Hello."

"Amaryllis is coming over to see you. She's very anxious about you. You look drawn. This is a terrible business."

I was silent.

"Have you just come from Eversleigh?" he asked. "I suppose the parental wits are being exercised to fullest capacity."

"What do you mean?" I asked.

"This kind of situation . . . it's always difficult for the spouse in the case. It's a commentary on marriage, I suppose, that when a man or woman dies mysteriously, the first suspect is the wife or husband."

I hated him, with his cool supercilious eyes. How could Amaryllis love such a man? How could I myself have ever considered him romantically?

He was a man who could change his personality as easily as most changed their clothes. It was the secret of his success.

"I have no doubt," he went on, "that your parents will extricate you from any difficult situation in which you find yourself. How fortunate you are to have a father who is not only doting and determined to save his daughter from any predicament into which she may project herself, but has the influence to do something about it!"

"The truth will be told," I said. "That is what I want and what my father wants."

"The truth? The whole truth and nothing but the truth?" he asked, lifting his eyebrows.

"We want the truth," I said.

"There is one little aspect which I think it would be wise to keep secret. You know to what I refer for we have discussed that matter before."

"What do you want now?" I said.

"I am no blackmailer. I just seize opportunities. And I would be a fool to blackmail you with staunch Papa standing guard. You and I share secrets about each other. What I want from you is perpetual silence. Suppose . . . just suppose . . . all goes well at this inquest and you and your lover are exonerated from all blame. Suppose you marry. Then you might say, 'What does it matter now if the whole world knew that I took a lover before my husband's death? The verdict is given. The matter is closed. What then? Why should I not tell what I know of Peter Lansdon and his less than respectable activities in London Town?' I do not take risks. I want a vow of perpetual silence from you, Jessica, and I want it now before the inquest.''

"And if I do not give it?"

"Then I shall be forced to tell the coroner that you had a motive for wanting your husband out of the way, that I had discovered . . . quite by chance of course . . . that you and your lover used to meet surreptitiously in London. So . . . I shall be obliged to hint that you had a reason for wishing him out of the way.''

"You're despicable.''

"One has to be ruthless sometimes to fight one's way in the world.''

"I wonder what Amaryllis would say if she knew the sort of man she had married.''

"Amaryllis is devoted to the man she has married. She has never had a moment's regret on that score.''

"That is strange to me.''

"Then it should not be. We all appear differently to different people. To you I am the abandoned sinner. To Amaryllis I am the hardworking and successful businessman who at the same time is the perfect husband and father. You judge too superficially. I am all that when I am with Amaryllis just as I am the wicked adventurer when I am with you. I am both these people, Jessica. Life is like that. Of course, I do not believe that you administered the fatal dose. But what of that other who would gain his desires by so doing, eh? What of the passionate Jake? Come on . . . give me your word. Forever more you keep my secret, and I shall not come forward at the inquest and tell what I know of you and Cadorson.''

I remembered then one day long ago when we had met Leah and she had told our fortunes. She had said that Amaryllis would go through life happy because she could not see the unpleasantness and danger all around her. How right she was! I supposed Amaryllis had always been like that. It was why life had always seemed so good to her. She saw no evil and therefore for her there was no evil.

I remembered that Aunt Sophie had seen nothing but evil

and how unhappy she had been; and it occurred to me that people made their own happiness or otherwise in this life; and that it was in the hands of us all to shape our own lives. And this was never more true than when one was passing through a situation such as this which now beset me.

"Well," said Peter, "what is it going to be? Let us both take the vow of silence, eh?"

I said slowly: "I will never tell what I know."

He leaned towards me. "Nor I of you, dear Jessica."

He lifted his hat and rode away.

The day of the inquest came at length.

Jake was there; so was Amaryllis with Peter Lansdon. James and Toby would be called as witnesses, as I should with Jake. We had been the last to see Edward alive.

I sat between my father and mother. My father's face was set and grim. He looked old and tired. How much of that was due to sleeplessness and anxiety I did not know. I knew he had been deeply worried by the danger which hung over me.

I watched Jake giving his evidence. He told how he had helped Toby to get Edward to bed. It was explained that it was James' duty but because of his strained back Toby had been called in. That was all.

Then James said that he had put the dose into the glass of water and left it at the bedside on top of the cabinet. He had gone out with Toby, Sir Jake had remained behind for a few minutes, chatted with Mr. Barrington and then he had gone.

It was my turn. I told them that I had returned to the house on Christmas night and my husband had been brought out of the carriage and put into the wheelchair to go into the house. After he was in bed I had visited him which was a normal practice. The water containing the sleeping draught had been on the top of the cabinet and I had handed it to him as I usually did before I said goodnight.

Had there been anything different about it?

I had noticed nothing.

Had my husband noticed anything?

"He grimaced when he took it, but then he had done that before. He said the draught had a bitter taste."

Had my husband ever said to me or implied in any way that he might take an overdose?

"Never," I said.

That was all.

The sensation came with Toby's evidence.

He had been a gardener, he told them, when Mr. James Moore had strained his back and could not easily lift Mr. Barrington. He had given up his work in the garden and had been solely employed in the sick room ever since.

Had Mr. Barrington at any time given the impression that he might have considered taking his life?

"Yes, he did on one occasion."

"When was that?"

"The night before Christmas Eve."

"What did he say?"

"He looked at the glass and said, 'Sometimes, I feel I am a burden to so many.' He asked what I thought of the morality of taking one's own life; and he said, 'Was morality more important than common sense?' "

"Was the bottle containing the sleeping draught within easy reach of Mr. Barrington?"

"It was in the cabinet. Not exactly within *easy* reach. But Mr. Barrington could just about reach the bottle . . . by stretching over."

"Was it wise to leave it in such a place?"

"It would not have been possible to remove it without Mr. Barrington's knowing that it was done," said Toby.

It seemed the bottle was there where he could reach it, and he had considered the possibility of taking his own life.

Suicide was the verdict.

I sat in the garden of the old *château* in Burgundy. I could hear the shouts of Charlot's children and those of Louis Charles as they played some ball game in the field near the old castle. I could look ahead to the vines with their ripening grapes.

In a few weeks the vendange would begin.

I had been here for eight months, and had left England with my mother and father soon after the inquest on Edward. They had said it was best to get away for a while.

My parents had sustained me during those months when I needed help. They knew that in my heart I did not believe that Edward had taken his life. He had always been stoical. He had accepted life. Even had he known of my love for Jake he would have accepted that, too, as inevitable. But he would never have taken that way out. I knew that someone had put that extra dose into the glass on that night.

My mother, with Mrs. Barrington, had made hasty arrangements. They had both agreed that I must get away for a while. For one thing I needed a change of scene, and for another there was the question of Jake.

Whatever the verdict, suspicions would remain. I could not go to Jake so soon. Nor could I see him every day. I was unsure of my feelings. There would always be a doubt in my mind. He had been there . . . alone. He had had the opportunity and I could not forget that he had said most vehemently: "I will find a way."

All my life I would be haunted by those words.

So my mother had said: "We must get away. Why not go to Charlot? He has often said we should. You would like to see the place, Jessica. It is so interesting. And the children are fun. You will love it."

I knew it was a great sacrifice for my father to leave England. He had always disliked the French and France, and I guessed that he must be longing for England, but his desire to be with my mother and me was greater than that; and he agreed that it was better for me to get as far away from Grasslands as possible.

I felt too listless to think for myself and I allowed them to make the arrangements.

Tamarisk went to stay with Amaryllis at Enderby; she was happy enough, I believe, because she saw a great deal of Jonathan who had said he would keep an eye on her. The Barringtons went back to Nottingham, taking Clare with them. They were going to stay in Scotland with Irene and her family.

Jake went to Cornwall. I had heard from him. In fact I had had several letters. I only had to say the word and he would come and get me, he reminded me. There was a convention that a widow should allow a year to pass after her husband's death before she remarried. He did not care a fig for such conventions. He was ready for me now.

"You will come here," he wrote. "You will be far away and on the other side of England. I am waiting for you, longing for you. I hope you are thinking of me. No one here will know what has happened; and when we pay our visits to London it will all have been forgotten. Who cares for conventions, anyway? True lovers never did."

To read his letters brought him back to me so vividly. I thought of him constantly during the long hot days and dreamed of him at night.

If he came, I asked myself, how should I feel? Should I ever be able to see him without seeing also that room in Grasslands with the cabinet by the bed and the glass standing on it?

What had happened that night? Should I ever know? Could I love the man who had murdered my husband? Had he? Could I suspect the man I loved of such an act?

I was unsure of myself.

Perhaps that was why my mother had brought me here. That was why my father curbed his impatience and tried to suppress his longing for home.

I accepted their care of me. I leaned on them. I had to. I dared not go back . . . yet. I had to discover my true feelings.

If I went back it would be a sign to Jake to come to me. And if he did . . . what should I feel? What should I do? I would say: "Jake, tell me the truth. Did you kill Edward?"

He would answer No. And would I believe him? I was not sure. If I loved him, would I be unsure? Yes. But if I loved him truly would anything he had done make any difference to me?

Now the culmination of the season was upon us. I had helped with the vendange. I had seen the grapes gathered; I had watched the peasants who had come in from miles round to help with the wine harvest.

It was a warm night and they were celebrating the successful gathering in. I was in my room. There was a stone parapet outside my window and I could step out onto this, and leaning over the wrought iron rail I could smell the scents of the night. I could make out the pepper pot towers at the east side of the *château* which Charlot and Louis Charles had so lovingly restored. I could hear the strains of violins in the distance and the singing of the workers.

There was the sound of wheels on the cobbles of the courtyard. Then . . . I saw Jake.

He looked up and for a few seconds we were silent, gazing at each other. Then I turned and ran down to him. He caught me in his arms.

"I'm here," he said. "No more partings."

"Jake . . .Jake . . ." I gasped. He was holding me so

tightly that I could scarcely breathe. "How . . . how did you get here?"

"On the wings of love," he answered and laughed. "Actually it was by the usual tedious way. I wanted to be with you so much. I am not going . . . until you come with me. No more waiting. Nothing matters . . . except that we are together."

I knew then that I did not care about anything. It did not matter what he had done. I only cared that he had come to me.

The Understanding

Jake took me down to Cornwall and we were married there. His house was like a castle, set high on the cliffs; it stood facing the sea, defiant and formidable as a fortress, and the gardens which wound down to the shore were a blaze of colour in the spring and summer; yellow gorse bloomed almost all the year round and in season there were the rhododendrons, azaleas and hydrangeas.

The house was almost feudal. I marvelled afresh that he had once left such splendour for a life with the gypsies. But that was Jake . . . unaccountable, the complete individual. It was one of the reasons why he was so exciting to be with.

I had no doubt that I loved him absolutely, that no matter what he had done I would follow wherever he led.

My parents had said it was right for me to go with him. It was the only way in which I could be cured of my melancholy. It was the only way I could forget the past and begin my life afresh.

That made the way easy for me.

My mother had decided that it would be best for Tamarisk to go to Amaryllis. She was rather fascinated by Jake, but Jonathan was the most important person in her life. She was a different girl with him—softer, more reasonable, humble, even biddable. "She reminds me of myself when I was a girl and loved Dickon," said my mother. "We were separated because they thought it was best, but I never forgot him . . . all those years when we were both married to someone else. It was only when we came together that I knew fulfilment and complete contentment. I understand Tamarisk. Let her stay near us. She grows more mature every day and she is a precocious girl. I believe she will marry Jonathan one day. There is no need to worry about Tamarisk. She will always take care of herself. My dear Jessica, you have now to grow away from all that has happened. You have to put the past behind you. You have to be happy."

The Barringtons had left Grasslands when we came to France. They said they would not want to come back for it could never be the same to them after Edward's death. In time they would see what they would do about the house.

And when I married, my parents suggested putting it up for sale.

Jake and I did not go back to Grasslands. We left France with my parents and parted from them at Dover—they to go to Eversleigh, Jake and I to Cornwall.

My mother's parting words were: "Be happy."

My father's were: "You'll be all right. Jake's the man for you. He'll look after you."

I wondered what their thoughts were about Edward's death. What did they say to each other when they were alone? Did they accept the theory of Edward's suicide? Toby's evidence had made that seem almost plausible. Yet I who knew Edward so well, had my doubts. I wished I could throw them aside but they lingered with me . . . and they came back to me in odd moments. Even when I was most happy, they would intrude.

We went to London now and then and my parents always contrived to be there when we were. That first Christmas after Edward's death they came to Cornwall. It was hard to believe then that it was only a year after that fateful night.

It was scarcely a merry Christmas to me. There were too many echoes from the past. I lived it all again, returning from Eversleigh, going to Edward's room, talking to him, handing him the glass. And the morning's discovery. Then I must go over the questions which crowded into my mind. Did Edward do it because he knew? Had he realized that Jake and I were lovers? Was I to blame?

When my son was born how proud I was! How proud was

Jake! We called him Jake and he was soon Jacco which in Cornwall means a conqueror. He certainly conquered the hearts of all who saw him. The servants adored him and Jake thought him the most perfect child who had ever been born; and although I laughed at him and said he saw in Jacco an image of himself, I shared his view of our infant son.

I should have been completely happy. I was . . . almost. It was just that now and then the doubts would come. How had Edward met his death? Could it really have been that the decision to die had been his?

Always . . . always . . . the same niggling doubt.

The months passed quickly, and when I knew I was to have another child I was delighted. Jacco was now eighteen months old and a bonny boy.

And then I achieved what I had wanted so much. I had a daughter.

It was three days after her birth. I lay in bed with my little girl in her cradle beside me. Jake was at my bedside when one of the servants came in to say that there was a gentleman who wished to see me. He had come from a long way and was a stranger in these parts. "A foreigner," the maid called him; but that could apply to anyone who was not Cornish.

Jake said he would go and see who it was.

It must have been about ten minutes later when he came back to my room and the stranger was with him. Jake brought him to the bedside and gave him a chair.

"This is Mr. Tom Fellows," he said. "I have brought him because he has something to say to you."

"Mr. Tom Fellows," I said, looking at him intently for his face was vaguely familiar.

He said: "You are wondering who I am, Lady Cadorson," he said, "and I must apologize for calling on you at such a time. But this is a matter of extreme importance. It is due to a deathbed promise that I am here."

I remembered the name Fellows. It was a Fellows who had hanged after the Nottingham riots for his part in them.

He said: "I see you are wondering who I am. We met once in Mr. Barrington's factory when I was with my father guarding the looms."

My mind went back to that momentous day. Yes, I had seen the looms and the man named Fellows guarding them.

"I remember," I said.

"You know my brother. He came to work for you. He called himself Toby . . ."

"Toby! Your brother!"

"Yes, he was my brother. After your husband's death he came back to Nottingham."

"But he was not Toby Fellows . . ."

"He changed his name. His own was known. When he came back he worked in horticulture. He was felling a tree in the forest. There was an accident and he was badly hurt. He lived for a week and during that week what he had done weighed heavily upon him, and he made me swear that I would find you and give his confession to you in person."

"What . . . was his confession?"

"Let me explain. He was a young lad when our father was hanged. Ten years old. He adored his father. He used to listen to him for hours. Our father was a leader in a way. He used to talk to the men and rally them together."

"Was he one of the leaders of the Luddites?"

"No. He saw the folly of breaking up the looms. He said that improvements had to come. On that day he was caught up with the rioters. He worked with them. You know what happened. He was sentenced to death. My brother never got over it. That was Tobias . . . Toby for short. He became obsessed by revenge. He used to say 'an eye for an eye, a tooth for a tooth.' Yes, he wanted vengeance. Your husband represented the enemy. He would not be content until a life had been taken for the one his father lost. You know the rest. He came to work for you. He had decided that only when Edward Barrington or his father was killed would justice have been done. He was always a strange lad—going in for boxing at the fairs, and he thought it was a heaven-sent opportunity when he was asked to work in the sick room. He killed Mr. Edward Barrington in just retribution, he said, for the murder of his father. But faced with death himself he was horrified by what he had done. He said he could not rest until you were told because suspicion hung heavily over certain people, including you from whom he had had nothing but kindness. He prevailed on me to find you, to bring you to him that he might confess all and when that could not be done he begged me to find you and tell you in person."

"It was good of you to come," I said. "I understand the poor young man's feelings."

"I wish I could have found you before he died. I wish I

could have gone back and told him I had seen you. He excused himself by the fact that Mr. Barrington was an invalid who would never recover, and he insisted that he would not have stood by and seen someone else accused of the crime which he had committed. He said he had made it appear as suicide.''

''Then my husband never said what Toby told the coroner he had. I found it hard to believe that he would discuss such a matter with him.''

''My brother said he had tried to make it so that no one would be accused. He would never have allowed anyone to stand trial for murder. He just wanted justice done . . 'an eye for an eye.' He kept stressing that.''

Jake had stood up. ''I think my wife is a little tired. Our daughter is but a few days old.''

''Forgive me,'' said Tom Fellows. ''But I had this duty to discharge.''

''How can I thank you for coming,'' I said.

''I will see that you are given some refreshment,'' Jake told him and turned to look at me with a rather special smile.

I lay in my bed. I could see my baby's cradle—it was on rockers, the cradle which had been used by the babies of the family for the last two hundred years.

I was glad of those few moments alone for I was filled with an emotion which I should have found it impossible to hide.

The haunting fear had been swept away now that I knew the truth. It was dazzling, revealing and irrefutable.

Jake came back.

''The poor fellow hadn't had a meal for twenty-four hours,'' he said.

He came to the bed and taking my hand smiled at me.

''Well,'' he said, ''so now you know. I didn't do it.''

''Jake,'' I said. ''I'm so glad.''

''I always used to tell myself that you believed I did it and yet . . . you married me all the same. I was hurt to be under suspicion, but I always said to myself, 'She loves me truly. She has married me even though she believes I may be a murderer.' What more could a man ask for than that his love should take him, sinful as she believed him to be!''

''I'm sorry, Jake.''

He kissed my hand.

''Forgiven,'' he murmured. ''I have no regrets . . . now. I

shall always remember you loved me enough to take me as I am . . . to risk your future . . . just to be with me. That was enough for me. And now that you have learned of my innocence you will love me more than ever, will you not?''

"No, I couldn't, because I loved you completely and utterly before.''

"Well spoken,'' he said. Then he stood up abruptly and went to the baby's cradle because I am sure he did not want to show the depth of his emotion.

"Do you know,'' he said, "I believe she takes after me.''

"Well,'' I said, as moved as he was, "she might do worse.''